THE ELIXIRIST

A Novel

Avraham Azrieli

ISBN: 978-1-953648-03-7

This book is lovingly dedicated to Talya, Benjamin, Elan, and Adam.

BOOKS BY AVRAHAM AZRIELI

Fiction:

The Masada Complex
The Jerusalem Inception
The Jerusalem Assassin
Christmas for Joshua
The Mormon Candidate
The Bootstrap Ultimatum
Thump
Deborah Rising
Deborah Calling
Deborah Slaying
Deborah Leading
The Elixirist

Nonfiction:

Your Lawyer on a Short Leash – A Guide to Dealing with Lawyers
One Step Ahead – A Mother of Seven Escaping Hitler's Claws

Author Website:

www.AzrieliBooks.com

THE ELIXIRIST

1

The boy kept his mouth open to avoid breathing through his nose. He held a clay bowl for his father, who scooped up the oily potion and rubbed it on the high priest's decrepit feet. The boy and his father were kneeling on the red mosaic floor by the daybed, while the high priest lounged back on oversized pillows and smoked a pipe.

Placing the potion bowl on the stone floor, the boy picked up a jar of water. His father, meanwhile, flipped over a small sand funnel to measure the time. The boy watched the sand drain through the funnel. He wondered how any potion could possibly cure such an intensely foul foot odor.

When the last grain of sand passed through the funnel, the boy tilted the jar, producing a thin flow of water on a rag, which his father used to scrub the potion from the feet.

The high priest snapped his fingers.

A curtain over a rear doorway stirred, and a veiled woman appeared. The boy was surprised. In past visits, one of the high priest's wives, who didn't cover their faces, had come in to sniff his feet and pass judgement on the success or failure of the treatment. Was this a servant, or a new wife?

The bottom hem of her white robe hovered just above her leather sandals, revealing small feet with red toenails. The long sleeves, which came down over her hands, allowed him a glimpse of her delicate fingers, whose fingernails were painted the same red as the toenails. The headscarf, also white, covered her face, leaving only a narrow slit for her eyes, which the boy couldn't see as she kept her head down. Her modest height and slim figure made him realize she wasn't a woman, but a girl about his age, which was sixteen. His heartbeat quickened. Could this be An, the high priest's only daughter?

The girl paced soundlessly as if her sandals didn't touch the floor. When she came closer, her loose robe raised a slight breeze, which the boy felt on his face. He forgot to breathe through his mouth, but the air that entered his nose wasn't foul. Rather, it carried the fresh scent of lavender. He wanted to inhale again, but his breath arrested when she bent over the high priest's feet, and her robe clung to her body, bringing out the gentle contours of her rear.

Tugging at her scarf to lift it off her nose, she sniffed and straightened up, shaking her head vigorously, which loosened her scarf and set free a thick braid of golden hair. The end of the braid was secured with a red bow, which dropped all the way down and settled against the small of her back.

In his struggle to breathe, the boy uttered a sound that must have come across as a mocking chuckle. She swiveled and looked down, showing him for the first time her eyes, which were large, brown, and burning with contempt. The effect on the boy was like getting punched in the face. He lost his balance, dropped the jar of water, and fell backwards. His head hit the floor, he felt a sharp pain, and fainted.

He found himself in a rushing river that carried him downstream among whitecaps. His feet found the bottom, and he waded towards the side of the river, where the current was less swift. Along the embankment he saw many men and boys with shaven heads and bare feet, wearing only sleeveless long shirts. Their complexion ranged from pale to dark, and their facial features varied widely, with mouths, chins, noses, and eyes in shapes as different as the birds in the air and the rodents in the desert. They clawed at the mud and scooped it up to fill straw baskets. Sporadic fights broke out, and he could hear them snap at each other in languages as numerous and as strange as their features. The mutual incomprehension seemed to fuel their acrimony, and they sounded more like dogs barking than men talking.

Once the baskets were full, they heaved them onto their bent backs and joined a long queue, which advanced slowly around an inlet. Further downriver he saw a massive tower that rose up from the ground like a giant cone with many floors in gradually diminishing circumference. Counting the floors, he reached forty before the tower disappeared in the clouds. A serpentine ramp was constructed around the exterior for the slaves carrying the mud baskets, as well as oxen pulling wagons heaped with pale-red stones. The wagons came from a redwood ship anchored at the riverbank, where a huge contraption of beams and ropes unloaded the stones from the ship onto the wagons.

Looking back at the tower, the boy was mesmerized by its height. He'd never seen a building taller than three stories, and that was the king's own palace.

The current swept the boy into the inlet. At its center, a fountain burst out of the water, producing an arc of golden water – the same heart-stopping hue of gold as the girl's braided hair.

A dwarf stood at the threshold of the inlet, where the arc of the fountain came down. His hair was white, but otherwise he appeared ageless. In his little hand was a chalice made not of clay or wood, but of a transparent material similar to glass beads. The line of slaves with full baskets passed by the dwarf, who gave each one of them a sip from the chalice. After drinking, the slaves stopped bickering and spoke quietly. Their newfound comprehension of each other softened their harsh features.

The dwarf offered his little hand to help the boy out of the inlet. "Welcome, Sall."

"Thank you." The hand felt firm despite its miniature size. "Am I dreaming?"

"Dreaming? Why?"

"You know my name, but we've never met."

"Haven't we?" He held forth the chalice. "You must be thirsty."

Taking a sip, the boy was surprised by the sour taste of the golden water, which he had expected to taste like honey.

Refilling the chalice, the dwarf asked, "Would you like some more?"

He shook his head. "What language are the slaves speaking now?"

"They speak many languages."

"How did they suddenly become fluent in all these languages, then?"

"Fluent?" The dwarf served the next slave in line. "People can understand each other without a common language."

"Does the golden water make it possible?"

"Water? This isn't water."

"What is it?"

"Elixir."

"Is it made of liquid gold?"

"Gold?" He raised the transparent chalice up against the sunlight. "Is that what you see?"

The boy nodded. "Don't you?"

"I see blue."

"That's impossible. Why are you lying to me?"

"Lying?" The dwarf kept serving the slaves. "Why would I lie to you, Sall?"

"I don't know why, but this elixir is golden, and you deny it."

"Look again." He held the chalice between them. "Better?"

The liquid distorted the dwarf's eyes, making them large, oval, and yellow. The boy imagined a whitehaired owl with little hands. It made him laugh. The dwarf also laughed at what he saw from the opposite side of the chalice.

"I think I understand now," the boy said. "We see different things, even when we're looking at the same thing."

"How true. And what are you looking for, that you've come here today?"

"A girl knocked me out with her eyes."

"Ah, yes, it happens. In the right circumstances, eyes are as fierce as lightening." The dwarf scratched his head as if reminiscing on his own brush with such eyes.

"Are you a healer, like my father?"

The dwarf refilled the chalice while the column of slaves crawled forward. "Mixing potions is a craft, whereas creating elixirs is an art."

The boy understood that the dwarf meant to praise his own vocation above that of a healer, but in his opinion, craft was more valuable than art, though he didn't say it out loud, lest the dwarf took offence.

"If you aren't a healer, what do people call you?"

"The Elixirist."

"Elixirist? I've never heard of such a profession."

"It's not a profession. It's who I am."

The boy finally understood why his dream had brought him here. "Can you mix an elixir that will turn a girl's contempt into love?"

"If you wish to change how another person feels about you, start by changing yourself."

The idea hadn't occurred to the boy before, and he mulled it over in his mind. What had the girl seen? A skinny boy with reddish hair and freckled cheeks, kneeling on the floor, holding water for his father to wash the high priest's odorous feet. As long as he remained the same scrawny boy, her disdain would persist. The dwarf was right – to change her heart, he had to change the way he looked.

"Can you create an elixir to help me look better?"

"Better?"

"Much better."

"In what way?"

That was an easy question to answer. "In every way."

The dwarf looked him up and down, put down the transparent chalice, and stepped up to the edge of the inlet. Leaning forward, he opened his mouth and drank directly from the fountain's arc of golden water. In an instant, his white hair turned lustrous black, his translucent skin gained a vigorous tan, and his bony arms and legs lengthened, swelling with wrought muscles.

Marveling at this transformation, the boy felt powerful craving to gulp a mouthful from the golden fountain and similarly transform into a tall, muscular, and mysteriously dark young man. He imagined the girl gazing upon such a strapping young man while the contempt in her large brown eyes turned to rapt admiration, possibly even love.

The Elixirist shrunk back into his former dwarfish self.

"That was perfect," the boy said. "How did you know to change into what I wanted?"

He chuckled. "I didn't change at all."

"But I saw it."

"You saw what you wanted to see."

The boy understood. "We see different things, even when we're looking at the same thing."

"Yes, we do." The dwarf moved aside. "Your turn."

The boy stepped to the edge of the inlet and opened his mouth wide to let in the golden water, but the flow suddenly intensified, flooding his mouth and gushing into his throat. Choking and spitting, he struggled to breathe while the fountain, the inlet, and the dwarf faded away, and his father's worried face appeared above. He was holding an empty jar of water.

Coughing hard, the boy sat up.

They were on the street outside the high priest's house. Dull pain pulsated in the back of his head where it had hit the floor. He felt a swollen bump. The coughing subsided, and he wiped his face while lamenting the disappearance of the golden fountain before he could drink from it.

"I am disappointed." His father helped him stand up. "You poured oil on the fire of disdain the high priest already feels for us."

"I don't want to be a healer," he blurted without thinking.

"You'll learn to accept it." His father took his arm and led him downhill. "Priests would rather have sick people pay for prayers than for healing."

Recalling the contempt in the girl's eyes, the boy shuddered. "I'm never going be a healer."

"You've been a healer since the day you were born and will remain a healer until the day you die." His father let go of his arm. "You can stop being a healer as much as you can stop being Sall, my only surviving son. A person cannot stop being what he was born to be, and if he tries, the betrayal will make him rot from the inside out."

"I don't want to rub potions on smelly feet."

"How do you think I feel?" His father sighed. "The high priest insists on wearing his old leather boots, not only in public, or during temple sacrifices, but all the time, even to bed. The stench has bored into his soles and under his toenails, too deep for my potions to reach."

"Why doesn't he air his feet?"

"Bad habits are like comfortable old boots that you keep wearing despite the worn soles, gaping holes, and bad odors."

It occurred to the boy that being a healer could also be a bad habit.

"The Gods love us," his father said. "We channel their healing powers to help those who suffer."

"From stinking feet?"

"Bad odors could be a torturous source of discomfort."

The boy crinkled his nose.

"You wouldn't be so averse to treating odorous feet if they belonged to the high priest's daughter, would you?"

He blushed, embarrassed, but also happy to learn that the girl wasn't a new wife. "Her feet don't smell," he said.

His father laughed. "You'd be surprised what foul smells sometimes emanate from beautiful girls."

Beautiful. The word made his heart race. Had his father treated An for an illness? Had he seen her without the veil? The boy wanted to ask, but was afraid his voice would tremble.

"A healer doesn't choose whom to help," his father said. "The people line up in front of our door every morning, bent over with pain and worry. Our potions calm their upset stomachs, cool their deadly fevers, and mend their broken bones. Yes, it's more gratifying to heal severe conditions, but our duty is to help others no matter what afflicts them, including smelly feet and bad habits.

2

At home, the boy's mother made him lie on his stomach. She placed a wet cloth over the back of his head. He told her what had happened, bemoaning his clumsiness with the jar of water under the girl's glare.

Umm-Sall replaced the wet cloth with a fresh one, cool and soothing. "At least you didn't try to kiss her again."

He sat up. "What?"

"Lie down, Sall." She adjusted the cloth and smoothed his hair. "Many years ago, when you turned five, we were invited up to the royal balcony at the temple of Qoz during a celebration of the king's recovery from a stomach ailment, which your father had healed. The high priest's youngest wife brought her little daughter along. When you saw An, you whispered to me, "She's very pretty, mommy." Next thing I knew, you ran over and kissed her."

"I did?"

"On the lips, no less." Umm-Sall chuckled. "Everyone laughed, especially the king, but her father has not allowed her out of the house since, not even when he chose her mother to be given to ... well, that's another story."

He tried to remember the event, but couldn't, which left him feeling both frustrated and excited. "If An was beautiful then, she must be even more beautiful now, right?"

His mother made a vague sound.

"Didn't you see her at the fertility sacrifice?"

Once a year, on the ninth full moon, the high priest officiated over a women-only sacrifice at the temple, initiating into maidenhood the girls who had experienced their first female bleeding during the previous year. No males were allowed inside the temple, and the women danced and sang to Qoz to celebrate the new girls joining the circle of female fertility.

The boy rose on one elbow. "Tell me."

"She's as thin as a reed."

"Slim as a graceful doe," he said. "And she has the most mesmerizing eyes."

"You should sleep now." Umm-Sall went to the doorway. "Better forget about her, son."

When his mother was gone, he whispered the name to himself. "An." It was a fitting name – noble yet reserved, proud yet unassuming. It made him think of a gold nugget he had seen once, which needed no enhancements or decorations to attract attention or proclaim its preciousness. Did she know his name? Probably not, which was good, because there was nothing noble about his name. "Sall," he whispered. It sounded like hissing. For her, he would change his name and choose a new one – a gallant name, a name befitting a tall, dark, imposing yet mysterious man – a name that would make her look up with awe, not glare down with contempt.

He fell asleep and dreamed that he was back in the river, carried by the current towards the distant cloud-piercing tower, but the tower didn't grow closer despite the rushing water, even when he tried to row with his arms. The tower remained distant, and he could not even see the old dwarf, let alone speak to him. He tried to kick the water with his legs, and the futile exertion woke him up.

Dawn glowed faintly in the window, which surprised him. He was tired as if he had gone to bed only moments ago. The dream had left him shaken. Did the tower, the river, and the golden fountain actually exist, as he felt they did, or were they part of an illusion, as he feared they might be?

He slipped his feet into his sandals and left his bedroom. Passing down the hallway, he heard his father snoring in the bedroom on the right and, on the left, his mother's dogs sniffing the air, too lazy to get up from the rug at the foot of her bed. He heard the servants speak quietly in the kitchen. The three of them had been with the family since long before his birth. Without families of their own, they lived in the house and were named for their jobs. He recognized the voices of the two women, Laundress and Cook, who was starting on the morning meal. They were explaining something to Horseman, who was slowing down in his old age.

The great Jujube tree in the front garden teemed with birds. He hurried downhill, his sandals clapping the stones pavers as the street crisscrossed the steep hillside upon which the city was built. A breeze came through the valley from the mountains in the east, clearing away the cloud of smoke from numerous fire pits that had burned overnight. The houses along the street grew smaller and denser as he approached the bottom of the hill. The king's horse stables and the soldiers' barracks, which faced each other across the open area inside the gates, were bustling with men and animals despite the early hour.

The gates had opened at dawn. He exited the city and walked to the fairgrounds. Several merchant caravans camped along the outer edge of the fairgrounds. He approached the nearest one, where a woman was feeding a handful of goats, two donkeys, and a horse. Noticing the boy, she put down the sack of straw and went into a tent. A moment later, a man came out, rubbing his eyes. His nose was unusually long and pointing aside.

Sall tried not to stare at the broken nose. "Qoz's greetings upon you, sir."

"It's early, boy." The man spoke the Edomite language with a harsh accent, which the boy recognized as coming from Moab. "I'll have my stall set up soon with soft Egyptian cotton, salted fish from Philistia, and sweet pomegranates from the Hebrews in Beersheba. Could you come back a little later?"

"I don't have any coins to spend."

The woman came out with a tray of fruit, but the merchant dismissed her. "If not coins, what else have you to trade for my goods?"

"I'm not here to shop."

The Moabite merchant snorted, wiping his crooked nose, and turned to go into the tent.

"Please, I only have a question."

A child stepped out of the tent. He was about six, naked and barefooted.

The woman reappeared, murmuring apologetically, wrapped the child in a blanket, and tried to lead him away. He resisted, clinging to the man, who smiled and picked him up.

"What's your question?"

"In all your travels, have you seen a great tower being built near a river by slaves from many nations, who drink from a fountain with golden water?"

The merchant shook his head. "Who told you of such a tower?"

"I saw it in a dream."

"A dream needs interpretation to discover what it means."

"Can you help me?"

"Perhaps. What's your name?"

"Sall. I'm the healer's son."

"The healer's son walks around without coins?"

The boy blushed.

"How old are you? Ten?"

"I'm sixteen."

"You don't look it."

His face burning, the boy spoke rapidly. "About the dream, it happened when I was helping my father yesterday at the house of the—"

"These are nice." The merchant pointed at the boy's sandals. "My son could use them."

They were fine sandals, made of leather and rope, a gift from General Mazabi, the chief of the king's army, who was a childhood friend of Umm-Sall. The boy hesitated, but he wanted an explanation for his dream more than he didn't want to lose his sandals. He took them off and handed them to the woman, who delighted in strapping them onto her child's small feet.

"Good," the merchant said. "Very good."

Sall felt sad about his sandals. "May I tell you my dream now?"

"What for? I don't know how to interpret dreams."

His sadness turned into bewilderment. "What about my sandals?"

"That's for telling you where to find a dream reader." He pointed north. "In Moab, about a ten-days' ride from here."

"In a city?"

"On a mountaintop overlooking the Sea of Salt. It's a long journey. You'll need a donkey, food, and water." The Moabite merchant snorted and wiped his nose. "I'll sell you everything you need for a fair price."

"How much?"

"Three silver coins. Can you get them?"

"I think so."

"And three more silver coins for the dream-reader's fee."

"Will you tell me how to get there?"

"First, bring the coins." The merchant grinned. "Don't wait too long. We're leaving at sunrise tomorrow."

3

A queue of customers already stretched across the front garden when Sall returned home. He went straight to the workshop and pulled down the cloth curtains from the windows. The interior walls were covered with wooden shelves. Additional standalone sets of shelves took up most of the large space. Hundreds of jars and small bowls filled the shelves, each containing a quantity of dry powder that had been prepared from the organs of various animals, plants, or seeds. Small wooden cutouts in the shape of animals or plants were nailed to the shelves to identify each jar and bowl. Most of the powders were intended for potions that treated rare ailments, which the boy had not yet learned about. The majority of customers came with common fevers, upset stomachs, headaches, or injuries, which were treated with simple potions. It was his responsibility to mix those potions every morning before his father arrived.

He set up three clay bowls and began to measure the ingredients in wooden spoons of different sizes. Horseman brought in a large jug of warm water from the kitchen, and the boy added the required amounts of water to each bowl. Mixing the potions with the prescribed number of turns, he made sure that all the powders were completely absorbed.

"Good morning, Sall." His father paused, looking at the boy's feet. "Where are your sandals?"

"They started to smell." It wasn't a lie, but neither was it the truthful answer to the question. "I had to leave them behind," he added, which was closer to the truth.

His father was already checking the potions. He picked up each bowl, tilted it from side to side, sniffed a few times, and stirred the potions with his forefinger. Mixed correctly, the potions had specific densities: the one for upset stomachs as thick as barley stew, the one for headaches as smooth as goat milk, and the one for fevers as cloudy as lemon juice. The last one he always mixed in the largest bowl, because feverish customers were most common, and his father made them drink a whole goblet on the spot so that the bad spirits would be flushed out with excessive sweat and urine.

"The ingredients are correct, but the mixing was rushed." His father sat down, which indicated acceptance despite his criticism. "Always remember that the dry powders we use are living things – animals and plants – in temporary dormant state. They need time to absorb the water, become animated again, and reignite their natural powers."

"I'm sorry, father."

"I was your age once, too." His father sighed. "Young men think life is a race, but a good life is measured not in speed, but in depth."

The customers came in one at a time. The boy poured the potions into cups while his father examined each man, woman, or child, offered comforting words and provided instructions on how and when to take the potions by mouth, or apply them to the skin over the affected area. He cleaned open wounds with wet rags and smeared a mix of honey and black seeds from the red flowers that grew in pots under the jujube tree in the front garden.

Payments were made in silver or copper coins, collected in a clay jar on the table.

Most of the morning was a blur of routine aches and pains, fevers, and injuries. The boy mixed additional bowls of potions as needed.

At midday, Cook brought a plate of bread, cheese, and fruit, as well as a cup of milk for the boy and a goblet of wine for his father. They consumed the food and drinks quickly and called in the next customer, who was suffering from tooth pain. After examining the tooth, his father summoned Horseman. The boy usually stepped outside in such situation, but today he stayed and watched his father place a thin iron rod against the side of the ailing tooth and hammer it with a stone while Horseman held the man. The tooth tipped sideways and tore out of the gums, chased by a gush of blood.

The boy became lightheaded, his forehead suddenly sweaty. Inhaling deeply, he took advantage of his father's focus on stemming the blood and slipped his hand into the payment jar. His hand was halfway out with a fistful of silver coins, when he paused, remembering the words of the dwarf: "If you wish to change how another person feels about you, start by changing yourself." Stealing the coins would turn him into a thief, which was the way to make the girl's contempt more justified, not less.

He dropped the coins and pulled his hand out of the jar.

The man left with a rag in his mouth, and a woman came in with a feverish child. There was still a long line behind her, and they continued working until the sun touched the horizon. While he washed the bowls and cups, swept the floors, and covered the windows, his father counted the coins.

"Father," he said. "Aren't young men entitled to get paid for their labor?"

His father gave him a searching look. "Yes, they are."

The boy felt his face burning. "What about me?"

"You're being paid with a place to sleep, ample food, and an apprenticeship in a lucrative profession." His father patted his cheek. "Perhaps it is time for a raise. Take what you feel is fair."

Alone in the quiet workshop, the boy finished covering the windows, took six silver coins from the jar, and closed the door. For a moment, he stood there, plagued by doubts. He had never journeyed away from the city without his father and loyal servants. Often, he'd seen travelers come to seek help with severe injuries inflicted by prey animals, venomous critters, or predatory outlaws. Would he end up lying by the roadside, far from home, bleeding, moaning, and gasping for air while tears of regret ran down his cheeks?

The coins clinked in his shaking hand while he recalled the golden fountain and the old dwarf transforming into a robust young man.

After the evening meal, he went to his mother's room and told her about the dream and the journey he considered taking to consult a dream reader. Umm-Sall was not a woman who held back her opinions. He expected a sharp rebuke, but she stayed quiet, took him in her arms, and pressed her lips to his forehead for a long moment. He felt her tears trickle down onto him.

4

Shortly before dawn, Sall woke up and found new sandals at the foot of his bed. He dressed and left his room. His father's door was closed, though no snoring sounded behind it. His mother's door was open, her bed empty. He assumed she was with his father, but found her waiting in the front garden with a saddled donkey, loaded up with sacks of food and bulging waterskins. Sitting by her side was one of her dogs – a young female with gray fur and sharp fangs, about the size of a goat.

Umm-Sall kissed him on both cheeks. He felt her lips tremble, and her eyes were moist. She handed him the donkey's reins and the dog's leash. "May Qoz watch over you."

He wanted to answer, but a lump formed in his throat. Across the garden, he stopped by the tall hedges that hid the street and looked back. His mother was on her knees before the effigies under the great jujube tree, praying silently to the Gods.

On the street outside, as he mounted the donkey, the leash slipped from his hand. The dog bolted through the hedges back into the garden. With dawn already breaking, he didn't stop the donkey as it started downhill.

"Sall!"

His mother caught up with him, pulling the reluctant dog along, and handed him the leash and a slice of dry meat. He tore off a piece and offered it to the dog, which ate it quickly and sniffed his hand for more.

"Don't let anyone else feed her," Umm-Sall said. "A dog's loyalty, once earned, is limitless."

He gave the dog another piece. "I'll bring her back to you, mother. I promise."

"Actually, I'm counting on her to keep you safe, wherever the road takes you."

The words offended him at first, but he understood she didn't mean to imply that he was less capable than a dog, but was merely seeking a ray of hope through her darkest fears. He still did not understand why she had acquiesced to his journey and opted to help him, rather than try to stop him or, worse yet, inform his father.

"Farewell, my son," she said. "You'll always be in my heart, whether you return or make a good life someplace else."

Her strange words shook him, and he hesitated, unsure how to respond.

"Go now, before your father comes out. It's hard for him to accept that you aren't a child anymore."

"And you?"

"Do I have a choice?" Her voice trembled. "A young man must follow his heart's journey, or his heart will go without him, lost forever."

After consuming a third piece of meat, the dog followed him willingly. When he looked back over his shoulder, his mother was gone.

At the bottom of the hill, near the gates, the horse stables and soldiers' barracks were quiet, unlike the previous morning. He rode out to the fairgrounds, where the Moabite merchant was taking down the tent.

"I have the coins," Sall said. "However, my mother surprised me with a donkey and all the supplies."

"No problem. Keep your silver. We're honored to host the healer's son on the journey." He tugged at the ropes securing the food and waterskins to the donkey and nodded in approval. "Everything looks good."

The dog bared her teeth, growling at the merchant. Sall pulled her back and patted her.

"Keep your dog tied up." The merchant snorted and spat. "Any more growling, and we'll have a roasted dog for dinner."

The abject cruelty shocked the boy, and he began to doubt the wisdom of travelling with a man capable of making such a threat. At that moment, the merchant's little son ran to the dog, which rolled on the ground and put her paws up in the air, making him laugh.

The mother smiled. "What's your dog's name?"

Umm-Sall did not name her dogs, but this one was his now, and he decided to give her a name. Trying to come up with something meaningful, he looked uphill towards his home, but couldn't make it out in the early dawn among the mass of white houses with copper roofs. The city of Bozra, which covered the whole mountainside, was waking up to a new day with columns of smoke from cooking fires, dogs barking in hunger or boredom, and men trickling out through the gates to work in the farms. He breathed deeply, taking in the sights, sounds, and smells of the city, and the answer came to him.

"Bozra." He shook the leash to make the dog stand up. "Her name is Bozra."

They travelled east through the valley in a convoy with four other merchant caravans. The road passed between lush fields and verdant orchards heavy with fruit. As they neared the eastern end of the valley, a group of riders came fast down the road from the mountains, trailed by a wake of dust. The merchant caravans veered off the road, and as the riders galloped past, the boy recognized the giant man at the lead. It was General Mazabi, the chief of the king's army. Unlike his soldiers, who wore helmets with red-horsehair rooster combs, the general wore no helmet on his gray mane, which fluttered in the wind behind him. In his right hand he carried a long spear – not the common crude wooden rod, but one forged from copper ore with a sharp point at the top and a bulging bottom.

While passing the caravans, General Mazabi pulled hard on his horse's reins, coming to a stop amidst a swirl of dust.

"Sall?" He turned and rode over, his massive horse towering over the donkey. "Going away, are you?"

The boy nodded.

"Did you kiss your mother goodbye?"

"Yes, but not my father—"

"Did I ask about your father?"

He shook his head.

"Never feel compelled to answer a question no one asked."

The Moabite merchant dismounted and bowed. "We will keep him safe, sir. You have my word."

The general ignored him. "Go in peace, boy, and take your time. Don't come back to Bozra before the sixth full moon comes around."

The words could have been in jest, except that the general's tone wasn't lighthearted and the specificity of a sixth full moon, not a fifth or a seventh, sounded like a warning. The moon last night had been a thin crescent, which meant it would take weeks until the first full moon, and a lot longer until the sixth one. The boy wanted to ask why he shouldn't return home sooner, but General Mazabi spun his horse around and took off towards the city. In the morning sun, Bozra's copper roofs were as red as the rooster combs on the soldiers' helmets.

Once they climbed to the crest of the hills and down the eastern slopes, all traces of greenery disappeared. Soon after, they reached the main trade route and turned north, travelling slowly over a barren land of sand, rocks, and dry thorn bushes. The sun beat down mercilessly, and the heat made breathing difficult. At midday, they stopped at an isolated oasis to fill their waterskins and take a brief rest. Near sunset, they reached another oasis and made camp in a tight cluster.

Bozra started barking, and Sall looked around to see what upset her. It was a cat, which an Egyptian merchant travelling with a wife and several children had kept in a straw basket until now. The cat was released to roam the campground, and it hissed at Bozra. She followed it from a distance, which was wise, because soon the cat was battling a snake near a rock cropping nearby. Bozra skulked back, and the cat won its battle, dragging the dead snake to the Egyptian merchant, who threw it in the fire.

Petting Bozra's head, the boy ate his food and thought about home.

At night, the men took turns standing guard. They didn't ask Sall to participate. He lay down next to the Moabite family's tent, but the merchant's snoring was too loud and kept him awake. He wondered how the merchant's wife and child managed to sleep in the same tent. After moving to the other side of the fire, he fell asleep.

During the following days, he allowed the merchant's young son to play with Bozra, but not to feed her. He made her earn her food by portioning it out as rewards while training her to sit tight until he summoned her with a whistled tune he had invented. Every night, he ate alone and slept near the fire, Bozra lying by his feet. She no longer chased the Egyptian merchant's cat, watching it from afar as it stalked the desert snakes, which often found an ignominious death by its sharp feline claws.

On the seventh night, they camped by the southern shore of great body of water. The Moabite merchant called it the Sea of Salt. The shoreline was coated with a white crust that glowed in the meek moonlight.

Stripping down to their loincloths, the men stepped into the dark water. The boy fed his donkey and dog, gave them fresh water, and followed the men. It was a strange sensation to immerse in water that was warm and thick, almost like soup. A few scratches on his legs and arms burned at first, as did his inner thighs, which were chafed from the long hours in the saddle. He licked his finger, marveling at the saltiness of the water. The bottom was rocky, but it didn't matter because the water lifted him off his feet and cradled him. Imitating the men, he lounged back, his toes sticking out of the water, and waded gently, careful not to splash.

In the morning, three of the caravans took the road west, while the Moabite merchant headed east with one other caravan. At midday, they split again and turned north alone, traveling on a narrow path into the mountains above the eastern shore of the Sea of Salt. Once in a while, the boy could see a glimpse of the water through the gorges descending to his left. In the evening, he helped the merchant start a fire, and they took turns nursing it through the night to keep predators away.

After two more days of slow northward progress, they camped for the night in a narrow passage between tall peaks. The air grew exceptionally cold, which worsened the merchant's snoring and caused him fits of coughing and spitting. Sall stayed awake much of the night, with Bozra keeping his feet warm.

While the wife prepared the morning meal, the merchant emerged from the tent wrapped in a wool coat. "What a night," he said. "Going this way has been more trouble than I expected."

"I'm grateful," the boy said.

The merchant grunted as if doubting it. He pressed one side of his crooked nose and blew, spraying snot on the ground.

"Are we close to where the dream reader lives?"

"An honest man shows gratitude with something of value."

The implication was obvious. Sall took out three of his six silver coins and gave them to the merchant.

"That's better." He pointed at a goat trail. "Follow it all the way to the summit. That's where you'll find the dream reader."

When the merchant's young son realized his four-legged playmate was departing, he cried and clung to her. His mother tried to pull him away from Bozra, but he wailed and held on.

The merchant reached into a sack, pulled out a red headdress, and offered it to Sall. "It's made of fine Egyptian cotton and dyed in your national color – a fair payment for the dog."

The boy declined. "She's my mother's dog. I can't sell her."

"She belongs to my son now." The merchant stuffed the headdress back in the sack and tied a rope around the dog's neck. "Leave quickly, or I'll take your donkey, too. And your food, water, and coins."

In the Moabite merchant's harsh tone, the boy heard the same abject cruelty as when he had threatened to roast Bozra. And judging by the wife's nervousness, his threats were not idle.

The donkey needed a firm shove to get going up the rocky trail. Bozra barked, and as the distance grew, her barks turned to yelps, which sounded almost human. Still, he kept climbing the trail, careful to bypass any rocks that could trip his donkey.

When he no longer heard Bozra's barking, the boy veered off the trail into a dry ravine and followed it for some distance. He placed a clutch of straw in front of the donkey and began to whistle Bozra's tune.

Moments passed.

He kept whistling and hoped his mother had been right about dogs' hearing being superior to men's.

Finally, rapid tapping of paws sounded, and Bozra appeared, panting hard, a rope dangling from her neck. He untied the rope and gave her water in his palms. When she calmed down, he fed her morsels of meat.

Bozra's ears pricked up, and she looked in the direction of the trail. He scratched her neck, and she didn't bark. He didn't know how long the Moabite merchant would search for her, but the man was bound to give up eventually.

The sun was a third of the way up when Bozra showed no further signs of alertness towards the trail. The boy led the donkey out of the ravine and continued the climb. Bozra followed, sniffing the ground along the trail.

Every time he thought the top of the mountain was near, the next turn revealed another steep slope. At one point, the trail narrowed, passing between a boulder and a sheer drop to distant rocks below. The donkey refused to proceed. Bozra, on the other hand, went ahead without concern and returned to check on him.

Sitting down to rest, the boy contemplated his predicament. Leaving the donkey here alone could attract coyotes, or even a tiger or a bear, which shied away from people and dogs, but could easily bring down a donkey. He would have to leave Bozra with the donkey, but to be an effective defender, she would have to remain free while not following him up the mountain. Lastly, he considered the possibility that the merchant had deceived him, and no dream reader lived at the top of the mountain. The last possibility made the most sense to him. Why would a dream reader reside on a distant mountaintop, far away from any village or town where people were more likely to seek his services?

He decided to press on until the sun reached the highest point in the sky. If he didn't reach the top of the mountain by then, he would accept defeat, descend the mountain, and search for someone to ask about the dream reader.

He tied the donkey to a rock and gave it more straw. Bozra obeyed his order to sit still. He worried she would lose patience and follow him, but she didn't, and he kept going while the sun continued to rise higher.

5

Placing one foot ahead of the other, the boy continued up the steep trail, hunched over under the beating sun. His muscles burned, his mouth tasted of dust, and he was unprepared when the trail suddenly flattened, causing him to lose his balance and fall.

Back on his feet, he shielded his eyes from the sun and looked around.

The summit was flat and clear of rocks. It was about the size of the front garden back home. Approaching the opposite edge, the boy felt awed by the view. Below him, on the left, the dark-blue Sea of Salt contrasted with the desert cliffs that jutted up from its shores. On the right, north of the Sea of Salt, a long valley was flooded with greenery. It took him a moment to make out the palm trees — thousands of canopies intertwined in an expanse of green fronds, except for a town that, from his lofty vantage point, seemed to be made of tiny houses and ant-sized people.

Across the water and the valley of palms, great mountains rose up in jagged peaks and scarred gorges. Only a single distant peak was as high as the one he was standing on. Gazing at it, he could make out the miniature outlines of buildings against the blue horizon.

"Jerusalem," a woman said behind him.

He turned sharply, almost losing his balance again.

Her flowing gray hair framed a deeply tanned face, creased as a dry raisin. She was wrapped from neck to feet in a wool blanket that was out of place in the midday heat.

Recovering from the initial shock, he said, "I don't understand."

"Ah, you're from Edom," she said in his language. Her right arm emerged from under the blanket. It was missing the hand, and she pointed with the blunt wrist. "You were looking at the highest peak in Canaan. That city on top is called Jerusalem."

He forced his eyes away from her wrist and gazed to the west. "Who lives there?"

"The Hebrew tribe of Benjamin. Its territory comes all the way down to this valley."

"Do the men of Benjamin own all these palm trees?" He gestured at the valley below.

"Only those on the west bank of the river," she said.

Scrutinizing the valley below, he made out a snaking river, which continued south until it entered the Sea of Salt. "What river is that?"

"The Jordan River." She slipped her right arm back under the blanket. "The palm trees on the east bank belong to my tribe, Reuben. Our territory is much larger than Benjamin's. It goes all the way to Rabbath Amon."

"Is that where the Jordan River comes from?"

She laughed. "You don't know this land, do you?"

His face flushed.

"The river flows down from the Sea of Galilee." Her left arm emerged from under the blanket. It also missed the hand, and she used the wrist to point north. "Several days' ride."

"The river seems small."

"It used to be bigger, but the tribe of Manasseh has diverted much of the water to their land, which extends from the west bank to the Great Sea and from the east bank all the way to Aram."

Unable to resist, he stared at her wrist, which was covered in skin as if a hand had never been attached to it. "Why does Benjamin allow Manasseh to take the water?"

"The men of Manasseh made a pact with the enemies of our God, the Canaanites, who control the northern territories. Do you see those shadows in the distance?"

He nodded.

"The Galilee Mountains. On a clear day you can see forests of cedars, oaks, and every imaginable fruit tree. The valleys in between are lush with dark soil and countless springs." She pointed west. "See the blue haze along the far horizon between the Galilee and Jerusalem? What do you think it is?"

He didn't know.

"The Great Sea. Ten days' ride from here, and you can walk on soft sand and swim in the same salty water as the Egyptians in the south and the Hittites in the north."

"Have you been there?"

"Once, a long time ago, before I came here to live with Moses."

Looking around, he saw no one.

"Don't you know Moses?"

He shook his head.

"There has never been a greater man than Moses, none more righteous, or wiser. Would you like to meet him?"

He nodded.

"Come with me."

She walked over to the north-west corner of the summit and sat cross-legged beside a chiseled slab of rock, level with the ground. The boy realized she was speaking of a dead man. He recalled the stories his father had told him of the Hebrew prophet Moses, who had once led the Hebrews through Edom during their Exodus from Egypt.

"Forty years he wandered in the desert," she said. "Right here, his journey ended."

"Why here?"

"It's the only peak from which you can see all of Canaan without actually setting foot on its soil." She brushed dust off the slab with her wrist. "Moses spent his life dreaming of Canaan, but he never realized that dream."

"Did you interpret his dream?"

"How old do you think I am?" She laughed, which made her look younger. "In fact, Moses was long dead when he appeared in my dream. He held my hands and asked me to join him here so that he can help me understand all the dreams of men and women. No one had ever held my hands before, or since, not even in my dreams. I immediately understood what the dream meant. If I came here, I would no longer be the crippled girl, born without hands, pitied by the righteous, feared by the superstitious, and mocked by the malicious. Here, I would be a person sought by all for her rare skill. The next morning, I left my village and came here. As Moses had promised, people climb the mountain to bring me gifts and discuss their dreams."

"That's why I came, too." He took out the three silver coins. "These are for you."

She patted the gravestone of Moses. "Tell me your dream."

He put the coins on the gravestone and told her what had happened at the high-priest's house, as well as the details of his dream, ending with the dwarf's transformation into a strapping young man.

"Obviously, your dream means that you wish to transform your body, as the dwarf did, but why? You're not old or ugly."

"I'm small and weak, like a child half my age. That's why An glared at me with contempt."

The dream reader rested her chin on her wrist, thinking for a moment. "Why do you care what that girl thinks of you?"

"Because I'm in love with her."

"In love? How could an angry glare from a veiled girl make you fall in love with her?"

He blushed, remembering the contours of An's rear as she bent over her father's feet, and the glistening marvel of her thick, golden braid, swaying down her back with the red bow at the bottom.

The woman poked him with her wrist. "Answer me, boy. We don't have much time."

"I saw her without a veil a long time ago."

"How long?"

"I was only five."

"Do you remember her face?"

"No, but according to my mother, I said she was very pretty and kissed her."

"All little girls are pretty. We're back to her glaring eyes."

"It's not only her eyes." He had difficulty speaking and cleared his throat. "It's everything about her. What I saw made me fall in love with her."

"Because she's beautiful?"

"Yes, and if I change into a handsome, dark, and muscular young man, her heart will change from contempt to love."

"You're growing into a handsome young man without any help, and there's nothing wrong with your complexion." She reached over and ruffled his reddish hair with her wrist.

He tilted his head out of her reach.

"Your feelings aren't true love," she said. "Men often mistake their lust for love."

"There's no mistake. I know how I feel about her. It's love."

"Love is like the sun – a blinding new glow in the morning, a tiresome sweatiness at noon, and a chilly twilight by evening."

"My love for her will never go cold."

"Tell me, boy, is your mother beautiful?"

The question upset him. He didn't want to think about his mother. "I don't know."

"How do men treat her?"

He remembered General Mazabi holding an empty wine jug in his hand and proclaiming that Umm-Sall was the most beautiful woman in all of Edom.

"Yes, she is."

"And your father, is he exceptionally handsome?"

Growing uncomfortable, the boy shook his head.

"Yet he won the heart of a beautiful woman, didn't he?"

"My father is the greatest healer in all of Edom."

"A wise man?"

"Yes."

"Kind, too?"

"Of course."

The dream reader brushed back her gray hair, exposing a deeply creased forehead. "Don't look away. I know I'm ugly now, but in my youth, I was very beautiful. Every young man who saw my face ran to my father and asked for my hand in marriage." She chuckled, holding up both her handless arms. "How do you think he answered them?"

The boy lowered his eyes.

She shook her head to get her long hair away from her face. "Men fall in love with what they see – a woman's external beauty, in which they perceive all kinds of imagined internal virtues. Women fall in love with what they hear – a man's voice, in which they seek his wisdom and humor, his tenderness and strength."

Desperation flooded him. "I'm not wise or funny, and I don't know how to be tender, or strong."

"Then these are the traits you must acquire, rather than height, muscles, or fetching features." Her wrist poked his chest. "And while you're at it, change the way you appraise girls."

"There are no other girls," he said. "I'm not wrong about the high priest's daughter. In her eyes I saw everything I needed to see. She is wise and strong. In time, she'll be tender, too."

"She's not funny, though, is she?" The dream reader got up. "Be warned, boy. Some girls' pretty eyes are mere ornaments fixed in empty heads."

He got up, as well.

"What is your name?"

"Sall."

"A good name," she said. "A spiritual name. It will serve you well in life, Sall. Now, go home and contemplate the love between your parents."

"What about my dream."

"Oh, that. Yes. Your dream has the flavor of reality. An interesting dream."

"What does it mean?"

"A dream that feels real isn't really a dream, but a memory."

"A memory of something I had never seen? How?"

She leaned forward and placed her forearms on his shoulders, pressing inward on the sides of his neck. The coolness of her wrists surprised him, and the proximity of their faces gave him a close view of her gray eyes, which reminded him of clouds.

Her blanket began to slip off her shoulders, and when she did nothing, he grabbed it.

"You're safe with me, Sall." She kissed his forehead. "Don't be afraid."

"I'm not afraid." He felt the pressure of her wrists on the sides of his neck, and his chest tightened with the urge to let go of her blanket and move away, but he didn't, dreading the possibility that she wore nothing underneath. "I'm not afraid," he repeated.

"Fear also comes from deep memories." Her lips curled in a smile that deepened the creases in the corners of her mouth and eyes. "I can feel your blood pumping up and down between your head and your heart."

He inhaled, holding it in, and exhaled slowly. "Will you answer my question?"

"Doesn't a newborn remember how to breathe, before taking his first breath? Or how to suckle, before latching onto his mother's breasts for the first time?" Her eyes glistened. "Memories reside in our hearts — not only the mechanical memories of how to breathe or suckle, which are necessary for survival, but also memories of dramatic events, which etch indelibly in the flesh and pass down the generations from parents to children like our hair color and the shape of our toes."

"Even if my dream was a memory, what does it mean?"

"When you have a dream that feels like a memory, it's not the dream's meaning that you should ponder, but its reason for surfacing into your awareness at this particular time."

"What is that reason? Will you tell me?"

"How can I? It's your memory."

"How would I know?"

"Find the tower that pierces the clouds. It may nudge more memories up to the surface."

The breeze suddenly picked up, turning into a gusty wind, which lashed them with prickly grains of sand. She withdrew from him, hugged the blanket to her chest, and hurried across the flat summit to the other side. He followed her down a short distance to a small cave between boulders. She crawled in and sat on the ground, bent under the low ceiling. There was no room for him as the rest of the cave was stuffed with jars, straw baskets, and rolls of parchment.

He had to yell over the howl of the wind. "How will I find the tower?"

She tilted her head towards the north.

"The Galilee Mountains?"

"Damascus."

He assumed it was the nearby town among the palm trees in the valley. "Is there another dream reader in Damascus?"

She shook her head. "Find the Sailor of Barada."

A violent blast of wind made her pull up the blanket over her head. He wanted to stay and ask her more, but his concern for Bozra and the donkey propelled him to move. He buried his face in the crook of his arm and felt his way up to the flat summit, across to the eastern side, and down the trail, where the wind wasn't as ferocious as at the top. He resisted the urge to run, knowing that a fall could result in an injury that would leave him stranded in this desolate place.

The lower he descended, the calmer the wind became. Coming around the large boulder over the precipice, he laughed as Bozra sprinted over and licked his face, wagging her tail. The donkey, on the other hand, didn't even glance in his direction. He gave both of them water, drank some himself, and started downhill again.

It took them the rest of the day to get down from the mountain. While twilight faded into darkness, he found the charred remnants of an old fire near a willow tree, added dry twigs and a few fallen branches, and used two flintstones to ignite a flame.

With darkness came the cold. He ate some bread and lay down by the fire, his hand reaching out from under the blanket to caress Bozra's head. He wondered if she missed home as badly as he did.

Late at night, the boy woke up to hear Bozra growling. Her ears were pricked up, and she sniffed the cold air in short, rapid intakes. He added fuel to the fire and, after a while, she calmed down. He fell back asleep, but woke up when she growled again. The donkey shifted restlessly, which added to the boy's dread.

It went on like that for the rest of the night, and he bolted up repeatedly to stare into the surrounding darkness and rekindle the fire, before lying down again, wrapped in the blanket, trembling.

6

At the first hint of sunrise, Sall got up, relieved to have survived the night. Whatever predator had stalked them, the fire and Bozra had kept it away. He gave her a piece of bread, stomped the embers, and packed up the donkey. The morning chill and the lack of sleep combined to cloud his mind, making it hard to think. He tried to calculate how many nights he would have to sleep in the desert, haunted by wild animals for their next meal, before reaching home. Two weeks seemed like a reasonable estimate, which was much sooner than the six full moons of General Mazabi's cryptic warning.

With a cheerful bark, Bozra ran a short distance northward and paused to look back. She was right, he thought. Giving up now would mean that he was forever destined to remain a cowardly boy, deserving a girl's contempt. Besides, Damascus wasn't far, and the proximity to the Sea of Salt and the Jordan River explained why a man would be called Sailor. Was Barada the name of his tribe, or his original place of birth? It didn't matter. Either the Sailor of Barada knew where the colossal tower was, in which case the quest would continue, or he didn't, which would leave no choice but to head back to Edom.

Fortified by this measure of clarity about the near future, the boy mounted the donkey and followed Bozra. The road was narrow and rocky, wedged between steep slopes. The sun rose over his right shoulder, its rays thawing the chill of the night.

They reached a fork in the road. He decided to take the left branch, which followed a dry creek downhill. Along the path, he noticed horse dung, cold campfires, and trash from travelers, but he didn't run into anyone.

When the sun was near its peak, the path emerged into the open, and the green valley of palm trees lay below, much closer than from the tomb of Moses on the mountaintop. He marveled at how straight the long lines of brown trunks were, shaded by the thick canopies of palm fronds. Workers climbed the tall trunks to clip dry fronds and harvest bunches of ripe dates, which dropped down onto sheets of cloth. Other workers removed the dates from the stems and packed the fruit in tall clay jars.

The trail ended at a wide road that ran north-south along the foothills. The air smelled of rotting fruit and smoke. He whistled Bozra's tune and clicked his fingers to make her walk beside the donkey.

They followed a group of workers, who carried loaded jars. The road curved to the left, and he heard the sound of water. A pair of stone pillars welcomed them to a wooden bridge over the river. The opposite end of the bridge was secured to another pair of stone pillars.

The donkey stopped and brayed, refusing to go on, whereas Bozra ran across the bridge, turned left, and went down to the water, where she jumped right in. The current swept her downstream. Sall dismounted and ran across the bridge and to the left, along the side of the river. He caught up with Bozra just as she managed to reach the opposite bank. She climbed out and shook, spraying drops of fresh water that glistened in the sunlight. She looked at him, and he feared she would jump back in to cross over. He walked back towards the bridge, waving at her to do the same. After a moment of hesitation, she did, and they reunited on the bridge. She smelled the way wet dogs did, but he still hugged her with great relief.

The workers laughed and cheered. A foreman arrived and began yelling. The workers picked up the clay jars and hurried on. One of them tripped and dropped his jar, which shattered, letting out a heap of fresh palm dates. The foreman whipped the worker. Bozra ran over, barking at the foreman, who stepped back, swinging his whip to keep her away. Sall whistled her tune, and she ran back.

The other workers put down their jars and collected the dates. The clay shards were tossed into the water.

The donkey, meanwhile, relented and ambled across the bridge.

A short distance further, they arrived at the town he had seen from the summit the previous day. Its walls had crumbled, forming a ring of rubble around the houses. A few merchant caravans camped in a field near the entrance to the city. He saw no fairgrounds, but the main street was teeming with shoppers and merchants' stalls as if the whole town was its own fairgrounds.

He dismounted, tied Bozra to the saddle, and pulled the donkey along while walking up the main street. The people spoke Hebrew, which he recognized from hearing it while helping his mother shop in Bozra's fairgrounds. She had always sought the Hebrew merchants from Canaan for their honey, cheese, olive oil, grape wine, figs, pomegranates, and palm dates.

One of the stalls was piled up with various items, but his attention was drawn to one in particular – a red headdress, which hung from the corner of a stall. He felt a pang of fear and quickened his steps.

"Not so fast, boy!"

It was the Moabite merchant, coming around the stall, his mouth twisted into a smirk under his crooked nose.

Bozra started barking.

The merchant raised both hands in mock surrender. "Don't worry, little dog. We're all friends here."

"You can't have her," the boy said.

He made a dismissive gesture. "Anyone can see that this dog is completely loyal to you."

"She is."

The merchant made to pet Bozra, but she growled and bared her teeth. He retreated, snorting and spitting.

Sall scratched her neck, calming her down.

"Well, boy, did the dream reader solve all your problems?"

He blushed. "She told me to seek a man who might know what I'm looking for."

"Who?"

"The Sailor of Barada."

The merchant lifted a copper plate and offered it to a woman who was eyeing his merchandise, but she shook her head and walked on.

"Do you know where I can find him?"

"Who?"

"The Sailor of Barada."

"Never heard of him."

The boy was disappointed, but he knew that the merchant was a visitor, like himself. "It's my first time in Damascus. Can you introduce me to one of the locals?"

"Damascus? Why do you speak of Damascus?"

"Isn't this Damascus?"

"This town?" The merchant laughed and poked Sall's chest with a forefinger. "You're dumber than I thought, boy. What's wrong with you?"

"What town is this, then?"

"Jericho."

He felt foolish, remembering the praise everyone had always showered on the exquisite date palms from Jericho. "And where is Damascus?"

"Farther than the moon, you feebleminded boy." The Moabite merchant was still laughing. "Go back home before you lose your head altogether."

It was hard to keep back his tears as he walked away, the merchant's mocking laughter ringing in his ears.

Further into the city, the stalls gave way to wooden shops filled with merchandise – cloth, carpets, furniture, tools, produce, bread, cheese, and even one store filled with parchment scrolls. Beside it was a garden, where a bearded man read aloud from the scrolls to a group of boys, who repeated every sentence after him. The garden reminded Sall of home, and the memory caused him to lose the battle with his tears, which flowed down his cheeks. He was, as the Edomite merchant had said, a feebleminded boy on a foolish quest, who should go home before he literally lost his head.

Retracing his steps down the street, Sall decided to wait by the road outside the city and inquire for a caravan heading south to Edom. He still had some food left and could fill up the waterskins in the river before the journey.

A dog chased them from behind, barking madly, and jumped on Bozra. The knot on her leash loosened from around the saddle horn, and Sall was too slow to grab it in time. She took off with the other dog, turning down a side street. It happened fast, and his attempted whistling failed. He yelled her name and gave chase, pulling the donkey along.

At the end of the side street was a workshop with smoking chimneys and a solid wooden fence. The gate was open as several men were pulling out a flat wagon loaded with clay jars, similar to the ones used by the workers to store the harvested dates. Bozra chased the other dog into the workshop, and a great noise of shattering clay followed. The two dogs reappeared, leaped over the wagon and toppled all the clay jars, which hit the ground and broke into pieces, as well, raising a cloud of clay dust.

"Bozra!" He stepped on her leash as she ran by him. "Enough!"

The other dog circled back, but the boy, while holding Bozra's leash, threw a stone, chasing it away.

A bare-chested man, his arms covered in clay dust, burst out the gate, wielding a club and cursing bitterly. Seeing Bozra, he rushed over to beat her with the club. The boy sheltered her with his own body. The men who had pulled the wagon hurried over and held the man back. He sat on the ground and buried his face in his hands, while the others congregated around him, unsure what to say. A bunch of children came out of the house attached to the workshop, followed by a young woman, and gazed silently at the spectacle of destruction.

7

The judge of Jericho, a fat man wearing a white cap, heard litigants at the entrance to the city. The potter was the first to plead his case, but before he even started, the Moabite merchant appeared beside Sall and announced his willingness to serve as an interpreter, which the judge accepted.

The potter's name was Ishkadim. According to the merchant, who whispered an abbreviated translation to the boy, the potter claimed to be "as shattered as my jars," having lost a month's worth of production, because the boy had failed to keep his dog on a leash. Without the sales proceeds from the ruined jars, he would soon run out of raw clay and wood for the ovens, as well as food for his wife and children. The judge looked at the boy and asked a question, which the merchant translated.

"Do you deny the allegations?"

"There was another dog. That's why my dog ran off."

"Nonsense," the merchant said. "She ran because you didn't tie the leash properly."

The judge waited a moment for translation, but when the Moabite merchant shook his head, he passed judgement in rapid Hebrew and waved his hand to dismiss them.

"I warned you, boy." The merchant snorted and spat. "Now, you've lost not only your head."

"What did the judge decide?"

"He gave the potter your dog, donkey, and everything else you own."

The potter led the donkey away. Bozra, whose leash was tied to the saddle, was dragged along, looking back at the boy. He thought of the promise he'd made to his mother and struggled not to cry. Would his safe return be enough to comfort her for the loss of her dog?

He turned to the Moabite merchant. "Do you know of a caravan that's heading to Edom? I want to go home."

"Home? Jericho is your new home." The merchant pointed at the departing potter. "Follow your new master."

"I don't understand."

"The judge made you a slave for twelve months."

"A slave?" The whole thing seemed unreal. "Twelve months?"

"That's if you work hard enough to pay back the damages you caused, but if you're lazy, the potter may keep you longer, possibly forever." The merchant cackled and shoved him roughly. "Go on, boy, serve your master."

Back at the pottery, Sall didn't wait to be told what to do. He picked up all the clay shards, making a tidy pile in the corner of the yard, and swept away the small pieces and dust. Meanwhile, the potter unpacked the donkey, taking the waterskins and what was left of the food, tied Bozra to the gate post, and put the donkey in a corral in the back of the house with a few goats, nibbling at a pile of straw.

Bozra started barking.

Sall went over to pet her. "Don't worry. We're staying here together until we're free again, and I'll bring you back home as I promised my mother."

Bozra barked again, and he realized someone was standing behind him. It was the potter, staring down at him, pointing at a low heap of wooden logs near the ovens. Sall understood. He was being told to bring more wood.

He left the town and walked to the palm orchards in search of a fallen tree. The first few trees he found lying on the ground were too fresh, and it took him a long time to find one whose trunk was dry enough to break under pounding with a rock.

He made multiple trips carrying logs until the pile was as tall as he and his hands were badly blistered. Sunset was coming, and not a moment too soon. As he returned to the pottery with the last load in his arms, he saw the Moabite merchant at the door to the house, talking with Ishkadim, who kept shaking his head. The boy watched from the gate with a foreboding sense that the day's series of misfortunes had not run out yet.

After some back-and-forth, the potter accepted a few copper coins from the merchant, who ignored the boy, went to Bozra, and untied her leash from the fence post. She barked and pulled towards the boy. The merchant kicked her and heaved the leash violently, making her yelp.

Sall put down the wood and ran over. He dropped by her side and hugged her. She pressed her body to him, licking his face, whimpering. The Moabite merchant pulled hard on the leash, plucking her out of the boy's embrace and sending her rolling on the ground. She tried to bark, but the leash tightened on her neck, and only a pitiful shriek came through.

Sall, still on the ground, wailed, "Don't hurt her!"

The potter hurried over and took the leash from the merchant. He handed it to Sall and said something in Hebrew, pointing down the street.

"Come on, slave." The merchant sneered, which made his crooked nose twist even further to the side. "Your master wants you to deliver this stupid dog to my son."

The field outside the town was packed with merchant caravans, preparing for the night. The Moabite merchant's young son ran to Bozra. She sat, tolerating his affection patiently, her eyes on Sall. He tied the leash to a tent peg, kissed her snout, and stumbled away, blinded by tears. She barked, and he covered his ears to block off the sound.

That evening, he lost his new sandals, his clothes, and his hair, which was shaved off with a dull blade by the potter's young wife. She did it gently, murmuring apologetically whenever he flinched in pain. When it was over, she gave him a sleeveless shirt and a blanket, and pointed to a thin mat on the floor by the door.

He lay down and close his eyes. The mat did little to soften the hard floor, and the air was pungent, with all the children sharing one bed. His mind simmered with images and sounds – the two dogs toppling the jars off the wagon, the explosion of shattering clay, the potter's rage and despair, and the judge's verdict, translated by the disdainful Moabite merchant: "The Hebrew judge made you a slave for twelve months." Bozra's whimpers echoed in his mind, fading as she was left behind, never to be seen again.

8

Waking up before dawn, at first Sall felt relief, certain that those terrible events had been a nightmare. A moment later, however, he touched his shaven scalp, saw his surroundings, and realized it had all actually happened. He was a slave to a Hebrew potter for at least a year. His second thought was, therefore, to run away. He hadn't forgotten General Mazabi's warning not to return home until the sixth full moon, but whatever reason the general had, it couldn't possibly be worse than slavery. He could take off now without the donkey, who would slow him down, whistle for Bozra to escape from the Moabite merchant, run out of Jericho towards the Sea of Salt, and hide somewhere until a merchant caravan passed by.

And then?

With his bald head, bare feet, and sleeveless shirt, they would immediately recognize him as a slave. How did the Hebrews treat runaway slaves? In Edom, the measures included lashing with a leather whip, scolding with boiling water, cutting off the ears and, for the most persistent escapees, amputating a foot. He had no reason to expect lighter punishments here.

Outside, he washed his face with water from the well and stood by the wooden fence, gazing at the quiet street. Escape was tempting, but futile. Rather, he should send a message to his family with a merchant heading to Edom. There was no question that his mother would want to help him, but would his father agree to travel all the way to Canaan, or hire others to go, and pay a substantial sum to the potter for his freedom after he had run away without permission?

Sall recalled his father's admonishment while they had walked home from the high priest's house: "You're the son of a healer, which makes you a healer from the day you were born until the day you die. You can stop being a healer as much as you can stop being Sall, my only son, or cease to be an Edomite. A person cannot stop being what he was born to be, and if he tries, the betrayal will make him rot from the inside out." And that's exactly what he had done by leaving his family and apprenticeship on a quest to change himself into a different person altogether. Reflecting on his actions, Sall had no doubt as to how his father thought of him now: a rotten son, not worth saving.

The potter's wife came out of the house. She pointed at herself. "Timna."

"Sall." He wiped his eyes. "I'm from Edom."

Timna appeared to be not much older than him. While preparing the morning meal, she pointed at each item of food and kitchenware and told him the name in Hebrew. She stoked one of the ovens, repeating the words for hot, cold, oven, wood, and fire, then drew from the well and recited the Hebrew words for well, water, rope, and bucket. He repeated each word while helping her bake flat breads and cut slices of cheese.

Done with the meal preparations, Timna showed him how to break off chunks from a large lump of clay, which he had mistaken for regular rock, and the way to crumple the chunks into powder and add water while stepping on it the same way vintners stepped on grapes.

The children came out one by one, drawn by the smell of fresh bread. There were eight of them, the oldest about twelve. Timna was obviously too young to have given birth to all of them, but she kissed each one affectionately and gave them food.

When the potter came out, the children ran to him, and for the first time since yesterday's disaster, his grim face broke in a smile. He picked the children up two at a time and murmured quiet blessings in their ears. When he saw Sall, his smile faded. He sat in the only chair, and Timna served him food while the children sat on the ground around him, eating and talking. She brought Sall a cup of goat milk, pointed at her husband, who was feeding one of the children pieces of cheese, and said, "His name is Ishkadim, which means a man of pottery."

After the meal, the workday began. Sall and the older children watered and stepped on lumps of clay, creating wet paste. Timna pulled aside a curtain from the open end of a shack in the back of the yard. Inside was a contraption Sall hadn't seen before. It was made of a wooden wheel, similar to a wagon wheel, but set horizontally, close to the ground. The short axle was fixed in a hole that had been carved into a heavy slab of rock. On top of the flat wheel, at the center, was a large wooden plate with a smooth face. Ishkadim used a stick to spin the wheel. He didn't stop, making it go faster and faster until it spun at a speed that blurred the outer edge.

Timna filled a bowl with clay paste and brought it into the shack. The children stopped working and came to watch. Sall did the same.

Ishkadim scooped up a palmful of wet clay and slapped it at the center of the spinning plate over the wheel. He added five more fistfuls in rapid succession. To Sall's amazement, the wet clay began to spread outward evenly. Ishkadim placed his hands around the spreading clay, blocking its way and causing it to start rising around the edge, creating a rim. With one hand at the rim, he pressed the other hand in the center, making the bottom thinner while pushing more of the wet clay to the sides, where the rim was now as tall as a man's knee. The potter's large hands shaped and reshaped the clay with quick, precise positioning that resembled a dance and belied his rough appearance. He moved around the spinning wheel and the fast-forming jar, continuing to adjust the rising wall of clay. When it was as tall as a man's hip, he shaped the upper rim as a lip, curled outwards, and put a hand inside to push the middle out and give the spinning jar it's final form.

Timna inserted a thin piece of wood under the jar. Together, they carried it to a table out in the sun. The children stood around the table, gazing up at the moist new jar.

Ishkadim clapped. "Back to work!"

Sall resumed stepping on chunks of clay while one of the children fetched water from the well and poured it on. Meanwhile, Ishkadim started making another jar.

During the morning, men came by to buy jars, but the potter had none to sell. He pointed at Sall while talking to his disappointed customers. At midday, Timna built up the fires in the ovens and started transferring the newly made jars into the ovens.

Every part of Sall's body was hurting, and some of the blisters on his hands and feet burned as if on fire. He remembered seeing red flowers in the field outside the yard. Going out to check, he was relieved to discover they were the same flowers that his father grew in the front garden for its medicinal powers. He removed a few of the small pods from the stems and returned to the yard.

Timna noticed him and asked if he needed anything. He asked for a bowl and made buzzing sounds to indicate bees while licking his finger as if they were dipped in honey. She brought him an empty bowl and a small jug of bee honey. He popped the flower pods to extract the tiny black seeds, ground them with a rock, and mixed in the honey. After washing his hands and feet, he smeared the potion on his blisters. He recalled his father's warning not to put any of it in his mouth unless he wanted to become numb and sleepy. Right now, however, the prospect of numbness and sleepiness was appealing. He wiped the bowl with his fingers and licked them clean. Soon, his aches and pains faded away, and he could barely stay awake to finish the evening meal.

9

When Sall woke up at dawn, his blisters were much better, but his sadness only darkened. He thought of Bozra being fed by the Moabite merchant's son, who would soon earn her total loyalty. He also thought of Bozra, the city, where life continued without him. Had his mother confessed to his father about her part in his departure? How would she excuse it? "Do I have a choice? A young man must follow his heart's journey, or his heart will go without him, lost forever." In retrospect, it was hard for Sall to believe the reason his mother had given, because she did have a choice – to tell him about the dangers of the road, the dishonesty of men, and the cruelty of the Gods. Why had she let him leave home, betray his father, and throw away his future?

He thought of the customers queuing up in the front garden to seek relief for their ailments. How long would it be before his father took on someone else as an apprentice, to groom as the next healer? A month? A week? Or had he already chosen a new apprentice – perhaps one of his older-sisters' husbands, or a more distant relative?

This thought in particular unsettled Sall. He felt foolish to have abandoned such a wonderful life and the prospect of an honorable profession among his family and neighbors, all in a futile quest to find an imaginary dwarf who had actually admitted the truth: "Elixirist is not profession."

Sitting up on the hard floor, he wiped his eyes and thought of the high priest's daughter, her golden braid, and the contours of her body. He imagined her beautiful face under the veil, a face befitting her mesmerizing eyes, and felt a forceful urge to hold her in his arms as only a husband was permitted to do. It would never happen, of course. What respectable father would give his daughter to a boy who had betrayed his own father?

He recalled the dwarf's advice: "If you wish to change how another person feels about you, start by changing yourself." The irony was that he had sought to change himself by leaving home on this failed quest, whereas the change he should have sought was possible at home, under his loving mother's care and his wise father's guidance. By transforming from a boy to a full-fledged healer like his father, or an even greater healer than his father, he would have had a chance to change how An felt about him, as well as how her father would consider such a match. That possibility was forever lost, even if, by some miracle, he would survive this slavery and find a way to return home, humiliated and ridiculed.

Sall hugged his knees to his chest and wished he could bow before an effigy of Qoz and plead with the greatest God of Edom to help him. Why had Umm-Sall not pack a small effigy with the food on the donkey?

Timna woke up, and he followed her outside to help prepare the morning meal, which was meager compared to the previous day. She marveled at his quick recovery. Using his broken Hebrew and hand gestures, he told her about the simple potion he had learned from his father.

When Ishkadim came out of the house, he gave the children their morning blessings and examined the new jars. Two showed thin cracks and had to be discarded. The remaining eight were placed along the wall where a dozen new jars had shattered two days earlier.

Timna served her husband bread, cheese, and grapes. She called Sall over, pointed out his healing blisters, and explained the boy's knowledge of potions. Ishkadim nibbled at his food for a while and gave the rest to the children. He kept glancing at Sall, his expression no longer hostile.

After the meal and a short prayer, Ishkadim beckoned Sall and walked to the main street of Jericho. Timna tagged along. As they walked by the merchants' stalls, Sall's eyes searched for the Moabite merchant, but didn't find him.

Ishkadim stopped at a local vendor of baskets who knew the language of Edom. Between Timna and the vendor, Sall managed to understand Ishkadim's questions, which centered on what kind of ailments he knew how to treat. In response, he explained that blisters, like all skin scrapes and injuries, can be treated with the potion he had mixed from bee honey and black seeds of certain red flowers. He could also mix other potions for upset stomachs, fevers, and various aches, provided he found the required ingredients in the surrounding areas, or purchased them from travelling merchants.

Before they left, the basket vendor spoke to Ishkadim in rapid Hebrew, and the potter responded. The ensuing argument grew in intensity, and Timna explained to Sall that the basket vendor is upset because the Hebrew God, Yahweh, frowned upon healers, who tried to ease the ailments He meted out to people as punishments. When the boy looked around for an effigy or a statue, she laughed and said that their God was everywhere all the time and didn't need a physical body.

Ishkadim ended the argument with a dismissive wave of his big hand and walked over to another stall, where he bought two jugs of honey.

Back at the pottery, while everyone else continued making clay jars, Sall collected black seeds and mixed a large bowl of potion for treating wounds. Ishkadim sent the two oldest children to announce all over Jericho that a skilled Edomite healer was available to treat injuries for a modest fee.

As the first few customers arrived, Sall's knees grew weak. In Edom, his father had done all the talking, taken care of all the ailments, and earned the people's gratitude and admiration. "Memorizing the right ingredients," his father had told him, "and mixing potions correctly, are two skills anyone can learn. To become a true healer, however, a man must learn to truly listen. A good listener opens not only his ears, but also his heart."

Sall crouched behind the fence, out of sight. How could he truly listen to those Hebrews strangers, who spoke a foreign language and worshiped an invisible God?

Timna brought a bowl of warm water and clean rags, which he had asked for, and a jar to collect payments. She squatted beside him, her face twisted in pain, and touched her lower abdomen.

"What's wrong?"

"Nothing." She smiled. "I'm with a baby. The first time is the hardest, they say. What about you?"

"No baby," he said, making her laugh. "Where is the mother of the children?"

"She died in labor." Timna took a deep breath. "Are you nervous?"

He nodded.

She got up, went back to the house, and returned with his sandals, as well as a clean robe and a headdress to cover his shaven head. He changed quickly, delighted to dress as a free man.

"You look nice," she said.

"I'm not my father. He is the real healer, not me."

"Did you assist him?"

"Every day."

"Did you watch him when he treated the people in your city?"

"All the time."

Timna pulled the gate open. "Can you pretend to be him?"

Sall stood beside her and glanced out at the waiting customers. "My father enjoyed taking care of his customers."

"We have a saying." Timna leaned against the gatepost. "A blessed man starts every day with a new song in his heart."

Forcing a smile onto his face, Sall imagined that he was his father, welcoming a new day of healing the people.

Ishkadim came out of the shack and looked at Sall, obviously surprised to see the boy no longer in the sleeveless shirt. His hands were covered in wet clay. He wiped them on his robe, picked up the chair he used at mealtime, and carried it to the gate. Gesturing for Sall to sit in it, he stepped back to watch.

The boy hesitated, glancing at Timna, who needed to sit down more than he did. She smiled and beckoned the first in line.

Sall sat down and recalled how his father welcomed the customers. "Good morning," he said, imitating his father's gracious tone. "How can I help you today?"

Timna translated his words to Hebrew.

The man lifted his robe and exposed a long cut over the front of his thigh.

Remembering his father's method of explaining to each customer the condition and how he would treat it, Sall said: "The skin along the cut is a bit red, but there's no swelling yet and no oozing pus. All we need to do is clean the wound, apply the potion, and dress it."

Timna translated it.

Sall used a wet rag to clean the wound, spread potion over it, and bandaged it with a dry rag. The man bowed in gratitude and dropped a coin in the jar.

Next were a mother with her son, about ten, whose knees were scraped almost to the bone from a bad fall. Sall welcomed them in Hebrew, making only one mistake, which Timna corrected with a whisper.

He remembered his father's rule: "The worse the injury, the more positive the healer's words must be." And the explanation: "Fear hinders healing, whereas the expectation of a full recovery is self-fulfilling."

"It looks much worse than it is," Sall said, reciting one of his father's favorite phrases.

As Timna translated, Sall repeated the Hebrew words after her, which elicited laughter from those who were close enough to hear. He cleaned the wounds with a wet rag, and the child started crying, holding on to his mother, who looked distraught. Timna comforted them in Hebrew, and Sall realized he was using too much force, forgetting to imitate his father's gentle manner.

"I'm sorry," he said. "I'll be more careful now. May I continue?"

Timna translated, and the mother nodded.

With a light touch, he applied generous layers of potion. Timna helped with the bandages.

For payment, the mother handed over a small basket of pomegranates, indicating that the basket itself was included.

The new robe felt hot, and he wiped sweat from his face. Feeling more confident, he turned to the next person, an older man with an open sore on the back of his hand.

When sunset approached, Sall had treated more than three dozen injuries and turned away a similar number of customers, whose ailments required different potions. Timna invited them to return for treatment after the Hebrew holiday of Passover, which was starting that evening and would last seven days.

10

That night, the evening meal did not include bread, but flat pieces of hastily baked unleavened dough, which had the texture of tree bark and the taste of nothing. On the other hand, the coins in the jar had paid for chunks of lamb and goat kid, as well as fish from the Jordan River – delicious as long as he avoided looking at the dead eyes. During the meal, Ishkadim told the children stories about the Hebrew slaves in Egypt and how their God inflicted ten plagues on the stubborn Pharaoh until he freed them.

The children were growing sleepy as the potter went on to recount the forty years of following Moses in the desert, which involved wars with several nations, but not with Edom, whose king allowed the Hebrews safe passage on account of their shared ancestor, the patriarch Isaac, whose sons Esau and Jacob had begotten the nations of Edom and Israel.

At this point, Ishkadim passed a cup of wine to Sall. "Thank you, boy!"

Sipping the wine, he thought of the tomb of Moses at the top of the mountain, overlooking all of Canaan, guarded by the handless dream reader. Her advice, to seek the Sailor of Barada in Damascus, no longer mattered. The Hebrews would be celebrating their exodus from Egyptian slavery again before he regained his freedom. By then, he would be too homesick to go to Damascus, which was more distant than the moon, according to the Moabite merchant.

In the morning, Timna explained to Sall that, during the seven days of Passover, the Hebrews didn't work, farm, or conduct trade. The affluent men had gone on a pilgrimage to the Holy Temple in Shiloh, and the rest made sacrifices at the local temple. She suggested he spent the holiday stocking up on ingredients for his potions.

With a basket over his shoulder, Sall left the pottery after the morning meal. He searched the main street and among the caravans outside Jericho for the Moabite merchant and his family, but they were gone. He longed to see Bozra, but found comfort in knowing she was loved by the merchant's son. He also asked if any of the caravans were going to Edom, but none were.

For the next seven days, he explored the foothills alongside the Jordan River for plants he remembered his father using. He decided not to try trapping animals, which would require him to dissect them for their internal organs, dry the organs in the sun for days or weeks, and grind them into powders. His knowledge was too limited, and he feared making an error, remembering what his father had said while treating a man whose skin rash had gotten much worse after visiting a healer in a village near Bozra: "A healer's first duty is to avoid making things worse." The rule, Sall realized, wasn't only moral and fair, but also important for the healer to avoid the wrath of enraged relatives and the risk of a fate worse than slavery.

Sall dried the plants he'd found and ground them into powders. Timna brought a few bowls, jugs, and a pot from the kitchen. He set up stones in a small circle and collected wood to make fire for boiling water. All the while, he practiced his Hebrew with her until he was able to translate many of the words and phrases his father had used with the customers in Edom.

Occasionally, Timna sighed and pressed her hand to her lower belly, but those moments of discomfort passed quickly, and he sensed that she didn't want him to pry.

After sunset on the last day of Passover, Ishkadim lit up torches and erected a shack for shade outside the gate. He also dragged over a few boulders for feeble customers to sit on.

The next morning, shortly after sunrise, a queue of ailing and injured people waited outside the gate. Sall was ready with several bowls of potions and jugs of warm tonic. He took a deep breath, imagined he was his father, and whistled Bozra's tune as his own private song of joy at starting a new day.

Timna beckoned the first in line.

Having organized everything in advance, Sall's work moved along smoothly. For the common skin cuts and scrapes, he had mixed a large bowl of potion with bee honey and black seeds from the red flowers. He gave a spoonful of the same potion to those with a broken arm or leg, before fixing the limb between two straight branches, secured by strings, which he had weaved from dry palm fronds. He served a tonic made with powdered willow-tree bark to treat back pains and aching joints, forcing down two full cups for those whose skin felt warm. For chest pain and heavy coughing, he made them inhale small amounts of powdered myrtle leaves. He also mixed a myrtle tonic for customers who had trouble urinating and those who had worms in their feces, which was more common than he expected. For those with stomach pain or swelling, either with constipation or its opposite, and for men with pain when urinating, he gave a tonic made of honeysuckle flowers, which was also helpful for any kind of fevers, boils, or sores, on which he also applied honeysuckle powder with a bit of honey to make it sticky. Remembering his father's warning to avoid making things worse, he told them to come back if they had trouble breathing, vomited, or developed diarrhea.

By the day's end, the queue was gone, the payment jar was full of silver and copper coins, and the shack was stuffed with payments in kind, such as fruit, vegetables, cheese, and a few farming implements. When Ishkadim saw all of it, he dropped to his knees and chanted a song of gratitude to his invisible God.

11

Getting up before dawn, Sall went to mix the potions and boil the water for the tonics. He expected only a few customers, considering how many he had treated the previous day, but a queue started growing at sunrise.

After the morning meal, with Timna at his side, Sall took a moment to adjust his mind to imitating his father, smiled at the first customer and asked, "How can we help you today?"

One after another, he treated the people, but the line didn't get shorter. The day grew hot, and the potions and tonics ran low. He told Timna how to mix new batches while he continued treating people, his Hebrew now sufficient, except for an occasional word he didn't understand.

In the late afternoon, when all his supplies were exhausted, the few remaining customers had to be sent away, disappointed. Sunset brought about the Sabbath, and he was relieved to know there would be no customers the next day.

The evening meal was a happy one, with abundance of food and wine, which Ishkadim drank to excess. After a restful night, Sall left the house with a large basket, knowing he wasn't bound by their religious rules that mandated complete rest until sunset. Jericho was quiet, with no merchants or shoppers, craftsmen or laborers. The morning air was cool and clear, without a trace of smoke, because the Hebrews did not start fires during their Sabbath.

Taking his time, he peeled bark from willow trees and collected red-flower seeds, myrtle plants, honeysuckle, and wormwood. Back at the pottery, he spread the plants on several rocks to dry in the sun and started to grind the bark into powder.

Consumed by the work, his back to the beating sun, Sall was startled by a shadow on the ground beside him. Turning quickly, he saw a bearded old man leaning on two walking canes. He wore a white robe with blue fringes and a wooden breastplate fixed with a dozen gems. Behind him, a group of men stood together, their faces grim.

The old man raised one of the canes and pointed at the bowl in which Sall was grinding the bark. "What is this?"

While he already understood the Hebrew words, Sall hesitated to answer.

"Speak up, boy."

"It's willow bark for a potion."

"What potion?"

"To help people." Sall's eyes were drawn to the glistening gems in the breastplate. "I'm a healer."

Lifting one of his canes straight up, the man pointed at the sky. "Yahweh is the only healer."

The men behind him voiced their agreement.

"Good Sabbath, priest." Ishkadim came out of the house, wiping his eyes and yawning while he walked over. "Aren't we supposed to rest today?"

His casual tone surprised Sall. No one in Bozra would dare speak like this to a priest.

"Have you forgotten Yahweh's decree?" The priest creased his eyes in concentration while reciting the words. "And when you come to the land that I promised you, do not imitate the ways of the gentiles in doing magic, gazing at stars, believing in false signs, or performing wizardry – and a wizard among you shall be put to death."

The words terrified Sall, who retreated deep into the shack.

Ishkadim, however, didn't seem concerned. "The boy is not a wizard. His father is a famous healer in Edom. They know what plants help sooth some ailments, that's all." He gestured at the plants drying on the rock. "Myrtle, wormwood, honeysuckle – didn't Yahweh create them for us to use?"

The old priest glared at Sall. "An Edomite!"

"What's wrong with that?" Ishkadim pointed at the sky. "Didn't He create the Edomites, too?"

Laughter came from the men behind the priest.

Enjoying himself, Ishkadim continued. "And didn't Yahweh send this boy to Jericho to teach us how to use these plants that He created?"

As fearful as he was, Sall couldn't help but admire his master's arguments, which seemed to have won the day with the men, if not with the priest.

"Very good." Ishkadim clapped. "Shall we go back to resting on this holy Sabbath?"

The men turned to leave.

The priest knocked on the breastplate with his cane. "And on the Sabbath, you shall rest, together with your slave and your livestock and all that you own." The priest pointed the cane at Sall and turned it slowly towards Ishkadim. "And the man who violates the Sabbath, he shall be stoned to death."

The bemusement faded from Ishkadim's face, and Sall realized that the priest had made a winning argument.

"Look at all this." The priest waved the cane at the drying plants, the half-ground willow bark in the bowl, and the boy in the shack. "Your slave has been working on the Sabbath."

Ishkadim opened his mouth to respond, but didn't seem to find the words.

The men behind the priest advanced closer, spreading in a half-circle as if to block any escape.

The priest grinned.

Sall pressed his hands together to stop them from shaking. He tried to think of something to say, or do, but was paralyzed with dread. He shut his eyes and imagined that it wasn't him standing in a shack at a Hebrew town away from Edom. Instead, it was his father, who had dealt with all kinds of men, including Hebrews and priests. He would know how to diffuse an intense situation like this.

"Excuse me." Sall stepped forward, bowed before the priest, and spoke in the conciliatory tone his father often used. "Please, holy man of Yahweh, let me help resolve this unfortunate misunderstanding."

The priest and his companions looked at him with astonishment, but Sall didn't pay attention, his mind busy recalling his father's method of dealing with unhappy customers. First, he always restated the issue in mild terms. Second, he flattered the customer. And then, he proposed a solution to the problem.

"Sabbath," Sall said. "It's a wonderful day of rest."

"A holy day," the priest said.

"Indeed." He forced a smile onto his face. "Your God is wise and merciful to give you a holy day of rest. It's a generous divine blessing, given only to you, the Hebrews. He surely loves you more than any other nation."

The priest grunted, visibly pleased, and his companions murmured in agreement.

"You're truly blessed," Sall continued. "I wish the Sabbath was for me, too, but I must work, because I'm not a Hebrew man."

"But your master is." The priest pointed his cane at Ishkadim. "And he violated Yahweh's laws when he made you, his slave, work on the Sabbath."

Sall knew exactly what his father, proud man that he was, would say in response. "I am no one's slave."

A long moment of silence followed his statement.

One of the priest's companions spoke up. "That's a lie. I heard the judge pass judgement, giving the potter ownership of this Edomite boy."

"I was there, too," another man said. "The judge made him a slave for twelve months."

The priest and his companions stared at Ishkadim, who looked at Sall with a mix of surprise and resentment that reflected his dilemma: confirm his ownership of the boy and risk being stoned to death for violating the Sabbath, or acknowledge the boy's freedom and risk losing a newfound source of wealth.

Waving his hand, Ishkadim chuckled. "Is he wearing a slave's shirt? Is he barefooted?"

"His head is shaved," one of the men said.

Sall touched his bald pate. "I had lice."

Even as the men laughed, Sall knew he made a mistake. There was no question that the judge had made him a slave, which was the reason his hair was shaved off.

Ishkadim laughed. "The boy is joking, of course. He was my slave, it's true, and his head was shaved, as with any other slave. The judge made him my slave for twelve months, because we thought it would take that long to earn back the damages his dog had caused, which was a reasonable estimate with manual labor. I mean, what is the value of another pair of feet stepping on my wet clay? Even a year wouldn't be enough, don't you agree?"

Some of the men nodded.

"But then, I discovered he's a gifted healer." Ishkadim slapped Sall's shoulder. "And hardworking, too. In a few days, he brought in more than enough coins and goods to compensate me for the damages. I'm a righteous man, am I not? How could I celebrate the miracle of our Exodus from Egyptian slavery while continuing to enslave a boy who no longer owed me anything?"

The priest leaned forward on his canes. "All those coins and goods belongs to God, who is the only healer!"

"We all belong to God," Ishkadim said. "We and everything we have, blessed by His name. Good Sabbath to you!"

12

After the priest and his companions departed, Ishkadim came into the shack and sat on the ground, his back against one of the support beams. Sall sat across from him. Timna, who had watched from behind the fence, joined them.

Ishkadim looked at Sall. "How does it feel to be free again?"

Sall didn't know what to say.

"Wife, bring us wine."

Timna went to the house.

"Don't worry, boy." The potter grinned. "I can't take back what I said to the priest, even though we both know it was a lie."

Sall dug in the soil with his fingers and filled his hand with dirt. "Which part was a lie?"

"The part about me releasing you from being my slave. Have I released you?"

"You allowed me to dress as a free man." Sall held his palm up and looked at the dirt, which was brown and dry. "And what about your claim of being a righteous man? Was that a lie, too?"

"Am I not righteous?"

"And the part about me having earned enough to recover your damages?"

Ishkadim waved in dismissal. "Who has the time to calculate such things?"

"Is calculating also forbidden on your Sabbath?"

The potter laughed. "Fine. That part was true, too. You've done well for me, boy."

"One half lie, two full truths." Sall let the dirt trickle between his fingers. "We have a saying in Edom. A liar lies even when he tells the truth."

The potter's face reddened, but he didn't yell or wave his fist, which was three times bigger than the boy's. "It's the truth now. You're free."

Exhaling slowly, Sall was overwhelmed by this sudden reversal of fortune. He was free!

"Free," Ishkadim said. "But poor."

It was true, Sall realized. Freedom allowed him to leave the potter's house, but a journey home would require a donkey, food, and water, as well as a fee for a caravan leader to let him tag along all the way to Edom."

Timna returned with a jug of wine and two cups.

"Three days," Ishkadim said. "That's how long we have."

They looked at him, waiting for an explanation.

"People don't like the priest. Their ailments don't heal by making sacrifices at his temple, despite his promises." Ishkadim glanced up at the sky. "Sorry, God, but it's true."

Timna shook her head, murmuring a prayer.

"The people will keep coming here," Ishkadim continued. "They won't stop just because the old priest quotes the Holy Scriptures and waves his cane, but in three days, the judge will be back from the Holy Temple. His word is the law, and he won't go against the priest."

Sall understood what the potter was hoping to achieve. "Why should I work for three more days if I'm already free?"

"To help the people," Ishkadim said with a hint of a smile.

Sall did feel compassion for the ailing customers, but his own situation wasn't much better. "Fine. I'll continue to treat people for three days, and you'll give me one-third of the earnings."

"One-tenth."

Having expected the potter to bargain, Sall was ready with a response, which he had heard his father say often: "When the price is fair, bargaining is an insult."

"You're full of surprises, young man." Ishkadim offered his hand. "One-third it shall be."

Sall noticed the change from "boy" to "young man." As they shook hands, he wondered about it. Did the potter see a change in him, or was he merely tossing in a dose of flattery?

Timna poured the wine.

Raising his cup, Ishkadim recited a blessing on the wine and drank it. Sall took a sip, hesitated, and drank the rest. The wine warmed his chest, the same way wine always did at evening meals with his family. He imagined arriving back home in two or three weeks. He would enter the front garden, and his mother would look around for her beloved dog while his father would gaze back at him with accusatory eyes and decide his punishment. What was the appropriate punishment for a son's betrayal?

The next three days passed quickly. He treated countless men, women, and children, many of them from other towns and villages. They spoke Hebrew in slight variations from Timna's manner of speaking. She explained that they came from several tribes, because Jericho was at the eastern edge of Benjamin's land and close to the territories of Judah, Ephraim, and Manasseh on the west bank of the Jordan River and to Reuben and Gad on the east bank, reaching as far as the borders of Amon and Moab.

On the evening of the third day, after the last customers had been treated, Ishkadim gave him a purse full of coins and told him that his old donkey would be ready for the journey in the morning, loaded with food and water.

The family ate together in the yard, singing Hebrew songs, which Sall already knew. After the meal, while Timna cleaned up, Ishkadim shared a jug of wine with Sall. The potter told him about meeting first wife. She had been washing clothes in the Jordan River on the eve of the Sukkot holiday, her wet robe clinging to her body, which made his blood boil. Her father understood his desperation and drove a hard bargain, demanding three years of labor in exchange for her hand in marriage. She was worth it, Ishkadim said, giving him eleven children in all. Some had died before she passed away while delivering the twelfth child, who was stillborn.

Ishkadim wiped his eyes and took another gulp from the jug. "I submit to Yahweh, but I seethe at His cruelty."

The wine loosened Sall's lips, as well, and he told Ishkadim about the high priest's daughter and how she knocked him out with her eyes, leading to the dream of the old dwarf, whose golden elixir not only gave people the power of understanding others, but transformed the dwarf into a young man.

Sall was about to confess his own wish to change into a striking young man with wrought muscles and dark skin, instead of the short, skinny, freckled boy that he was, but the doubtful expression on the potter's face made him remember how foolish his wish was and what a failure his quest had been.

That night, Sall had trouble sleeping while his mind travelled ahead, imagining the journey he would begin in the morning. Eventually, his exhaustion won over, and he slept soundly until a scream woke him up.

13

The scream came from Timna. Ishkadim got up, rekindled the fire in the stove and lit two torches, which he fixed to the wall. The light revealed a pool of crimson blood on the cot between Timna's thighs. She stared at it wide-eyed, her hand pressed to her mouth.

Ishkadim began to sob.

Timna moaned.

Sall knew he was looking at death, which came back to the potter's house to kill another wife and her unborn baby. He ran out and vomited by the side of the house. He could hear the children wailing and the potter pleading with his God.

For a moment, Sall considered pulling his donkey out of the corral and leaving this doomed house before death noticed him, too. He gagged on a piece of half-digested food that became lodged in his throat, coughed hard, and spat it out. Resisting the urge to flee, he went to the well, pulled up the bucket, and poured it over his head.

The cold water straightened him out. He recalled waking up at home one night when a terrified young husband brought his pregnant wife, bleeding profusely. Sall's father had spoken soothingly to the girl and made her drink a lot of water while the servants boiled a pot with the chopped pieces of a root.

What kind of a root?

The wailing inside the house made it hard to think.

There was something pretty about the name of that root. Sall struggled to remember. His mother had also spoken about that root and its virtues, and then she kissed him on both cheeks and on his forehead. Why had she kissed him?

Lovage.

His father had given the woman a tonic made of the lovage root.

Sall ran inside and paused at the sight of the children clinging to Ishkadim, who was on his knees beside Timna, whose face had gone completely white.

Back outside, Sall refilled the bucket in the well, carried it in, and splashed Ishkadim.

Astonished, the potter stopped crying.

"It's only blood," Sall said, keeping his voice even and soothing as his father had spoken to the woman and her husband back in Bozra. "It's not as bad as it looks. You've seen blood many times, haven't you?"

Ishkadim nodded slowly.

"And most people don't die from a little bleeding, isn't that true?"

He nodded again.

Sall filled a cup with water. "You're a good husband and I'm a good healer, right?"

More head nodding, faster now.

"We can help her, but we have to work together. Are you ready?"

The children let go of their father.

"Take a torch and a shovel," Sall said. "Go to the fields, find a lovage plant, and dig out the root. Also, pick up a handful of nettles. Do you understand."

"Root of lovage and some nettles." The potter took a torch and a shovel and ran out.

"Sall," Timna whispered. "I don't want to die."

Imitating his father, he patted her arm gently and smiled. "Didn't you hear? It's not as bad as it looks."

"You're a poor liar."

"It's the truth," he said with a straight face. "I've watched my father help many women in this condition. You'll be fine, I promise."

His lies brought a glint of hope to her terrified eyes.

He held the cup to her lips and helped her drink. When the cup was empty, he filled it again and dropped in a lump of salt, which he had seen his father give to men who had lost a lot of blood.

Timna took the cup and held it with both hands, sipping from it.

He filled a pot with water from the bucket and put it on the stove to boil. The sour smell of blood sickened him, and he started breathing through his mouth the way he had done when treating the high priest's rancid feet.

She handed him the cup.

He topped it off. "Keep drinking."

Her eyes on the pool of blood between her legs, she asked, "Is the baby dead?"

"I think so."

Tears flowed down her cheeks.

He pressed her forearm. "There will be other babies, boys and girls, and they'll make you very happy."

The words came out easily, even though he didn't know if she would survive, let alone have more babies. Lying was necessary to help her heal, as his father had said: "Fear hinders healing, whereas the expectation of a full recovery is self-fulfilling."

Wiping her eyes, Timna spoke haltingly. "Did the baby suffer before dying?"

The loaded question had no ready answer, except one that would comfort her. "Not at all," he said. "You barely started to show, which means there was only the beginning of a baby."

She sniffled. "That's good."

He wondered if the fetus had come out with the blood, or was it still inside her? Once, he had watched a goat give birth, and the bleeding only stopped after the farmer had pulled out the sack in which the kid had lived inside the goat. He remembered the farmer saying that it would have started to rot if left inside, causing high fever and death. Looking closely, Sall saw nothing but blood, which continued to trickle through her loincloth. He knew what he had to do, but the thought of actually doing it repulsed him.

"Children, let's go." He helped them get up and handed the youngest one to an older girl. "It's time to go outside and look at the stars. They're very bright tonight."

When the children were out of the house, he helped Timna pull her robe up above her hips. Her loincloth was completely soaked with blood. Keeping his eyes averted, he removed it and gave her a rag to press between her legs.

Ishkadim returned, holding the torch in one hand and a bunch of greenery in the other. He stopped and stared at his young wife, naked from the waist down.

"We need your help." Sall took the nettles from him. "Chop up the lovage root and add it to the water on the stove."

The potter rushed to do it.

Tearing the nettles leaves to pieces, Sall gave them to Timna. "Chew on the leaves. It'll slow the bleeding. And keep drinking the water."

She did as he said.

Sall kept his eyes averted to a point where he was still able to see from the corner of his eye. He nudged her legs apart and removed the rag. When his fingers first touched the bloody mess, he retched, but managed to keep it down. By touch, he scraped off several lumps of congealed blood, clearing the way. Feeling inside her with his fingers, he detected something elongated, like a pinky. Was it the baby's leg? An arm? He tugged on it, but it wouldn't come out of her. Getting a firmer hold on the tiny limb, he pulled harder. It was connected to a larger lump, and as the whole thing slipped out, it made a swishy sound, and Timna whimpered.

"Don't look." He used the rag to wrap it up. "We have to get everything out, or you could get high fever."

He had to reach deeper to find the sack. It slipped out easily, followed by a gush of blood, but then, she stopped bleeding, just like the goat.

Placing the cup near her lips, he made her drink more water with salt.

Ishkadim brought another full bucket. Sall got behind Timna and held her under the arms while the potter washed her private parts, put on a clean loincloth, and slipped a fresh robe over her head. They carried her together to a clean cot. Sall bunched up the bloodied linen, loincloth, robe, and rags. He placed the bundle in one of the ovens outside and rekindled the fire. His hands and forearms were crusted over with dry blood. He drew more water from the well and scrubbed until his skin hurt.

The children were allowed back in. They cuddled together on their bed. Sall poured some of the lovage-root tonic into a cup and gave it to Ishkadim, who helped Timna take sips.

Feeling dizzy, the boy sat on the floor, his back to the wall. He looked at his small, pale hands, so different from his father's strong, capable hands. Remnants of dry blood lined the edges of his fingernails.

Timna fell asleep. The potter put away the cup, sat on the floor beside Sall, and put his arm around the boy's shoulders. "Thank you for saving my wife's life."

The words tugged at the taut strings that held him together, undoing the knot of determination to imitate his father's measured method of thinking, calm manner of speaking, and mastery of battling death, who snapped its bony fingers in giddy anticipation of an error. Sall began to tremble. Hugging his folded legs, he rested his forehead on his knees, and wept.

14

At sunrise, while Timna remained asleep, Ishkadim helped Sall saddle the donkey and secure the sack of food and the waterskins. Leading the donkey along, they walked together to the main street, which was still quiet, and down to the field where the merchant caravans camped. There was a well and a water trough near the field. The donkey stopped to drink.

"He's a strong one." Ishkadim patted the donkey's hump. "It's a long way to Edom."

"Not long enough."

"Are you not eager to return home?"

Sall felt his face grow hot. "I left without my father's permission."

"Would he have given it, had you asked?"

"No."

"It's better to dare and suffer, than to live with regrets."

"Is it?"

"I speak from experience." The potter waved around. "This valley is all I've seen in my life. You, on the other hand, are young and free. Follow your dreams now, because freedom is a gift that shrinks with age."

Digging in the soil with the tip of his sandal, Sall said, "It's too late. There's only regrets for me."

"Why?"

"Because I failed."

The donkey stopped drinking and turned his head to look at the boy.

"How do you know that you've failed?"

"It's a fact."

The potter shook a finger. "Failure only happens when you give up."

Sall pulled the donkey's reins, but the animal didn't move. "It's all up to the Gods."

"The Gods?" Ishkadim chuckled. "Let me tell you a story about a poor man who cried to God every night until, after weeks of this nuisance, God roared from above. "What do you want?" The man said, "I bought a cow with my last coins, but she gives no milk, and my children are hungry. If you make her give milk, I'll be your faithful servant forever." God was tired, so he agreed and said, "Starting tomorrow morning, she'll give you plenty of milk." The man was very happy, but the following night, he was crying for God again, and when God appeared, the man yelled, "You broke your promise!" God became upset. "That's impossible. I did what you asked." The man argued, "No, you didn't. My cow still gives no milk!" God thought for a moment and asked, "Have you squeezed her teats?"

Sall laughed. He understood the message, but how could he persist in his quest after everything that had happed?

"Believe it," Ishkadim said. "The Gods clear the way for those who chase their dreams."

"Our mightiest God, the great Qoz, is not with me. That's why I can't succeed."

"Funny you should say that." Ishkadim reached into his pocket, pulled out a small object, and held it out in his open palm. "I bought it yesterday in the market, a farewell gift for you."

Looking closely, Sall was delighted. It was a miniature clay figurine of Qoz, down to the three short horns and bulging eyes in a humanlike face, small breasts of indefinite gender, and a three-pronged thunderbolt.

"Thank you." Sall kissed the effigy. "It will keep me safe on the way home."

"What if Qoz wants you to resume your quest?"

"I was supposed to look for a man in Damascus."

"Damascus?" He clapped. "Aram's blooming city in the north."

"The Moabite merchant told me that Damascus is farther than the moon."

"Let me quote a wise boy," Ishkadim said. "A liar lies even when he tells the truth."

Looking around the vast field, Sall counted three caravans that were packing up for departure, whereas the rest were docile except for the women preparing the morning meals. He pressed Qoz to his chest and walked to the first of the three. The merchant, a young man with a short beard, was folding up the tent.

"Good morning," Sall said. "Where are you heading from here?"

The man pointed east, across the Jordan River. "To the Hebrew towns of Heshbon and Beser."

Sall looked in the direction the man was pointing and saw the trail he had arrived on after visiting the dream reader. "And after that?"

"We're going to Rabbath Amon for the summer. And you?"

"I'm not sure." Already walking away, Sall spoke over his shoulder. "Have a safe journey."

The second caravan was larger. An older man sat on a rock with a cup of milk, while a group of younger men took down the camp. They had bushy red beards and white caps.

He approached the old man. "Good morning. Where are you heading today?"

The response was a vague gesture towards the mountains.

One of the younger men came over. "Yahweh's blessings upon you."

"And you," Sall said.

He tugged at his red beard. "You seem like one of us, but you speak not as a son of Judah."

Sall realized his light skin and freckles, which usually went with red hair, made him look like a member of the tribe of Judah. He hid his hand with the effigy of Qoz. "I've lived here for a while. Which direction will you travel today?"

"Back home to Hebron. We still have a few jars of olive oil, if you wish to buy."

"Not today," Sall said. "May you travel safely."

Approaching the last caravan that was packing up, his heart pounded, and he pressed Qoz to his chest. The moment of truth was upon him. If the third caravan was heading south, he would join it and go home to Edom, but if it was going north, it would be a sign that Qoz wished him to continue on his quest.

The merchant had dark-brown skin and hair which was tightly curled like raw wool. He wore a light-brown robe, made of an unusually smooth fabric, and smiled with glistening white teeth.

"A wonderful morning, isn't it?"

"It is," Sall said.

He put a hand to his heart. "I am Li'uli."

The name was unusual, and the boy wasn't sure he heard it right.

"Lee-You-Lee?

"Correct." He laughed. "Most people mispronounce it."

A young woman with the same dark complexion was sitting by a fire with two infant girls and a baby boy, whom she was nursing. A glimpse of her exposed breast made Sall look away.

"That's my wife, Li'iliti."

"Lee-Ee-Lee-Tee?"

"Correct again. What's your name?"

"I am Sall."

"So-All?"

The boy nodded. Nearby, two young men were pulling out the pegs and folding the large tent. They wore only loincloths, and under their dark-brown skin they were bones and muscles. Each had a short, curved sword stuck in the loincloth against the left hip.

"My servants," Li'uli said. "They don't have names."

With the tent down, the boy saw the merchant's animals tied to a tree — a few goats, a horse, and a camel, which was rare.

"Where are you travelling today?"

"Up the river," Li'uli said.

Turning towards the river, Sall got his bearing. "North?"

"To the Sea of Galilee," Li'uli said. "To swim in its sweet water."

The two servants rolled up a long rope that slithered on the ground.

"I'd like to learn how to swim," Sall said.

"Would you like to join us?"

"Yes, please. I can pay."

"Companionship is more precious than coins." Li'uli took the rolled-up rope from the servants. "First, we must eat. A journey is easier to start on a full stomach."

"I don't wish to impose."

"My wife insists on plentiful meals." Li'uli winked. "She's a chief's daughter, you know."

Sall glanced at Ishkadim and the donkey.

"Your friend is also invited." Li'uli beckoned the potter. "I can tell he enjoys eating."

They sat around the small fire with Li'iliti. The baby had fallen asleep, and the two girls climbed into Ishkadim's lap and tugged at his bushy beard while he tickled them. A pot of barley stew was simmering on the fire. The servants came over to serve the meal.

The barley was cooked in goat milk and mixed with raisins, whose sweetness was balanced with garlic and pepper, giving it a flavor unlike any Sall had tasted before. Instead of wine, they drank water mixed with bee honey and spiked with a squirt of lemon, also a novelty for the boy.

Ishkadim managed to enjoy the food and drink while the girls continued to play with his beard. He smacked his lips, shaking his head in wonder at the taste. "The flavor of your food comes from a foreign land, but you speak our language. How is that?"

Li'uli smiled. "Hebrew isn't very different from Egyptian, which is spoken in my father's house. And we've been travelling among your tribes for several months now."

"One day," Ishkadim said, "I'll make a pilgrimage to the Holy Temple in Shiloh. Have you been there?"

"No, we came from the south along the coast of the Great Sea through Gaza to the land of Simeon, where the judge of Beersheba hosted us in his home for several weeks. Then, we went through the land of Judah to Gezer, Bethlehem, and Hebron, where your patriarchs are buried in a magnificent cave. From there, we entered the territory of the tribe of Benjamin and stayed in Jerusalem for a month."

"Oh, Jerusalem!" Li'iliti's soft voice complimented her beauty. "It's magical."

"And windy," Li'uli said. "It's perched on a steep mountaintop, with open views over all of Canaan. And the most unfathomable thing? A bubbling spring under the highest peak. It's impossible to believe unless you see it with your own eyes."

"Please God," Ishkadim said. "May I live long enough to see Jerusalem."

Sall reminded the potter what he'd said moments earlier: "The Gods clear the way for those who chase their dreams."

The two servants cleared the dishes and resumed packing up the camp. They didn't utter a word, and Sall wondered if they were mute.

"Take care of my young friend." Ishkadim patted Sall's shoulder. "He is a capable healer."

Li'uli's eyebrows rose. "A healer?"

"My father is," Sall said. "I imitated him for a while, but it's over now."

"It's only starting," Ishkadim said. "Let me tell you about another young man, Ehud, son of Gerah, who lived here many years ago. At that time, Jericho was occupied by King Eglon of Moab, who oppressed our Hebrew tribes on both banks of the Jordan River. One night, Ehud dreamed that God told him to revolt against Eglon and liberate the people. But Ehud was left-handed and had never wielded a sword. He travelled to Shiloh, told the high priest about his dream, and asked, "How can I liberate Israel, when my hand is weak, and my heart is meek?" The high priest told him to change, to turn himself from a crippled coward into a brave swordsman. Ehud cried, "How?" Now, do you know what the high priest told him?"

When they didn't answer, he did. "Imitate until you mutate!"

"That's heavenly advice," Li'uli said. "Imitate until you mutate. I'll remember it."

Sall didn't think that pretending to be another person could actually lead to changing. He had imitated his father out of necessity, but had no illusions about actually acquiring his father's wisdom and healing abilities.

"Tell us," Li'uli said. "Did Ehud become a great warrior? Did he liberate your people?"

"Look around you." Ishkadim gestured at Jericho. "Are we not free?"

The boy recalled what the potter had said earlier, that freedom was a gift that shrank with age. Was it only personal freedom, or was the same true for a city, a tribe, or a people?

"I must return to my family." Ishkadim got up. "May your Gods keep you safe."

15

Li'uli tugged on the ropes that secured the sacks, baskets, jars, and waterskins to the camel. When he was satisfied, his wife and children mounted the camel, sitting between its two humps. Li'uli mounted the horse. He took the lead, followed by Sall on his donkey, the camel, and the goats, which were tied to each other and to the camel. The two servants took the rear on foot, naked but for their loincloths and curved swords.

They rode north along the Jordan River, leaving Jericho behind. Thick palm orchards provided shade, keeping them cool through the hottest hours of the day.

In the late afternoon, a group of armed men blocked the road in front of the caravan. They carried a pole with a cloth flag that was completely black except for a white antelope with straight horns. The men wore no caps on their heads, which made Sall assume they were not Hebrews, but their leader announced that this was the territory of the Manasseh tribe, and merchant caravans wishing to pass must pay one silver coin or ten copper coins, whatever the caravan leader carried.

Dismounting his horse, Li'uli told the leader that he was not a trading merchant, but a prince on a peaceful expedition on behalf of his father, King Nigusi of Kush, a vassal state of Egypt. He pulled a stone tablet from a side pocket in his saddle and showed it to them.

Sall came over to look.

The tablet was etched with symbols he didn't recognize. At the top was a carving of a lion and a lioness on their hind legs, facing each other—either fighting or embracing, it was hard to tell.

Li'uli pointed at the carving. "This is our ancestral seal, symbolizing our ancestral patriarch, whose parents were the king and queen of all animals."

The soldiers' leader was shaking his head, but he stopped when Li'uli started reading aloud from the tablet, his finger moving under the words. His language sounded like a staccato of guttural throat-clearing and tongue-clucking.

Sall was intrigued by the tablet and the strange language, but he had his doubts about Li'uli's royal claim. A real king would not send his son off to roam the roads across foreign lands with a beautiful wife and young children, risking death or slavery, for the questionable gain of learning about distant tribes. And what use would such knowledge be in a faraway kingdom?

The soldiers listened raptly to the language of Kush and smiled at Li'iliti, obviously charmed by her.

Their leader turned to Sall. "You don't look like someone from Kush." The others laughed.

He grabbed the boy's wrist, pulled up the sleeve, and plucked a few strands of reddish hair from his forearm. "I know this color," he said, holding the hairs up between a forefinger and a thumb. "Shouldn't a boy of Judah know not to enter our land?"

Sall was too terrified to speak.

Li'uli burst out laughing, and Li'iliti joined him, clapping her hands.

The leader looked at them, his eyes creased.

Taking a cue from the hollering couple, Sall inhaled deeply and started to imitate the guttural throat-clearing, tongue-clucking language while gesticulating with his hands and contorting his face in the manner of a passionate argument.

The soldiers and their leaders seemed stunned, but Li'uli and Li'iliti laughed even harder, and their two girls, too. When he ran out of air, Sall bowed to Li'uli, hoping he would take over.

Still laughing, Li'uli said, "This boy isn't one of your Judah rivals."

"He looks like them," the leader said.

"Back in Kush, his mother is albino. That's why he looks like cheese." The soldiers laughed.

"He's one of the court jesters," Li'uli continued. "The king sent him with us to find new material for royal amusement."

One of the soldiers approached the two servants, who stood motionless in the rear of the caravan, staring forward. He circled them, grinning, and reached for the handle of one of the curved swords. With the speed of a striking snake, the servant drew his curved sword and placed the blade against the soldier's neck. The other servant, with equal rapidity, drew his sword and aimed it at the soldier's crotch.

The other soldiers aimed their spears at the two servants.

Li'uli addressed his servants in the throaty language, and they stepped back, lowering their swords.

"That's better," he said. "Now, how about some gifts?"

The soldiers lowered their spears.

From a sack on the camel's back, he took out a pouch, pulled a few white figurines, and handed one to each soldier and their leader.

"These are elephants," Li'uli said. "In real life, an elephant is several times bigger than a camel and has two white tusks, like curved horns. Our artists make all kinds of things from the tusks."

Sall remembered hearing about elephants from an Egyptian merchant, who sold a piece of tusk to his father to make a remedy for discolored toenails and thinning hair.

The leader signaled the soldiers to step aside and let the caravan pass.

Sometime later, Li'uli said to Sall, "A clever move, to imitate our language."

Behind them, perched atop the camel, Li'iliti clapped. "You're a good mimic."

Sall blushed. "My throat is still hurting."

"It gets easier." Li'uli chuckled. "We'll teach you."

And they did, practicing with him the words one would use most often, such as greetings, food items, and how to say, "I love you," which involved three tongue-cluckings and a sucking sound with the lips pursed as in kissing.

A village by the Jordan River provided a safe place to camp. The two servants set up a large tent, as well as a small one for Sall. Li'iliti supervised the meal preparations while Li'uli and Sall sat by the river and the two little girls played in the mud nearby. After the meal, the servants cleaned up. One of them remained awake, standing at the entrance to his master's tent, and the other lay on the ground beside him, his hand on the handle of his carved sword. Settling in for the night in the small tent, Sall felt safe for the first time since leaving home.

They continued north in the morning. The valley on both sides of the Jordan River became wider, and the jugged mountains became rolling hills. Vast groves of palm trees lined the river, similar to what he'd seen around Jericho, but the farmers of Manasseh went further than the naturally moist land near the river. They dug channels to deliver water to the foothills east and west, turning dry land into arable fields. He saw men plowing with donkeys or oxen, and others tending orchards of trees heavy with pomegranates, figs, lemons, and plums. Further up the hills, where the land was steep, creviced, and strewn with rocks, he saw rows of grapevines and silver canopies of olive trees. Once in a while, a shepherd passed by with his goats or sheep. Many of the houses had corrals with cattle, as well.

That night, they camped near another village, where Li'uli bought fresh bread, cheese, fruit, and vegetables. After the evening meal, Li'iliti took the children into the tent to sleep.

Sall gestured south, where they had come from. "When the soldiers of Manasseh suspected that I was from a rival tribe, why did you start laughing?"

"Why not?" Li'uli lit up a pipe and drew smoke from it.

"They could have killed us."

"That's why we laughed." Li'uli took another draw from the pipe and blew smoke upward at the night sky. "It's a good defense."

"To laugh?"

"Yes, to laugh, or to cry. To reason politely, or to howl like a madman. To play mute, or to start talking in a strange language with passion and conviction as if it's the most normal thing in the world."

"I don't understand."

"It depends on the situation, boy, but the principle is the same." Li'uli pointed at him with the pipe. "When facing a powerful enemy, always do the unexpected."

16

On the afternoon of the fourth day, the hills to their left flattened, and a vast valley opened up to the west. Further up the road, a group of armed men appeared, brandishing Manasseh's banner – a white antelope against black background.

One of them asked, "Are you the prince from Kush?"

Sall was shocked that word about them had already reached this place.

"I am." Li'uli did not get off his horse. "Take me to your leader."

Continuing north, the road passed by man-made ponds and a network of channels that irrigated fields and orchards. Up ahead, in the middle of a vast valley, Sall saw a steep hill with a wall around the top. He imagined the distant views one would enjoy from up there.

The road split, and the men led the way to the left, where a large encampment abutted the road. Many more armed men were about, fixing their weapons or practicing their use. They stopped to watch the caravan go by.

At the center of the camp, two soldiers guarded a sizable tent. A tall pole flew a large banner Manasseh. Li'uli dismounted, took the stone tablet out of the saddle pocket, and beckoned Sall to join him.

Inside the tent, a man was lounging on cushions, holding an open scroll against the light of an oil lamp. His face was creased, his beard was gray, and his head was covered with a white cap. Noticing them, he put the scroll aside and gestured at the cushions. They sat, and he clicked his fingers. Several women came in, bearing trays with dates, figs, and pomegranates, as well as jugs of water and wine.

"Don't worry," he said. "My women will assist your wife, and my men will take care of your animals."

"Why should I worry?" Li'uli popped a fig into his mouth. "Is there a better host than a paragon of faith and justice?"

The man laughed. "Either my reputation precedes me, or you're a gifted flatterer."

"Or both." Li'uli joined the laughter. "It's an honor to finally meet you in person, Judge Ben-Dor. Tales of the wise leader of the Manasseh tribe have reached all the way to my country, the kingdom of Kush."

Sall was impressed that Li'uli knew the judge's name, but he had a feeling the praise exaggerated.

"My father is King Nigusi, and this is our ancestral seal." Li'uli handed him the stone tablet.

Judge Ben-Dor gazed at it for a long moment and gave it back. "I'm honored."

Li'uli kept the tablet in his lap. "On behalf of my father, we invite you to visit our magnificent kingdom and hunt for a prized animal of your choice – a lion, a tiger, or an elephant."

"I'm grateful, but our God forbids us from ever again leaving the blessed land, lest we become slaves of another nation, as we suffered under the Pharaohs for four hundred years."

"Your God is wise."

"And what brings the prince of Kush all the way here?"

"The Sea of Galilee, of course, whose water is reputed to be sweeter than honey, its color bluer than the sky, and its fish fatter than a cow." Li'uli held his hands apart to demonstrate the size.

"The Sea of Galilee is a marvel of our land, indeed, but are there no sufficient wonders in your own country, that you would take to perilous roads in foreign lands?"

"My father said: "You only learn to appreciate home after traveling far away from it." That's why he sent me to visit all the wonders of the world, from the golden sands of the Sinai Desert to the Temple of Dagon in Gaza, from the seven wells of Beersheba to the hidden spring of Jerusalem, and from the boundless palm groves of Jericho to the magical water of the Sea of Galilee."

The judge smiled. "And after that?"

"The giant cedars of Lebanon and the blooming jasmines of Damascus."

At the mention of Damascus, Sall's chest swelled with excitement. He hadn't discussed Damascus yet with his travel companions, and hearing that they, too, were heading there made him think of what Ishkadim had said. "The Gods clear the way for those who chase their dreams."

"But first," Li'uli said, "we're eager to reach the Sea of Galilee."

"Not so fast, I'm afraid." The judge rolled up the scroll and set it aside. "We're in the middle of war here."

"With whom?"

"The men of Issachar, a troublesome tribe."

Sall wondered why the Hebrew tribes were fighting one another, but he dared not ask, because he was supposed to be a court jester from Kush who wasn't fluent in their language.

Li'uli sighed. "My children will be disappointed. Are you battling over the Sea of Galilee?"

"Much more than that." Judge Ben-Dor took a fig from the bowl, but didn't bite into it. "Come, I'll show you."

He led them outside and held his hand out to a handsome horse, whose wet lips picked the fig from the judge's palm.

Sall saw Li'iliti breastfeeding the baby while sitting with the children under a tree. The two servants stood guard behind them. Several women brought over bowls of food and jugs of drink.

Judge Ben-Dor led the way, with Li'uli following on his horse and Sall on his donkey. A small group of armed men walked behind. Once they left the camp, a narrow path took them up a moderate slope that concluded on a rocky ridge. The judge turned his horse and waited for them to come alongside.

With the late-afternoon sun behind them, the whole valley was in open view. At the center was the steep hill with the wall around the top. From this vantage point, Sall could see the roofs of many houses inside the wall.

A ring of small encampments surrounded the hill. Smoke columns rose from cooking fires while horses, cows, and goats nibbled the grassy ground inside makeshift corrals. He remembered stories about cities under siege from his father's nighttime tales of long-ago conflicts between Edom and Egypt.

"An impressive blockade," Li'uli said. "What's the name of this fortified city?"

"Beth She'an," Judge Ben-Dor said.

"Never heard of it."

Again, Sall had a feeling Li'uli was lying. Why would the prince of Kush pretend not to have heard of this place?

"It was a famous city when Canaan was part of Egypt," the judge said. "The Egyptian governor's palace still stands inside those walls, as do the homes of his administrators and military leaders."

"An Egyptian governor ruled here?" Li'uli raised his eyebrows. "Are you sure?"

"It's the intersection of the trade routes from other lands they controlled." The judge pointed as he spoke. "Damascus in the north, Amon in the east, the Jordan Valley in the south, and behind us, the fertile Jezreel Valley and the Great Sea, where the Egyptians had built a coastal highway along the shoreline all the way south to their capital city, Memphis."

"Why did they leave?"

"The Philistines attacked them from the Great Sea, the Arameans pushed down from the north, and the Canaanites became rebellious. Pressed on all sides, the Egyptians withdrew."

"When was it?"

"A long time ago, but the local Canaanites still tell fables about Egyptian convoys as long as rivers, carrying untold riches back to the Pharaoh. They were gone when our tribes returned to Canaan, and the men of Issachar conquered Beth She'an from the Canaanites."

"And now you want to take it from Issachar?"

"God wants us to have it." Judge Ben-Dor glanced up at the twilight sky. "He favors us over Issachar."

"How do you know that?"

"Because He helped us conquer all the lands around here, ten times more than Issachar."

"Why would the Hebrew God favor one tribe over another?"

"Because our patriarch, Manasseh, was the firstborn son of Joseph, who was Jacob's favorite son."

Li'uli stayed quiet for a moment. "How long have you besieged the city?"

"Since the fall. I had hoped they would accept my offer of safe passage and leave during the winter, but they didn't. Passover came and went, and we're still waiting. My men want to return to their farms for the spring harvest. I had to form an alliance with King Javin of Hazor. He's sending a thousand soldiers with siege machines. They'll be here in two days."

Inside the walls of Beth She'an, torches lit up, and voices rose up as the men of Issachar began to chant the evening prayers to the invisible Hebrew God.

"I like alliances," Li'uli said. "As long as the price is right."

Judge Ben-Dor's face hardened. "I told the men of Issachar they may resettle in peace north of here, where the rest of their tribe lives, but they're stubborn, like donkeys. They forced me into this alliance with idol worshippers. In two days, Issachar will become slaves to the Canaanite king, and we'll have Beth She'an. From behind its walls, we'll control the trade routes."

"A worthy conquest justifies a risky alliance."

"Risky?"

Li'uli clutched his hands together. "An alliance only holds until the common enemy is defeated, at which point the allies often turn on each other, and one of them enters a new alliance with the beaten enemy against the former ally."

17

Back at the main camp, several hundred men were waiting for Judge Ben-Dor, who led them in prayers and slaughtered two goats on a makeshift stone altar. The edible parts of the goats were roasted and shared around between the men. A tent was put up for the guests. It was large enough for Sall to sleep inside with the family.

At dawn, he woke up, heard commotion outside, and went to look.

A group of men gathered near the judge's tent, their horses ready to go. Judge Ben-Dor was talking to the men. When he finished, they mounted the horses and rode off to the west.

Li'uli came out of the tent and stood with Sall, watching the riders until they were gone. He patted Sall's shoulder. "Prepare yourself, boy, for a memorable day."

The judge noticed them and beckoned. They joined him inside his tent, where a pleasant scent welcomed them. It was lavender, and Sall thought of the high priest's daughter, who didn't even know how far he had journeyed to win her heart.

A woman brought in a bowl of sliced pomegranate and a plate with bread dipped in olive oil, as well as a jug of wine and three cups. Sall was startled when a bunched-up blanket on the bed shifted and a girl sat up, holding the blanket to her chest. She flipped aside her long black hair, yawned, and lay back again, pulling the blanket over her head.

"Don't mind her." Judge Ben-Dor chuckled. "She's of the Cainite Clan. Her services are a gift from King Javin, who is their current protector."

"A lovely gift," Li'uli said.

"As my honored guest, you can borrow her any time."

"Thank you." He dipped a chunk of bread in the olive oil and took a bite. "Did your soldiers leave for their farms?"

"No. I sent them to meet up with the Canaanite army on the road from Megiddo and lead it here. I'm told the Canaanites have machines that hurl boulders big enough to crush men and animals as if they were made of clay." He sighed. "I wish there was another way. There are women and children up there, but what can I do? They won't surrender."

Li'uli ate some pomegranate and wiped the red juice from his lips. "Why are they holding on so stubbornly?"

"Isn't it obvious?"

"They're afraid you'll use the fortified city against them."

"Yes, even though I've given them my word. Truth is, I wouldn't trust them, either. The strife between our tribes goes back dozens of generations to the original sibling rivalry between our tribal forefathers, the twelve sons of Jacob."

"Rivalry over what?"

Judge Ben-Dor raised three fingers. "Jealousy. Greed. Pride."

"For generations?"

"The small is jealous of the big. The rich is greedy for more. And everyone seeks primacy over the others."

"Your God must be upset."

The judge took a deep breath. "Of all the nations in the world, He chose us, the People of Israel, to give us His divine laws, the Torah of Israel, and promised us His best creation, the fertile Land of Israel. Alas, we're a stiff-necked people, clinging to tribal enmities, the way Issachar is doing now with blatant impunity, forcing me to make an alliance with the wretched Canaanites."

Taking a sip of water, Li'uli swished it in his mouth before swallowing. "I heard that King Javin subjugated some Hebrew tribes in the north. What if his alliance with you is a trick to take Beth She'an from Issachar and subjugate Manasseh, as well?"

The judge tugged at his beard. "We're a powerful tribe with large territories. Only a fool would challenge us."

The girl wrapped herself in the blanket and left the tent.

He watched her leave and chuckled. "She'll be back. I'm a generous customer."

"And a generous host," Li'uli said. "As a token of my gratitude, I'd like to try and negotiate with your opponents inside the city. Perhaps they'll listen to a neutral guest from a distant land, whose only interest here is a peaceful resolution so that his children can swim in the Sea of Galilee."

"You have my blessing," Judge Ben-Dor said. "Their leader, Judge

Yerakh, might not be as gracious."

Li'uli patted Sall's shoulder. "My young companion is a potent good-luck charm."

The servants were up already, building a fire to prepare the morning meal. They readied their master's horse and Sall's donkey, which they loaded with two sacks of food.

Riding slowly, they crossed the siege ring and approached the hill. Up close, the sheer slopes appeared to have been cut into the rock to make it impossible to climb. The height seemed equal to twenty men standing one on top of the other, if such an act was possible. At the top, the defensive wall was built right at the edge, surrounding the city. A steep ramp led up to a wooden gate. Swaying lazily from a beam above the gate was a blue banner with a yellow sun surrounded by a ring of white stars.

They stopped some hundred steps back from the hill and waited.

A man yelled from above. "Who are you?"

"Visitors," Li'uli said, his deep voice reverberating. "Call your leader."

"We're at war, haven't you noticed?"

Laughter roared up behind the wall.

"Would you like this food?" Li'uli pointed at the sacks tied to the donkey's saddle.

After a while, the man yelled, "Leave your animals and come up with the food."

At the top of the ramp, the gate cracked open to let them in and closed behind them.

Foul odor made Sall gag.

A crowd of men closed in, dirty and thin, staring at the sacks of food.

"Make way!" It was the sonorous voice that had spoken to them from the top. "Move!"

As the crowd parted, Sall expected a gray-haired man with the stature of Judge Ben-Dor. Instead, a young man appeared, radiating health and vigor, wearing a clean robe.

"I'm Kohav, son of Yerakh," he said. "Who are you?"

"Li'uli, son of King Nigusi of Kush, here to visit your father."

"He's dead. I'm the new judge."

Some of the men around them hung their heads.

Kohav gestured at Sall. "Your servant can hand over the food now."

Li'uli nodded, and Sall put the two sacks of food on the ground before

Kohav, who signaled to two men. They took the sacks and walked down the main street of the city. The crowd followed them, joined by women and children, all of them emaciated and dirty.

"God bless you for this generosity," Kohav said. "Go and tell the cursed Judge Ben-Dor that we will never surrender, because Issachar is first and center among the tribes of Israel, whereas Manasseh is only half the tribe of Josef."

"In our language," Li'uli said, "my name means Prince of Peace, which is my aspiration."

"When you mediate between enemies, you risk becoming enemy of both."

"True, but I'm a stranger, passing through your land, having no stake in your conflict, only sadness at watching brothers kill one another."

"Worry not, prince of Kush. No killing will take place, because this city is an invincible fortress."

"History is littered with the ruins of invincible cities."

"Beth She'an will be the exception." Kohav skipped up a set of stairs onto the top of the wall. "Come, see for yourself."

They followed him. Sall glanced down over the edge and stepped back, dizzy from the immense height. He looked straight out, and the dizziness passed. From this high, the siege ring of men, tents, and animals seemed too small to pose a threat.

Pacing on the wall around the city, Kohav pointed as he spoke. "We can track anyone coming down the road through the Jezreel Valley from Megiddo, the Gilboa Mountains, Mount Tabor, or the Great Sea. And there, to the south, we can see all the way down the Jordan River almost as far as Jericho." Coming around, he pointed again. "The east bank of the river is as clear as the palm of my hand. Our watchmen can alert us to any coming threat from the Hebrew tribes that live there, Gad and Reuben, as well as the king of Amon."

They reached the opposite side of the city, and Kohav pointed north. "This is my favorite view. On a clear winter day, you can see the white snow on the Golan Heights beyond the Sea of Galilee, and even make out the road to Damascus."

Sall shaded his eyes, gazing at the distant Golan Heights, which were not white this time of year, and imagined the road he would follow soon on his quest to find the Sailor of Barada, who would lead him to the cloud-piercing tower and the golden fountain.

"You see?" Kohav waved his arms at the surrounding views. "We can shoot our arrows and hurl our spears at anyone approaching this city, and no man can possibly scale the sheer slopes of this hill to try breaking through our stone walls. Why should we fear Manasseh?"

Li'uli stepped down from the wall into the crowded street. "What about the Canaanites' boulder-hurling machines?"

His words ignited anxious murmuring among men standing nearby.

"That's a myth," Kohav said. "Those machines don't exist."

"They exist," Li'uli said. "I've seen them with my own eyes."

"Where?"

"In Egypt, and I heard the Canaanites have them, too."

The murmuring grew into fearful muttering.

Kohav descended the steps from the wall and walked down the street. Li'uli and Sall hurried after him, and the crowd followed.

Sall noticed that the houses along the street were old yet grand, with masonry first floors, second floors built of wooden beams, large windows, and airy balconies. At a closer look, the wood appeared dry and brittle, some of the second floors were crumbling, and the thatched roofs were too thin to provide protection from the sun. Between the houses, people used every patch of dirt to grow vegetables or keep scrawny goats, fed with leaves and twigs.

At intervals along the street were tall jars marked with a splash of red paint. Li'uli lifted a cover of one and looked inside. Sall looked, too. The jar was filled with water.

"That's wise." Li'uli put the cover back. "The dry wood and thatched roofs could easily catch fire, placing the whole city in danger."

"My father thought of it," Kohav said. "We can put out a fire in moments, if we want to."

The comment was cryptic. Why would they not want to put out a fire? Sall looked at Li'uli for an explanation.

The prince smiled. "Fire is a mighty weapon of attack, or of defense, but not at the same time."

Kohav turned into a stone-tiled square with a well in the center, where a queue of women stood, holding jugs and waterskins. In the back of the square was the ornate façade of a great palace. Sall gazed in awe at the massive edifice. It was built of huge square blocks of white stone, set in straight lines of true alignment. The columns at the entrance were carved with intricate images of various animals. At the top of the left column was a massive bust of a lion's head, and on top of the right column, the head of a lioness. Above the entrance was an even larger bust of a bird's head with a disk above it.

Li'uli looked up. "A Falcon crowned with a sun – that's Ra, the Sun God of Egypt."

Kohav heard him and stopped, also looking up at the bird's head. "Is that what it is? We thought it was just a decoration." He pointed at one of the men. "You, get a stepladder and a hammer and smash this false God above the entrance."

As they walked into the palace, he added, "Maybe that's why Yahweh has been unkind to us. He'll be pleased when we destroy it."

"If it's a false God," Li'uli said, "why would your God care about it?"

Kohav led them down a wide corridor. "He forbids us looking at false gods, lest we fall into idolatry like our neighbors."

Tall wooden doors, etched with a scene of cats pawing snakes, let them into a great hall. Kohav walked across the empty hall and sat in a large stone throne. There were no chairs, and they had to stand before him as supplicants before a king. Behind them, a hushed crowd filled the rear of the hall, ushering in a wave of stench. Sall resorted to his old trick, breathing through his mouth.

Kohav seemed too small for the stone throne. The seat and back were smooth, but the armrests were carved like legs of a powerful animal, ending with mighty claws. The back was very tall, and the part visible above Kohav's head was etched with an image.

Sall leaned forward, peering at it.

The carving showed a lion and a lioness standing on their hind legs, facing each other. Their heads were close, their jaws open, and their front legs intertwined in either a fight, or an embrace. Sall realized he was looking at the same image as the one etched on Li'uli's tablet, commemorating the legend of his royal ancestor.

Pointing at the image above Kohav's head, Sall turned to Li'uli, who smiled and put a finger across his lips.

Behind them, through the open entrance, the sound of hammering entered the great hall and echoed from its walls and high ceiling.

18

Li'uli gestured around the hall. "This grand remnant of past glory, where powerful Egyptian governors ruled over Canaan and its neighbors, proves that this city is not invincible."

"It proves nothing," Kohav said. "Beth She'an has never fallen."

"Because its past dwellers may have left before their enemies arrived. You, on the other hand, will soon watch Canaanite soldiers setting up machines capable of hurling boulders as big as bulls over your walls."

"Yahweh is invincible to machines and boulders."

"They won't be aiming at your God." Li'uli gestured at the back of the hall. "Your people are in danger."

"They won't be the first to die for this city."

"Men, women, and children will be crushed."

"It's a price I'm willing to pay."

A collective groan came from the crowd.

Kohav got up, raising his voice. "Do you want Manasseh controlling the roads to Jericho, Shiloh, and Megiddo? Preventing us from taking our goods to the markets? Blocking our pilgrimage to the Holy Temple?"

No one responded.

"I admire your courage," Li'uli said. "Especially in light of your elective isolation amidst Manasseh's territory, while the rest of your tribe plows the fertile land by the Sea of Galilee."

Li'uli's mix of effusive praise and implied disparagement exacerbated Sall's confusion over the presence of Li'uli's ancestral seal on the Egyptian governors' ancient throne.

Lounging back, Kohav opened his arms. "What choice do we have?"

Li'uli sighed, scratched his head, and gazed at the ceiling which, Sall noticed, showed faded paintings of hunters and beasts. He wondered how the Egyptian craftsmen were able to paint intricate scenes on a ceiling that high.

"Indeed," Li'uli said. "It's a difficult situation."

Sall almost laughed. He was certain that the brown prince had conceived a plan before entering this sieged den of smelly Hebrews.

Kohav leaned forward eagerly.

Li'uli held his hands together, fingers intertwined as if in prayer. "What do you think of Judge Ben-Dor?"

"He's an enemy of Issachar." Kohav spat on the floor. "His hands are covered with the blood of our people, who died here of starvation and disease, including my father, rest in peace."

Li'uli nodded, sighing sadly. "Did your father hate Judge Ben-Dor?"

The question stumped Kohav, whose face reddened, before he answered in a low voice as if he didn't want the people in the back to hear. "My father hated no man."

"Not even the enemy of Issachar?"

"Hatred is a stool with three legs: malice, stupidity, and shortsightedness. That's what my father said when I asked him how could he not hate Judge Ben-Dor."

The statement shocked Sall, but there was no reaction from the men behind, who must have heard it from the late judge.

"Now I understand," Li'uli said. "Neither you nor your opponents know for sure where your God stands."

Kohav nodded.

"And neither of you wants those idol worshipers from Hazor getting a foothold here." Li'uli gazed at the ceiling again. "The Canaanites would be a threat to both tribes' freedom of trade and pilgrimage, aren't they?"

Another nod.

"What if I ask Judge Ben-Dor to take an oath on the scrolls of your Holy Scriptures that Manasseh will never prevent Issachar from taking goods to the markets or making pilgrimage to the temple?"

"Trust the judge of Manasseh?" Kohav laughed bitterly. "The one who made an alliance with the Canaanite king to slaughter us?"

A shuffling noise came from behind, and Sall turned to see an old woman making her way slowly to the front. She kissed Kohav's forehead and spoke in his ear. Sall imagined himself one day, facing a similar situation, his beloved mother whispering words of wisdom in his ear. He chuckled to himself, knowing he would never be in a position of power like this young Hebrew judge, or be required to make a decision for a city full of desperate people.

Kohav got up, helped the old woman sit on the throne, and turned to Li'uli. "Go and ask the judge of Manasseh. If he agrees, I will accept, but on the condition that our priest will administer the oath."

"You chose wisely," Li'uli said, turning to leave.

"Wait," Kohav said. "One more thing."

"Yes?"

"Our people will be allowed time to pack up and leave the city before any man of Manasseh sets foot inside these walls."

"How long?"

"Let's say, until sunrise tomorrow."

Sall watched Li'uli's face and noticed a hint of a smile at the corners of his mouth.

19

When the gate closed behind them, Sall hurried down the ramp after Li'uli. They mounted the horse and donkey and rode towards the siege ring.

"Your ancestral seal," Sall said. "How is it possible—"

"Not now, boy."

"But—"

"I'll explain later."

Li'uli's response confirmed that the similarity wasn't a coincidence, making it even more intriguing.

Judge Ben-Dor listened to Li'uli's full report, recited a brief Hebrew prayer for the late Judge Yerakh, and agreed to take the proposed oath and allow the men of Issachar until sunrise tomorrow to pack up and leave Beth She'an.

Li'uli walked back across the field, stood below the cliff, and delivered Judge Ben-Dor's response to Kohav, who listened from the top of the wall.

The sun was already high in the sky when the men of Manasseh gathered from all around the hill of Beth She'an, leaving their siege positions, and gathered behind their elderly judge. Many men of Issachar joined their young judge on top of the wall to watch the proceedings below. A priest came out of the gate and walked down the steep ramp in his white robe and white cap, a bejeweled breastplate hanging from his neck and a bundle of scrolls held in his arms. He paused at the bottom of the ramp and looked at the mass of armed men facing him. Li'uli and Sall walked over and accompanied the priest. He held the scrolls forward for the judge to lay his hands on them.

"I, Judge Ben-Dor, leader of the Manasseh tribe, descendent of Josef, son of Jacob, hereby take this oath." His voice boomed across the valley, echoing from the chiseled cliffs. "I swear in the name of Yahweh upon these Holy Scriptures that no harm shall come to the men, women, and children of Issachar as long as they leave Beth She'an by sunrise tomorrow and join their tribesmen near the Sea of Galilee. I further swear that Manasseh shall never prevent Issachar from passing through our land to bring your goods to the markets in Jericho and Megiddo, or from making pilgrimage to the Holy Temple in Shiloh."

The men of Issachar above and the men of Manasseh below joined in a roaring cheer.

The priest hugged the scrolls to his chest and hurried back across the field and up the ramp to the gate, which opened to allow him in and slammed shut behind him.

Judge Ben-Dor stood for a long moment, gazing up at the city. Around him, hundreds of men were hugging each other while reciting prayers of gratitude to their God for ending the conflict peacefully. They went back to their siege encampments, packed up the tents and supplies, and gathered the animals. Within a short while, they began to leave, either west towards the Jezreel Valley, or east towards the Jordan River. Sall wondered if there was a bridge nearby, like the one in Jericho, to cross over to the east bank of the river, shortening the way back to their towns and villages.

In the main camp, the judge sent a group of men on horses to inform the Canaanite force that its help is no longer needed. He summoned the remaining men to sit in the shade of a large tree near his tent. Sall estimated their number at about fifty.

"Wonderous are the ways of Yahweh," Judge Ben-Dor said.

The men grunted in agreement.

"His divine wisdom is never ending."

There was more grunting.

Li'uli leaned over and whispered in Sall's ear, "What about my wisdom?"

"I agonized for a long time," Judge Ben-Dor said. "Would it not be a grave sin to invite idol worshippers to spill the blood of fellow Hebrews, even for a just cause?"

The men watched him, waiting.

"A fond memory helped me overcome my doubts. My first wife, Zifra, makes the most delicious sheep stew, which I eat until my belly is about to burst." He patted the front of his robe. "It's sweeter than honey, and if my sheep weren't giving the best wool in Canaan, I would have slaughtered every last one of them to supply my wife with meat for her magical stew."

They laughed, wiping their lips.

"Every woman in Megiddo asked Zifra what she put in her stew, but she wouldn't tell them, because it was a secret family recipe from her mother. One day, after eating a whole bowl and wiping it clean with bread, I ordered my wife to tell me what was that magical ingredient that made her stew so incredibly sweet to my palate. Do you know what she said?"

Someone said, "Honey."

The judge shook his head.

Another one said, "Palm dates."

"No."

Others tried to guess.

"Pomegranates?"

"Figs?"

"Raisins?"

"Dried plums?"

"Diced apples?"

He kept shaking his head, smiling. "Do you give up?"

Everyone yelled, "Yes!"

Judge Ben-Dor pulled something from his pocket and held it up. "Horseradish root."

The men cried in surprise.

"Yes," he said. "The most bitter herb, which brings tears to a grown men's eyes, was the secret ingredient that sweetened Zifra's sheep stew."

Sall was captivated by the story, but he couldn't understand how it was related to the Canaanite army. He looked at Li'uli, whose eyes were actually focused on the top of the hill, where a cloud of dust formed above the wall. It was a curious sight, but whatever was happening inside Beth She'an could not be seen from the camp due to the height difference. The most likely answer, the boy decided, was that hundreds of feet were drumming up dust as the people of Issachar rushed here and there to find their loved ones and fetch their belongings ahead of their hasty departure.

"This is our delicious stew." Judge Ben-Dor pointed at the fortified city atop the hill. "Starting tomorrow, we'll sit in the great palace the Egyptians had built, sleep in their lavish houses, and wield our weapons from the top of the wall to cement our control over both banks of the Jordan River and all over the Jezreel Valley. Manasseh will dominate the trade routes north, south, east, and west, making us masters of central Canaan from the Great Sea to the Gilead Mountains in the far east. Such victory, sweeter than any stew, required swallowing a bitter herb – accepting help from the Canaanite idol worshippers."

The men nodded, voicing their agreement.

"And what does our almighty God bring me instead?" Judge Ben-Dor pointed at Li'uli. "A different idol worshipper!"

The men burst out laughing, and Li'uli smiled, taking a playful bow.

The judge raised both hands towards the sky. "He saw the pain in my heart and sent us the Prince of Peace, all the way from Kush, at the right time and the right place and with the right peacemaking skills. Can this be a coincidence? No! It's the hand of God!"

20

Back near the tent, Li'uli's two servants were lashing sacks, jugs, and waterskins to the camel, the horse, and Sall's donkey, while the goats nibbled at the grass nearby. It would be unusual to depart in the afternoon, but Sall didn't mind. He was eager to resume the journey, even if they would stop to swim in the Sea of Galilee and detour to admire the giant cedars of Lebanon, before taking the road to Damascus. Besides, he didn't want to risk Judge Ben-Dor noticing Li'uli's ancestral seal on the ancient Egyptian throne in the morning, which was bound to cause suspicion.

Inside the tent, the children were taking a nap. Li'iliti spoke to Li'uli in their guttural language, and he replied in an appeasing tone. She glanced at Sall and lowered her eyes.

The black-haired girl of the Cainite Clan entered the tent. "The judge sent me," she said to Li'uli. "A gift of gratitude."

He smiled and gestured at the cot.

Rising from the cushions, Li'iliti left the tent. Sall breathed in the girl's scent of lavender and stepped out, thinking of An. He joined Li'iliti in the shade of a tree. The two servants left the animals and went to stand by the tent's entrance, as still as brown statues. The rest of the camp was quiet, everyone resting in their tents during the hottest part of the day. Through the thin cloth of the tent, Sall heard the girl moaning softly. He blushed, but Li'iliti kept her proud bearing as if nothing was happening.

When the girl left, her scarf covered her face.

Li'uli appeared between the two servants. He looked up towards the hill of Beth She'an, where the frantic activity continued behind the wall, dust drifting upward into the growing cloud that hovered in the stagnant air.

Li'iliti returned to the tent, lay down beside the sleeping children, and closed her eyes. Sall didn't know whether or not to stay, but Li'uli sat on a cushion and gestured for the boy to sit beside him. One of the servants came in with two cups of hot milk and handed one to each of them.

Li'uli raised his cup. "To victory."

Sall raised his. "To explanation."

Li'uli laughed.

Emptying his cup, Sall put it down on the ground beside the cushion. The warmth of the milk spread inside him. It was pleasant and soothing.

"You're a clever boy," Li'uli said.

"And curious."

"Yes, but other people will be curious, too."

"I won't tell."

"Swear by your God."

Sall took the effigy of Qoz from his pocket. "I swear in the name of the mighty Qoz that I won't repeat what you tell me."

"Fine," Li'uli said. "If you can guess half of it, I'll tell you the rest."

Having spent the whole time pondering possible explanations, the boy was certain of one fact. "You're a descendant of the Egyptian governors who ruled here generations ago, but your arrival at this particular time, when the Hebrew tribes are fighting over it, is too much of a coincidence."

"Go on."

His excitement rising, Sall sat up, thinking. "Maybe your father heard about this fight and sent you to interfere before the city was destroyed in a battle."

"How would my father hear about this?"

"From travelling merchants, I suppose."

"And why would my father, King of Kush, care about saving Beth She'an from ruin?"

"I don't know," Sall said. "He could be hoping to rule over Canaan again, but that would be impossible without the backing of Egypt, which already gave you the throne of Kush."

"Impressive." Li'uli brought the cup to his lips, but put it down without drinking. "You're an unusual boy, my friend."

"Am I right?"

"You are."

"Then you have to tell me everything."

Li'uli chuckled. "My great-grandfather eight times back, also named

Li'uli, was the last Egyptian governor of this region – from the Great Sea through all of Canaan to Lebanon and Syrian, well beyond the Tigris and Euphrates rivers, as well as the lands known today as Amon and Moab. At the time, Pharaoh Akhenaten became the new Pharaoh while he was still young and weak, unable to defend Egypt's shores from the sea people, those you call Philistines, or from the Hittite armies in the north. When he abandoned Egypt's Gods in favor of a single God named Aten, the angry Gods punished him with the loss of many battles to the Hittites, forcing him to withdraw from this region. Governor Li'uli had to flee back to Egypt, and Akhenaten's heir, Pharaoh Tutankhamun, gave him a small Egyptian dominion along the upper Nile River."

"Kush?"

"Correct. My father is the seventh heir to the throne of Kush, but it is a poor and wild region that lacks fertile lands or useful quarries, whereas it's abundant with deadly reptiles and warlike tribes who feast on human flesh. Now you understand why we've never ceased to dream of returning to our ancestral palace in Beth She'an and rule over Canaan and its rich environs."

"I'm here because of a dream, too."

"That's why we're brothers in spirit," Li'uli said. "Your dream, however, is young, while our family's dream has lived on through eight generations. We have questioned merchants who traveled through this region, and we've pled with every succeeding Pharaoh for a military campaign to reconquer this whole fertile region for the glory of Egypt and the restoration of our house to its rightful governorship."

"And the current Pharaoh agreed?"

"More than just agreed. Pharaoh Ramesses the Fourth is the son of the greatest leader Egypt has had in all its glorious millennia. He won many battles against invaders from the Arabian lands and pushed the Philistines north to the coast of Gaza. And now, as we speak, his army is marching from Giza to the Sea of Reeds."

"The Sea of Reeds is on the southern border of my country."

"Correct," Li'uli said. "Edom is Egypt's gate to Canaan, because the coastal road is blocked by the Philistines."

"Will you wait here for Pharaoh's army?"

"My mission is to prepare the ground here and elsewhere."

"Isn't it dangerous?" Sall yawned, covering his mouth. "The Hebrews will kill you if they find out."

"Risk and gain go hand in hand."

"What about the risk to Li'iliti and your children?"

"A foreign man traveling with two armed guards raises suspicion, but no one suspects a friendly prince touring the trade routes with his wife, children, and servants. And having our court jester adds to the credibility of my cover, don't you agree?"

The unravelling facts should have upset Sall, but he felt too tired to be upset and struggled to keep his eyes open. "You deceived me," he said, yawning again.

"When lying is necessary, it's not a lie."

"What will happen to the Hebrews?"

"One person's dream is often another person's nightmare." Li'uli handed him his own cup of milk. "Here, drink mine, too. I'm not thirsty."

Sall drank half the cup and put it down. "Why did you make peace between them?"

"To prevent this stronghold from falling into the hands of the Canaanite. King Javin of Hazor would have used it to entrench his forces and fight Egypt's army. The quarrelling Hebrew tribes, on the other hand, will be easy to crush."

"Judge Ben-Dor is formidable." Sall kept yawning. "By morning, he'll rule the fortified city."

"I'm not worried about that."

Wiping his eyes, Sall asked, "Won't he use it to entrench his forces and fight Egypt, like you feared the Canaanites would?"

"Beth She'an won't be of much use to him."

"No use?" Surrendering to an irresistible sleepiness, he closed his eyes and lounged back on the cushion. "Why not?"

"Because it will burn tonight."

"Burn?" Alarmed, Sall tried to sit up, but his body wouldn't cooperate. "Why?"

Li'uli chuckled. "It's easier to capture a burnt fort and restore it, than to conquer it whole."

21

The shouting woke Sall up from a dream in which he was already in Damascus, standing atop a wall overlooking a wide river with many sailing ships. He sat up and looked around. The tent was empty, other than the cot he had slept on. The other cots, the cushions, the children, and their parents were gone. Were they outside, waiting for him?

He yawned, wishing for more sleep, but the shouting outside persisted. Through the entrance he could see twilight, tinged with red. It was evening already, too late to start traveling. They would have to unpack the animals and spend the night here.

Getting up, he became dizzy and almost fell. Holding on to the center pole, he recovered and stepped out of the tent.

The air was cold, which was odd as the heat of the day usually lingered through sunset. His donkey, saddled and loaded with his sack and waterskins, was tied to a nearby tree, but Li'uli's horse, camel, and goats were gone. Had they left without him?

He took a deep breath and coughed. It was smoky, but without the pleasant smells of cooking food.

More shouting made him turn.

On top of the hill, Beth She'an was on fire. Flames soared high above the walls, casting a red glow over the whole valley. Beyond it, he saw a thin orange line over the mountains in the east, hinting of a new dawn. He had slept not only through the afternoon and evening, but through the night, as well.

How could it be?

The hot milk!

Sitting down on the ground, Sall cradled his aching head in his hands. He remembered drinking the milk from his cup, as well as from Li'uli's cup. What had they put in the milk? The boy had seen his father mix a potion for people who had trouble falling asleep. Was the sleeping potion known in Kush, as well? Or in Egypt, where Li'uli's family had originally come from?

Snippets of yesterday's conversation came back to him, with Li'uli saying, "It's easier to capture a burnt fort and restore it, than to conquer it whole."

How had Li'uli guessed that Kohav would burn the city before leaving? Had it been the exchange about the water jars on the street? The young judge had said, "We can put out a fire in moments, if we want to." The prince's words had been similarly cryptic: "A fire is a mighty weapon of attack or of defense, but not at the same time."

The ferocity of the flames filled the boy with terror. He struggled to breathe. Pulling the effigy of Qoz from his pocket, he pressed it to his lips.

Judge Ben-Dor, accompanied by several men, rushed by and entered the tent.

Sall slipped the effigy back into his pocket.

The men came out, and two of them pulled Sall up by his arms.

The judge asked, "Where is the brown prince?"

He was too terrified to speak.

The judge slapped him across the face with a heavy hand.

Shocked, the boy cried, "I don't know."

"You speak our language." The judge slapped him again. "No more lies, boy. Where is your prince?"

"He's not my prince. I only met him a week ago."

"You're of Issachar, aren't you? An agent of Kohav, right?"

"No." His cheeks hurt from the slapping, but he feared worse if they found out he wasn't a Hebrew. "I've never been north of Jericho until now. I worked there for a potter, Ishkadim of Benjamin. He released me and—"

"Where did the brown prince and his family go? Which direction?"

"They gave me hot milk with something in it that made me fall asleep."

"Look," one of the men said. "His donkey is ready for the road. He was going to slip away, too."

Judge Ben-Dor stared at the boy. "Why did he trick us?"

"He tricked me, too."

The judge slapped him again. "Was he paid by Issachar? Did Kohav hire him to deceive us?"

"Nobody paid me, I swear in the name of—" He almost said Qoz.

"Don't invoke God's name in vain." The judge's hand flew again, this time hitting the side of the boy's head. "Tell me why the brown prince did it and where he went, or my men will make you talk."

The men clustered closely, glaring, their fists clenched.

As tempting as it was to tell everything he knew, Sall could not bring himself to break his vow. He had no ally here except Qoz. Besides, the rage in the men's faces told him that they would attack him no matter what he said.

"I'm sorry he tricked you," Sall said. "He tricked me, too."

"You will talk, boy." Judge Ben-Dor turned to his men. "Get the donkey ready."

Early sunrise was breaking when they removed everything but the saddle from his donkey, tied one rope between the saddle horn and his bound ankles, and a second rope between the donkey's neck and the trunk of a tree. One of the men kicked the donkey, jolting it into a run, which pulled the boy's legs from under him and dragged him along. His robe tore off, and the skin ripped from his back. He screamed. The donkey ran around the tree, the men hitting it with sticks. At one point, Sall's head hit a rock, and he lost conscience.

Someone poured water on his face. The sky above was bright, and he was in more pain than he imagined possible. He tried to cry, but couldn't take more than a shallow breath.

The judge leaned over him, his bearded face hiding the sky. "My questions are simple: Why did the brown prince trick us? Who paid him? Where did he go?"

"I can't," Sall whispered. "Please. I can't."

Someone hit the donkey, and the torture resumed. Above him, Sall saw the sky spinning against the outer branches of the tree. He felt his body bouncing on the rough ground and heard his voice screaming.

Everything went dark again.

22

They tied Sall to a wooden stake, a rope under his armpits to keep him upright, facing the hill of Beth She'an. The defense wall surrounding the top was intact, but behind it, the flames had not abated, leaping to great heights and bellowing black smoke that drifted south. His robe and sandals were gone, as were the donkey and all his belongings. He tried to lean forward against the rope to keep his flayed back off the tree trunk. The sun blinded him, and he shut his eyes.

A man came over and poured oil on him, smearing it all over his exposed chest, arms, and legs. Soon, the sun's scorching rays started to bake him alive. At the same time, his earlier injuries sent waves of pain from his legs, up his back, to his head, pounding him with frightful jolts. He wondered who took his robe with the effigy of Qoz in the pocket. He needed all the Gods of Edom now to join forces and transport him to Damascus or, better yet, directly to the fountain by the giant tower, where a sip from the golden elixir would transform him into a handsome, muscular dark man, or, at least, heal his wounds and make him whole again. Surely the golden elixir could do that much, couldn't it?

"It could do anything you want it to do." The voice came from a ball of glowing haze. "That's the whole point."

The boy tried to speak, but no words came from his parched throat.

"I'm waiting for you." It was the old dwarf's voice, but the glowing haze hid him. "Hurry up. Time is running out."

What was the hurry? What would happen when time ran out?

Before he could ask, the ball of glowing haze faded, and a man poured oil on him again while demanding answers to the judge's questions: "Why did the brown prince trick us? Who paid him? Where did he go?"

All the boy could do was shake his head and pray to the Gods.

Blisters began to pop on his chest, the skin peeling off in brittle layers. He cried for his mother and his father. He tried to whistle Bozra's tune, begging her to come and save him.

The black-haired girl of the Cainite Clan appeared and held a cup of water to his lips. When he finished the water, she hurried away. He fainted again, and when he woke up, the men of Manasseh were tying a few captives in tattered robes to tree trunks nearby. Beatings began in earnest with sticks, clubs, and knotted ropes. The captives groaned through clenched jaws, except for the youngest one, about Sall's age, who cried out loud.

An older captive hushed him. "Men of Issachar don't cry."

The youth quieted for a while, but the man of Manasseh who was beating him took it as a challenge and intensified his efforts. The youth resumed crying, and the older one hushed him again.

"Let him cry," another captive said. "We're as good as dead anyway."

With the sun at its full force, Sall's arms and legs blistered up like his chest. He felt the skin puff up on his cheeks and forehead, as well. The pain had lost its edge, and he kept blinking, trying to clear his eyesight, which had shrunk as if he watched the world through a porthole.

Judge Ben-Dor came over and showed Sall the shattered remains of the effigy of Qoz in his hand. Tears flooded the boy's eyes as the clay fragments fell to the ground by his bare feet.

"You're an Edomite." Judge Ben-Dor stepped on the fragments, pushing them into the dirt. "A descendant of Esau, slithering back to the land of Jacob's children to cause mayhem. Now, for the last time, answer me. Why did the brown prince trick us? Who paid him? Where did he go?"

The boy wanted to explain that he had no desire to cause trouble, that he was merely passing through on his way to Damascus, and that he had taken a vow not to reveal what Li'uli had told him, but his throat was too dry and his breath too shallow to utter a single word.

Judge Ben-Dor turned to the oldest among the men of Issachar. "Will you talk, or do you need more beating?"

The captive cocked his head back, cleared his throat, and spat at the judge.

The others laughed.

Plucking a leaf from a tree, the judge used it to wipe the mucus off his cheek. Meanwhile, his men converged on the captive and clubbed him until his bones were broken and his head was oozing blood.

Judge Ben-Dor approached another captive.

"We had no choice," the man said. "Judge Yerakh died, and Kohav didn't bother citing the Holy Scriptures. Anyone who disobeyed him starved to death."

"Did the brown prince from Kush tell him to burn the city?"

The captive seemed confused. "Didn't you send him to us?"

"What do you mean?"

"Kohav was certain he was your agent, trying to trick us."

"Then why did Kohav agree to leave? And why did he burn the city?"

"We had to go before the Canaanites came and killed us, but there was no way he would leave the fortified city for you to dwell in and use against us."

"But I took the oath he had asked for. Did he not trust me?"

The man hesitated.

"I won't hurt you for telling the truth."

"He said you're as trustworthy as a Canaanite idol-worshipper."

The words made Judge Ben-Dor's shoulders sag. "He was wrong. I would have honored our truce, but now that Issachar broke it, Manasseh will be forced to take revenge."

"Our tribe is blameless," another captive said. "Kohav alone decided what to do. He ordered everyone to tear off wooden beams from houses, break up beds and chairs, and pile pillows and linen for fuel. He selected seven men to stay behind and light the fires with candles and torches late at night, once he and the rest of the people were too far for you to catch before they reached the territory of Issachar."

Judge Ben-Dor's face hardened. "Are you the ones who started the fire?"

"We couldn't refuse."

"Why not?"

"He threatened our families."

The judge counted them. "I see only six of you. Where's the seventh?"

"He died in the fire."

"Good," one of the Manasseh men said. "And now we'll burn the rest of you."

His friends voiced their support.

The young captive whimpered.

Turning away from them, Judge Ben-Dor looked up at the burning city.

Sall imagined he was contemplating the captives' fate. Was his own fate being decided now, too? The boy's mind was fogged up, and he couldn't think straight. His eyes descended to the clay fragments on the ground. What hope did he have without Qoz?

The men of Manasseh watched the judge in silence, waiting for his orders.

"Yahweh is watching us." Judge Ben-Dor turned back to face his men. "The fifth of the Ten Commandments is simple: Do not kill! We must never spill the blood of another Hebrew man or woman except for the specific sins listed in the Holy Scriptures."

His men shifted, visibly disappointed.

"The fire started before dawn." He gestured at Beth She'an. "It was still their city to do with as they wished. Yes, their leader broke the truce he made with me, but he cleverly avoided taking an oath to fulfill his part. Either way, these captives didn't violate the Holy Scriptures by setting fire to Beth She'an. They are free to go."

One of his men pointed at Sall. "What about him?"

"He must pay for deceiving us. Tomorrow morning, you may take him up to the city and throw him into the fire."

The men of Manasseh released the captives and untied the dead one, whose body fell to the ground. Two of the others picked up the corpse, and the group hurried away, glancing back warily as if expecting Judge Ben-Dor to change his mind.

The sun started its descent behind Sall, but the damage it had caused could not have been worse. The blisters all over the front of his body had burst, oozing clear liquid that soon dried into a yellowish crust. He shut his eyes, trying to dream again of the river, the tower, and the old dwarf. He slumped forward, the rope cutting through his armpits. His consciousness slipped away, and he heard a woman weeping in the distance. Was it his mother? He couldn't tell.

23

A whisper tickled Sall's ear, the rope that held him to the stake gave out, and someone grabbed him around the chest, causing a sudden explosion of pain. He was draped face-down over something hard, which pressed on his abdomen, causing more pain. It shifted and moved. Through the cloud of agony, he noticed the familiar odor of his donkey, mixed with a pleasant scent of lavender. It was nighttime and, in the moonlight, he saw the bottom of the donkey's belly and, on the other side, his own bare feet. Sall understood that he was lying over the saddle, his head on one side and his legs on the other. The scent of lavender came from the girl pulling the donkey, and he caught a glimpse of a dark robe and delicate ankles in leather sandals. He thought of An, who had also smelled of lavender and walked in sandals over her delicate ankles.

He fainted again.

When he came to, the sun was rising. The donkey stood at the edge of a pond, drinking noisily.

Water!

Thirst hit him with a desperate craving. He tried to speak, but only a faint sigh emerged. The Cainite girl supported his head and held a waterskin to his lips. He drank a bit, coughed hard, and drank more. The world started spinning, and he lowered his head next to the donkey's belly. The raw flesh over his chest and abdomen rubbed on the saddle, and he imagined this was how it felt to be burned alive.

Drifting in and out of consciousness, his mind registered their onward movement through the day and into the next night, with occasional stops for water. He heard dogs barking in the distance, birds chirping in trees above, and once, the soft voice of the Cainite girl singing in a language he didn't recognize. During the night, a brief shower woke him up, the wounds on his back sizzling as if sprayed with boiling oil, not raindrops.

The next time he woke up, gentle hands lifted him off the saddle, carried him into a tent lit by a single candle, and put him down on his right side with his arm prone. It was the only part of his body still covered in skin. They were women, he could tell by their pleasant scents, subtle movements, and hushed voices. One of them cradled his head while another held a cup of water to his lips. They removed his loincloth and started to wash him, which hurt even more than the rain. He was too weak to cry.

When Sall opened his eyes again, it was light outside. His whole body was smeared with a potion that smelled of honey. A woman was fanning him with a palm frond. Like the Cainite girl that had saved him, the woman had long black hair and a pale face.

Another woman came in and helped him drink a cup of milk, which was still warm from the goat. The effort exhausted him, and the wounds on the back of his neck flared up from craning his head. He rested his cheek against the cot and closed his eyes, wishing to leave his broken body. He imagined being in his room at home in Bozra, the clean sheets cool against his skin, kitchen smells wafting in, Laundress and Horseman talking outside his window, making each other laugh. He wondered, what was Cook making for dinner?

It was his last coherent thought for many days and nights as high fever attacked him. His mind simmered with images and noises that made no sense and left only snippets of memories – the women of the Cainite Clan trickling milk or water on his tongue, washing his wounds, and chanting strange tunes by his cot. Once in a while, he heard men talking, singing, or laughing. A few times, the voice of the old dwarf told him to hurry up before it was too late, but as hard as he tried to wade through the glowing haze and find the dwarf, he was never successful.

When the fever started to subside, the Cainite women took him outside at night and put him on a bed of straw by a small fire while they cooked and sang melancholy songs. The cool night's air felt good on the scabs that covered his wounds. The morsels of bread, meat, and cheese they placed on his tongue had no taste, but he chewed them slowly and swallowed with difficulty. One night, he noticed that the moon was almost full, but couldn't figure out whether it was the first, second, or third full moon since he had left home.

A few days later, the girl who had saved him came into the tent. Her scent of lavender brought back contrasting memories from Bozra and

Beth She'an.

He cleared his throat and spoke with difficulty. "Thank you for rescuing me."

His voice was hoarse and husky as if it belonged to an old man.

She smiled. "You were more dead than alive. We didn't expect you to survive."

He coughed hard, and she went out and brought him a cup of milk, which he drank slowly until it was empty.

The girl took the cup. "Would you like some more?"

He shook his head. Sitting up, he held out his hand to her. "Will you help me stand up?"

She did, and he wobbled on his weak legs. They stepped out of the tent and into a crisp, sunny morning. His donkey was nearby, sharing a corral with two other donkeys, as well as goats and sheep. There were several other tents, spread out a good distance from one another. He saw a man step out of one of the tents, reach into his pocket, and give a coin to the woman who came with him. She had long black hair and pale face like the other women of the Cainite Clan. Sall wondered where the men of the clan were staying.

Through the trees he noticed a mountain shaped as a giant woman's breast. He shaded his eyes with his hand, gazing at it.

"That's Mount Tabor," the girl said. "And behind us is the Sea of Galilee."

He turned and, to his astonishment, saw blue water through the trees, far downhill from where they stood. He felt dizzy and wanted to sit down. Touching his rear, he felt scabs, which would break if he sat. The girl understood and helped him back to the tent, where he lay down on his left side. It took him a moment to catch his breath before he could speak.

"Why did you save me?"

The girl reached into her pocket and brought out a handful of turquoise stones. "The brown prince gave them to me. They're more valuable than silver coins."

"In exchange for saving me?"

She shook her head. "He only asked that I plead for your life with the judge."

"When did he ask you? While you were in his tent?"

"He really is a prince. His hand never touched me, and I moaned only in case someone was listening. He told me that you would be captured and accused of spying, but that you are innocent. Then, he rehearsed with me what to tell the judge." She paused, recalling Li'uli's exact words. "How could a young boy from Edom know to be wary of a crafty foreigner, if the wise judge of Manasseh didn't see through his scheme?"

"And the judge allowed you to take me?"

"Yes, but only if I could sneak you out of the camp without any of his men noticing. He said they were too thirsty for your blood, and he would let them have you if they caught us."

"Why did he agree to let me go?"

"He is a faithful Hebrew. They have a mighty God who can see everything and expects them to be fair and just towards other people."

"It would have been fair and just to punish me for my part in the burning of their city."

"Judge Ben-Dor said that your injuries were punishment enough." She shrugged. "He spoke about your nation, Edom, which had allowed the Hebrews to pass through unharmed on their exodus from Egypt."

"That was many generations ago, long before I was born."

"He said you were smart, speaking the Hebrew language almost as a native, and also brave, resisting torture to keep the brown prince's secrets, even though he had betrayed you, too. The judge saw greatness in you and hoped that, when you return home, you'll do something vital for Edom, which would repay the Hebrew debt of ancient times."

Her words sounded to Sall as if they described another person. He wasn't smart or brave, and there was no greatness in him, no chance of doing some vital deed for Edom. At the same time, he was grateful for being alive, no matter how misguided the judge's reasons had been.

"You shouldn't return to Edom, though." She took the empty cup and got up to leave. "The brown prince said it wasn't safe, not for a while."

"Why not?"

"He didn't explain."

That night, in his dream, Sall was standing on the royal balcony at the Temple of Qoz in Bozra with his parents. They were much taller than him, but before he could ask them about that, a little girl appeared on the balcony, her golden hair framing a pretty face with large brown eyes and red lips that drew him with an irresistible urge to kiss her, which he did while taking in her scent of lavender.

24

Early one morning, the Cainite girl rushed into the tent, pulled Sall off the cot, and took him outside. Several of the women were up, hurrying from one tent to another. The girl pushed him into the bushes and put her finger across her lips. He only had his loincloth on, but her distress kept him from arguing.

The drumming of hooves came from the direction of Mount Tabor. A few moments later, a group of riders appeared at the edge of the camp. Their hair was pasted to their scalps and cut at the shoulders, their faces were clean-shaven, and their bare chests glistened with either sweat or oil. They wore short skirts, dyed with horizontal lines in different shades of gray, and carried weapons – wooden machetes, battleaxes, and short spears.

The women of the Cainite Clan lined up. The riders dismounted. One of them, whose saddle was decorated with colorful strings, paced in front of the women and pointed at the girl who had saved Sall. She led him into one of the tents. Some of the others went with the remaining women into tents, and the rest sat by the fire.

One of the soldiers walked around the camp, twirling his spear, and came close to where Sall was crouching. He retreated further into the bushes, careful not to step on a twig, and crouched on the ground. The scabs all over his body itched badly. He didn't scratch, only pressed lightly on the scabs, which eased the itching for a moment.

A long time passed. He heard men's voices, women's laughter, and a horse neigh, but not the sound he hoped to hear – the drumming of hooves fading away.

As the day progressed, he became thirsty and nauseated. The world began to spin around him. A rustle in the bushes nearby scared him, and he scurried back to the camp on all fours, scraping off the fresh scabs on his knees.

At the clearing, he held on to a tree and stood up. Several Canaanite soldiers sat around the fire, drinking from jugs, their weapons on the ground nearby. One of them saw him, laughed, and beckoned. The boy approached them, bent over with nausea and dizziness.

A soldier held a jug up. "Have some wine, old man."

Sall understood the words, spoken in the language of the Canaanites, which he had learned while helping his father care for merchants and laborers from Canaan. He glanced over his shoulder, assuming the soldier was talking to someone else, but there was no one behind him. He realized his scabbed skin had made him look like an old man. Laughter burst out of him, not intentionally, or with any joy behind it, but a croaky laughter triggered by the outrageousness of the situation and the dreamlike state of his mind, right at the verge of fainting.

The girl hurried over, a smile plastered on her pale face. "He got lost," she told the soldiers. "His mind is feeble."

"The tent," said. "Please. Take me."

"Don't be silly." She grabbed his arm and pulled him up. "You're too old for the tent."

He didn't understand what she meant.

The girl led him towards the animal corral. "Come, your donkey knows the way home."

"Home? It's too far."

"Be quiet," she whispered.

His donkey was inside the corral, chewing on a leafy tree branch over the fence. The saddle was off, and flies swarmed over the areas where the hard leather had rubbed off the fur. Several goats were drinking from the water trough. Sall pushed between them, bent over to drink, and lost his balance, falling in head first. The girl pulled him out, and he coughed badly. Behind him, the soldiers hooted.

When the coughing stopped, he cupped his hands and drew water from the trough, gulping it down while much of it dripped all over his chest.

One of the soldiers imitated him, and the others laughed.

The girl helped Sall mount the donkey's bare back.

He held on to the plume of hair on the back of the donkey's neck while she pulled on the reins, walking out of the corral.

The soldiers quieted down and watched.

"Old man is confused," she yelled towards them. "Forgot his donkey here yesterday."

They lost interest and resumed drinking.

She led the donkey out the other end of the camp, away from the soldiers, circled around through the trees, and joined a trail that led downhill towards the water. When they were out of the soldiers' sight, she gave him the reins and hurried back.

"Wait," he said. "I don't have a robe, a saddle, or food. I have nothing."

"You have your life. Go now."

"When can I return."

"They're part of a large Canaanite force conducting drills near Mount Tabor. They'll be here for weeks."

"Why do you let them stay in your camp?"

"Their king is our protector, and his soldiers do with us as they wish. If you come back, they'll toy with you the way children toy with a sick bird before killing it."

"Then leave with me."

She smiled sadly. "I'm a woman of the Cainite Clan. We are outcasts, don't you know?"

He didn't know, and before he could think of what to say, she was gone.

"Thank you," he whispered and tapped his heels at the donkey's ribs.

The trail ended in a road that ran along the shore. The Sea of Galilee was enormous, a vast expanse of turquoise water, a shade brighter than the turquoise gems that Li'uli had given the girl. A fresh breeze from the north ruffled up the surface of the water. Across the sea, its distant eastern shore gave rise to precipitous mountains, shrouded in a green haze.

With a tap of his right knee and a shake of the reins, Sall turned the donkey left and headed north towards the Golan Heights, where Kohav had pointed out the road to Damascus. It wasn't a choice the boy made because he was smart or brave, in pursuit of greatness or the opportunity to perform a vital deed for Edom. He turned north because there was little doubt in his mind that death was coming for him today, and he would rather die while chasing his dreams than while making a futile retreat towards a home he would never see again.

25

The donkey paced along the left side of the road under overhanging trees, which teemed with chirping crickets and twittering birds. On the right was the shoreline, heavily populated by croaking frogs. The afternoon heat made Sall sweat, and the scabs that covered his scraped back and sunburned front itched maddeningly. Unable to resist, he scratched a few places, and fresh wounds opened, drawing flies. He stopped the donkey, dismounted, and walked down to the water, pebbles stabbing his bare feet, frogs leaping out of the way.

When the lukewarm water reached his thighs, he crouched, soaking in for a moment, and walked out. Back on the shore, the breeze blew on his scabs, cooling them and easing the itch. He walked back in and dunked all the way to his chin, tilting his head back to wet the short hair that had started to grow during his time with the Cainite Clan. The water was soothing. He lifted his feet from the rocky bottom and floated on his back. The sun had descended behind the mountains, and twilight turned the water from turquoise to gray. He closed his eyes and listen to the little waves shuffle the pebbles on the shore. He felt no itching or pain, only an overwhelming exhaustion.

The donkey brayed, startling Sall, who jolted up and splashed water into his eyes. For a moment, he was blind and disoriented, his feet seeking the bottom, his hands hitting the surface of the water. The donkey brayed again, and the sound told the boy where the shore was. He opened his eyes, stood up, and got out of the water. The donkey put its head down and drank from the sea.

On the road again, Sall paced beside the donkey while holding his arms up in the air, allowing the breeze to cool him down even better than the palm fronds the women had fanned him with in the tent. He noticed wild grapevines growing along the road and ate some grapes, which revived him. He considered trying to start a fire, but even if he succeeded, the fire would die out soon after he fell asleep, naked and alone, leaving him without protection from the cold and wild animals.

While he lingered by the grapevines in indecision, the donkey resumed walking north, and he followed.

With darkness descending on the Sea of Galilee, Sall noticed lights ahead. The donkey walked faster, and they approached a walled town. For the first time in his life, he saw boats, secured to shore with ropes. They were nothing like the great ships in his father's stories of the Philistines, sailing all over the Great Sea to trade with distant nations. These little boats seemed too flimsy to keep men above water.

Cooking fires glowed behind the town walls. The gates were locked for the night. Above the gates was a pale-red banner with a drawing of a deer, which meant this town belonged to neither Manasseh, nor Issachar. Smoke from roasting meat and voices of people drifted over the walls. He banged on the wooden gates.

A man peeked over the wall beside the gates, holding up a torch. "What do you want?"

"Shelter for the night," Sall said. "A robe, or a blanket, if you can spare it."

The guard disappeared.

Exhaling in relief, Sall patted his donkey's head.

Behind the gate, someone asked, "Who is that?"

"You won't believe it," the guard said. "A cursed one wants to come inside."

He wanted to tell them he wasn't cursed, only unlucky.

A hand appeared over the wall and threw a pebble, hitting Sall in the head. He cried in pain and shock. Other hands rose up, throwing stones over the walls. He turned and ran away, chased by stones and jeers. The donkey panicked and took off down the road, its hooves pounding the dirt. The boy was slower, but he kept running until he tripped and fell, his face slamming the dirt.

Pulling himself up, Sall brushed off the dust. His chest, arms, and legs hurt where the scabs tore off. He stepped down from the road into the water up to his hips and rinsed his face and fresh wounds. Feeling his head with his hand, he discovered a swelling where the first pebble had hit him.

A full moon rose over the mountains across the sea, its face reflected in the water. Back on the road, Sall walked slowly, keeping his eyes ahead of his feet to avoid stepping on a sharp stone or, worse yet, a snake. The night was cool, but not as cold as he had feared. There was no sign of the donkey, but he expected to see it soon, drinking on the shore or chomping at the bushes by the road. He recalled the morning of his departure from Bozra, his mother waiting for him in the front garden with the packed donkey and her favorite dog. Fighting back tears, he inhaled deeply and looked around, trying to take his mind off the memory.

He noticed that the birds had stopped twittering, while the crickets' chirping came in waves, rising and falling in loudness, as did the frogs' croaking. The two sounds alternated as the crickets grew louder and the frogs quieted down, and then, the opposite, again and again. At first, he thought it was his imagination. Why would these two species, of which one preyed on the other, be taking turns with their noisemaking? Was it all part of a mass ritual, thousands of insects mocking their would-be predators, which taunted them back before eating them?

Braying sounded ahead.

He quickened his steps.

The braying repeated, rising to a pitch, like a cry of pain.

Sall ran.

There was no more braying, but as he came closer, he heard crunching, like twigs breaking underfoot. He slowed down as, in the moonlight, he saw his donkey lying across the road ahead under a large animal with dark fur. The donkey's rear legs twitched the air. Sall's first instinct was to rush forward to save his donkey, but the urge passed instantly when he comprehended that he was looking at a large bear, which no man could beat back. There was nothing he could do to save his donkey.

He retreated slowly, trying to make no noise.

The bear stopped eating and glanced back at him.

The boy froze.

Howling, the bear stood up on its hind legs like a giant man with fur, jaws, and claws.

Sall turned and ran, his ears filled with the bear's howling, the massive paws pounding the ground, getting closer, sharp claws reaching for his back—

Glancing over his shoulder in sheer terror, he saw nothing. He stopped, held his breath, and heard no howls or paws. The crickets' chirping was on the rise, overwhelming all other sounds. He waited, and as the chirping declined and the toads' croaking started to rise, he heard the distant noise of crunching bones.

On the side of the road opposite the shore, he found a great tree and pulled himself up onto the lowest branch. He climbed further up and chose a wide branch to sit on, his legs dangling to the sides, his back against the trunk. His panting gradually subsided, and the alternate swells of chirping and croaking lulled him into sleep.

26

A bird landed on his shoulder and twittered into his ear, waking him up with a fright that almost toppled him from the high branch. Sall grabbed the trunk of the tree and collected himself while the bird hopped off to perch on a nearby branch.

He climbed down from the tree, crossed the road, and went down to the water, which sparkled with the first rays of the sun. He drank his fill, rinsed his face, and got back on the road, heading north. Hunger made him weak, and his body ached. Many of his scabs had been ripped off, leaving open wounds that attracted flies, whose tiny legs tickled him incessantly.

Up ahead, the donkey's ribcage appeared on the road like a gaping jaw with long teeth. Black scavenger birds picked at the carcass. He stepped down from the road to the waterline and bypassed the scene of death. Back on the road, he made frequent stops to rest. Later on, he came upon an apple orchard, picked one off a tree, and took a bite. It was fleshy and sweet. Juice dripped down his chin. He finished it and picked another, biting it, savoring the taste. As his stomach was filling, his heart swelled with relief that Qoz hadn't abandoned him despite what Judge Ben-Dor had done to its effigy.

His gratitude to Qoz only intensified when, in the afternoon, he saw a small village ahead, built on a low bluff between the road and the shore. A pole carried the same pale-red flag as the walled town of evil men who had stoned him the previous night, but he hoped these people, who didn't hide behind a wall, would be kinder and give him a chance to explain his circumstances. He longed for a clean robe, a hot meal, and a cot for the night.

A group of women stood in the water, washing clothes. A few children, who were playing near the women, ran towards him. Suddenly, the women began screaming for the children to come back, which they did.

Sall stopped, shocked by the intensity of their behavior. Was the bear following him? He turned quickly and scanned the road and the woods alongside it, but there was no sign of the bear.

The women herded the children into the houses while men rushed out, armed with clubs and shears, and advanced in his direction.

One of them yelled, "Don't come any closer!"

"I don't need much," he yelled back. "A robe, something to eat, a cot to sleep on. Have you no mercy?"

Holding their weapons with one hand, they used the other to pick up stones and hurl them at him. He turned and ran.

Once out of sight, Sall stepped off the road into the woods and began a long trek around the village. Those people had no hearts, he decided, only cruelty and malice. They were even worse than the other Hebrew tribes he had encountered.

The vegetation was thick, and he broke off a tree branch to beat the bushes to chase away any critters or snakes. He passed by more orchards and felt no remorse for picking the fruit of his tormentors' labor. He ate several plums, pomegranates, carobs, figs, and a particularly sweet bunch of grapes from a small vineyard abutting a rocky hillside.

When Sall was on the road again, walking north, a caravan came from the opposite direction. The leader veered off the road and stopped. Several women and children dismounted and clustered together, facing away from him while he walked by. One of the children dropped a small fish he was holding and tried to pick it up, but a woman pressed him to her bosom. Sall wanted to tell them he was no threat, but the leader was already rushing them off to the south, away from him.

The sun was low over the horizon when he saw a shack by the shore. A boat bobbed in the water behind it. In front of the shack was a wooden stall with a pile of fish.

A man came out of the shack. He was tall and very thin, with shaggy gray hair and an unkempt beard. Sall stopped, expecting the man to react with hostility and reach down to collect a rock.

"Come, come." His long-fingered hand beckoned. "Would you like to buy a fish?"

The boy approached warily. "I have nothing."

"You still have your body." The man smiled. "It could use a wash, though."

Looking down, Sall was embarrassed by how soiled he was with mud, blood, and flies.

"It's not your fault, boy. People are cruel to those they fear."

"Why do they fear me? I'm small and have no weapons."

"Everyone fears leprosy."

Leprosy! The word hit Sall worse than the Hebrew judge's heavy hand. It explained everything and offered no hope, because it would take months for his bloody sores to heal and for new skin to emerge and look normal. Until then, he bore the stigma of the most terrifying pestilence, a literal invitation to be killed by strangers crazed by fear and revulsion.

He felt weak with despair, and his knees bent under him. As he sat on the ground, a dog ran out of the shack. It wasn't pretty like Bozra. Its fur was patchy with bald spots, its left ear was folded, and its jaw drooled as he licked Sall's face, wagging its tail.

The man laughed. "His name is Dugdug."

"He's so happy." The boy scratched the dog's head. "I used to have a dog, too."

"He can tell you're a friend."

Sall turned his head, and the dog licked his ear, tickling it and making him laugh.

"If Dugdug likes you, everyone here likes you." The man waved around. "Welcome to Naum's village."

Sall didn't see a village, only the shack and fish stand.

"It's only me for now," the man said. "Yahweh hasn't yet given me a wife to bear my children, who will procreate and populate a village on this shore, named after me."

"Naum?"

"That's me. Do you know what it means?"

"No." The boy cradled the dog's snout in his hands and kissed its nose.

"Naum is a man being consoled, treated with compassion, which is a blessing that comes with a parallel duty, as God said." He pointed at the evening sky. "Treat others as you wish to be treated."

Sall stood up. "Aren't you afraid of lepers?"

"I can tell the difference between leprosy and boils. My family's patriarch, Job, had boils all over his body, just like you, but his boils came from Satan, not from malicious men."

"They dragged me behind a donkey, and then, they oiled my skin to help the sun burn me."

"God have mercy," Naum cried. "Who did that? The men of Naphtali in Rakkah?"

Sall pointed south. "Is Rakkah the walled city by the shore?"

Naum nodded.

"They only threw stones at me. The torture was done by men of Manasseh near Beth She'an."

"The fortified city?"

"It's in ruins now, burnt down."

"And they blamed you for it?"

Sall nodded.

Nahum shook his head. "I can tell you're not one to squash a noisy cricket, let alone burn a city."

"It doesn't matter. My life is over."

"You're alive, aren't you?"

"Not for long, the way things are going."

"That's what Job thought."

"Your patriarch?"

"Yes, thirty-six generations ago."

"Why did Satan give him boils?"

"The boils were the final test. In the beginning, when Job had been wealthy with land, livestock, and beautiful children, Satan teased God that Job loved Him only because He gave him everything. To prove Satan wrong, God allowed him to take away Job's wealth and kill Job's children, but Job wouldn't turn his back on God. At last, Satan gave Job boils from his feet to the top of his head. Job's wife saw him sitting on ashes, scratching himself with a shard of clay, and she told him, "Are you still holding on to your faith? Curse God and die!" But Job wouldn't, and he told her, "If we accept all the good things from God, then we must accept the bad, too." And when God heard it, he mocked Satan and healed Job, giving him a new wife, Dina, daughter of Jacob, who bore him many children while he became wealthier than he'd been before his suffering."

Of this long tale, which was meant to encourage him, Sall found only one morsel of hope. "If you descend from a daughter of Jacob, not a son, does that mean you're not a member of any of those nasty Hebrew tribes?"

Naum laughed, tugging at his beard. "It seems to me that your wretched appearance hides a very clever boy."

"I'm already sixteen," Sall said.

"A clever young man, then, who is dirty and hungry." Naum pointed at the Sea of Galilee. "Why don't you take a cleansing dip in this blessed water while I cook us some fish."

27

Dinner consisted of minced fish, which Naum had prepared by cooking several fish on a fire, deboning each one meticulously, and chopping up the fluffy white meat with rosemary and olive oil until it had the consistency of stewed barley, only richer in flavor and softer in texture. Sall went to sleep with a full belly on a comfortable cot under a soft blanket, the dog lying by his feet.

In the morning, he found a clean robe by the cot. He put it on and went outside.

Naum was in the boat, out on the water, the rope having been let out to its full length. Kneeling in the boat, Naum dropped pieces of leftover minced fish over the side with one hand, while in the other hand he held a stick with a net, which he abruptly swept down, coming up with a fish. Dugdug ran back and forth at the water's edge.

"Sorry." Naum dropped the fish into a bucket inside the boat. "This one is a keeper."

He got ready again, dropped a few crumbs in, and waited a brief moment before swinging his net. This time, the fish was small, and Naum tossed it to the dog.

The sun was a quarter of the way up when a caravan appeared up the road. Sall retreated into the shack, and Naum pulled on the rope to bring the boat back to shore. He carried out the bucket, which was full of water and live fish, and put it on the wooden stall.

From inside the shack, Sall watched a merchant and two women come over to look at the fish. After some haggling, they gave Naum a loaf of bread and a handful of figs in exchange for three sizable fish, which one of the women wrapped up in a piece of cloth.

When they left, Naum came into the shack with the bread and figs. He divided the food into two bowls and took a jug of wine out of a sack hanging from one of the support beams.

The boy hesitated to touch the food.

"Why aren't you eating?"

"I have nothing to pay you with."

"Did I pay for it?"

"Yes, with the fish you caught."

Naum pointed at the sea. "Plenty more fish in there."

They ate in silence. When they were done, Naum gave him a piece of cloth to cover his head in the sun, and they went into the boat together. As the rope was let out, the boat drifted from shore.

Dropping crumbs of food was easy, but there was an elusive skill to swinging the stick with the net quickly enough to catch the jittery fish. After a dozen attempts, Sall was tired.

"I can't do it. The fish knows what I'm about to do before I do it."

"That's right." Naum chuckled. "And the opposite is true, too."

The boy looked at him, confused.

"If you don't know what you're about to do, the fish doesn't know it either."

"How would I know what to do, if I don't know it?"

Naum threw his head back and laughed.

On the shore, Dugdug barked.

In the water, Sall sensed a ripple under a morsel of food and swung the net into the water. It came up with a fish.

"That's it." Naum grabbed the fish and hurled it to the dog. "Do you understand now?"

"I did it without thinking."

"Exactly. A skilled hand can perform a perfect job without premeditation. It's true for catching fish in the sea, or for shooting arrows at enemies."

Sall continued to practice his fishing skills, which improved as he learned to let his hand swing as soon as his eye caught a hint of movement underwater. When the bucket was full, Naum pulled the rope to bring the boat to shore. They sat in the shack and drank wine while Naum discussed the subtleties of fishing. Every long while, a caravan would stop to buy fish. Occasionally, local farmers would pass by, either on foot or mounted on a donkey, but none of them stopped. Sall assumed they knew how to catch fish for themselves.

In the afternoon, when the wine ran out, he felt lightheaded and relaxed. Naum asked about his life in Edom and the reason for his journey.

Sall told him what had happened with the high-priest's daughter, the dream behind his quest to find the Elixirist, the meeting with the handless dream reader on the mountaintop, the slavery under the potter in Jericho, and the events that precipitated his suffering in Beth She'an, followed by the weeks he spent under the care of the Cainite women. At last, he bemoaned having to postpone his quest for many more weeks to avoid the wrath of men terrified of leprosy.

After a few moments of silence, Naum got up and beckoned Sall to follow him.

Crossing the road, they climbed the hillside, Dugdug following behind. There was no trail, but Naum was confident of the way. Reaching a massive carob tree, he picked a couple of carobs and gave one to Sall. A few steps from the tree was a wall of thick vegetation. Naum parted it with his hands to let the boy to pass through.

In the middle of a clearing was a pool of fresh water, which came from a lively spring nestled between the rocks. Beside the spring was an open cave. The water gave off a sharp odor that Sall did not recognize.

Naum removed his sandals, took off his robe and loincloth, and stepped into the pool. Sall did the same. The warm water made his skin tingle all over, not in an unpleasant way like the incessant itching under the scabs, but like caressing by soft hands. He dipped his head in and held his breath while the tingling spread over his injured scalp and sunburnt face.

They stayed in the pool for a while, chewing on the carobs, which were as sweet as bee honey. The carob tree provided shade, protecting them from the hot sun while the evening approached. At sunset, they got out and dressed.

On the way back to the shack, Naum asked, "Are you feeling better?"

"My skin doesn't itch as much." He pointed at his knees. "And the sores aren't bleeding."

"You must swear never to tell anyone about this place."

"I swear, but what is it?"

"Job's Bath. That's where God sent our family patriarch to heal after Satan had been proven wrong. Job slept in the cave and dipped in the pool during the day. His boils healed within thirty days. Tomorrow, I'll take you back, and you'll stay in the cave and bathe in the pool every day as Job did many generations ago."

His mind refused to believe the power of Job's Bath, but Sall could not deny the improvement it had brought about already.

"There's one condition, though." Naum stopped walking and faced him. "You will not leave for Damascus until after you have found me a willing wife."

Finding a wife for this strange man wasn't something the boy thought possible. He didn't even know where to start on such a mission. In Edom, an old man sometimes took a young wife, but only if he had the means to support her and any children she might bear him. Naum had nothing but a crude little boat and a rickety shack. No wife could be found for him, Sall realized, but he didn't say anything, remembering the advice General Mazabi had given him at the outskirts of Bozra: "Never feel compelled to answer a question no one asked."

The sun was already down when they returned to the shack. The unsold fish had died in the hot bucket, and Naum emptied it into the sea. For the evening meal, they ate what had remained of the bread and figs from the morning. As there was no wine, Naum boiled water on a fire, mixed in mint leaves, and filled two cups.

They sat by the fire, looking out at the moonlit Sea of Galilee. Dugdug rested his head in the boy's lap.

"I was wondering," Sall said. "Do fish sleep?"

"They do, but they keep swimming slowly."

"Have you tried to catch fish at night?"

"I can't even sell the ones I catch during the day." Naum sighed. "They die for nothing, poor fish."

"If you cook them, they won't go bad."

"Who's going to buy cooked fish?"

"Why not?"

"People want fresh fish, right out of the water."

"They don't eat them fresh. They cook them. Perhaps some people would prefer buying them already cooked and ready to eat." Sall was getting excited about the idea. "You can even sprinkle some rosemary and olive oil on the fish, as you did yesterday for our dinner. Come to think of it, maybe some people would want to try your minced fish, too. It's delicious."

Naum emptied what remained in his cup into the fire, which hissed. "You're talking nonsense, boy. Let's go to sleep."

28

At sunrise, Naum led Sall back to Job's Bath. He gave him a knife that, according to family lore, Job had with him during his stay. Unlike Job, though, Sall also had a dog, because Dugdug refused to leave with Naum.

During the first day, Sall soaked in the pool under the carob tree while the dog watched him from the edge. They shared a few carobs for an evening meal, drank water directly from the spring, and went into the cave for the night. He listened to the noises outside. There were less frogs here than near the shore, but the crickets were as numerous, judging by the ruckus of their chirping. He worried that a bear could approach undetected under the noise of the crickets and the running spring. And if not a bear, then a lion, a wolf, or a pack of laughing jackals, eager for an easy prey.

The dog wagged its tail as if responding to the boy's fears with a reminder about dogs' superb hearing, sharp fangs, and complete loyalty.

Sall calmed down and slept through the night. He started the second day with another long soak in Job's Bath. Later, having eaten some carobs, he became bored. Scratching lines on the rocks with the knife provided little amusement, but it gave him an idea. He broke a thick branch from the tree and started carving it.

It took many failed attempts to hone the wood to the image he had in mind. Every day, he soaked in the pool while carving and, intermittently, sharpening the knife on a hard stone under water. It took him eighteen days to learn how to carve and produce a correct effigy of Qoz, with its oversized head sprouting three curved horns, its eyes rounded in a blank face, its chest hinting of breasts with shallow protrusions, and its throne equipped with a bull and a cow for armrests. The hardest part was the delicate carving of a multipronged thunderbolt in the effigy's left hand, with which the mighty Qoz controlled light and darkness, storms and rain. The complete effigy was about the size of his hand.

Meanwhile, the scabs covering his body gradually melted away, exposing new skin, which was red, tender, and blotchy. The wide canopy of the carob tree protected him from getting sunburnt again.

On his twentieth day at Job's Bath, Sall started carving another, more complicated effigy. Kothar-wa-Khasis, the God of craftsmanship, was his favorite among the Gods of Edom. He had oversized hands, each bigger than his body. The fingers were carved into tools: Hammer for metalworking, measuring ruler for engineering, inkwell and feather for inventions, bowl and crusher for potion making, wand for spell casting, saw and chisel for woodworking, and a key to open the window through which Ba'al Ammon sent rain to nourish the land.

On the twenty-fifth day at Job's Bath, when Sall finished carving the final delicate point of the key, a rainstorm came. He took shelter with Dugdug in the cave and watched the downpour, which left the rocks, bushes, and trees gleaming with moisture.

During the last five days, he soaked in Job's Bath while telling Dugdug, Qoz, and Kothar-wa-Khasis all that had happened to him along his journey so far. He discussed how each experience had felt, down to the most minute details of the injuries and pain, as well as his mental impressions, terrors, and revelations. The more he talked, the more his mind cleared of all fears, worries, and despair, leaving behind a clarity of purpose, which he had not felt since saying goodbye to his mother many weeks before. Meanwhile, his skin gradually cleared up and all the red blotches and tender spots faded away.

On the morning of the thirty-first day, Sall put on his robe, collected the two effigies and the knife, and held the hedges apart for the dog. "Time to go home," he said.

Dugdug led the way through the trees and bushes. Sall walked slowly, his eyes on the ground ahead of his bare feet. He smiled in anticipation of Naum's excited reaction to a living, walking proof of the healing powers of Job's Bath. He imagined the lanky fishmonger, first tugging at his unkempt beard in bewilderment, then throwing back his head of tangled gray hair and laughing heartily at the sight of the boy's clear skin, raising a toast with a jug of wine, if he had any.

In the back of Sall's mind, a nagging voice asked how he intended to find a wife for Naum before leaving for Damascus. The boy had no plan. He didn't know any of the farmers in the area, and even if he did, what father would give his daughter to a disheveled aging fisherman who could barely feed himself? The voice kept nagging, but none of it penetrated through the shield of calm that had formed around him over the last thirty days, fortifying his heart with unassailable hope for the future. As Ishkadim had said, "The Gods clear the way for those who chase their dreams." Sall looked at the two effigies in his hands and asked them to convince the poor fisherman to release him from that unfulfillable promise to find him a wife.

The dog sped ahead, and Sall noticed the scent of the nearby Sea of Galilee. He heard knocking sounds, not in regular intervals, but a staccato, as if rocks were falling from a cliff, or being thrown by men. The scent of the sea was now mixed with the smell of smoke. He quickened his steps, wondering what trouble had Naum gotten himself into. Was it related to hosting him? Sall imagined the evil men from the walled city of Naphtali converging on Naum with stones and torches, accusing him of harboring a leper, stoning him to death, and burning his shack.

Sall started running. He heard men yelling while the knocking sounds grew louder and the burning smoke denser.

When he reached the road, the sight stopped him in his tracks.

The shack was gone. In its place was a half-built house of four or five rooms, extending up the bluff overlooking the water. The walls grew slowly as several men hammered stones into fresh mud in straight lines. An oven had been built next to the house, and a woman attended to it, cooking fish over the smoky embers. A short distance from it, a new stall stood by the road, larger than the old one, with a roof for shade. Naum was serving a customer while several others waited. They must have been local farmers, not only because their donkeys were tied to the bushes nearby, but because Sall could see only one caravan, whose leader was sitting with his family under a tree, sharing a large bowl of minced fish.

Naum noticed Sall and left the stall to cross the road. His appearance had changed completely. The tangled hair and long beard had been trimmed neatly, his tattered robe was replaced by a blue coat, and he wore new sandals.

He checked out the boy from head to toes. "It's really true, then. Blessed be Yahweh."

Sall slipped the two effigies into his pockets.

Throwing an arm around the boy's shoulders, Naum led him across the road. "Look at my new life – it's all your doing, my clever Edomite savior!"

It finally dawned on Sall that he was looking at the realization of his idea to sell cooked fish, either whole or minced, sprinkled with rosemary and olive oil, ready to eat.

"Hurry up," one of the customers called from the stall. "We're hungry."

The fisherman rushed back to serve them, but on his way there, he yelled to the woman, "That's Sall, the boy I told you about."

She smiled. "Thank you for everything."

He nodded, unsure what to say.

"I am Shuva, wife of Naum."

Reaching into his pockets, Sall touched the two effigies and thanked them silently.

Back at the oven, Shuva's hands expertly flipped over the fish before they burned, tossed rosemary and olive oil over them, and removed the ones that were cooked through. She wasn't very young, but not too old to be a fruitful wife. Sall hoped she would be the wife Naum had prayed for and bear him the children he counted on to build on this bluff a flourishing village, which would carry his name for many generations.

29

After sunset, with the customers and construction workers gone, Naum and Sall sat by a fire near the water, and Shuva served them food and wine. She had already won the affection of Dugdug, who followed her everywhere while she kept feeding him.

The fisherman ate and drank with relish. "Why aren't you eating?"

"I've eaten only carobs for a month." Sall took a tentative bite and chewed slowly.

"You don't look any worse for it."

"I feel well."

"Ready to resume your quest?"

"Yes."

"If anyone can succeed, it's you. Look at what you've done for me."

Sall recalled Ishkadim's story of the man who complained to God about his dry cow. "It's not me," he said. "Your God needed you to start, so that He could help you."

"But you made me start." Naum chuckled. "When I came back from Job's Bath without you, I looked at my dirty shack and meager belongings and realized the emptiness of my lofty words, the delusion of my plans for a large family, and the improbability of a flourishing Naum's Village on this shore. I thought to myself, how in the world can that poor boy find a wife for a scrappy pauper like me? Would I hold him here as a prisoner to a promise no one could fulfill? Would I deprive him of realizing his dream on account of my failure to realize mine? I tore down the shack, which stood for everything that was wrong with my life, and went to sleep in the boat, but in the middle of the night, I had an unexpected visitor."

Sall sat up, alarmed. "A bear?"

"The old dwarf, the one you told me about."

"The Elixirist visited you?"

"In my dream."

"Oh."

"I recognized him immediately, because he was holding the transparent cup you had mentioned, and it was filled with the golden elixir that you had tasted."

"Did he give you some of it?"

"He said I didn't need it, that I could change my life without drinking any elixir."

"How?"

"By taking your advice."

"Cooking the fish?"

"And making minced fish, too."

"Did you tell him it was nonsense, like you told me?"

"I did."

"Did he go away?"

"No. He said the purpose of his visit was to make sure you can leave for Damascus and find him before it's too late."

"Late for what?"

"I don't know, because at that point, he pushed me off the boat." Naum pointed at the water. "Right there, I sank underwater like a stone. If it was any deeper, I would have drowned, but it was shallow, and after a lot of coughing and cursing, the truth managed to penetrate through my hard skull. I got back into the boat and started fishing – at night, another one of your ideas, which worked because the full moon helped me see the ripples on the surface where the sleeping fish swam slowly. I caught more fish than ever before. In the morning, I collected wood, built a big fire, and cooked the fish with rosemary and olive oil, the way you liked it, and minced about half of them. An hour later, some local farmers started showing up, salivating like dogs in heat, because they'd never smelled my fish cooking in the morning, when they're in the fields nearby."

"Did they buy the fish?"

"Did they?" Naum clapped. "By noon, I sold everything and had to go fishing again. By sunset, I was rich, but I didn't lie down to rest. I went fishing, and by the next morning, I was ready with three times the quantify of fish. The customers didn't stop coming, some of them all the way from Rakkah in the south and Migdal in the north. Those who didn't have coins paid me with produce, wine, clothes, and wood for fire. Others offered me their labor." Naum waved his hand at the half-constructed house, whose walls reflected the red glow of the fire. "After a week, a man came by to offer me his daughter, whose husband had died and left her idle at her father's table. A customer trimmed my hair and beard, another brought me a new coat, and a third was a hungry priest who married us for a meal. Soon, she'll be with a child, and if it's a son, can you guess what his name will be?"

The boy shook his head.

"Sall, son of Naum, because I wouldn't have him if not for your help."

Touching the effigies in his pockets, the boy said, "The Gods have been kind to both of us."

Rather than go to sleep, they got in the boat, let out the rope, and went fishing. Sall discovered that night fishing, as Naum had said, was completely different from fishing in daylight. He learned to trust his instinct and let his hand swing as soon as he sensed the presence of a fish under the moonlit surface. The more skilled he became, the more joy he derived from each catch. In the end, he was disappointed when the bucket was full.

Back on shore, Naum poured the water and fish from the bucket into a large barrel and added a few buckets of water.

Watching this, Sall had an idea. "We can build a fish corral."

Naum's dismissive gesture paused in midair. "Here I am, rejecting your idea without thinking. What is a fish corral?"

"A pool that's bigger than a barrel."

"More room won't help." Naum used the net to pull a small fish out of the barrel and tossed it to the dog. "They'll still die of heat by midday."

His eyes on the net, Sall had an idea. "We can build a corral with nets inside the water."

"In the sea?"

"Right next to the shore, where it's shallow. I'll try tomorrow."

Sall was up at sunrise. He went across the road and searched for branches that were straight and about half his height. He carved each end into a sharp point and stuck them in the bottom where the water was lower than his knee, creating a circle about ten steps across. He pounded each stick with a rock to push it deeper until it stood up solidly, the top end showing above the water. Shuva knitted a net from threads, and the boy secured it to the sticks all around. He pulled one fish from the barrel and put it in the new corral. The fish swam at the net, turning away from it again and again until it gave up and began to peck the bottom for food.

Watching this, Shuva clapped.

"That's it," Naum said. "Now you really made it possible for us to build a village here."

"Naum's Village," Sall said. "When I grow old, I'll come back to visit."

"You'll be an honored guest." Naum reached into his pocket and took out a ring. "Here, this is for you."

Sall took the ring and looked at it closely. It was made of copper, which was stained with age, and its miniature seal showed a man in a boat, casting a net into the water.

"Put it on," Naum said.

"What is it?"

"The Ring of the Fisherman."

"I can't accept it. It looks ancient, like a family heirloom.

"Yes, passed from father to son, with the instruction to give it to a stranger who proves to be the true fisherman. And until I met you, boy, I didn't know how to recognize a true fisherman."

Slipping the ring onto his index finger, it felt heavy for a moment, but then, Sall experienced a burst of hope as bright as a new sunrise.

The next four nights he spent fishing, his nightly hauls filling the fish corral to capacity. During the days he slept in the shade while Naum and Shuva cooked the fish and served customers. They asked the leader of every merchant caravan that came from the south whether he was heading to Damascus. None of them were until the fifth day. Naum woke Sall up and called him over.

It was a large caravan of horses, donkeys, and pack camels with heavy loads. The leader said they were Arameans on the way home to Damascus. He agreed to take the boy and asked for a free serving of fish for the large family, which included three grown sons, several women, and a few children. Shuva provided the food while Naum took Sall aside and gave him a long-sleeved robe, a headdress that fell over his shoulders, a pair of good sandals, and a fat purse.

Sall peeked inside the purse, which was full of coins. "I can't take this."

"Why not?"

"It's your money."

"Mine to give, isn't it?"

"You need it to build your village."

"I am making more every day. This is your fair share." Naum rested his hands on the Sall's head. "May the Gods, yours and ours, watch over you and assist your quest."

Shuva came over with a warm bread, put it in his hands, and kissed him on the cheeks. Dugdug barked, and Sall kneeled down and had his faced licked thoroughly while scratching the dog's belly.

Sall walked behind the caravan, glancing back over his shoulders at Naum, Shuva, and the dog, standing by their new house. He imagined coming back one day to the Sea of Galilee to visit a prosperous Naum's Village by a shoreline dotted with fishing boats and playing children.

30

The caravan stopped for the night in Kinneret, a town by northern shore of the Sea of Galilee. The merchant, whose name was Anis, invited Sall to join the evening meal. With the sun gone, the boy could take off the oversized headdress and roll up the sleeves of his robe in order to enjoy the fresh breeze coming from the water.

He sat with Anis and his sons around the fire. The men spoke the Aramaic language among themselves, but it had enough common words with his native language and Hebrew that he understood most of what they said. He learned that they were returning home to Damascus after travelling throughout Canaan to purchase goods that were in high demand in Aram. They had a fair quantity of palm dates from Jericho, packed in large clay jars, six on each camel. In Emanuel, a fortified city of the Ephraim tribe, they had bought sheep's wool, which was compressed into sacks, four on each donkey. In Aphek, the largest city of Manasseh, they had bought fine leather hides, which were rolled up in cloth sheets and secured to the horses behind the saddles. They had planned to travel by Megiddo to purchase jugs of bee honey from the Jezreel Valley, but once Anis heard that Beth She'an had burnt down in a dispute between Issachar and Manasseh, he decided that the additional profit wasn't worth the risk of getting caught in a war between the two Hebrew tribes. The sons were unhappy about skipping Megiddo, but he said, "Greed is a stairwell to self-destruction."

Although they stopped arguing, the young men didn't appear convinced. Sall wanted to tell them that their father was right, but he couldn't reveal what Li'uli had told him about the coming Egyptian invasion. How long would it take for an Egyptian army to march up from the Sea of Reeds through the deserts of Edom and the Jordan Valley to Beth She'an? Would the Hebrew tribes put up a fight, or scatter before Pharaoh's might? And what about the Canaanite army? Was the king of Hazor strong enough to resist Egypt? Sall wished he could have asked Li'uli all these questions.

For now, however, Anis was only worried about thieves. He took the first shift guarding the camp, followed by each of his sons. They didn't ask Sall to take part, and he wasn't offended, because they had met him that day and had no basis to trust him.

In the morning, the fairgrounds came to life with local farmers hawking their produce, as well as artisans and craftsmen setting up stalls and workshops. Beside the few traveling merchants, most of the vendors were Hebrews from the tribe of Naphtali, but the town did not fly the tribe's pale-red flag. Most men carried a short sword or a spear. Some of them were Canaanites, recognized by their oiled hair, cut straight at the shoulders, and the absence of beards.

Walking around the fairgrounds with the purse hidden under his robe, Sall bought a donkey, as well as a good saddle, food, and four waterskins. As he passed by a stall of jewelry and precious stones, the vendor noticed the ring and came around his stall to look at it.

"Interesting," he said. "What is it?"

"The Ring of the Fisherman. That's what it's called."

"I'll give you a silver coin for it."

Shaking his head, Sall resumed walking.

"Two coins," the vendor said.

"It's not for sale."

The vendor followed him. "Three silver coins, boy. It's more than it's worth, trust me."

People glanced at them curiously, which made Sall uncomfortable. He slipped his hand into his pocket and quickened his pace, pulling the donkey along, and was relieved when the vendor didn't pursue him.

North of Kinneret, the road split, and Anis turned north-east. The mountains ahead were steep. Coming closer, Sall was surprised to see black cliffs under the vegetation. Climbing up, the road twisted back and forth in tight turns. At the top, rather than jugged peaks, a high plateau extended as far as he could see.

In the early afternoon, Anis turned off the road onto a narrow path that seemed to lead nowhere, but ended abruptly at the edge of a gorge, which was only noticeable up close. At the bottom was a dark pool, fed by a tall waterfall.

Everyone dismounted, and the men took the children down to the pool.

Sall joined them. The water was very cold. He stayed in the shallows, but the men ventured in, swimming with ease while holding the children. He watched them swim and tried the same motions in the shallow water, keeping his head above the surface. It wasn't easy, but he was getting better. It reminded him of Ishkadim's advice, which Li'uli called "Heavenly" back in Jericho: "Imitate until you mutate!" The memory bolstered Sall's confidence, and he ventured deeper, imitating Anis's sons, only to go under and swallow a lot of water before surfacing and scrambling out of the pool.

31

That night, they reached a town called Golan. Sall saw two flags flying from poles by the gate: a black flag of Manasseh with the white antelope, its horns long and straight like arrows, and a second flag, which was divided into three colors — white, black, and red — and bore a drawing of a square with rows of dots, which reminded him of the Hebrew priests' bejeweled breastplates.

Anis pointed. "That's the flag of the Levi tribe, whose men are the priests of the Hebrews. The breastplate is called Urim Ve'Tummim. I heard that their High Priest in the temple wears the original breastplate from their first priest, who wore it during their exodus from Egypt, with real precious gems — rubies, emeralds, topazes, sapphires, and crystals."

Beside the two flags, another oddity was the fence around the city, which was fit for an animal corral, providing no meaningful defense.

Sall asked, "What's the purpose of this fence?"

"It marks the city boundaries," Anis said. "Apparently, the God of the Hebrews told the priests to designate shelter cities, where a man who killed someone by accident would be protected from revenge by the dead man's family." He pointed at the gate. "As soon as a fugitive gets through the gate or over the fence, his pursuers may no longer take a life for a life."

"Who decides if the killing was intentional or not?"

"There's a trial. If he's found guilty of murder, they send him out of the city to be killed by the victim's family, but if the judge rules that the death had been accidental, the killer pays compensation to the victim's family, and the matter is closed." Anis chuckled. "It would never work in Aram, where full revenge is always taken, priests or no priests."

They made camp in the fairgrounds near the gate. After the evening meal, Anis asked the boy to take the second shift in guarding the camp. Sall was excited and couldn't fall asleep until Anis came to summon him to take over the watch.

It was strange to walk around while everyone slept. There were three other merchant caravans spending the night. They didn't post guards, either because there weren't enough men to share the responsibility, or because they didn't have much to steal. One caravan, from Egypt, had two cats pacing around their tent with predatorial self-importance befitting a fully-grown tiger.

He circled the fairgrounds and came back to check on the animals and the goods, which were covered with cloth. His donkey snorted, and Sall brought some straw and water to pacify it.

A strange sound attracted his attention. It came from up the road. He stared into the darkness, holding his breath, listening. It was a combination of heavy breathing and grunting. Was it a bear? Or worse, a lion? He rekindled the fire and picked up a burning branch to defend the camp and the animals.

He noticed a drumming of hooves, fainter than the breathing and grunting. About to wake up Anis and his sons, he stopped when a vague blotch of gray appeared up the road, gradually coming into sight. It was a man, running slowly, panting heavily, glancing repeatedly over his shoulder. The drumming hooves sounded in the darkness behind him, further up the road.

At the gate of Golan, someone yelled, "Fugitive on the run!"

The man was about to pass on the road by the fairgrounds, when a horse came into view, bearing two riders in a halting trot that told of an arduous journey.

The gate creaked as it opened, and several men stood on both sides, shouting, "Faster! Faster! Faster!"

Sall assumed they were encouraging the fugitive, but then, one of them yelled, "You can catch him! Ride faster!"

The rider up front whipped the horse frantically, alternating left and right, while the one behind raised a sword, ready to slash down on their prey.

As the fugitive passed in front of the camp, Sall saw the sheer terror on the man's sweaty face. He glanced back and ran faster, his sandals raising dust from the road.

The men at the gate hooted.

The fugitive had about twenty steps left to reach the gate and keep his life. However, with the horse speeding up under the vicious whipping, Sall estimated that they would catch up to him a few steps before the gate.

The fugitive was doomed.

The pursuer with the sword leaned to the side of the saddle, tilting the blade, grinning with the certainty of a hunter at the final moment of the chase, already envisioning the inevitable slaying, the blood spraying, the prey writhing in death throes.

There wasn't any time left for contemplation, Sall knew. Either he acted now, or the fugitive would be slain.

As the horse flew by, Sall hurled the burning branch, hitting the horse's rear below its raised tail. The beast neighed, jerked both hind legs up, and kicked the air behind. Its head was literally even with the fugitive, and as the horse tilted forward and lost its balance, it catapulted the two riders up and over. Had the fugitive not swerved quickly, the men would have landed on top of him and crushed him, or delayed him long enough for a deadly strike with the sword. But he was agile, and while the two pursuers fell hard and rolled on the ground, he sprinted the remaining few steps and crossed the line between the gateposts into the city of shelter.

The men at the gate booed.

Sall ran into the road, picked up the burning branch, and ran back, dropping it in the fire. He crouched behind his donkey and watched.

The two pursuers got up, patted down their robes, and helped their horse stand. The boy was relieved to see the horse walk about, having sustained no lasting injury.

The fugitive stood just inside the open gate, catching his breath, watching his pursuers, standing only a few steps away, well within striking distance, yet barred from touching him. He cheered and began to dance in place. Sall could only imagine the overwhelming rage the two men felt and was awed by their restraint, abiding by the Hebrew God's prohibition on hurting a fugitive inside the city of shelter. He was grateful they hadn't noticed him hurling the burning branch behind them, or they would have taken all their furious frustration on him.

Turning around with his back to the two men, the fugitive bent over and lifted his robe to show them his buttocks. Sall could see the fugitive's laughing face upside down between his spread legs.

Perhaps it was having his head upside down like this, right after the extreme exertion of running for hours, but the fugitive lost his balance, fell backwards on his exposed behind and rolled over and out the gate. He tried to scramble back in, but his pursuers sprung forward and pounced on him. They dragged him a further from the gate, kicking and screaming. While one of them held the fugitive down, the other one picked the sword from the ground and drove the blade into his gut, running it through. He uttered a terrible scream, rolled over, and crawled towards the gate. They took turns stabbing him in the back until he stopped moving and went silent.

The locals watched silently from the gate while the two men got back on the horse and rode up the road, disappearing into the night. The corpse of the fugitive remained in the dirt near the gate.

The commotion had woken up Anis and his sons. They looked at Sall, but he was too shaken to talk. Lying down on his cot, he pulled the blanket over his head and took deep breaths, trying to divert his mind away from when he had just seen, but the fugitive's last scream kept playing in his ears until he touched the Fisherman's Ring, which brought up pleasant memories from his time in the boat with Naum and the peaceful weeks at Job's Bath with Dugdug.

32

They spent the morning making steady progress northward on the plateau. Up ahead was a great mountain with a white cap of snow. Anis said the Hebrews called it Mount Hermon. Along the road were farms and small villages, all of them flying Manasseh's black flag with the white antelope.

In the afternoon, the road split, and they took the right branch to the north-east. Shortly before sunset, the plateau gave way to a moderate decline that stretched far ahead. The vegetation thinned out as the ground turned rocky and dry. There were no farms or villages in sight. They camped by the roadside and fanned out to collect twigs and dry shrubs to feed the fire through the night.

When darkness came, Anis pointed out distant lights. "That's Damascus. We'll be there by tomorrow evening."

At night, a pack of jackals stalked the camp, and their laughter echoed in the darkness. The donkeys brayed and clustered closely, the horses neighed and pulled on their reins, but the camels seem indifferent. Sall imagined how, if not for the lively fire, the jackals would have stormed the camp and killed some of the animals.

In the morning, despite the restless night, everyone chatted happily while taking down the camp, eager to start down the road to Damascus. Sall was eager too, though he felt a pinch of envy, wishing his own home was also nearby.

When the caravan got going, he prodded his donkey to catch up with Anis. "How many people live in Damascus?"

"More than three thousand," Anis said. "And for each person there are a thousand blooming jasmines. You'll see. It's the world's greatest city in trade, beauty, and scent."

In scent, perhaps, Sall thought, but not in trade or beauty, which Bozra surpassed all other cities with more than five thousand inhabitants and the largest fairgrounds between the River Nile and the Euphrates, according to his father.

"I'll be looking for a certain person."

"Who?"

"He's known as the Sailor of Barada."

Anis chuckled. "No one sails the Barada River anymore. Many generations ago, the river became too shallow for ships."

"Why?"

"From all the diversions to farms along the way."

"Does the river start in Damascus?"

"The name should give you a hint. The Barada River starts in Lake Barid, and Barid means cold, because the lake is fed by a spring at its bottom with water from the snowy mountains of Lebanon."

"Is the lake near Damascus?"

"A couple of days away." Anis pointed to the north-west. "It's the coldest lake you'll ever swim in, if you're foolish enough to do it."

"Are there any ships there?"

"Where would they sail? There's nowhere to go."

All this was of little use to Sall. The picture he had drawn in his mind of a wide, deep, flowing river, busy with merchant ships like the ones his father had described in tales about the Philistines, existed only in his imagination. The reality was dramatically different. As he absorbed the new image of the Barada River in its pitiful shallowness, he feared that his journey to find the Sailor of Barada was a fool's errand.

Disappointment and sadness descended on the boy like a dark mist. He let go of the reins, and the donkey slowed down while Anis and the rest of the caravan kept going. From behind, the camels looked fat and ungainly with the large jars of palm dates secured to both sides of their humps, in addition to other packages of goods and sacks of straw.

The morning sun bore into his eyes. He pulled down the headdress over his face and trusted the donkey to follow the caravan while he closed his eyes. He wished for the dream of the Elixirist, either as an old dwarf or a handsome young man, but neither came to him. Instead, he dreamt of crossing a river whose muddy water barely reached his knees. As he advanced towards the middle of the river, the water grew hotter, and his feet began to burn, but he couldn't stop, hoping that the great tower was on the opposite bank, though he was unable to see it because of the drooping headdress that covered his eyes. He tried to lift the edge of the headdress to get a peek at the column of workers with their heavy loads, waiting to drink from the magical elixir of understanding, but his hands didn't work, and the headdress kept his eyes in the dark, preventing him from seeing for himself whether or not the workers and the tower actually existed. He tried to shake his head to shift the headdress, or bend over to make it fall off, and while he was struggling against this maddening blindness, someone grabbed his robe and pulled on it, causing him to fall over – not into the scalding water of the shallow river, but on hard ground. His breath knocked out of him, and pain shot through his body, yet his eyes were still smothered by the headdress. He wanted to pull it off, but froze in terror, sensing a predator's hot breath on his neck.

A bear?

A wet tongue tasted his skin.

A jackal?

A moist snout probed under his earlobe.

Was he still dreaming?

No, a dreamer didn't wonder if he were dreaming. This was real. He was about to suffer the fate his donkey had suffered by the Sea of Galilee.

A paw landed on his chin, the sharp claws pricking his skin.

He didn't move, playing dead.

The paw scratched at his face under the headdress, the claws plowing his cheek, the wet snout prodding his neck, the hot breath making him sick with fear.

A terrible noise exploded in his ear, louder than anything he imagined possible. Screaming, he rolled away and scrambled to his feet just as the noise repeated, but now, as it wasn't projected right into his ear, he recognized it.

A bark!

Tearing off the headdress, he Bozra, who jumped into his arms, her jaws open, her tongue dangling out. He stumbled back, sitting on the ground, laughing and crying, while she pressed herself against him, licking his face and barking. He hugged her and gave her kisses as one would a beloved child. She collapsed in his lap and panted while he scratched her all over.

"It's really you, girl." He wiped his tears. "How is it possible?"

Her ribs felt hard under the skin, and he realized she had become very thin.

"What are you doing here?"

She barked.

He looked around for the Moabite merchant, his family, and his animals but there was no one nearby. And where was Anis's caravan? Gazing down the road, he saw the caravan far away, approaching Damascus. Had they not noticed he had fallen behind? Or were they too impatient to reach their home?

Bozra rolled off his lap and stood, wagging her tail.

Sall patted her head. "Where's your little Moabite friend?"

She walked a few steps and paused, looking back.

He pulled the donkey along, following Bozra to a mound of rocks, about one step across and four steps long. On top of it rested a pair of sandals. Looking closely, Sall recognized the sandals he had given the Moabite merchant and recalled the mother strapping them onto the small feet of their little boy.

"Oh, no." He knelt by the mound of stones. "Poor child."

Barking again, Bozra took a few steps and stood by another mound, longer than the first. On it rested a pair of woman's sandals.

The mother was dead, too.

Looking around, Sall didn't see a third grave. Had the Moabite merchant died with no one to bury him?

"Show me where he is," Sall said.

Bozra barked and led him towards a clutch of small trees and bushes, which indicated the existence of water, though not much of it. He saw a half-collapsed tent under a tree. Beside it was a pile of cold ambers. Further back he saw the skeletons of a horse, two donkeys, and several goats. A sour stench made him cover his nose. He stopped, hesitating to go closer.

Bozra barked.

Pulling aside the flap of the tent, he saw bunched up blankets, soiled clothing, and empty jars, but no corpse.

Barking again, Bozra circled the tree trunk several times.

Sall peered at the surrounding land, trying to locate the remains of the merchant.

A snore startled him.

It came from above.

Looking up into the tree, he couldn't see the source, but then, another snore sounded, and he recognized it from the time they had travelled together. With Bozra's barking having no effect, Sall picked up a fist-sized stone and threw it at the canopy.

Nothing happened.

He threw another stone, and another, until a face appeared above. It had the Moabite merchant's crooked nose, but otherwise wasn't recognizable. Matted hair and beard framed a shrunken face with sharp bones and oversized eyes.

"The healer's son?" His voice was scratchy and weak. "Am I hallucinating?"

"No. Come down."

His legs were like twigs, trembling as he climbed down. The rest of him was also bones and skin, covered with a shredded robe.

He leaned on the trunk, gazing at the boy. "How do I know if you're real?"

Sall picked up another stone.

"Fine, you're real, but it doesn't matter. You're too late to help us."

"I was busy being a slave and a few other things. What happened here?"

"Our boy became ill on the road to Damascus, so we made camp. He died, and then, my wife died, too. I buried them, but I was too sick to keep a fire going, and my animals fell prey to a pack of jackals. I climbed into the tree to wait for my own death, but the Gods decided to prolong my suffering until you arrived here to witness their divine justice."

"Justice?"

"Punishment."

"For what?"

"For what I did to you."

"Taking her?" Sall gestured at Bozra, who sat by his side, looking up. "The Gods wouldn't kill a child and his mother over a dog."

"I forgot how dumb you are, boy."

Sall looked him up and down. "Between the two of us, who's looking dumb now?"

"That's harsh. You've changed, boy. Have you become a man?"

Not bothering to respond, Sall turned and walked back to the two graves, where his donkey had waited, grabbed the reins, and headed back to the road.

"Wait, you hotheaded Edomite." The merchant followed him, tripping on the bushes and rocks. "Slow down."

"Leave me alone."

"Listen, my punishment wasn't for taking your dog." He fell and struggled to get up. "What I did was much worse."

Pausing, Sall turned. "Go on."

He stayed down, panting. "The other dog, the one that lured yours away, that wasn't a wild dog."

"What?"

"I saw it in one of the yards, tied to a stake, pulling hard to get to your dog. I released it. That's why your dog broke away from you and shattered all the pottery. It was my doing."

Watching this shadow of a man, sitting in the dirt, admitting his malicious actions, didn't make Sall angry. The confession was like a light coming on, illuminating everything that had happened to him with clarity of cause and effect, pain and reward, or, as Li'uli had said, "Risk and gain go hand in hand." Becoming a slave to the Hebrew potter, which had been devastating at first, gave him courage to become a healer in his own right, which in turn transformed his angry master into an admiring friend, who gave him freedom to continue his journey. His suffering in Beth She'an, though terrible in itself, taught him that men could be devious and cruel, but also honest and benevolent. The weeks of feverish ailment in the care of the women of the Cainite Clan showed him that outcasts, despised by all others, could be the kindest of all people. And that, in turn, prepared him to survive his own torment as an outcast suspected of leprosy, which led to sheltering with the compassionate fisherman, who shared with him the secret of Job's Bath, which cured his body of its many wounds and healed his mind from debilitating doubts. And when Naum taught him how to fish by trusting his feelings, he came up with ideas that turned the fisherman's life of poverty and childlessness into riches and hopes, giving Sall confidence in the value of his own ideas even when others mocked him. And now, learning that this crooked merchant had caused the slavery that started the cascade of torturous events, Sall felt no anger, because all that suffering had changed him from a fearful boy into something else entirely.

"Nice ring," the Moabite merchant said. "What is it?"

"The Ring of the Fisherman." Reaching into a sack on his donkey,

Sall pulled out a chunk of bread. "With this, I'm buying my dog back from you."

He ate it quickly, snorting in pleasure like an animal.

Bozra waited patiently while Sall tied a rope around her midriff and secured it to the saddle horn. Mounting the donkey, he urged it towards the road.

"Wait, boy. If you give me a more food, I'll tell you another secret."

"Keep your secrets." Sall stopped the donkey, reached into his sack, and gave him another piece of bread. "Here, for staying quiet."

The merchant took a bite. "I'll tell you anyway."

"I'm not interested."

"You'll be very interested in this one." He spoke while chewing. "Do you remember what I promised in exchange for your sandals?"

"Yes." Sall glanced at the small mound of stones. "To take me to the dream reader."

"Not true."

Thinking back to that day in Bozra's fairgrounds, he remembered. "You promised to tell me where to find the dream reader."

"Correct." He snorted. "And what did I actually do?"

"You took me there."

"Why would I take a foolish boy on a long journey through the desert? Out of the kindness of my heart?"

"Not likely."

"Correct again." The merchant held out a shaking hand. "Do you want to know why?"

The boy gave him another piece of bread, which he shoved in his mouth and swallowed without chewing. "I did it for silver."

"Whose silver?"

Again, he put out his trembling hand, accepted a piece of bread, and gulped it down. "Do you want to guess?"

Sall shook his head.

The merchant grinned. "Your father."

Sall felt dizzy and held on to the saddle horn. "That's a lie."

"I'll prove it to you."

Feeling sick, Sall gave him what remained of the bread, which the merchant consumed quickly, before he spoke again.

"Do you remember telling me you're the healer's son?"

Sall nodded.

"You shouldn't have told me that."

The merchant pointed a bony finger at a waterskin, and the boy gave it to him. Tilting it up, he drank all of it in noisy gulps, his visible ribs rising and falling. He put down the empty waterskin and breathed heavily for a while before talking again.

"That night, I went to have a chat with your father, the famous healer of Bozra, expecting him to reward me for warning him about his son's reckless plans. At first, I was disappointed, because he already knew."

"That's impossible."

"Your mother had told him. I turned to leave, thinking I wasted my time." He snorted and wiped his nose on his forearm. "Imagine my delight when the opposite happened."

"Opposite?"

The merchant pointed at another waterskin, which he also drank whole. Oddly, where his sunken abdomen had been, a bulging belly extended out of his skeletal body, resembling a skinny girl at full term with her first baby.

"Your father gave me eighteen silver coins to keep you safe for the length of the journey."

"You're lying."

"Why would I lie? Your stupidity was making me rich."

"I don't believe you." Even as he said it, Sall knew it was the true. "My father needed me at his side and expected my complete loyalty. Why would he facilitate my departure?"

"He was afraid for you."

"Afraid of what?"

The merchant dropped the waterskin, groaned, and grabbed his newly extended belly.

"Tell me, what was my father afraid of?"

"I had a son, too." Tears appeared in his eyes. "I would have sent him away, too, rather than see him suffer."

"Suffer from what?"

"If only the Gods gave me that choice, as they had given it to your father."

Sall didn't understand, but there was no point in pressing for an answer, because the Moabite merchant fell over and remained motionless, no longer breathing.

Bozra whimpered and lay down, resting her head between her front paws.

As shocking as death could be, this death didn't unsettle Sall at all, not because he wished for the Moabite merchant to die, but because the man had already been dead for all practical purposes, except for the opportunity to confess his actions and come clean with the boy about what had really happened in Bozra and Jericho.

A smelly blanket from tent served as makeshift shrouds. Clasping the edge with both hands, Sall dragged the corpse to a spot next to the two graves and began to cover it with stones. When the mound was sufficient to keep out scavenging animals, Sall stepped over to the child's grave and knelt beside it. He took the effigies of Qoz and Kothar-wa-Khasis out of his pockets and placed them next to the sandals on top of the stones.

"Thank you for taking care of our dog," Sall said. "May you rest in peace, little man."

The road to Damascus stretched before him, the city resting in a lush valley ahead. He urged the donkey forward and reflected on the revelation that his father had known of his impending departure and supported his quest. It meant that no one at home considered him a rotten traitor. The dread of facing hostility and mockery upon his return to Bozra had lifted, and a future reopened of resuming his apprenticeship and, in time, succeeding his father as a famous healer. His chest swelled with happiness, and he longed to return home and embrace his loving parents. At the same time, the revelation added to the mystery of General Mazabi's order not to return for six full moons and Li'uli's message that it wasn't safe for him in Edom. What stood behind these warnings?

33

As Anis had said, Damascus was like a giant garden of blooming jasmines that emanated a scent as intoxicating as anything Sall could have imagined. The rolling fields of white flowers around the city were complemented by flower beds along the roads and potted jasmines on every windowsill and roof ledge. Anis was also right about the Barada River, whose path through the city carried shallow water, which was clear and cool, not muddy and hot as in Sall's dream.

The city walls, which had a red tinge, were curved to create a giant circle around Damascus. Two sets of gates provided access, one next to the river's entry point and another where the river exited the city. The river itself wasn't blocked, but massive guard towers on both sides could accommodate many soldiers, ready to rain rocks, spears, and arrows on any invaders. He rode down the main street along the river from the north gate, marveling at the stately houses and abundant shade trees. Bozra barked at any dog she saw, but the rope kept her alongside the donkey. He dismounted and walked through the lively market, buying figs, bread, and cheese.

Leaving Damascus through the south gate, he continued along the riverbank, stepping over irrigation channels that branched out of the river towards fields and orchards. At the point where each channel connected to the river, a wooden barrier was fixed in upright tracks, allowing it to be moved up or down to adjust the flow of water from the river into the channel. He wondered who was in charge of the barriers, because that official might know whether any part of the river, even far upstream or down, was still navigable by ships and, therefore, allow men such as the Sailor of Barada to plow their trade.

Sall rode up a small hill, dismounted the donkey, untied Bozra, and sat down with a fistful of figs and a waterskin to watch the river. Excited by her new freedom, Bozra ran around and sniffed the trees and rocks.

Late in the afternoon, he saw a hunchback proceed along the

riverbank, stopping at the channels to adjust the barriers. It was a slow process, and Sall waited until the hunchback was further down the river, before tying Bozra to the saddle horn, mounting the donkey, and following him at a distance.

As the sun was setting, the hunchback headed to a solitary house on a hill near the river. He sat in the front garden, surrounded by blooming jasmines. A woman served him food, while children played in a sandbox under a tree.

When twilight turned to darkness, the woman and children went into the house. The hunchback sat by a small fire and smoked a pipe. He noticed Sall and beckoned with his pipe.

"What brings you here, young man?"

Sall tied the donkey to a tree and gave Bozra a piece of bread to keep her pacified. "I have a question about the river."

"What gift do you have for me?"

Sall took a coin from his purse and handed it to him.

The hunchback wouldn't accept it. "Floodmaster may only accept coins from farmers - one coin per year for each channel – no more, no less. Keeps you honest."

"Floodmaster? Is that your job?"

"That's who I am. Floodmaster. That's who my father was, and his father, as many generations as Damascus has existed. It's an important responsibility, backbreaking work." He burst out in a croaking laughter. "Backbreaking, get it?"

Chuckling politely, Sall put the coin away.

"And who are you?"

"My name is Sall."

"Not your name. Who are you? Farmer? Baker? Clothdyer? Shepherd? Butcher?" He grabbed the boy's hand and held it to the light of the fire. "Look at these virgin hands. Who are you, boy? Priest?"

Sall shook his head.

"Prince, then." The hunchback dropped the hand. "You princes are like rabbits in season."

"Healer," Sall said. "That's who I am."

"Is that right? Can you heal me?"

"Of what?"

"Good answer." The hunchback chuckled. "And what about my gift?

Don't you have something for me?"

"Like what?"

"Look at this." Reaching to a side table, he picked up a small white item. "My previous visitor gave me this beautiful figurine."

In the light of the fire the boy saw a miniature elephant, carved of a white tusk, similar to the ones Li'uli had given to the soldiers of Manasseh on the road to Beth She'an. He took a branch from the fire and looked at the figurine closely. The resemblance was uncanny, but how could it be? Li'uli, here at this hunchback's house? He remembered the hunchback saying, "You princes are like rabbits in season." Now it made sense.

"Was your previous visitor a brown prince from Kush?"

"That's the one." The hunchback put down the tiny elephant, his gaze lingering on it. "Beautiful, isn't it?"

Anxiety gripped Sall's chest as the memories came rushing back of Li'uli giving him warm milk with a sleeping potion, leaving him behind to be dragged by the donkey and roasted by the sun. He could feel the searing pain and imagined being taken again, right here, by the men of this city, who would blame him for whatever disaster Li'uli was about to bring on Damascus. What new ways would they find to torture him for the brown prince's trickery? Sall couldn't breathe for a moment, but then, he thought of his escape from Beth She'an, his survival, and his ultimate healing. He touched Naum's ring and managed to take a deep breath.

"About the river," Sall said. "Is it deeper elsewhere, enough for ships to sail on it?"

"Healer and Sailor?"

"I'm not looking to sail, but to find a man who does."

"I know all the men of this river. What's his name?"

"Sailor of Barada. Do you know where he lives?"

The hunchback laughed.

"What's funny?"

He struggled to speak while laughing. "Where he lives? That's what you're asking?" He laughed harder.

Not taking offense, Sall smiled and waited.

"It's not a man," the hunchback said. "Sailor of Barad is the name of a ship."

"What ship?"

"A mighty ship. The last ship to sail the river."

"When was that?"

"Long before I was born. Many generations ago, in fact."

Sall knew he was at a dead end. Had he misunderstood what the dream reader had said? "Find the Sailor of Barada." Those were her words, after telling him to go to Damascus. There was no room for confusion, but here he was, talking with a man who knew all there was to know about this river. Sailor of Barada was a ship, not a person, and that ship had been gone for generations, together with any sailors who had worked on the Barada River.

The hunchback puffed on his pipe. "Do you want to see it?"

"See what?"

"The ship?"

The boy was confused. "But you said it was gone."

"No, I said it was the last ship to sail the river."

"It still exists?"

The hunchback pointed upriver. "In the lake near the great falls. It's a sight to see, if you know how to get there through the forests, which almost no one knows."

"Is it on land now?"

"Stuck at the mouth of a gorge like a dam. There's more water in the lake behind that ship than in the whole river below."

A frightening thought came to Sall, but he kept his tone mild as he asked, "Did you tell the brown prince of Kush about the ship?"

"Why not? He gave me a lovely gift and introduced me to his beautiful wife and children. Charming family."

"Did you show him the way to the ship?"

"I did."

"Why?"

"He said it was his aspiration to swim in every sea and lake along his journey. I warned him that the water there is colder than ice and will paralyze his muscles, but he assured me it would be a short and vigorous swim."

"When was that?"

"Many weeks ago, perhaps as long as two full moons. Is he a friend of yours?"

"He pretended to be," Sall said.

"It was a silly question." Drawing on the pipe, the hunchback gazed at the elephant figurine. "Royals can never be true friends."

Reflecting on their last conversation before the warm milk put him to sleep, Sall remembered Li'uli's words: "One person's dream is often another person's nightmare." Was he planning to stage a nightmare for the people of Damascus, as he had done in Beth She'an, in further preparation for the Egyptian reconquest?

"I must see the Sailor of Barada."

"The forests are dense. You'll get lost."

"Will you show me the way?"

The hunchback puffed smoke and watched it rise towards the dark sky. "A nice gift always makes me happy."

Sall looked at the miniature white elephant. "I swear by Qoz," he said. "My gift will make you happier than any gift before it."

"That's a tall order. I've received some valuable gifts over the years."

"Have any of the gifts been as valuable as all of Damascus?"

34

Sall slept under a tree near the house. At sunrise, as he was packing up the donkey for the road, a hunchbacked boy of about ten came out of the house, went to the stable, and brought out a diminutive horse. It was about the size of a donkey, but stouter and more irritable, snapping at Bozra with its big teeth. She dodged easily, and the frustrated horse whinnied in a high-pitched tone.

The hunchbacked boy held up a carrot, and the horse snatched it, almost biting off his fingers.

Floodmaster joined them. "An irritable beast," he said. "Only calms down once we get going, and by noon, doesn't want to go anymore. Lazy as a donkey. You'll see."

With a whistle of their secret tune, Sall summoned Bozra. She sat before him, wagging her tail, and he tied her to the donkey's saddle.

"Thank you, son." Floodmaster patted the hunchbacked boy on the cheek. "I'll be back in a few days."

Sall mounted his donkey. "I'm grateful for your help."

"It's my duty." He climbed the little horse with difficulty. "All my life, no one had asked me about the Sailor of Barada. I only know about the ship because my late father took me to see it once so that I understand its power over the river. And now, two strangers from distant lands come asking about it within weeks. I need to know the reason."

They travelled north along the river. Once in a while, the hunchback dismounted and adjusted a barrier up or down. There were many of them on either side of the river, and he clearly remembered each one and knew where the river was safe to cross.

Approaching Damascus from the south, the boy marveled again at the abundance of blooming jasmine, which infused the crisp morning air with an invigorating scent. The city itself was humming with activity. Along the river, the streets were filled with vendors, shoppers, and animals. Men waved at the hunchback, or called from afar, "Good morning,

Floodmaster!" A few came over to hand him a piece of fruit, a slice of cheese, or a chunk of honey cake, which he shared with the boy.

Once they left the city through the north gate, tranquility returned. Lush fields and orchards spread in every direction. The road continued upriver on an almost imperceptible rise towards the mountains. The willow trees along the riverbank were teeming with birds, and deer nibbled at the drooping branches, darting away at the sight of the riders. The hunchback continued to stop at the irrigation channels and adjust the barriers. Occasionally, a farmer would come over to discuss the water needs of his fields or orchards.

They approached the mountains in the afternoon. The road veered off the river into a thick forest. The little horse confirmed its owner's prediction and slowed down to a crawl. The hunchback dismounted and pulled it by the reins up the road. When they turned onto a narrow path, Sall also dismounted. He untied Bozra, trusting her to follow, and led the donkey along. The path meandered up into the mountains through a dense forest of mature cedar trees. At sunset, they made camp in a clearing, built a fire, and settled down for the night. Sall woke up often to Bozra's growling and rekindled the fire before returning to sleep.

In the morning, they resumed the slow progress along the path. Whenever it split, the hunchback chose a direction, but sometimes realized he'd been wrong and backtracked. Occasionally, a fallen tree blocked the way, and they had to cut off all the branches and help the animals over the trunk.

At midday, Sall heard a distant rumble, which he recognized as a waterfall, like the one he'd seen on the plateau near the Hebrew shelter city of Golan. Here, however, the path ended at the bottom of the waterfall, which was was many times bigger than the one on the plateau. It hit the water with a thunderous roar, raising a cloud of cold mist. The surrounding cliffs hid the sun, shrouding the place in perpetual twilight.

They tied the horse and the donkey to tree trunks, but left Bozra free to run around.

Stepping to the edge of the water, Sall felt a chill. Before him wasn't a pool, like the one he had tried to swim in back at the plateau, but a huge basin of dark water, surrounded by rocky cliffs and giant trees – a natural barrier that was taller and more impenetrable than any defensive walls around a great city.

The hunchback said something, but the noise from the waterfall drowned his words. He proceeded a short distance along the shore, away from the roaring waterfall and the cold mist, and pointed. Sall followed with his eyes.

At the opposite side of the lake was a ship. It was made of redwood, just like the ship in his dream, and lay across a narrow gorge, its bow and stern lodged against the opposing sheer walls of the gorge. The ship looked as if it were floating on the lake, with most of its hull below the waterline. A solid railing ran along the side of the deck with slats for oars, some of which were still in place. Above the middle of the ship rose the wide canopy of a tree that, he assumed, was growing at the mouth of the gorge just beyond the ship.

Walking along the water's edge, further away from the waterfall, Sall shaded his eyes to see better. He was in awe of the ship's size.

"Sailor of Barada." The hunchback rubbed his hands. "Impressive, isn't she?"

"How did she get here?"

"According to the story that has come down the generations, when the Egyptians ruled this region, they ran a huge quarry near here for red marble. They sent shipbuilders from the River Nile to build this ship for transporting marble from the quarry to Damascus and bring slaves and supplies back here. The river was much deeper, and this basin was accessible through the flooded gorge. The ship was built of solid redwoods, treated with oil and sap, making it stronger than a rock. It moved by sails, rowers, or horses pulling ropes from the riverbanks. Eventually, when the Egyptians had to withdraw from this area under pressure from the Hittites, they turned the ship sideways and blocked the mouth of the gorge."

"Why?"

"Sore losers." The hunchback made a dismissive gesture. "Stuck like this, the ship can never be sailed again."

"And they blocked the river."

"Legend says that the Barada River was dry for three years before the water level reached the crevice."

Gazing hard, Sall could see water flowing out through a narrow crevice in the side of the sheer wall of the gorge near the ship's bow. "I need to visit the ship."

"Go aboard?"

"Yes."

"Give it up. There's no way. Look at the walls of the gorge. They're straight up, impossible to climb. And the water is too cold to swim across. It will paralyze you, and you'll sink like a stone."

Sall dipped his hand in the water. It was painfully cold. Did he really need to reach the ship? Thinking back to his meeting with the dream reader, he recalled her exact words: "Ask for the Sailor of Barada." That's all she had said, leaving him with the assumption that it was a man who would direct him to the giant tower and the golden inlet. However, knowing now that the Sailor of Barada wasn't a man, her words could only mean that the ship itself, or something aboard it – an artifact, a relic, a message carved into the hull or written on a scroll tucked between the beams – would help him with his quest.

The hunchback hacked at the vegetation. "I'm going around the edge to see if the brown prince left any hints to his visit's purpose."

Sall told Bozra to stay put and hiked back up the path, leaving it to go around the base of the cliffs and up the other side. It was steep and traitorous, but he made it to the top on the east side of the gorge. Down on his belly, he crawled to the edge and poked his head out over the side to look down.

The ship seemed much bigger from above. It had a flat deck surrounded by a waist-high railing. There was a large opening in the middle of the deck. He assumed that's where the quarried marble stones were lowered into the ship's cargo hold with the enormous cranes that he had seen in his dream.

The tree he had thought grew over the ship from the bottom of the gorge was in fact growing inside the ship. The trunk came up through a large cargo hatch in the middle of the deck, and the canopy cast a shade over most of it. He noticed fruit on the branches, dark and elongated, and realized it was a carob tree, as abundant with fruit as the one at Job's Bath.

Near the side railing at the rear of the ship, he saw a child's robe on the deck, secured with stones to keep it flat. It seemed whole and clean as if someone had washed it recently and laid it to dry in the sun.

Crawling back from the edge, Sall sat up and contemplated what he'd seen. Did the robe belong to one of Li'uli's children? Were Li'uli and his family hiding inside the ship? How had they managed to reach it? For what purpose? And where had they left their animals?

Sall advanced again to the edge. He shaded his eyes and noticed the hunchback about halfway around the lake, beating back the shrubs and willow branches to make way. Further to the right, a family of antelopes came to drink.

On the ship below, he saw no sign of life. He picked a stone and dropped it over the edge. It passed through the canopy of the carob tree and hit the deck.

Nothing happened.

He did it again, and again.

A distant voice yelled, "What are you doing?"

Scanning the ship, Sall saw no one.

"Over here."

It was the hunchback, yelling from the shore, his voice echoing from the cliffs.

Sall waved at him and dropped another stone on the deck of the ship. There was no response. He looked again around the basin for Li'uli's horse, camel, and goats, seeing none of them. The most likely explanation, he decided, was that Li'uli had built a boat, visited the ship with his family, and while there, washed one of the children's robes, but forgot it when leaving back to shore, where the boat was scuttled or hidden in the bushes.

Satisfied with this explanation, which opened up the possibility of using the same method to reach the ship, he crawled back from the edge and made his way down the rear of the cliffs to the bottom and through the path to the water.

Bozra received him with barking and tail-wagging, while the donkey and the little horse continued to nibble on leaves. He patted Bozra, gave her a piece of bread, and tied her to the donkey's saddle.

"Keep him safe, girl," he said. "He's not smart like you."

She barked once and sat down.

"Come over here," the hunchback yelled. "I found something."

Sall followed the trail of hacked branches and stomped bushes. When he reached the hunchback, the antelopes were only a few steps away. They were white and graceful, with straight horns and a smooth fur.

The hunchback threw a rock into the water, and the antelopes scattered, disappearing into the thicket.

Sall was disappointed. "Why did you do that? I've never seen them so close."

"And I've never seen anything like this." The hunchback pointed at a narrow gap in the dense vegetation, leading into a clearing. "What do you make of it?"

The clearing was surrounded by tall shrubs and shaded by trees. No one would have stumbled on it unless they were looking. The ground had been cleared of rocks, and the thin layer of leaves seemed no older than a few weeks. Most of the clearing was taken by six tidy piles of twigs and branches. Each pile was as tall as Sall's shoulder. Looking closely, he could tell that many of the twigs and branches were not completely dry yet.

"It's firewood," the hunchback said. "Someone's stocking up."

Looking up at the canopy of trees, Sall shook his head. "Whoever starts a fire here will end up burning the whole forest, including himself."

"You could manage a small fire here."

"For cooking food?"

"Or burning a sinner," the hunchback said. "A solid stake in the middle, and the convict would burn to ashes."

The image sent a shudder through the boy, reminding him of the stake he had been tied to in Beth She'an. He crouched beside one of the piles and noticed a rope hidden underneath. Teasing it out, he pulled a section of about five steps long. It was tied to something underneath the pile. He sat on the ground, raised his legs, placed the soles of his sandals against the side of the pile, and shoved, toppling it over. Below the pile was a square platform, about six steps across, made of wooden logs tied together with strings. He grabbed the rope, dragged the platform from the clearing through the narrow gap to the edge of the water, and pushed it in. It floated.

"It's a raft," he said.

"Look at this." The hunchback bent over and dug in the ground by the water's edge with his fingers, prying out a blue pebble. He peered closely. "I've never seen turquoise stones in the river. Merchant caravans sell them in the market for high prices. I think they come from distant islands in the Great Sea."

"I know how it got here," Sall said. "The brown prince had a few of these with him."

"That means it was him who built these rafts, but why?"

Sall quoted Li'uli: "A fire is a mighty weapon for attack or defense, but not at the same time."

The raft drifted away from shore. They watched it move across the water slowly until it reached the great ship at the opposite end and bobbed against the wooden hull.

"There's our answer," Sall said. "What would happen if the ship caught fire and broke up?"

The hunchback's face turned red, and he clenched his fists, raising his short arms in front of him in a violent gesture of aggression that would have been funny if not for the sheer fury on his face. The boy felt awe at Li'uli's audacious cleverness. In Beth She'an, he had manipulated the men of Issachar to burn the city, making it uninhabitable and no longer an obstacle for the Egyptian invaders, as he had explained with a cold rationale: "It's easier to capture a burnt fort and restore it, than to conquer it unharmed." Here, he planned to cause a flood that would wash away the population of Damascus, relying on a similar rationale, which Sall put into words: "It's easier to take a flooded city and dry it out, than to conquer it whole."

"Thousands of people will drown," the hunchback said through clenched teeth. "Including my family."

The image of countless corpses floating in the streets of Damascus among a white carpet of jasmines caused Sall to shudder. It might have been clever to manipulate opponents to burn down an old fort, but to drown thousands of innocent people was utter evil.

A gust of wind whipped them with cold mist from the waterfall.

They went back into the clearing and pulled out a second raft to the water, got in beside it, and with a joint effort heaved one side so that all the twigs and branches toppled into the water and floated way. They let go of the raft and went to bring the next one.

After toppling the sixth pile off its raft, Sall held on to the rope. "The brown prince's plan depended on surprise. Now you know the danger."

"Thank you for this gift. You were right – it is as valuable as all of Damascus."

"You're welcome. I think you should tell the city elders to post guards here."

"And what shall I tell them about you?"

"Tell them you took a curious traveler to see the waterfall and stumbled on the rafts." Sall picked two large branches, put them on the raft, and climbed on it. "We made a lucky discover, that's all."

"Where are you going?"

"To look for clues on the ship to help me on my quest. Do you want to come?"

"Good luck, my friend." The hunchback shoved the raft from shore. "I'd rather watch you from here."

The raft drifted across the water, whose surface was littered with twigs, branches, and the other rafts. Sall used the branches as oars, steering the raft to the middle of the ship. As it got close, he stood on the raft, which rocked from side to side, and reached up to grab the railing. He was too short, so he jumped up to reach it, inadvertently pushing down the edge of the raft, which tilted sharply and sprang backwards from under him. He managed to hold the railing with one hand, but his fingers slipped, and he dropped into the water.

The coldness shocked Sall. His head went under, and he aspirated water. Flailing with his hands and kicking with his legs, he resurfaced briefly, and in a fit of coughing, sank in again. He told himself to imitate the movements of Anis and his sons in the water near Golan. Back on the surface, he reached for the ship, scraping the hull with his fingers, but the wood was covered with a slimy layer, providing no traction.

He heard Bozra barking and glanced back. The raft bobbed in the water a short distance away. He tried to swim over, but his arms and legs moved too slowly, and he sank again. His mind no longer had control over his limbs, which felt like wooden logs.

His descent was gradual, the light from the surface dimming, the darkness below rising to engulf him.

A silvery fish passed by, looking at him sideways with an unblinking eye.

He descended into the dark, but another light appeared below, deeper in the water. It grew brighter, and he realized it came from the side of the ship underwater. Further down, when he reached the same level, he saw that the light came from within the ship through an opening.

Inside was a table with candles.

Someone was sitting at the table.

No, standing by the table.

It was a small boy, perhaps seven or eight. His head was shaved clean, and he only wore a loincloth, which explained the child's robe on the deck. Otherwise, nothing made sense. What was this young boy doing inside an ancient ship? Where were his parents? And why didn't the water flood the ship through the opening?

The little boy looked back at Sall through the opening. His eyes were too large for his head.

Sall knew he would soon sink lower than the opening and enter complete and final darkness. He gathered all the life that remained inside him and kicked the water, sending himself forward, but instead of going into the ship through the opening, his head banged against an invisible barrier. He kicked again, and his head butted the same transparent barrier.

Next to his face, the silvery fish reappeared, also gazing into the candlelit ship's hold. At the table, the boy raised a goblet, which wasn't made of wood or clay, but of a transparent material like the dwarf's goblet in Sall's dream. He realized that the opening before him was fitted with a window made of the same transparent material as the goblet, blocking his only path to survival. In a fit of rage, he kicked the water one more time, ramming the transparent window with his forehead so hard that flashes of light danced in front of his eyes.

A crack appeared in the transparent barrier.

Putting down the goblet, the bald boy went from the table to the window and climbed a stepladder next to it, disappearing above. A moment later, a horizontal wooden plank, which Sall understood to be the upper section of the window's frame, came down from the top of the opening. He felt himself being sucked forward with the water over the descending horizontal plank, together with the silvery fish, into the ship. They hit the hard floor. A moment later, the waterflow shrunk down to nothing.

He was lying in a puddle of water on a wooden floor. The water drained through slats between the planks. Next to his head, the fish was thrashing, its mouth gaping and closing. Sall tried to breathe, and a bit of air entered his chest with a gurgling sound.

Above, the bald boy tightened a large wooden wheel atop the square frame of the transparent window. He climbed down the stepladder, rolled Sall onto his belly, and hopped on his back, jumping up and down, stomping his small feet, until a jet of water shot out of Sall's mouth, and he began to cough violently. His chest burned and his body hurt as badly as when the donkey had dragged him around the tree in Beth She'an.

35

The bald boy stepped off Sall's back, knelt beside his face, and smiled with bare gums. "There's no question, young man, that you're the biggest fish I've ever caught in my clever contraption."

His voice wasn't soft, but weak and tremulous, broken by brief pauses for air. Sall also noticed that his head was bald not because it had been shaven, but because no hair grew on it. The eyes weren't too big for the face, but the opposite, the face had shrunken around the eyes. The skin on the bare chest, arms, and legs wasn't milky for lack of exposure to the sun, but had the coarse texture of parchment and clung to the bones like the skin of a sickened goat. All those facts added to the conclusion that he wasn't a small boy, as Sall had mistakenly assumed, but another dwarf, much older than the dwarf in his dream, who had a full head of white hair and a set of good teeth.

Embarrassed to be staring, Sall looked at the square frame holding the transparent window. It was attached to a contraption of ropes and pulleys, which were connected to the large wooden wheel above the frame. The rest of the ship's hull was made of logs and beams, smeared with dark paste along the joints to prevent the water from seeping in through the cracks.

"Look at that." The dwarf peered at Sall's hand. "The Ring of the Fisherman, isn't it?"

Sall nodded.

"That makes me a fisherman's fisherman." He cackled. "You're a good catch."

The ship's cargo hold was cavernous, but Sall saw only a few broken slabs of red-tinged marble in the low area along the deep centerline of the ship. In the middle was a large wooden box filled with soil from which the carob tree grew, its trunk rising through the loading hatch above. The wooden ceiling, Sall assumed, was the underside of the deck he had seen from the top of the cliff earlier.

Not much light came through the loading hatch because of the tree canopy, but he could see well enough to look around for anything helpful to his quest for the tower, the inlet, and the golden fountain. He saw nothing of note, but had a fleeting notion that the presence of a transparent goblet in the hands of another dwarf, albeit much older than the dwarf from his dream, meant something important. His mind, however, was too foggy to figure it out.

Picking up the silvery fish with his tiny hands, the dwarf tossed it into a bucket of water. "The fish had no choice, but you could have come in over the railing. It would have been a lot easier, though less dramatic, of course."

Sall tried to explain what had happened, but started coughing instead.

The dwarf held the goblet to his lips, and he sipped a little wine, which warmed his chest. He cleared his throat, and the words came out halting. "A tower. I'm looking for it. Very tall tower."

The dwarf helped him out of the wet robe. "Why do you need the tower?"

"I had a dream. Or a memory."

"Which was it? A dream, or a memory?"

"A dream that's really a memory. That's what the dream reader said."

The dwarf unfolded a blanket. "Which dream reader?"

"I don't know her name. She had no hands."

Draping the blanket over the boy, the dwarf asked, "Is she still watching over Moses?"

"Yes." Sall untied his wet loincloth under the blanket and took it off. "She told me to look for the Sailor of Barada so that I can find the tower with the inlet and golden fountain.".

"The tower collapsed many generations ago."

"Are you sure?"

"The Gods made the earth shake, because men were trying to reach heaven and conquer it."

"It was still standing in my dream."

"Must have been a memory that came down from your ancestors."

"The tower is really gone?"

"You saw its ruins with your own eyes."

"Did I?"

"The circular walls of Damascus sit on the foundations of the great tower." The dwarf looked up in contemplation. "It was a beautiful tower, but the Gods were right to destroy it, because its height caused men to become arrogant and think they were divine, too."

"You saw it?"

"I did a bit more than seeing it."

"What do you mean?"

"Suffice is to say that the Gods banished me to make sure no one would ever again make the building of such a tower possible by helping strangers understand each other."

Looking at the goblet again, Sall began to understand. "The Elixirist was your father, or grandfather, many generations back, right?"

The dwarf chuckled. "Craftsmen can bequeath their trade down to their sons. The art of creating elixirs passes only when the Gods choose a worthy successor."

Sall recalled asking the Elixirist if he was a healer, to which he had responded: "Mixing potions is a craft, whereas creating elixirs is an art." Could this ancient bald dwarf be the same one from in his dream – the whitehaired dwarf he had been seeking, the real Elixirist? If so, where was the golden elixir? Looking around the ship's hold, Sall saw nothing golden, only pale-red slabs stacked at the bottom and scattered dry carobs that had fallen from the tree.

"If you are the Elixirist, where are your elixirs?"

The dwarf waved his tiny hand dismissively. "At my age, I only mix an elixir once a year. The Jasmine Elixir. I pour it into the river slowly over the last few weeks of winter. When spring begins, I wait for the wind to blow the scent of jasmines upriver, and its strength gives me some indication of how well my Jasmine Elixir had worked."

"It's working very well. Damascus is a magnificent garden of jasmine."

"Magnificent, is it? I'm determined to see it with my own eyes before they close forever."

With every moment, Sall saw more resemblance to the dwarf from his dream. "When did you lose your hair?"

"Lose? I didn't lose it. It's here somewhere, though not attached to my head anymore."

"How old are you?"

The dwarf put a finger across his lips. "We don't speak of age, but I'll give you a hint: my favorite cousin, Methuselah, died in his youth, relatively speaking."

"Why don't you drink the golden elixir and become young again?"

"What for? To grow old again?" He shook his head. "One life is enough, especially a long life like mine, don't you agree?"

Sall didn't know what to say.

"Fortunately, my heir has been chosen by the Gods. Once I pass on the knowledge, I'll be free to leave this watery tomb and see the jasmines of Damascus before I die."

"If you don't mind, while waiting for your heir, could you help me?"

"Help you?" He chuckled. "You're the one who's helping me."

The dwarf's words made no sense, but Sall's purpose in coming here wasn't to understand the dwarf's convoluted life story. "I fell in love with a girl, but she feels only contempt for me. In my dream you told me what to do." He quoted from memory. "If you wish to change how another person feels about you, start by changing yourself."

"That's a good rule to follow."

"I want to change in the same way you changed when you drank the golden elixir. I'm certain that, if I'm no longer this scrawny, freckled, redhaired boy, but rather a tall, strong, and exotically dark young man, she would look at me not with contempt, but with awe, passion, maybe even love. That's why I need to drink from the golden elixir."

"There's none left. I'm sorry."

"Can you make a fresh dose for me?"

"It's not as simple as that."

"Then tell me what ingredients you need, and I'll bring them to you, or I can drink directly from the fountain if you tell me where to find it. No matter where it is, how far, or what dangers await me, I'll go right now."

"Your determination is commendable, but unnecessary."

"Why?"

"Because you're mistaken. The golden elixir didn't change my appearance. I remained a little person. The elixir changed the way you saw me, which was the way you wished to appear yourself, if one's appearance could be changed."

It took a moment for Sall to understand the dwarf's words. "I know what I saw. You really changed after drinking the elixir. I'm sure of it."

"A potent elixir makes you see what you wish to see, but we need not argue, because a change of appearance is like a change of clothes, which is no change at all. To change a girl's heart, you must show her that your own heart has changed."

"How?"

"It will be easy for you, because your heart has already changed in many virtuous ways."

Pressing his hand to his chest, Sall shook his head. "I have the same heart as before."

"The same, but different."

"That makes no sense."

"The day you left the safety of your sheltered life and started on a perilous journey, you began to change your heart, which grew both braver and more compassionate each time you overcame setbacks, confronted hazards, suffered injuries, and recovered from each disappointment and heartbreak. Yours is no longer the heart of a fearful boy, but the heart of a strong man."

"I'm not strong," Sall said. "Didn't I drown only moments ago?"

"And you kept kicking, butting your head against my precious glass window, which had taken me decades to fabricate but would have shattered in a moment had I not opened it to let you in with the water and the fish."

"I was desperate."

"You were determined to survive and continue on your quest."

"But I'm the same person."

"Let me use a local example," the dwarf said. "Have you heard of the Damascus Steel?"

Sall nodded. "The best in the world."

"Right, because they start with strands of weak iron ores, each one too soft to make a strong sword, but once the different ingots melt in the fire and are pounded together by a blacksmith's heavy hammer, the weak ores bind together into a gloriously hard blade. Same with you. Before you left Edom, you had many weaknesses, but along your journey, under the heat of the sun and the pounding of men's cruelty, all those weaknesses were seared and hammered together to forge a man as strong as the Damascus Steel. Never again will a girl look at you with contempt."

The last words were delivered with a conviction that made Sall reluctant to argue, but in his heart, he knew that An would see no change in him and treat him with the same contempt, unless his physical appearance changed completely.

"I'm grateful for your compliments," he said. "At the same time, I'd like to grow taller and more muscular and, if possible, darker, as well."

The dwarf took the silvery fish out of the bucket and laid it on the table, writhing frantically, its mouth gaping. "Do you know what's the best elixir for growth and strength?"

Sall shook his head.

"Food." With a short knife, he cut the fish open. "And you don't need to be an Elixirist to make it."

Gutting the fish with expert movements, the dwarf peeled off the skin and removed the bones from the flesh, which he sliced into bite-sized pieces on two wooden plates. Though he had never eaten uncooked flesh of any animal or fish, Sall didn't want to insult his host. He ate a piece and was surprised by its pleasant taste and texture.

Taking another piece, he said, "It's my first time eating uncooked fish."

"And my last," the dwarf said, chewing slowly with his gums. "Praise the Gods for choosing the new Elixirist."

Hearing these words, it finally dawned on Sall that, if the dwarf won't help him, the new Elixirist, whoever that was, could provide him with the golden elixir to change into a towering, strong, and exotically dark young man, capable of winning An's love. He ate some more fish while choosing his words carefully.

"Won't it take a long time to pass all the needed knowledge to the new Elixirist?"

"No." His little mouth made swishy noises as he chewed. "Not long at all."

"That's good." Sall hoped his intentions were not transparent. "When do you expect him to arrive?"

"He's already here. Would you like to meet him?"

"I'd be honored."

The dwarf left the table and went to the corner of the room, where he fumbled in a clay bowl filled with fishhooks, fire-starting stones, and a few knives. He returned to the table with a flat piece of wood, about the size of a grown man's hand. He turned it over, held it in front of Sall, and picked up a candle.

In the soft light of the candle, Sall saw his face for the first time since viewing it in his mother's mirror at home. He recognized his features and red hair, which was still short but growing. His face, however, wasn't as milky white as it had been, but soft brown, like clay, making his freckles less prominent. His chin appeared more pronounced, molded over a square jaw. His eyes were still gray, but cooler and unafraid.

"There you go." The dwarf put the mirror down. "How do you like the new Elixirist."

Sall laughed.

"It's not a joke."

"Me? The new Elixirist?"

"Who else?"

"But I don't know anything about making elixirs."

"Creating elixirs. I'll teach you everything."

"It's not me. You're mistaken."

"The Gods brought you here. Are they mistaken?"

"The Gods helped me on my quest, which is to win a girl's heart in Bozra, not stay here, buried in this old ship, eating raw fish."

"Carobs are plentiful, too, but that's irrelevant, because you're not staying here." The dwarf picked up the mirror again. "Now, let's teach you the art of creating elixirs."

"No, thank you. I don't want this. Find someone else."

"The Gods found you, not me." The dwarf positioned the mirror in front of Sall to reflect the flame of the candle. "Calm down, it won't hurt, I promise."

"I'm not afraid of pain."

"I know. Now, look at the flame in the mirror and try to calm down."

Sall wanted to argue, but there was something captivating in the way the reflection of the flame flickered in the mirror.

"That's good." The dwarf started swaying the mirror back and forth at a slow pace. "Watch the flame. Only the flame. It's all you see. It's very pretty. It's calming you down."

He watched the flame, and it did sooth him.

"Breathe slowly, deeply."

He did.

"Let your muscles relax, starting with your toes, your feet, your ankles, and your lower legs."

Inhaling deeply, Sall concentrated on relaxing his lower legs.

"Now, your thighs, your belly, and your back, calm and relax while you breathe slowly."

Following the directions, he felt completely at peace, and when the dwarf's voice told him to relax his chest muscles, his neck, and his jaw, the calmness became as complete as when he'd drunk Li'uli's spiked milk, which made it only natural to obey the last direction: "You'll fall asleep now, except for your ears, which will remain open, and your mind, which will remember everything I teach you."

36

Sall woke up on a soft cot, the blanket tucked around him. Rays of sun penetrated through the canopy of the carob tree, lighting up the ship's cargo hold. The transparent window was softly lit through the water. He saw a fish swim by. His robe and loincloth were folded on the floor beside him. They were dry, and he put them on.

He heard steps on the deck above and started climbing up the stepladder through the loading hatch. On a middle rung, he found a white miniature elephant. He took it with him up to the deck.

"Good morning, young man." The dwarf, now dressed in his child-sized robe, was tying together several old oars. "Are you feeling rested?"

Shading his eyes with his hand, Sall looked over the railing at the water. The six rafts Li'uli had built for his bonfires had drifted to the corner near the bow of the ship, where water flowed through the narrow crevice to the gorge below, feeding the Barada River. He peered across the water to where he had left Bozra and the donkey yesterday. They were gone. He whistled Bozra's special tune, but no barking came in response.

"Don't worry." The dwarf added an oar. "Floodmaster must have taken your animals home."

"You know him?"

"I knew his forbearers, all of them hunchbacks with the same nasal voice that I heard yesterday over the water."

Holding up the miniature elephant, Sall asked, "What's this?"

"An elephant from the land of brown people."

"Who gave it to you?"

"Your friend, Prince Li'uli of Kush."

"He's not my friend."

"Your admirer, then. An enchanting man."

"An evil man."

"Evil men enjoy harming others for no purpose, whereas good men regret harming others even when it's necessary for a lofty purpose." His small hands fumbled with the rope, trying to make a knot. "He told me that he had paid a girl to plead for your release, but later heard that they had dragged you behind a donkey and smeared you with oil under the sun. He regretted causing your death, but I knew you'd survive."

Looking at the intricate carving of the elephant, Sall thought of the long weeks of pain, fever, and delirium he had spent with the Cainite women. "How did you know I'd survive?"

"Because I survived similar calamities."

Sall handed him the elephant.

"Keep it." The dwarf threaded the rope between the oars again. "You deserve this gift more than me, having suffered the consequences of his actions."

The memories gave Sall a shot of fury. "He's evil, I don't care what you say, and I won't regret hurting him back, if I get the chance."

"Hurting another in anger is a permanent solution to a temporary problem." The dwarf held up two ends of a rope. "Do a double-ender sailor's knot, will you?"

Sall knelt on the deck and watched his own fingers manipulate the ends of the rope around the wooden oars and tie a complicated knot rapidly and without hesitation.

"Excellent," the dwarf said. "Do another one here."

While doing it, Sall said, "I didn't know I could do this."

"We had a productive night, you and I, which means that this morning you know many new things you didn't know yesterday." He added another oar from a pile, placing it next to those already bound together. "Go ahead, tie this one, as well."

Sall's fingers worked without the need for him to think about what to do. "Did you know Li'uli made six floating bonfires to be launched when the Egyptians arrive?"

"I could tell what he had in mind by the way he inspected the ship. And he was kind enough to set aside these old oars and new ropes for me to build a raft in case something happened to the ship." The dwarf tugged on the ropes to check the knots. "Nice and solid."

"I destroyed his fuel piles for the bonfires, but the Egyptians will make new ones when they come. If they burn the ship, it will collapse and all the water will rush down the gorge and flood Damascus, killing thousands of people."

"Don't worry about Damascus." He pulled two more oars from the pile. "These we'll use to row our little raft to shore."

"Aren't you afraid to die?"

"Not anymore." He tapped Sall's forehead with a tiny forefinger. "Right here, my knowledge is safe in its new home, and I'm ready to see the magnificent jasmines of Damascus before I take my eternal rest."

To Sall, the dwarf's claim to have transferred all the knowledge of an ancient Elixirist into his head sounded ludicrous. He felt no smarter or wiser than yesterday, and his concern for what could happen to the people of Damascus had not abated.

"What about the ship?"

"All in good time. Put the raft in the water, will you?"

He hefted the raft over the railing while the dwarf held the end of the rope. Dropping the two oars onto the raft, Sall raised one leg over the side to climb down to the raft.

"Not yet." The dwarf tied the rope to the railing. "We have one more thing to do."

Sall followed him down the stepladder into the hold, which seemed darker after the brightness above. Against the hull of the ship, on the opposite side from the transparent window, he noticed a large pile of dry leaves, twigs, and branches from the carob tree. The dwarf knelt by the pile and started to knock two stones together.

"What are you doing?"

The dwarf kept banging the stones together. "Get ready. We'll have to move quickly."

Sall knelt by him and put his hand between the stones. "What about the people in the city?"

"Didn't I tell you not to worry about Damascus?" He resumed banging the stones.

There was no way Sall could stop worrying about all the people he had seen yesterday in the city's busy streets. He crossed the hold to the transparent window and climbed the stepladder. Above the window was the large wheel that the dwarf had used to open the window.

"You read my mind." The dwarf kept banging the stones. "Wait for my signal."

Sall was even more confused. Why start a fire, only to douse it with water from the window.

"There it is." A spark ignited a dry leaf, and the dwarf dropped the stones. "I'm getting too old for this."

The fire spread quickly to the rest of the pile. The dwarf made his way to the stepladder and started to climb. Smoke rose from the fire to the ceiling, accumulating under it, and found its way out through the loading hatch and the tree canopy. Sall tugged on the wheel, which was connected by ropes and pulleys to the wooden frame of the transparent window. Nothing happened. He tried to turn the wheel with both hands, but it wouldn't move. The flames grew rapidly, the smoke bellowed and thickened, and Sall's eyes teared up. He pulled harder on the wheel with no success.

From halfway up the stepladder, the dwarf called, "Not yet. Let the fire grow."

The flames licked the inside of the ship's hull, which started to acquire a blue glow. Sall was choking on the smoke and wanted to jump off the ladder and run, but the thought of countless corpses floating in the streets of Damascus terrified him.

"Almost time," the dwarf yelled from the top of the stepladder.

The fire caught on to the beams and planks of the hull, and sparks flew from the black paste in the cracks.

Coughing, Sall yelled, "The wheel won't turn."

"Pull the stopper. It's the piece of wood at the top of the wheel."

Barely able to see through the smoke and his tears, Sall reached up, found the end of a short stick, and pulled it out. The wheel jerked. He turned it, applying more force to spin it faster. The roar of water made him stop. The transparent window was half-open, and water gushed into the ship.

"Run," the dwarf shouted. "What are you waiting for?"

Jumping down, Sall stumbled in the water, which flowed down to the lowest area along the centerline of the ship. He fell, his face in the water, and struggled to get up. The thunderous noise of the rushing water was terrifying. He got up and waded through the water. Reaching the stepladder, he climbed up, chased by the hiss of rising flames and the rumble of falling water.

On the deck, the dwarf was as pale as milk. Smoke bellowed through the loading hatch. He beckoned Sall to the opposite railing over the downriver direction of the gorge. On this side, there was no water against the ship, and its curved wooden hull was exposed all the way down, where the water that passed through the nearby crevice flowed at the bottom of the gorge.

The dwarf offered him a carob. "Chew, it'll calm you."

"You could have told me your plan."

"And spoil the suspense?" He clucked his tongue. "You figured it out by yourself. Feels good, doesn't it?"

They looked down over the railing, waiting. Below their feet, the ship trembled as water gushed into its cargo hold.

"Any moment now," the dwarf said.

A popping noise sounded, and a clutch of smoky wooden beams broke away from the side of the ship below them, followed by a jet of water, which arched down all the way to the bottom of the gorge below, joining the flow of the river.

"It worked," Sall said. "The new hole is not too big."

"About the size of the window."

"It's a clever solution, to let the lake drain slowly through the ship."

"And the river will only rise as much as it does during the rainy season."

"The Egyptians will be disappointed."

The dwarf leaned on him as they walked to the opposite railing. "I don't think so."

"Why?" Sall tugged on the rope to bring the raft closer.

"Pharaoh's army will never return to this region."

Sall lifted him over the railing and lowered him onto the raft. "Li'uli said they're determined to recapture all the territories they ruled eight generations ago."

"Determined?" He shifted forward to make room. "That's not going to help them, not this time."

Sall climbed down, careful not to rock the raft. "What's different this time?"

He dipped his tiny hand in the water and dampened his bald head. "This time, they'll be stopped long before reaching Canaan or Damascus."

Rowing alternatively on each side, Sall propelled the raft away from the ship. "Who will stop the mighty army of Egypt?"

"Who?" The dwarf smiled. "You, of course."

37

Sall carried the dwarf on his shoulders from the waterfall through the dense forest over the meandering path down the mountains. Once on the road along the Barada River, he noticed that the flow was faster than it had been during the trip upstream, but the water didn't overflow the banks or the barriers at the irrigation channels.

They stopped a few times along the way, drinking water from the river and eating grapes and figs that grew along the road. By the evening, Sall's shoulders hurt and his legs were wobbly. He made a fire and, while he slept beside it, the dwarf remained awake and kept the fire going.

The next day, Sall continued to carry the dwarf on his shoulders until the afternoon, when they saw Damascus ahead. The road passed through blooming fields of jasmine, and the dwarf inhaled loudly and exhaled with groans of pleasure. At the gates of the city, he insisted on walking, and Sall lowered him to the ground. They proceeded slowly through the bustling main street. In the marketplace, Sall noticed Anis and his sons at a stall loaded with the goods they had brought from Canaan.

He pointed at them. "That's the family I travelled with from the Sea of Galilee. The leader is Anis."

"I knew an Anis once," the dwarf said. "Go and greet them. I'll wait here."

Sall stepped over, and they received him warmly.

"We must beg your forgiveness," Anis said. "After you asked me about a sailor on the Barada River, I dosed off on my horse and only woke up when we approached the city. I asked after you, but everyone had also napped along the way, tired from the night with the jackals."

"I also fell asleep, and my donkey stopped." Sall decided not to mention the Moabite merchant and his dead wife and child. "It wasn't your fault."

"We're rejoiced to see you in good health."

"The feeling is mutual."

Anis patted his shoulder. "Well, then, have you managed to sail on the river?"

"Not yet," Sall said, going along with the joke. "But I tried swimming."

They laughed together.

The dwarf walked over slowly. Sall helped him sit on a stool, and Anis offered him a cup of wine.

"Thank you, my good man." He took a sip. "Tell me about your merchandise."

"With pleasure." Anis pointed as he spoke. "The jars contain the best palm dates from Jericho by the Jordan River. The sacks over there are filled with the finest wool from Emanuel in the Samariah Hills, and the leather hides, as any expert would confirm with high praise, come from Aphek near the Coastal Plain."

Reaching into his pocket, the dwarf pulled out coins, which glistened in the afternoon sun. He needed both hands to hold the coins, which were much larger than silver coins and had the color of pure honey. It took Sall a moment to realize he was looking at gold coins, which only kings and high priests possessed. Each such coin was worth many dozens of silver coins. There were seven of them in the dwarf's open palms.

Anis peered at the coins, and his expression turned to awe. "What do you wish to buy?"

"Everything you have."

While his sons looked at each other in amazement, Anis asked, "Everything?"

"Is it not for sale?"

"Yes, it is, but I didn't expect to sell everything to one person."

"The best expectations are those that reality exceeds."

Anis nodded in agreement.

"Go ahead," the dwarf said. "Take as many coins as you think is fair."

Looking at the gold coins with reverence, Anis took three out of the seven and bowed deeply. "Where should we deliver the goods?"

The dwarf turned to Sall. "Well?"

"Floodmaster," Sall said. "Do you know where he lives?"

"I do," Anis said. "What shall I tell him?"

"Tell him these precious goods are a second gift from the Edomite boy."

Anis glanced at the remaining coins. "Anything else we can do for you?"

"There is something," the dwarf said. "Do you know safe roads to take an important passenger from here to Edom?"

"The best are the eastern trade routes through the mountains of Ammon and Moab."

"Have you travelled them?"

"Several times."

"How quickly could you reach Bozra?"

"Twenty days, assuming we carry enough food and water, as well as the means to buy fresh horses to replace the tired ones along the way."

"When can you leave?"

"At sunrise tomorrow, if you wish." Anis paused and added, "It's a long journey of hot days and frosty nights, not easy, even for a young man."

"Only the boy will be traveling with you." The dwarf held up the four gold coins. "Will these be enough?"

With another deep bow, Anis collected the coins.

"When you deliver him safely to Bozra, there will be a generous bonus, as well."

Anis's eldest son cleared his throat and pointed at the coins. Anis held one of them up to the sunlight, examining it at length.

The dwarf smiled. "Is something wrong?"

Anis looked at the other coins, too. "They appear to be new."

"They've been in my purse since new."

"That's impossible," Anis said. "I have visited Egypt several times and know their pantheon of past leaders. These coins bear the image of Pharaoh Nebhepetre Mentuhotep the Second, who ruled many dozens of generations ago, which was the time they were minted."

"Minted?" The dwarf chuckled. "You know your pharaohs, but not how their coins were made in the old days. Coins were not minted, they were carved by hand and honed to perfection from bars of gold. Dozens of artists were chained to a great rock by the River Nile for their whole lives, lest they were tempted to ingest gold dust and flee. It was a sight to see."

The last few words cast a spell on Anis, who knelt on the ground, staring wide-eyed at the old dwarf, who reached with his tiny hand and patted the grown man's cheek as if he were a child.

"You have the handsome face of your ancestor."

"You knew him?"

"Anis of Lebanon? Of course. An honest merchant if there ever was one. He supplied all the cedar beams for the tower, whole forests of Lebanon, cut down and floated down to Damascus in the snow-melting season."

"Gods, have mercy on me," Anis whispered. "The stories were true — the great tower collapsed, but the Elixirist lived on."

"A long and tiring experience, but fortunately, at an end." The dwarf gestured at Sall. "This boy is the Gods' choice to take my place. He is due in Edom without delay — the survival of Damascus depends on it."

Showing no doubt in this outlandish warning, Anis got up and bowed to both of them. While he and his sons loaded the goods back on the camels, Sall helped the dwarf to a spot near the water, where they sat on the ground, surrounded by flowering jasmines. The packed camels ambled towards the city's south exit to deliver the gifts to the hunchback. When they were gone, Sall spoke.

"I can't go to Edom tomorrow. General Mazabi told me not to return until the sixth full moon, and the Moabite merchant revealed that my father had told him to keep me away."

The dwarf waved dismissively. "People tell you what not to do for reasons that seldom align with your best interests."

Sall thought for a moment. "Li'uli said that Pharaoh's army was marching to Canaan by way of the Sea of Reeds, which is on Edom's southern border."

"There's your answer." Reaching into his pocket, the dwarf pulled a fistful of gold coins. "War makes parents nervous."

"War? Why would there be war? Edom is at peace with Egypt, and there's plenty of empty desert for their army to travel through Edom peacefully."

The dwarf pulled out additional gold coins and added them to a growing pile on the ground between them. "Isn't Edom a rich nation of copper and iron ore that's worth subjugating?"

"We're also a strong nation with a mighty army. I assume the Egyptians need their army intact in order to reconquer the lands Pharaoh ruled in the past, not Edom, which they never ruled."

"Making assumptions and acting on them is like a lost traveler making up road signs to guide himself."

Shame filled Sall as he realized that the men of Edom were donning armor and training with weapons to defend it while he was chasing a dream, egged on by his parents and General Mazabi, who obviously viewed him as a cowardly boy, unfit for the battle to defend Bozra.

"Don't feel bad," the dwarf said. "Not every man makes a good soldier, but also, no good soldier ever won a battle by himself."

"No coward ever won, that's for sure."

"A coward? You?"

Sall nodded.

"A coward would have stayed at his father's knee, rather than pursue a dream through the harsh desert and up the steepest peak. A coward would have given up after the dream reader failed to interpret his dream." The dwarf took a deep breath and continued, his voice feeble, but clear. "A coward would have bent under the yoke of slavery, mourned his lost dog and all his belongings, and served his owner mindlessly until freedom was granted to him, or not." Another deep breath, the voice growing meeker. "A coward would have given up on his quest a hundred times along the torturous journey you have taken. No, boy, you're no longer a coward – if you ever were one."

The words made Sall feel better, but the result was the same. "I'm not with the other men of Edom, but here, on a foolish quest to change a girl's heart. The irony is that, had I stayed to fight like a man and defend Edom, she would have witnessed my courage and changed her feelings in my favor."

"What use is a girl's heart to a dead boy?"

"Dead?"

"Edom cannot beat Egypt in battle."

"You underestimate my people. General Mazabi's mighty arm can throw a spear and hit a target a thousand steps away, and our king is the best swordsman in the history of swords."

"Spears? Swords?" The dwarf found another coin in his pocket and added it to the pile, which had thirty or forty gold coins. "Pharaoh's soldiers are raised from infancy to fight. They spend every day of their lives training to win battles. Egypt's infantry will not be hindered by swords, its archers will not be diverted by spears, and its steel chariots will not be stopped by kings, generals, or brave boys freshly enlisted on the eve of battle."

"What are you saying? Edom is lost?"

"Lost? I didn't say that. No, Edom can be saved, but not by kings and generals."

"Then by whom? Wait, let me guess. By me."

"Correct."

Sall laughed bitterly. "It's a joke."

"A joke?"

"A bad joke that's not funny, because it makes no sense. How can a night of studying while asleep turn me into someone who can save a nation?"

"Oh, my dear boy, you are mistaken in your modesty." The dwarf sipped some water, his hands shaking. "The knowledge I passed to you overnight was merely the finishing touch. The underpinnings of an Elixirist were in you already."

"What underpinnings?"

"Your keen perception of the world, its blessings and curses alike. Your ease of connecting with human and animals, whether they're friends or foes. Your acute ingenuity and fertile mind, coming up with creative ideas no one else could conceive. And your personal charm, which is only beginning to ripen." He swayed, drained by the long sentence, and his little mouth remained open as he struggled for air.

In his mind, Sall knew the words were true, but his heart refused to accept them for a reason that made him ashamed. "I'm afraid," he said.

The dwarf took Sall's right hand between his child's hands, which were cold, dry, and tremulous. "Only a fool feels no fear." He spoke slowly, his voice barely audible. "Elixirist is what you are now. My gold, my knowledge, and my responsibilities are yours." His old eyes were misty, and his breathing was labored. "Go home to your people. When the time comes, you'll know how to save Edom."

An unfamiliar sentence surfaced from Sall's memory and came to his lips. "Courage is overcoming fear, not the lack of fear."

The dwarf smiled, his eyelids closed, and he slumped back, lying among the white jasmines. The whisper of his breathing quieted down until it was no more.

38

As the sun was setting, Sall carried the dead dwarf out of the city and found a quiet spot on a knoll budding with jasmines. While he was covering the body with stones, people gathered nearby and watched him in silence.

On top of the stones, Sall placed the miniature white elephant. He didn't know which Gods the old Elixirist had believed in. Instead of trying to recite a prayer, he spoke out loud the words that came to his lips from the night of sleep-study inside the Sailor of Barada: "How does an elixir work? An elixir works by eliciting the recipient's confidence in its powers. That confidence is the most important ingredient, whereas physical ingredients serve merely as inducements towards the desired effect. Sometimes water with honey and lemon will do, if the surrounding circumstances trigger a firm belief in the elixir's potency. Hence, the potency of an elixir depends on the recipient's belief in that potency, and that belief depends on the Elixirist's capacity for dramatic persuasion."

In the fading twilight, Sall walked south along the river. A small crowd trailed him, but when darkness descended, they gave up. He walked on, whistling Bozra's tune. Eventually, he heard barking, and she came running out of the night and jumped into his arms, licking his face with breathless excitement. Floodmaster appeared behind her on his little horse, trotting as fast as its short legs could manage. He carried a lit torch and wore a beautiful leather hide over his shoulders.

"Am I dreaming?" He dismounted and threw his arms around the boy, almost burning him with the torch. "Is it really you?"

"She thinks so," Sall said as Bozra stood on two legs and licked his face again.

"But how? I saw you drown, and you never resurfaced. When Anis came and told me that all those gifts were from you, and that he had just seen you in Damascus, I told him it's impossible."

"There was an old dwarf living in the ship. He opened a window underwater, and I poured in with water. He saved me and, by morning, I recovered."

"A dwarf living inside the Sailor of Barada? How long has he been hiding there?"

"Since the Gods destroyed the great tower."

The hunchback took the reins and turned the little horse back towards the house. "My father told me stories about a great Elixirist of tiny stature, banished by the angry Gods. I thought it was just a myth. Is he still on the ship?"

"He passed away a short time ago."

"Are you sure he's dead?"

"I buried him."

The hunchback contemplated for a while. "Legend says that he couldn't die until the Gods sent his replacement. Are you the new Elixirist?"

"He thought so, but I don't feel any different than yesterday, last week, or last year. I'm just a healer's son from Edom, and I must go back to enlist in the army and defend our nation."

"If only I could have met him before he died."

"Why?"

"To punch him in the face."

Sall laughed. "Why would you punch an old dwarf in the face?"

"Because he gave us this." He reached over his shoulder and patted his humped back. "For many generations, every firstborn male in our family had to live with this deformity."

"Did he give a reason?"

"Floodmasters should be crooked on the outside so that they're straight on the inside." The hunchback sighed. "That's what the Elixirist told our forefather, who was the first to take on the responsibility for the river."

They reached the house and sat by the fire, eating palm dates from a bowl and drinking wine. Later on, as the wine took effect, the hunchback asked Sall if he could make an elixir to straighten his son's back. Searching his memory, the boy found nothing helpful. Had the Elixirist intentionally left the hunchback-curing elixir out of the knowledge given during the night on the ship, or was the allegation that he had caused the deformity contrived, a way to blame some mythical wizard for a devastating hereditary defect? Sall didn't know the answer, only that he couldn't cure the hunchback's son.

At sunrise, Anis and his three sons appeared with seven horses, but without their women and children. Two of the horses were packed with food and waterskins. Sall transferred his few belongings from his donkey, which he decided to leave behind, to the horse they had saddled for him. He tied Bozra to the saddle horn with a long rope. The gold coins he split between his purse and a piece of cloth he tied under his robe.

Sall thanked the hunchback for his hospitality, accepted from him a fistful of date palms for a morning meal, and joined the caravan on the road south. Anis insisted that Sall ride up front with him. They rode fast, pushing the horses hard, with rests few and far between. Bozra didn't last long at such pace, and he had to carry her in front of him on the saddle.

The sun was setting when they stopped at a small town. Anis traded their horses for fresh ones. Sall found an empty sack and fashioned a carrier for Bozra by tying the sack to the side of the saddle. They rode on through the night with burning torches. The second day brought them to the city of Astarot at the southern edge of Aram. Anis paid a trader for replacement horses and fresh supplies, as well as a live pig, which his sons butchered and roasted on a fire put. They set up a single large tent, which everyone shared, including Bozra.

At dawn, Anis led the group east to circumvent the eastern territory of Manasseh, then south into the land of Amon. They pushed the horses hard, exchanging them when the opportunity came, and spent the next four nights in villages along the road. On the seventh evening, they reached Rabbath Amon, a walled city with a royal palace at its center. Anis and his sons obtained fresh horses, food, wine, and water. After a quick meal of barley stew, dried sheep's meat, fresh bread, and a cup of wine each, they slept until dawn.

When Sall got up, he was startled to see a line of people waiting in front of the tent.

Seeing him, a woman at the head of the line announced, "The Elixirist is awake."

Everyone bowed.

Anis and his sons were up, too. They didn't seem puzzled. The son who had the last guard shift held out his hand to the woman. She put a coin in his palm and knelt before Sall, holding up a very thin newborn baby whose face had a hole instead of the upper lip and nose. Sall had seen this deformity several times while apprenticing for his father and knew there was no cure. The child's inability to nurse brought death a week or two after birth.

"Return the coin," Sall said to Anis's son. "The Elixirist is dead. I buried him in Damascus."

The woman accepted the coin back, but her eyes filled with tears, and she wouldn't get up while the people in line started kneeling down, too.

He addressed all of them. "I can't help any of you. Forgive me and pray to your Gods instead."

Anis rested his hand on his shoulder and whispered, "Aren't you a healer?"

"The baby can't be healed, and for the others, they need potions and tonic, but in this arid area I haven't seen the plants we use for the required ingredients. I'm sure they have local healers who mix potions with ingredients they can find around here."

"Do something for them. Mumble incantations, chant blessings, whatever. They'll pay you anything you ask."

"They'll be paying for false hopes."

"False hopes are better than no hopes."

Lifting Bozra into the sack by the saddle, Sall mounted his horse and took off down the road, away from Rabbath Amon. Anis and his sons caught up with him after a while.

Skirting the territories of the Hebrew tribes of Reuben and Gad, Anis led them for five more days on narrow roads and rocky paths, arriving after sunset at the largest Moabite city, Dibon. The gates were already locked for the night, and the walls were manned by guards with burning torches. After setting up camp in the fairgrounds, they learned from travelling merchants that the Moabite ruler, King Bin-Lot, had put his soldiers on high alert due to rumors of an Egyptian army facing off with the army of Edom on the shores of the Sea of Reeds. Sitting around the fire after the evening meal, Anis used a twig to draw a map in the sand to show his sons and Sall how, once the Egyptians defeated Edom, there would be nothing to stop their march north to Moab and Canaan. When Sall objected, arguing that Edom's army was undefeatable, Anis shrugged and tossed the twig into the fire.

That night, they woke up to screams. At first, Sall thought that the Egyptians were attacking, which meant that the mighty army of Pharaoh had defeated Edom and trotted north at a lightning speed. The screaming, however, came from a woman in the neighboring tent. She ran out, clasping her neck, followed by the rest of the family. The other caravans woke up, as well. The woman ran around the fairgrounds, shrieking in a high pitch, while her family chased after her. She fell down, writhing and stuttering.

Anis looked at the Sall. "Won't you help her?"

"It's too late."

His words were met with an awkward silence. Snakebites usually took hours to kill, or even days, but the woman's reaction indicated an extremely bad case.

A moment later, she became still.

One of Anis's sons went over to check and came back, nodding at his father.

"You were right," Anis said to Sall. "How did you know?"

He pointed at the tent, where a dark snake slithered out under the side. "Black cobra. It bit her on the neck. The venom went straight to the head and the heart."

"Impressive," Anis said. "Did you learn this from the Elixirist?"

"From my father. I accompanied him once on an urgent call to the home of a man who was bitten by a black cobra under his ear. He also died quickly."

Several men followed the snake and killed it with rocks.

Anis grunted. "Did your father also kill the snake?"

"He said that snakes are needed to eat rodents, or our fields and orchards will suffer."

"What about biting people?"

"My father said that snakes don't waste venom on people unless they feel threatened."

39

From Dibon, they headed south along the main north-south trade route. Eight days of harsh desert trekking later, they turned right and took a switchback road uphill. In the afternoon, they reached the crest of the hills and stopped. A great valley spread below them. At the opposite end of the valley, covering a vast mountainside, the city of Bozra glistened with countless copper roofs, encircled by massive whitewashed walls. At the top of the mountain, the king's palace poked the skyline, adjacent to the Temple of Qoz.

Sall shaded his eyes from the afternoon sun ahead and gazed down at the valley. He saw no Egyptian infantry, archers, or steel chariots, only the familiar tranquility of checkered fields, lush orchards, and tidy vineyards, dotted with farmers and animals.

Bozra struggled to stand inside the sack by the saddle and barked.

Sall rubbed her head. "We're almost home, girl. You'll be free before sunset."

Urging his horse down the road, he reached the first switchback when he noticed that Anis and his sons remained at the top. He turned his horse and rode back up.

"You're safe now," Anis said. "We have to ride back."

"Why don't you come to the city with me? You'll be our guests for the night, and we'll arrange fresh horses for you."

"It will be an honor to visit you when peace returns."

Sall gestured at the valley below. "It's peaceful now."

"Before a storm, there's always serenity." Anis bowed his head. "Farewell, young man."

"Wait." He reached into his purse and pulled out a gold coin. "May the Gods deliver you safely to Damascus."

He watched them disappear down the east face of the mountain range. Bozra popped up again and barked, making him smile as he urged the horse down the meandering road to the valley.

When Sall reached the bottom, the sun was low over the city at the opposite end of the valley. Riding between fields and orchards, he realized that the farmers he had seen from high above were not men and boys, as was usually the case, but women and girls. It was the first visible confirmation of the rumors of war, as well as a stinging reminder of his shameful departure from Bozra on the eve of war. He felt his face flush at the prospect of entering the city while all the men and boys of Edom were at the Sea of Reeds, confronting the army of Egypt. He was determined to restore his honor by obtaining a sword, a spear, and a fresh horse, and riding south to serve under General Mazabi at the Sea of Reeds – no matter what his father, mother, or anyone else said. He would not listen, because he now understood that the old dwarf had been right about one thing: He was no longer a coward. And when An heard about it, she would be impressed, because no girl could feel contempt for a young man leaving home to defend his nation.

Already halfway to the city, Sall's attention was drawn to the hills along the southern edge of the valley. A single rider was making his way down a steep slope, his horse loaded with a long package tied across the back behind the saddle. It was an odd sight. Those hills were rocky and precipitous, lacking any proper roads, water sources, or shade trees. Why would a rider with a heavy load traverse those rugged hills through desolate wasteland instead of taking the well-trodden trade route from the south and the good road over the hills at the east end of the valley?

As if to confirm his concerns, Sall saw the horse stumble down the slope. Its front legs folded, then its rear legs, too. The fall knocked off the rider, who rolled downhill and remained motionless on his back.

Sall turned his horse and sprinted across wheat fields towards the hills. As he got close to the slope, he saw the fallen man's left arm, slumped sideways on the ground, but not the right arm. A dark cloth swaddled the right side of his upper body.

Reaching the base of the hill, Sall recognized the man and felt a chill despite the heat. It was General Mazabi.

He gazed uphill, hoping to see the rest of the king's army, but no one appeared.

The general breathed heavily. The dark cloth was a makeshift bandage, soaked in blood, pressed over the right shoulder. The mightiest arm in Edom, which could hurl spears to great distances, was gone.

The shock stunned Sall for a moment, but he forced his mind to focus on what needed to be done to save the general. Urging his horse up the slope to the fallen horse, he intended to remove the large package and leave it there, but now he could see that it was a man, lying face down over the back of the horse, an arrow sticking out of his shoulder through his red coat, which was threaded in gold.

The king!

Sall dismounted, took a waterskin, and knelt by the crouching horse. He poured water slowly into the palm of his hand while the horse, whose lips and tongue were cracked from dryness, licked the water. When the waterskin was empty, he helped the horse get up and led it the rest of the way down. The general's heavy copper spear was secured to the side of the saddle, and Sall wondered if it would ever be hurled again.

Taking a second waterskin from his own horse, Sall poured some water on General Mazabi's face, which was badly sunburnt. His eyes opened, blinking rapidly. Sall helped him sit up and held the waterskin for the general, who emptied it. With Sall's help, he got up, placed his boot in the stirrup and used his left arm to pull up and get back in the saddle.

Sall mounted his horse while Bozra peeked out of the carrier sack, staying quiet.

"Why are you here, boy?" The general swayed in the saddle. "I said six full moons, not four, or five."

"I'm not a coward. Had I known about the war, I would have stayed to serve."

"And to die."

The implication took a moment to sink in. "Is everyone—"

"They slaughtered our whole army."

Sall wanted to ask about his father. Had he joined the army's march to the Sea of Reeds, or stayed in the city to care for the women and children? It was unlikely that the king would go to war without the best healer in Edom, and the fact that the arrow had not been removed implied the worst about his father's fate.

The king groaned, startling Sall.

The general tilted his head towards the city. "Lead the way, boy."

He retraced his steps through the fields to the main road and turned west towards the city, the sun in his eyes. Glancing back to make sure they had not collapsed again, he could hear the dwarf's voice: "Edom can be saved, but not by generals and kings."

Closer in, Sall saw no merchant caravans in the fairgrounds, an ominous sign as Bozra was a popular stop for merchants from all the neighboring nations, as well as distant ones.

The gates were closed, but as the two horses approached, the guards opened them. Under the uniform, they were old man.

"Shut the gates behind us," General Mazabi said. "No one else is coming back."

One of the old guards sat on the ground and cried, "My son! My son!"

The other one hung his head and sobbed.

Inside the city, they passed by the king's empty horse stables and vacant army barracks and started up the main street, which crisscrossed the hillside. Women rushed out of the houses with their maiden girls and young children. They bowed to the fainted king and maimed general, before running down the hill to the gates to find their husbands and sons. The gathering crowd must have learned the tragic news from the guards, because Sall could hear a rising chorus of wails from the bottom of the hill.

On the street by his home, Sall saw sick women and their children trickle out of the front garden through the tall hedges. They bowed and hurried downhill. He felt sorry for them, but also relief, because the presence of the sick answered the question he hadn't dared asking. His father must be home, alive and safe, taking care of the people here, not lying dead on the bloodied shores of the Sea of Reeds with the rest of Edom's army.

He stayed mounted, riding into the front garden, followed by the general. The queue in front of the workshop was gone. The door was open, and he expected his father to appear, holding a bowl with the potion he had used for his last patient.

No one showed in the door of the workshop. Was he still caring for the last patient?

Dismounting, Sall took Bozra out of the sack and put her down. She barked and sprinted into the workshop.

A moment later, the servants rushed out of the house. Horseman helped General Mazabi dismount and lie down on the ground, while

Laundress and Cook surrounded Sall with tearful hugs and kisses.

His mother came out of the workshop. He felt a rush of conflicting emotions – joy for seeing her, dread for his father, and confusion over her assuming the healer's role.

Umm-Sall hurried over, hugged and kissed him, then stepped back to look him over.

"I'm fine, mother," he said. "As good as ever."

"Blessed be Qoz." She wiped tears, embracing him tightly. "But you shouldn't have come back, son. Not yet, anyway."

"My quest was successful." He looked towards the workshop. "Father?"

"He went with the army."

Sall felt dizzy, his worst fears confirmed.

She noticed the king slumped facedown over the second horse. "Gods, have mercy! What is he doing here?"

"They almost died in the hills."

"They?"

He pointed at General Mazabi, lying on the ground behind the horse.

"Him, too?" She bent over the general, inhaling sharply. "Your arm!"

Looking up at her, he smiled faintly.

"Who's leading the army?"

"There's no army." He reached up with his left hand to touch her cheek. "I'm sorry."

The chorus of wailing traveled up the hill from the gates, thousands of women crying for their husbands, fathers, and sons.

She moved away from his hand. "You've lost the whole army?"

He nodded.

"How?"

"Pharaoh's chief general, the Jabari, offered tribute for safe passage through Edom to Canaan. Our king agreed. The next day, while our men celebrated the peace, arrows suddenly rained down on our heads, steel chariots trampled our men, and hordes of Egyptian infantrymen swarmed our ranks." He glanced sideways at the miniature pantheon of stone effigies. "We fought back, but the Gods abandoned us."

"What about my husband?"

"He was in there."

"He may still be alive."

"No one could survive."

"You survived." Umm-Sall spoke deliberately, pronouncing every word. "Did you see my husband dead with your own eyes?"

"I saw him treating the injured. It was hopeless. I told him to run."

"Run?" She pointed at the horse. "This animal could run, not my husband. Why did you leave him?"

"I had to save the king."

Bozra nudged Umm-Sall with her snout.

Looking down at the dog, Umm-Sall petted her. "Yes, you did keep your promise."

"She did." Sall tried to smile through his sorrow. "It was touch and go for a while."

His mother stood and rested her hands on his shoulders. "Son, you're the man of the house now. That's why the Gods brought you back. I want to hear about your quest, but first, we must treat these cowards' wounds."

They carried the king into the workshop and put him face down on a long table. Umm-Sall sent Cook to bring hot water and started to cut a hole in his gold-threaded coat around the arrow's entry. The general was too tall and broad for a table, and they put him on the floor. The cloth covering his right shoulder glistened with fresh blood.

Sall saw his mother hesitate, her eyes go from the king, whose life equaled that of the whole nation, and General Mazabi, whose friendship extended back a lifetime.

"Don't worry," Sall said. "I'll take care of him."

"Do you know what to do?"

He nodded, and whatever doubts Umm-Sall harbored, she set them aside and focused on the king. The boy's own doubts were harder to quell, but he remembered the dwarf's words: "Courage is overcoming fear, not the lack of fear."

Kneeling by the general, he helped him drink water from a cup. When it was finished, he made him drink another.

One of the bowls his mother had prepared for the day contained the familiar potion he'd also used in Jericho, a mix of honey and black seeds from red flowers. He placed it on the floor beside the general and gave him a third cup of water.

"Drink this, too. I'm going to pull off the cloth, clean the wound, and dress it with a potion."

General Mazabi's remaining hand grabbed the boy's arm. "Leave me. Help your mother save the king."

"In a moment."

His grip tightened, becoming painful. "Now."

Sall peeled the general's thick fingers from his arm. "Lie still and don't talk."

There was dismay on General Mazabi sunburnt face. "Listen, boy——"

"I would let you die, as you have let my father die, but the people of Bozra will need you when the Egyptians arrive. Now, be quiet while I treat your wound, or I'll knock you out with a club on the head!"

The last words he uttered in anger. His mother and the servants looked at him, but Sall resisted the urge to apologize. He clasped the edge of the cloth and ripped it off the bloody shoulder.

The general groaned, and his head slumped back.

All the wounds and injuries Sall had seen while helping his father here and, later on, treating people by himself in Jericho, had not prepared him for this. As soon as the cloth was off, blood bubbled up from the thick stump of the right arm, which had been hacked off close to the shoulder. It looked like a sliced tree trunk with concentric rings – the inner ring of bone, surrounded by muscles, fat, and an outer ring of multi-layered skin. He pressed a fresh rag to stem the bleeding and put his ear to General Mazabi's gaping mouth, ensuring that he was still breathing.

Ready with a handful of potions, he uncovered the wound, smeared the potion, and replaced the rag, securing it with a long leather strap around the general's chest.

Horseman, Laundress, and Cook brought over a bed with a blanket and a pillow. Together with Sall, the four of them lifted General Mazabi from the floor into the bed without disturbing his wound, carried him to the house, and put him in Sall's old room. He was incredibly heavy, and Sall's arms hurt after putting him down.

He went back to the workshop and joined his mother at the table, where the king's back had been stripped. The arrow was stuck in his left shoulder blade. All the arrows Sall had seen before were made of thin tree branches, which were naturally imperfect and rough. The Egyptian arrow was different. Its shaft, about as thick as his pinky, was carved out of a larger log. It was perfectly straight and smooth. The tail end was notched for the bow's string, and just below it, fitted with two crossed feathers, one black and one white.

"Look at the entry," he said to his mother. "There's no extended wound."

"What does it mean?"

"A flint arrowhead would have caused an entry wound larger than the shaft. This one has no arrowhead. The shaft itself was sharpened to a point. It means we can pull it straight out." He pressed the flesh around the arrow. "Not much bleeding. That's a good sign. On the other hand, it's stuck in his shoulder bone, which makes it hard to pull out."

Her eyes went from the arrow to him. "How do you know all this?"

"The Elixirist taught me."

"You found him?" The astonishment in her voice was almost comical. "The Elixirist from your dream?"

"He was waiting for me."

"For what purpose?"

"To teach me everything he knew." Sall stopped there, not explaining that it happened overnight while he was in some form of sleep, or that he only remembered important information when it was needed.

"Why you?"

"He believed the Gods had chosen me as his heir." Sall pulled out his purse and the knotted piece of cloth he had hidden under his robe and put them on the table by her elbow. "These are gold coins that he also bequeathed to me. Each is worth more than a hundred silver coins."

She peeked inside the purse, and her eyes widened.

"Hide them somewhere safe, please." Sall took two rags and placed them on the king's bare back next to the arrow. "We must stop the bleeding as soon as the arrow is out." He moved the bowl of warm water closer. "To extract an arrow from a bone, it must be pulled straight up, or the tip might break inside. A piece of wood stuck in bone will rot and cause deadly fever unless the limb is amputated."

Umm-Sall rested her hand on his, stopping him. "Son, do you even understand what your mouth is reciting?"

"It's obvious. A shoulder cannot be amputated, so we must pull this arrow out in one piece." He clasped the arrow with both hands. "Ready?"

She gripped it, too, their hands alternating between the king's skin and the two feathers. Sall nodded, and they heaved it together straight up. The arrow came out of the bone in one piece, its sharp tip red, chased by gushing blood. Sall splashed the wound with warm water, wiped it with a rag, smeared the potion of honey and seeds, and pressed another rag to the wound to stop further bleeding.

His mother was staring at him.

"What's wrong?"

"An old dwarf might have taught you about arrows, but he couldn't teach your hands to do it all so perfectly." Her eyes filled with tears. "You have your father's hands."

He smiled. "Father trained me well. I healed many ailments and injuries in Canaan."

"By yourself?"

"It's long story. Bozra caused damage, and I was sentenced to slavery under a potter in Jericho, but his kind wife discovered that I was a healer's son. Word went around, and I became a busy healer, taking care of hundreds of people, and bought my freedom back."

The look on Umm-Sall's face went from amazement to pride. She took him in her arms and kissed his cheeks. "If only your father had lived to see you take up his work with such competence."

"Father is alive." He saw her face contort with a quick succession of hope and grief. "Don't ask me how I know it, but I do. Father is alive."

She gave him a searching look. "Perhaps the old Elixirist was right about you."

40

Umm-Sall went to check on General Mazabi. Bozra followed her, tail wagging. In the workshop, Sall revived the king by placing crushed mint under his nose. With Horseman's help, he propped the king up in a chair and gave him water with lemon juice.

The news must have reached the palace, because Sall saw through the workshop door two old guards driving the royal carriage into the front garden. One of them shouted in a hoarse voice: "Long live King Esau the Eighteenth!"

The king's young grandchildren, a boy and a girl, climbed down and ran into the workshop. They hugged their grandfather, who cringed in pain, but smiled.

Sall examined the bandage on his back and saw no fresh bleeding.

"Are you the healer's son?"

"Yes, my king."

"Aren't you the one who found us in the hills?"

Sall nodded.

"I came to when you helped the horse stand, then fainted again." The king sighed. "Did General Mazabi survive?"

"We cleaned his wound and bandaged it with a potion. He's sleeping in the house. If he avoids the fever, the wound will close, and his strength will come back."

"But not his arm." The king grunted. "You learned well from your father."

Sall bowed and winked at the children, who laughed and clung to their grandfather's legs.

The king drank some more water. "Well, boy, what shall be your reward?"

The question was unexpected, but Sall's response sprang to his lips. "A girl's hand in marriage."

"Presumptuous, but I'm a king without a kingdom." King Esau

caressed his granddaughter's head. "Princess Needa, do you like this redhead boy?"

The girl, who was barely as tall as Sall's hip, looked up at him for a long moment and nodded.

Blushing, he said, "I meant An, the high-priest's daughter."

Princess Needa swung her leg back and kicked him in the shin.

"Ouch!" Sall retreated before she could kick him again.

The king chuckled. "You'd rather marry that skinny girl?"

"My heart belongs to her."

"That's unfortunate." The king signaled his guards, who carried him to the carriage. "Don't you know your fathers hate one another?"

"Not more than other priests and healers, I assume."

"She's already betrothed to her brother, Qoztobarus." The king settled in the carriage, groaning in pain. "Choose another girl, and do it quickly, before the Egyptians arrive and take all our maidens."

The words shook Sall, but he was immediately distracted by the intensifying wails and cries from downhill. He followed the king's carriage out of the garden, but whereas it turned right towards the palace at the top of the hill, he turned left and walked downhill. The street, which switched back and forth across the width of the city, was deserted, as were the houses alongside it.

A dense crowd of women and children filled the open area between the vacant soldiers' barracks and dormant horse stables. From where he stood, Sall could see the open gates and a stream of burning torches down the road across the valley. He realized that women were coming from all the farms and nearby villages, seeking news about their men. Every time a new group reached the gate and learned that the whole army had been cut down by the Egyptians, new voices joined the wailing.

At one point, a woman pointed at Sall. "That's the boy who saved the king."

A group of women congregated around him, their tear-lined faces illuminated by the jittery flames of the torches, their eyes pleading with him desperately, as if by saving the king he had shown his ability to also save their men and bring them back from the dead. When the loud wailing of a newly arrived group attracted their attention, he slipped away and walked back up the hill to the house.

Umm-Sall was sitting in a chair next to General Mazabi, who snored loudly. The rag on his shoulder was dark with dry blood, but no fresh blood was visible. She kissed Sall and went to sleep in her room.

Laundress brought in a large bowl of hot water. She set a cot by the bed with white linen while he bathed with a wet sponge, wiping the grime and dust from two weeks on the road. When he finished bathing, she unfolded a clean robe for him. He put it on and hugged her. She had worked in the house since before he was born.

"Welcome home," she said. "I couldn't avoid hearing what you told Umm-Sall about your journey and the great Elixirist, who passed his knowledge to you. Did he teach you how to bring our men back to life?"

"The dead can never be revived."

She sniffled.

"I'm sorry."

"Are we doomed, then?"

A grunt came from the bed, and the general shifted. He no longer snored, but his eyes remained closed.

Sall stepped out of the room with her. "Don't worry. Qoz will not let Edom fall under Egypt's boot."

"Qoz didn't help our men at the Sea of Reeds. Who will fight for us now?"

Sall didn't know what to say.

"Run away again, boy. Please, run away."

Her words hurt like a slap on the face. "I didn't run away before, and I'm not going to now."

Laundress burst out crying. "I beg you, child, leave Edom before it's too late. Healers don't go hungry, wherever you go."

His arm around her shoulder, he led her to the servants' quarters in the rear of the house. Back in his room, he puffed on the candle and lay on the cot beside the bed, staring up at the dark wooden beams of the ceiling. Laundress's voice repeated in his mind. "Run away again, boy." Was this how everyone was thinking of him – a coward who fled Bozra to avoid war?

"She's right," General Mazabi said.

Startled, Sall sat up. "She's wrong. I didn't run away."

"She's right that we're doomed."

Lying back down, Sall said, "What kind of a general takes military advice from an old maid?"

"A general without soldiers is no better than an old maid." He coughed. "Without soldiers, there's no army. Without an army, there's no defense. Without defense, there's no survival. That's why we're doomed."

"The king has gold. He can hire mercenaries."

"It would take weeks, or months. The Egyptians will be here in days."

"We can defend Bozra until the mercenaries arrive. You can lead the people, tell them how to fortify the city."

"I'm as useless as a lame horse."

"Perhaps my mother was right when she called you a coward."

General Mazabi was silent for a long time before he spoke. "She's wrong. I'm worse than a coward. I'm a fool."

"A fool?"

"Several times over. Each mistake increasingly more fatal."

"What mistakes?"

"Enlisting every able man and boy, which left no males to replenish Edom. Marching the whole army, which left no one to defend Bozra. Failing to train them beyond the basics, which left us soft-bellied. Believing Egypt's fake peace tribute, which left us unprepared for the assault." He paused, inhaling deeply, and then said in a low, barely audible voice, "And saving the king instead of your father, which left me without your mother's respect."

The last sentence confused Sall, though it didn't surprise him, having grown up seeing the general visit the house frequently while showing effusive deference to Umm-Sall. What captivated Sall, though, was the general's succinct condemnation of his cascading military errors, which had led to the city's current defenselessness against the marching Egyptian army. He concluded that all those mistakes were caused by the genera's arrogance, which brought up a proverb in the old dwarf's voice:

"An error born of arrogance requires a correction devised in humility."

It sounded wise, but Sall could not figure out how to implement this principle in their current, desperate situation.

41

Waking up in the middle of a dream, Sall remembered the last part, which involved the dwarf drinking the golden elixir from the transparent goblet, causing him to gain a commanding height, a smooth skin, a dark complexion, and lush black hair that didn't stop growing until it reached hips that were wide and curvy, because the dwarf was transforming, not into a young man, but a young woman, who was as striking and as mysterious as the young man in Sall's original dream at the high priest's house.

A woman?

The dwarf's feminine transformation unsettled Sall, but his attention diverted to what had woken him up. Someone was banging on the front door, and the noise reverberated through the house. Beside him, General Mazabi continued snoring, undisturbed.

He stepped out of the room to the hallway and saw Cook and Laundress by the closed door, unsure what to do. Umm-Sall emerged from her room in a night robe. She tied on a headdress and signaled the servants to open the front door, which they did.

"Your son," a woman said. "Where is he?"

Another woman yelled, "His name is Sall!"

"Lower your voices." Umm-Sall stood at the doorway, blocking it. "General Mazabi is resting. He was badly injured fighting the Egyptians and saving the king."

The woman at the door lowered her voice. "Sall was the one who saved the king and the general. He can save all of us."

"Only the Gods can save us," Umm-Sall said.

"But the Gods made Egypt victorious."

"We'll pray they make Egypt merciful, too."

Sall eased his mother aside and stood at the door. The front garden was full of women of all ages. Their faces were bland in the meek light of dawn.

Umm-Sall held his arm. "Go back inside."

He removed her hand from his arm and kissed her fingers. "It's fine, mother."

The woman who had pounded on the door stepped back from the landing. "Are you a wizard?"

"No," he said.

"But people came down from Moab to look for you. They said you can do magic."

"They are wrong."

"Can you bring our men back to life?"

He shook his head. "Death is final."

An outburst of weeping swept the garden and continued outside on the street behind the tall hedges. He watched their faces, contorted with grief and fear. The depth of their despair was justified, not only for the loss of their fathers, husbands, and sons, but for losing the protection of the king's army, which spelled death or slavery for them, their daughters, and their small children. He wished there was something he could say to comfort their despair, but Edom's defeat at the Sea of Reeds had sealed their fate, as General Mazabi had said: "Without defense, there's no survival."

Was it the end of Edom?

He heard the old dwarf's voice: "When faced with a challenge, open your ears, eyes, and heart, and your mind will know what to do."

Following this prescription, Sall opened his ears to their voices in the garden and on the street, all through the city, and the deep reverberations caused by their cries told him there were many more women out there than he had thought, probably a few thousand. He opened his eyes, focusing on the women near him, noticing the details of their tearful faces, their burdened shoulders, and their hands, which were strong, with coarse skin from years of work at home and in the fields. And he opened his heart to their powerful yearning for survival and for a future as good as their past had been.

Having opened his ears, eyes, and heart, Sall looked up and wished his mind to know what to do. The surrounding noise receded into the background as he stared at the bleak sky, where the stars were still visible. Nothing came to him, other than a childish fantasy of turning all the twinkling stars into soldiers, who would make an army as numerous as any that had ever been assembled.

His mind blank of new ideas, Sall felt deflated, realizing he had been right in telling the dwarf he was not his heir. At the time, he had not wanted it, because his only goal had been to drink the golden elixir and change from a skinny redhead boy to a handsome, mysteriously dark man of great strength who would win An's heart. Now, however, with agonizing despair all around him, his quest seemed small and unimportant, and Sall needed the old dwarf to be right. He wanted to become the new Elixirist, who would know what to do for Edom.

A memory came to him of Ishkadim, quoting the Hebrew high priest's advice: "Imitate until you mutate!"

With that, Sall decided to imagine himself as the new Elixirist and act accordingly.

"Listen to me." He lowered his eyes from the stars and looked at the women. "Listen, please."

They hushed each other. Gradually, silence returned.

"I cannot bring back those who died," he said. "Only time will heal your grief for them, but time is short for all of us unless we have a new army, and for a new army, we need new soldiers. That shouldn't be too hard, should it?"

The women looked at him silently.

"Think about it," he said. "What are soldiers, if not people with arms, legs, and brave hearts. The rest – armors, shields, weapons – are mere tools and ornaments."

Speaking aloud helped him think. He recalled the disturbing end of the recent dream in which the dwarf transformed into a young woman, as striking and as mysterious as the young man in the original dream.

Suddenly, he knew what to do.

"Yes," he said. "We'll have plenty of soldiers."

One of the women asked, "Where will you find new soldiers?"

"Right here." He waved at the crowd. "You'll be the new army."

"Perhaps you haven't noticed," she said. "We are not men."

Her words won some laughter, but it stopped when they heard his response.

"I will turn you into men."

"How?"

The answer sprung to his lips without thinking. "Male Elixir."

The women looked at each other, then at him.

"You heard me," he said. "That's what I'll create for you. Male

Elixir."

They repeated it to each other, the words travelling out to the street and down to the gates.

"It's a potent elixir." Sall shook his finger. "Its mysterious powers are without comparison. And after you drink it, you'll be as strong and as fit for battle as men, maybe more than men."

Again, the words were repeated by countless voices.

A woman said, "We don't know how to fight."

"General Mazabi will teach you everything you need to know. He'll forge you into an army strong enough to chase away the Egyptians."

He waited for his words to travel far enough, and asked, "Are you ready?"

They clapped and cheered.

Umm-Sall stepped out of the house and stood beside him on the landing by the front door, watching the eruption of joyous hope.

In the midst of the clapping and cheering, Sall noticed a woman making her way from the rear through the dense, boisterous crowd. Her head was covered, her face turned down, and she was slim enough to slip easily between the others.

Umm-Sall leaned over and asked quietly, "Do you know what you're doing?"

"I don't, but the Elixirist does, and I'm imitating him."

"He taught you how to make this Male Elixir?"

Sall nodded.

"That's not healing. It's witchcraft. Your father would never allow it."

Placing his arm around his mother's shoulders, he put his lips near her ear. "Making potions is a craft. Creating elixirs is an art."

"It's unnatural." She pointed at the cheering crowd. "If you let a tiger out of the cage, you'll never be able to put it back in."

Raising both hands to quiet the crowd, Sall waited as the cheering subsided. The women looked up at him, except for the slim one, who kept advancing closer with her head down.

"My mother just told me words of wisdom," he said, watching the only woman who wasn't looking at him. "If you let a tiger out of the cage, you'll never be able to put it back in."

A wave of murmuring ran through the crowd.

He raised his hands again to silence them. "My response is simple.

Edom will rather die than live in an Egyptian cage!"

The women roared, waving clenched fists, shouting at the top of their voices, except for the slim one, now close enough for Sall to see that she had the narrow hips of a girl, not of a mature woman who'd given birth to children.

He put his hands beside his mouth to amplify his voice. "Are you ready to fight?"

The crowd roared in unison, "Yes! Yes! Yes!"

As the girl reached the front, her head still bowed and her face to the ground, Sall recognized the lightness of her steps and the contours of her body. She looked up at him through the narrow slit in the face scarf, her large brown eyes shining, not with contempt, but with awe.

The effect on Sall was as fierce as it had been at her father's house a few moons back, and if he were holding a jug of water, he would have dropped it. He swayed, almost losing his balance, his breath arrested in his tight chest.

The women at the front of the crowd noticed that something was happening and began to quiet down.

Before Sall had time to humiliate himself, the girl turned to Umm-Sall. "I am An," she said. "Daughter of the high priest."

Hearing her voice for the first time, Sall felt a pang in his chest, because her voice was as soft and as deep as her eyes.

"Welcome," Umm-Sall said. "Do you bring condolences from your father for my husband's death, or only glee?"

"Mother!" Sall was shocked by her vicious words. "Everyone is grieving today!"

"Not the high priest," his mother said. "Neither he, nor his sons have gone with the army."

All the women were completely silent now, listening to the exchange.

"I'm sorry for your loss." An bowed. "The king ordered me to come here and stay under your supervision while my father and brothers are away from Bozra."

"Of course," Sall said. "Our home is yours."

His mother glanced at him with raised eyebrows. "Come, girl, join our morning meal. We don't want you getting any skinnier than you already are."

Sall stepped aside to let her pass, and her scent of lavender engulfed him. "I have a question," he said, his voice sounding odd to his ears as if it came from someone else. "Where did your father and brothers go?"

Keeping her eyes down, An said, "They left with the king before sunrise."

Umm-Sall pulled the girl to the door. "Let's go inside."

"Wait." Sall stayed put. "Where did the king go?"

His mother glanced warily at the crowd of women.

"South," An said. "Towards the Sea of Reeds."

"Why?"

"Inside," Umm-Sall reached to take his arm. "Now."

"No, here." Sall waved at the crowd of women in the garden. "They deserve to know."

An spoke louder. "The king plans to welcome the army of Egypt on the road and offer gold and precious stones as gifts of surrender."

"Surrender," Sall repeated in disbelief. "On what terms?"

An looked up at him, and in her large brown eyes he saw not only awe, but also calm strength. "Edom will become a vassal state," she said. "Its people will serve as humble slaves to Egypt. The king will keep his crown, his palace, and his hereditary rule over Edom as servant of the Pharaohs in perpetuity."

Angry shouts came from the women.

Sall raised his hand to hush them. "And your father?"

"He'll keep his position, his property, and his perpetual right to bequeath the priesthood."

A few women booed, and soon hundreds more began to jeer the betrayal of Edom and its women by King Esau the Eighteenth and his high priest.

42

Inside the house, Umm-Sall went to wake up General Mazabi. The high-priest's daughter retreated to the corner of the room and stood with her head down, except for a quick glance at Sall when he entered.

The general groaned as he lowered his legs off the bed and sat up, rubbing his eyes with his left hand. The hair on his huge head was matted with dust and dry blood, his sunburnt face was peeling, and his bare feet were raw and dirty. Sall checked the bandage over the right shoulder. It was dark with dry blood.

"What's this noise?" General Mazabi tilted his head at the window.

"Thousands of very upset women," Umm-Sall said. "They heard that the king and high priest went to offer terms of surrender to the Egyptians."

"That was quick."

"You expected it?"

"Surrender is efficient. Egypt saves the expense of a siege, and the king saves his neck." General Mazabi lay back down. "They won't spare my head, though. And tell those women outside to stop shouting, go home, and slaughter their pretty daughters, because death is better than what's coming to them."

His shocking words caused An to inhale sharply, making a sound that was eerily similar to the unintentional sound Sall had uttered in her father's house, earning him a contempt-filled glare from her. She must have recalled the same thing. They looked at each other, and he heard her giggling under the scarf, which made him laugh.

Umm-Sall glowered at them. "What's wrong with you?"

The general, however, raised his head to look at them and smiled. "To be young and in love. Have you forgotten?"

In an instant, Umm-Sall's face crumbled, and tears filled her eyes. It took her a long moment to recover, and when she did, her voice was shaky.

"I forgot nothing," she said, looking at him.

"Good," he said. "A little comfort near the end."

"It's not the end. You have to get out of bed."

He sighed. "What can I do?"

"My son told the women that he will turn them into men, and then, you'll teach them to fight as an army and scare off the Egyptians."

Again, General Mazabi lowered his legs and sat up on the bed. He scratched his dusty beard, and his gray eyes rested on Sall.

The boy looked straight back at him, refusing to lower his eyes.

The general gestured at the window. "All those women, into men?"

"Yes."

"How?"

"Male Elixir."

"You know how to make it?"

"Yes. I found the great Elixirist near Damascus and he taught me everything."

"Why would he do that?"

"He was very old and believed the Gods had chosen me as his heir."

"You are the new Elixirist?"

"He believed it."

"Do you?"

"It doesn't matter. Right now, I must act like the Elixirist, or we'll be doomed."

"And by drinking your Male Elixir, our women will grow muscles, beards, chest hair—"

"No," Sall said, interrupting him before he went any further. "It'll give them confidence, courage, and aggression. They'll act the way men act, they'll dress in men's clothes, and they'll bear men's weapons."

"I see," General Mazabi said. "They'll imitate men the way you're imitating the Elixirist."

Sall nodded.

"And I'll make them into an imitation army, correct?"

"The Hebrews have a wise saying," Sall said. "Imitate until you mutate."

"The Hebrews?" General Mazabi sneered. "They believe in an invisible God, those fools."

"They're not fools," Sall said. "Every one of them can read and write, even young boys and poor beggars."

"Imitate until you mutate. It's catchy. Tell me boy, if you believe it, why don't you imitate a general and leave me in peace?"

"He might have to," Umm-Sall said. "Are you too afraid to face the Egyptians again?"

The bemusement faded from General Mazabi's face, and his expression turned to fury, which was fearsome. He reached for a jug of water next to the bed, lifted it, and tilted it over his head. The water poured out, soaking his hair and beard. He put down the jug and combed his wet hair and beard with his fingers.

The heavy copper spear was leaning against the wall by the bed. Umm-Sal picked it up, almost lost her balance due to its weight, and handed it to the general, who propped it as a walking stick with his left hand and stood up. The bottom of the spear was forged into a bulge, and he pounded it on the floor three times.

"Lead the way, boy," he said. "Time to inspect our army."

Sall left the room, walked down the hallway, and stepped out of the front door to the landing, followed by the general, Umm-Sall, and An. The women in the front garden parted to make way while the four of them walked out to the street, which was filled with women up and down the city.

General Mazabi spoke in a booming voice. "Brave women of Edom. We face a mighty enemy. It's true. But Egypt's army is less mighty than it had been before your beloved men fought it fiercely by the Sea of Reeds." He pounded the copper spear on the ground. "The boy Sall, standing here beside me, has travelled to Damascus and studied with the ancient Elixirist the secret art of creating elixirs. One of them is the Male Elixir, which will endow you with the strength, courage, and aggressive spirit that turns men into victorious soldiers. If you drink it, I will train you to be Edom's greatest soldiers since the days of King Esau the First."

They cheered.

The general pounded the spear again. "Tell us what you need to make this Male Elixir."

Waiting for complete silence to return, Sall asked, "Who among you are butchers' wives or shepherds' wives?"

The words were passed up and down the street, and several women made their way through the crowd.

He beckoned them closer and spoke in a low voice. "I need the male parts of sixty goats, thirty sheep, twelve donkeys, and six oxen."

They looked at each other, and one asked, "Which male parts?"

"All of it – the shaft and testes. But slaughter the animals first, so they don't suffer, and wash the area well before you slice it off. Make sure to pack the organs separately by the animals they came from."

"What should we do with the rest of the animals?"

"The city is full of hungry people," he said. "Roast the meat and let them eat."

The wives of butchers and shepherds hurried away.

Sall thought hard what else he could do to prepare for the arrival of the enemy army. What did he know about the Egyptians that could be used in a confrontation with them? A sentence came to his mind, told in the dwarf's voice: "Stay quiet as you learn the facts, causes, and effects, but when you devise a solution, fear not to open your mouth."

He had an idea.

"Who among you are wives of snake catchers?"

The profession wasn't a common one, and it took longer for word to travel further up and down the street, all the way to the gates.

From behind, Umm-Sall asked quietly, "Why snake catchers?"

Sall quoted Li'uli: "When facing a powerful enemy, always do the unexpected."

"That's good advice," General Mazabi said. "Relevant to our situation. But still, snake catchers?"

"During my journey, I noticed that Egyptians keep cats to protect them from snakes, which terrify them. It's a weakness. We should take advantage of it."

"How?"

"I'm not sure yet, but I have a feeling there are a lot more snakes in the desert around our city than there are cats in Egypt's army."

An laughed quietly behind him, and he turn to her, smiling.

His mother took the girl's arm and led her back to the house. Sall inhaled deeply, taking in the scent of lavender before it faded.

The general chuckled. "Who would have imagined? A foolish boy goes on a perilous journey and comes back a clever hero."

Three women appeared. One limped badly. The second had a lame hand that was as black as a burnt piece of wood. The third was very young and pretty, except for a deep scar on her cheek.

"Thank you for stepping forward," Sall said. "Can you tell me about your husbands' work?"

The limping one said, "Our home is near Punon, in the south. When snakes entered houses, or crawled under rags, people called my husband, and he took care of it."

The woman with the blackened hand said, "It's the same in Tamar, where we live. The snakes are out in the spring and summer, and in the winter, they congregate in pits, sometimes hundreds of them. One time, a horse stepped into a pit, got bitten, and bucked so high that the rider flew fifty steps away."

The pretty one touched the scar on her cheek. "We live here, in Bozra. My husband was paid handsomely. He taught our son, too, but now both of them are dead."

"Mine too," the limping one said. "I helped my husband when he was busy, but after a snake struck me, I was too afraid to help him anymore."

"We're all afraid," Sall said. "Courage is overcoming fear, not the lack of fear."

General Mazabi grunted, nodding in approval.

"I have some questions," Sall said. "How did your husbands remove the snakes from houses or pits?"

The pretty one answered. "With two long sticks, tied in the middle, like a vice, to grab the snake near the head and put it in a jar, or a sack."

The woman with the blackened hand said, "Sometimes my husband would tie a burning torch to a long stick and use it to make the snake crawl out of a tight spot or a pit."

Sall was surprised. "I didn't know snakes are afraid of fire."

"They like warm places, but crawl away from actual fire."

"Can you teach others how to catch snakes?"

The three of them looked at each other and nodded.

"Here's what I'd like you to do," Sall said. "Each one of you will gather ten girls, help them make the two-stick tool for catching snakes, and teach them how to do it without getting hurt. Go out to the desert, turn over rocks, uncover pits, ruffle bushes, and collect as many snakes as you can find. Put them in clay jars, and make sure they don't escape until we decide how to use them against the Egyptians."

The general pounded his spear and spoke to the crowd. "We need thirty girls who are too small to fight, but brave enough to help with a dangerous task."

While dozens of girls came to the front, he continued, "We also need clay jars and sheets of cloth. Bring them to the gates after we are done here."

The snake-catchers' wives took the girls with them and left.

General Mazabi pounded his spear again, keeping the women's attention. "I know many of you came from the city of Punon or from smaller towns, villages, and farms, which you have left unattended. From tonight until victory, every woman in Bozra shall open her house to shelter and feed our guests." He pointed at the rising sun. "Before it gets too hot, let's have our first drill. Go down to the fairgrounds outside the gates. Line up in rows of one hundred each, facing away from the sun. Each row will be a company of soldiers. The first in each line will be in command of the other ninety-nine members of the company. Her deputy will be the one at the end of the line. Go!"

43

Firing up the large oven in his father's workshop, Sall had Cook and Laundress bring in the wedding pot. It was a giant clay pot for cooking goat stew in quantities sufficient to feed hundreds of guests at a time — at weddings and, as often, at funerals.

Once the pot was in the oven and filled with water, he told Cook, Laundress, and Horseman to build five firepits in the garden and borrow wedding pots from five other wealthy families.

By the time the pot in the workshop began to boil, the butchers' wives started delivering the animals' male parts he had asked for, sorted in separate bowls for sheep, goats, donkeys, and oxen. They had removed the organs with extra skin, which they tied up in order to neatly seal the sac of each animal. The organs were bloody and odorous, but he felt no nausea or disgust as he added the male organs to the pot, counting ten of goats, five of sheep, two of donkeys, and one of oxen. He added three fists of salt, one fist of crushed peppers, and one fist of mint leaves.

In the garden, the five firepits burned under wedding pots filled with water. He added the same quantities of male organs and spices to each additional pot and asked the three servants to take turns stirring the six pots with wooden sticks.

Inside the house, Umm-Sall was waiting for him with a meal of boiled pigeon eggs, flat bread with cheese, and fresh cucumbers. He gobbled up the food and downed a full goblet of wine.

His mother chuckled.

"There isn't much time," he said. "We're creating an army out of thin air."

"Thousands of women aren't thin air."

"They are, as far as soldiering goes."

Bozra came into the kitchen, wagging her tail, and he gave her a piece of bread, which she chewed on while looking at him. He pecked her snout.

"You're wearing a ring," his mother said. "What is it?"

"The Ring of the Fisherman. It's a gift from a man who taught me how to fish." Sall tried to sound indifferent when he asked, "Where is An?"

"Fixing old robes with a needle and a thread."

"What? You put the high-priest's daughter to work?"

"Boredom to the mind is like drought to the land."

"Needlework isn't boring?"

"To you, it is. For a girl, it's a way to earn her meals and make herself useful."

"But she's our guest."

"Did the king put her under my supervision, or yours?"

He laughed.

"Nothing funny about it."

He picked up the wine jug and drank directly from it.

"Use the goblet, son."

"I'm not a child anymore." He took another swig.

His mother shook her head. "Where are your manners?"

"Maybe I lost them when my mother deceived me with lofty words about a young man's need to follow his heart's journey and a packed donkey. Or maybe I lost them in Jericho, together with my freedom. Or in Beth She'an, with the skin of my back. Or in Damascus, with my last breath under icy water."

She covered her mouth, and her eyes teared up.

Her sadness made him remorseful. Shifting his chair closer, he leaned over and rested his head on her shoulder. "My journey felt as long as three lifetimes."

She caressed his short hair. "I know, son. I know."

He recalled Li'uli saying, "You only learn to appreciate home after traveling far away from it." Now, feeling his mother's warmth, smelling her familiar scent, he understood what Li'uli had meant and hoped that the brown prince had made it safely back to his home in Kush, if only for the sake of Li'iliti and the children. Would he ever meet them again? Sall wasn't sure if he wanted to, or what he would say if they did meet in the distant future. Li'uli had caused much of his suffering and pain in Canaan, but had also shared his wisdom and knowledge, which Sall would not have acquired had they not met.

His mother's hand went from his hair to his chin and made him look up at her. "You and An, it's not possible, ever."

"Why?" He got up, stepping back. "I love her."

Umm-Sall groaned. "You haven't even seen her face yet."

"I did see it."

"When you were children, which you don't even remember."

"I do. It came to me in a dream."

"Another dream?"

"More like a memory of how her hair sparkled in the sun, how her eyes drew me with an irresistible force, how her lips tasted – better than honey. My heart has always belonged to her, I just wasn't aware of it until the Gods reunited us at her father's house."

"Over his smelly feet?"

"When she entered, there was only the scent of lavender. Believe me mother, An and I, we belong together. There's no one else for either of us. Our hearts are bound forever."

"Marriage is a matter for the mind, not for the heart. A match is arranged by parents through careful consideration of the families' compatibility, negotiations of the dowry and bride price, and determination of the couple's future living arrangements. Choosing a wife is the prerogative of your father, and in his absence, mine."

"I don't care who makes the choosing, as long as I marry An."

"No one can choose what isn't available. She's betrothed to her eldest brother, Qoztobarus, the next high priest."

"I know. The king told me."

Her eyes widened. "The king?"

"He offered me a reward for saving his life, and when I asked for An's hand in marriage, he told me she's betrothed and that I should choose another."

His mother stood up, her face pale. "Then why did he send her here?"

"Maybe he changed his mind. He's the king, after all, and he can tell the high priest—"

"Don't be naïve." Umm-Sall clasped her hands together. "The king sent her here because he assumed we're all going to die or become slaves. If your fantasy army of women somehow prevails and we survive, you must let her go. Otherwise, Qoztobarus will kill her and you."

The idea of letting An go seemed cruel and unjust to him. "Is that what happened to you and General Mazabi?"

His words made his mother groan. She sat down, grasping the edge of the table.

Cook appeared at the door. "The water is overflowing," she said. "What should we do?"

Sall hurried outside. The giant pots had grown heaps of foam over the simmering water, and some of it was running down the sides of the pots to the flames, making hissing sounds. He used a long plank to shift some of the wood out of the fires, except the one in the oven at the workshop, where the fire wasn't strong enough to cause the same problem.

"Keep stirring the pots," he told the servants. "I need them to simmer all day."

Back in the house, he went straight to his room and lay down on the cot next to the empty bed. He thought of An, sitting in one of the other rooms, bent over a torn robe or a ripped bedsheet, her eyes focused on the needle between her finger and thumb, her thick braid of golden hair falling on her back, or curled over her shoulder and down her chest, the red bow at the end resting by her narrow hips. He inhaled deeply, searching for the gentle fragrance of lavender.

44

It was twilight in the window when Bozra woke him up by licking his face. He laughed, pushing her away, and she barked, jumping on top of him. He wrestled her off, and she ran around the room, bumped into him, and rolled over on her back for a belly scratch, which he provided.

A distant chanting was getting louder, and he realized it was a chorus of many women shouting in unison, "Ee-Dom! Ee-Dom! Ee-Dom!"

Sall got up and went to the front door. Bozra turned into the kitchen.

It was warm outside, and the air smelled of stew, but it didn't make his mouth water, even though he usually liked stew.

The women entered the front garden in an orderly column, marching to the pace of their chanting, "Ee-Dom!" The column broke into rows, but the women kept marching in place while row after row filled up the garden. He could hear many more voices on the street outside and all the way downhill.

The sun was setting, and the fires under the five wedding pots were down to embers. He took a stick and stirred one of the pots. About a third of the water had evaporated, leaving a thick, lumpy stew. The three servants, as well as An and his mother, came out of the house. The girl's eyes glistened through the slit in the scarf, and he could tell she was smiling. He smiled back and asked the five of them to fetch wooden planks, wash them clean, and use them to mash up the cooked animal male organs into the stew until there was no piece larger than an olive.

The rows of women kept chanting, "Ee-Dom! Ee-Dom! Ee-Dom!"

General Mazabi entered the garden from the street and walked around the women to the front. His appearance had completely changed. He had washed, trimmed his hair and beard, and put on leather armor over his chest and back, as well as thighs and shins. A sword was strapped to his hips. On his head was the customary copper helmet with the red horse-hair comb. He used the copper spear as a walking stick, and over his left shoulder he carried a large bow and a quiver with arrows. Reaching the front, he nodded at Sall, turned to the women, and pounded the heavy spear three times.

They stopped chanting.

"Well done, soldiers," General Mazabi said. "Today you learned how to follow your company commander in an orderly march. For good soldiers, the commander is as mighty as all the Gods put together. If your commander falls, her deputy will step in. Remember that blind obedience is the key to victory. Understood?"

They yelled in unison, "Yes!"

"Excellent. I'm proud to be your general." As they resumed cheering, he leaned close to Sall and said, "They're useless. Like sheep. Is your elixir ready?"

"Yes, but you must understand that its powers are limited to—"

"Don't tell me about limitations."

Sall glanced at his mother, An, and the servants, who each stood by a wedding pot, pressing the wooden planks into the stew to mash up the solids.

General Mazabi pounded his spear to silence the cheers. "Take a good look at me. That's how a soldier of Edom looks when serving our nation. Each of you must look like this when the Egyptians approach Bozra. Search your homes, take your homes apart if necessary, and use everything you can to equip yourselves properly. Find a neighbor or a friend who knows how to bend tree branches into bows and hone sticks and logs into arrows and spears. Take apart leather saddles and make them into armor pieces and helmets. Do not go to sleep tonight until each and every one of you is ready with leather armor and helmet, as well as a spear, a bow, and thirty arrows in a quiver. If your man has left a sword, make a sheath and a belt for it. If not, strap on a knife, a plowshare, a sickle, a pick, or a pruning hook."

The women repeated his instructions down the rows, out to the street, and down the hill.

"Help each other," the general said. "Give away your time and share your belongings, because soldiers sacrifice everything for their brothers. Always remember this rule: Fingers are to a fist as soldiers are to an army – easy to break when separate, rock hard when clenched together."

With help from Horseman, Laundress, and three other women, Sall carried the sixth wedding pot from the workshop to the garden. Horseman used a plank to mash down the lumps in that pot, too.

"Soldiers," General Mazabi said. "The Male Elixir is ready for you. Those who fear drinking it, go home and resign to your fate. Edom only wants her brave women to take a stand."

The commanders shouted orders, rearranging their charges in six queues, one in front of each wedding pot. Sall sent Cook into the house to bring twelve cups, two for himself, and two for his mother, An, and each of the three servants. They held one cup in each hand and dipped them in the thick stew, which was no longer lumpy, but quite odorous.

The first two women in each line took the cups and drank the Male Elixir, followed by the others. Some gagged or retched, but none actually vomited it out. Sall counted in his head the women who drank the elixir from his wedding pot. Every time he reached one hundred, he put a pebble on the ground between his sandals. The process took a long time, well into the night, until all the women in the garden and on the street reached the front of the lines. The queues got shorter until the last few women drank their dose of elixir and left the garden. By that time, the pots were almost empty.

General Mazabi, who had sat in a chair by the house, got up with a groan. "How many?"

There were nine pebbles between Sall's sandals, and he had counted another eighty-seven since placing the last pebble. "My pot served nine hundred and eighty-seven women."

"Almost a thousand," Umm-Sall said. "Multiply that by six pots. You've turned nearly six thousand women into men."

The general grunted. "I hope you didn't poison them all, son."

"I trust him." An filled one of her cups with stew from the bottom of her pot. "Wish me luck."

"No!" Sall reached with his hand to stop her. "Don't!"

"Why not?" His mother tossed her two cups into the pot. "Is it unsafe?"

Sall felt his face flush. "It's perfectly safe."

"What's the problem, then?"

"I don't want her to drink it."

"You didn't mind the other six-thousand women drinking it."

General Mazabi chuckled. "He doesn't want her to change, not even temporarily."

"Please." An looked at Sall. "I want to defend Edom."

He lowered his hand.

She brought the cup under her face scarf to her lips and drank it up.

45

Before General Mazabi went to bed, he asked Sall to walk around the city, check on the preparations, and make sure the gates were locked up and guarded. An volunteered to accompany him, and Umm-Sall didn't object when they left together.

Out on the street, they saw women walking downhill with goods in their hands. Sall and An walked uphill. At the top, a crowd stood in front of the king's palace, where servants kept bringing out leather hides, saddles, cushions, coats, and boots, as well as colorful wall carpets and floor rags. Under burning torches, a group of women tore up the carpets and pulled out long threads. One of them explained to Sall that the gold and silk threads would make good strings for bows, and the red threads would knit nicely into rooster combs.

Walking back downhill, they saw fires burning and intense activity in every house. In one front yard, a line of women waited to have their hair cut short by the butchers' wives.

At the bottom of the hill, the army barracks were dark and quiet, but at the king's stables, a few women were arranging tall jars. Sall recognized one of them by her limp. She was the snake-catcher's wife from Punon. With her were several of the girls who had volunteered to catch snakes in the desert. He counted seventeen jars already fitted with tight cloth seals over the top.

The snake-catcher's wife recognized him, limped over, and bowed. Embarrassed, he glanced at An, who curtsied, which made him laugh.

"I see you got many snakes already," he said. "It's good, but haste could be dangerous."

She bowed again.

"No need to bow to me. Any problems so far?"

"One girl has been hurt."

"Snake bite?"

"A scorpion. She'll be fine."

"That's good."

"I have a question," An said. "How many snakes in each jar?"

"Twenty-five, most of them venomous."

An took a step back.

"They won't come out," the snake-catcher's wife said. "Snakes are lazy. They only move if they're hungry, or afraid."

"Afraid?" An glanced at the ground around her feet. "What could possibly scare snakes?"

"Predators and fire."

"What predators?"

"Cats, hawks, and us."

They heard banging from the main gates. Two girls ran over to open them. A group came in carrying sealed jars and burning torches. Some of the girls were smaller than the jars, requiring three of them to lug each jar. As they passed by to enter the horse stables, Sall heard hissing from inside the jars.

The girls put the jars down and went back out of the city into the night.

"So many snakes," An said. "I didn't know the desert was crawling with them."

"Especially near a city," the woman said. "They like rats and mice, which we attract with our garbage. My husband's best customers were those who didn't keep a clean house. The valley also draws them, because many rodents come to eat the fallen fruit in the orchards."

"Aren't they hungry now, locked up in the jars?"

"Snakes eat when they can, always ready to follow the scent of prey."

Sall thanked the woman and walked with An to the gates. In the room under the guard tower, he found the two old guards sleeping. He woke one of them and told him to take turns with the other one and raise the alarm if they saw anything suspicious.

He led An up a set of stairs to the top of the guard tower, which was about three times the height of the wall. The wooden platform was enclosed with a waist-high railing. A soft breeze brought over the chill of the night from the desert. In the distance, the dark hills were outlined against the moonlit sky. The great valley was dark, not a single fire burning in any of the farms, only a few dots of light where the girls where searching for snakes with lit torches.

"It's beautiful," An said.

He nodded and thought of the Egyptian army, camping for the night somewhere along the north-south trade route between Bozra and the Sea of Reeds. He imagined hundreds of fires in straight rows of a well-ordered military camp, divided by units according to their specialties – foot soldiers, archers, charioteers – a huge war machine, ready to crush any opponent. The enormity of the danger dawned on him, and he exhaled, resting his elbows on the railing.

"Don't worry," An said. "You'll figure out a way to win."

He looked at her, surprised that she had guessed his thoughts.

She took off the head scarf.

His heart raced, beating against his chest.

Her white teeth glistened in the dark.

He smiled back.

She pulled her long braid over her shoulder to the front, the bow at the end, resting by her right hip. Her face was pale in the moonlight, oval shaped with high cheekbones, a sculpted jaw, and full lips.

Feeling weak, Sall held on to the railing. "You're very pretty."

"Thank you."

"It's true. Really."

"Maybe that's why your mother doesn't like me."

Her words startled him, but she didn't speak in anger, and he didn't want to respond with dishonest denials. "She's worried for me, that's all."

"She said I caused you to risk your life on a foolish quest."

"That's ludicrous. She encouraged me to go."

"Why?"

"She said that a young man must follow his heart's journey, or his heart will go without him, lost forever."

"That's wise."

"In truth, she and my father had heard about the Egyptian threat from General Mazabi and wanted me to leave rather than join the army."

"Your mother loves you more than anything else in the world," An said. "I always wondered what kind of a mother mine would have been, had she lived to raise me."

A memory came to him of Timna crying in fear, blood pouring out between her legs, while Ishkadim wept like a child. "Did your mother die giving birth to you?"

"Shortly afterwards."

"I'm sorry. Sometimes it's impossible to stop the bleeding."

Again, there was hesitation before An spoke. "It wasn't the delivery. I was a few weeks old when she was given to Qoz."

"What?" Sall thought he misunderstood. "Your father sacrificed her to Qoz?"

"There was a drought. People were starving."

"But he's the high priest. He didn't have to sacrifice his own wife. He could have selected any girl."

"I asked him this question when I was old enough to know what happened. He told me that Qoz wanted my mother, because she was the most beautiful girl in Edom. And a few days later, Qoz brought rain, and the wells filled up again."

"Do you believe him?"

Gazing up at the moon, An sighed. "I'm already without a mother. If I allow myself to hate my father, what will become of me?"

Intoxicated by the scent of lavender, Sall struggled to resist an overwhelming urge to take her in his arms and comfort her.

"I hope your mother changes her mind about me." An sat down, her back to the railing, her arms hugging her knees. "Now, tell me about your quest. Everything."

Sitting beside her, Sall took a deep breath and told her what had happened from the moment she had glared at him with contempt at her father's house. He described his dream about the Elixirist at the fountain by the great tower, his decision to seek the golden elixir and change into a strong, tall, and darkly mysterious man – she laughed and squeezed his forearm with her hand, making his heart skip – and described the journey with the Moabite merchant, who tried to rob him of his dog. Next came the handless dream-reader's vague advice, Bozra's wild run, the resulting slavery in Jericho, the healing business that gave him freedom, and the journey with the brown prince of Kush. An covered her mouth, hearing about the torture he had suffered after the burning of Beth She'an, the kindness of the Cainite women during his weeks of recovery, and the abuse he received for appearing to be a leper. She nodded slowly when he described the magical healing at Job's Bath, the fishing success that launched Naum's Village, the revelations on the road to Damascus, the glory of the flowering jasmines, the kindness of the hunchback, the discovery of the Sailor of Barada, and the drowning he survived through the transparent window. She shook her head in awe as he spoke of the night of sleep-learning as he absorbed all the secret knowledge of the Elixirist, whom he then carried to Damascus and buried in a glorious field of blooming jasmines, before riding back to Edom and finding General Mazabi and King Esau on the southern slopes by the valley.

An took his hand and held it up to the moonlight. "This ring, you didn't tell me about it."

Her firm grip excited him, and he had to clear his throat before speaking. "The Ring of the Fisherman. It's been in Naum's family for many generations, waiting to be given to a true fisherman."

"You were his hero." Not letting go of Sall's hand, An gazed into his eyes. "And now you're mine."

Sall leaned over until his lips connected with hers.

46

Sleep eluded Sall as he lay on the cot in the dark, listening to General Mazabi's snoring. At first, he was too excited about winning An's heart, and then, as he replayed the magical moment in his head, he started to worry that her bold expression of affection might have been triggered by the Male Elixir, which imbibed women with men's confidence, courage, and aggression. He dismissed those worries, reasoning that, while the Male Elixir might have lowered some of the traditional inhibitions on how forward a girl might be, the feelings An had shown for him were genuine and sincere. Then, he worried that their time together might be short. Not only was Bozra about to face the mightiest army in the world, but even if they survived Egypt's onslaught, An might be forced to marry her brother. That prospect made him hot with fury, and he tossed off the blanket.

"What's wrong, boy?" General Mazabi sat up in the bed. "Bad dreams?"

Startled, Sall sat up, too. "I couldn't sleep. How are you feeling?"

"Thirsty."

The boy went to the kitchen and brought back a jug of water.

After drinking, the general relieved himself noisily in a bucket at the corner of the room. He returned to bed and lay down with a groan.

A cold breeze came in from the window, and Sall helped him pull up the blanket.

Back on the cot, he was still angry, but no longer hot.

"What's keeping you up, boy?"

"Egypt."

General Mazabi chuckled.

"Aren't you worried?"

"There's a time to worry, and there's a time to sleep."

While he understood the words, Sall didn't understand how the man in the bed, having already lost his right arm and his whole army, could sleep while holding in his remaining hand the fate of six thousand women and their children.

"When I was about your age," the general said, "we fought a series of bloody battles with the Hebrew tribe of Judah. My father commanded the king's army. The night before a decisive battle at Tamar, we lay in his tent, and I couldn't sleep. My father told me to chase away all worries from my mind by imagining being at home and playing with my favorite dog. I tried, but it was hard, because I knew the fierceness of the men of Judah. My father said something I never forgot." General Mazabi cleared his throat. "Commanding your own mind is harder than commanding an army."

Pondering the words, Sall tried to focus his mind on memories of playing with Bozra, but his thoughts kept returning to the view from the guard tower and the prospect of the great valley filling up with Egyptian foot soldiers, archers, and charioteers, advancing menacingly towards the city.

"Try harder," General Mazabi said.

"How long did it take you?"

He chuckled. "A little while, but it worked, and I slept well the rest of the night."

"How did the battle go?"

"The Hebrews killed my father."

Shocked, Sall sat up. "How?"

"A stone from a sling." General Mazabi held his hand up, making a fist. "This big, from a great distance, smack in the forehead. I heard the thud, like a hammer on wood, and saw him fall off his horse. My heart broke, but I remembered what he'd told me the previous night. I commanded my mind to focus on winning the battle. The soldiers looked up to me, and I took over his command to lead the charge."

"What happened?"

"We won. Then, I allowed my mind to think of my father and take revenge for his death. I burned Tamar to the ground and cut off their heads – all the Hebrew men, women, and boys."

The image in Sall's mind was horrific, but he noticed the general hadn't mentioned girls. "What about the girls?"

"The girls were kept alive for my soldiers, but I was forced to set them free." General Mazabi laughed out loud. "You won't believe it, but a Hebrew woman bent my will to hers."

"Didn't you kill all the women?"

"She was a healer. It's foolish to kill a healer, because you'd be killing all the people the healer could help in the future, which might include someone you love."

"I thought Hebrews don't have healers."

"Why?"

"The Hebrew priest in Jericho said the only healer is their invisible God, Yahweh."

"Different tribes, different priests, different rules." He sneered. "I heard that, during their exodus from Egyptian slavery, some of their priests started to worship a golden calf."

Sall imagined a Hebrew woman healer with the face of Timna, standing up to an enraged young General Mazabi, his armor and weapons covered in the blood of her people.

"How did she force your hand?"

"When I ordered her to treat my wounded men, she refused unless I sent all the Hebrew girls to a nearby city of Judah. No matter what I threatened to do to her, she persisted while my injured men were dying. I had no choice. Only after I sent the Hebrew girls off to Arad and took an oath not to chase them later, did she start treating my men."

Back under the blanket, turning on his side, Sall thought of his father and hoped that the Egyptians also didn't kill healers. He imagined seeing his father again, assisting him in the workshop, listening to his stories of distant travel and exotic nations.

47

There was sunlight in the window when Sall woke up. The bed was empty. He went to the kitchen and found General Mazabi with Umm-Sall, sitting at the opposite ends of the long table, sipping hot mint water from clay cups. An stood with Cook at the counter, kneading dough. She was wearing a headscarf over her hair, but her face was uncovered, and a wayward lock of her golden hair swept down across her cheek as she looked up at him and smiled. He smiled back, and his hip collided with the corner of the table, causing the dishes to rattle. His mother grabbed the pitcher, which was about to tip over.

General Mazabi chuckled. "Sit down, boy, before you cause real damage."

Umm-Sall poured a third cup. "You look pale."

He shrugged, slurping the hot drink, drawing warmth from it, and struggling not to look at An.

"Big day ahead." General Mazabi got up, reached with his hand between Cook and An, and grabbed a lump of dough, which he dropped on the table next to the pitcher. "Make us a map, boy."

"This represents Bozra." Sall put the pitcher at the end of the table where his mother sat. "And these will be the hills on the four sides of the valley." He tore off pieces of dough and formed them into lumps, which he arranged along the four edges of the rectangular tabletop. Cook handed him a cup of flour, which he sprinkled in a straight line from the pitcher through the middle of the table all the way to the lumps of dough at the opposite end, under the general's beard.

"We're here." Sall pointed at the pitcher. "Bozra covers the hills on the west end of the valley. And these are the hills on the south and the north." He pointed at the lumps of dough along the two long sides of the table. "The line of flour is the road that runs from Bozra, through the center of the long valley, to the hills in the east, climbs over them, and connects to the main north-south trade route, which would be behind where the general sits." Back near the pitcher, he spread some white flour on the table and drew a rectangle with his finger. "That's the open fairgrounds between the gates of the city and the beginning of fields and orchards in the valley."

An came over and spread breadcrumbs over the table on both sides of the road crossing the valley. "The fields and orchards in the valley."

Sall looked at her, taking in every detail of her face.

Umm-Sall cleared her throat.

"Right here." General Mazabi pointed at the top of the hills in the east. "At the opposite end of the valley from Bozra, that's where the Egyptian Jabari will stop for a view of his new conquest."

Sall gestured at the middle of the table. "He'll see our new army in the valley and know that we're not his new conquest."

"We don't want to show our hand too early." General Mazabi tapped on the pitcher. "We'll keep the women inside the walls, out of sight, until we find out if the king's negotiations were successful."

"How?"

"He'll be riding at the head of the Egyptian army with their Jabari."

"And if he wasn't successful?"

"They'll have his head on a pole."

"He deserves it," Umm-Sall said. "But they won't kill him, because they need a king to rule Edom and collect taxes for them."

"You're probably right," General Mazabi said. "We'll have to find a way to tell the king in confidence about the army of women. He'll decide what to do."

Sall was startled. "He's already surrendered."

"He's our king."

Umm-Sall sneered. "Our brave king."

General Mazabi knuckled the table. "Brave or not, he's the king, and I'm a soldier, duty bound to follow his commands. It's as simple as that."

"It's not simple," Umm-Sall said. "What if the king orders us to rest our throats under Pharaoh's axes and place our girls under his soldiers?"

"Then we obey. It's our fate."

"Fate is a choice, except for cowards and slaves."

The general's face reddened, but he didn't answer.

"The king chose to be a coward, and you?" Umm-Sall pointed at him from the opposite end of the table. "You chose to be the king's slave, which is why you saved him while leaving for dead your lifelong loyal friend, my husband."

"There is no king," An said. "By abandoning us, he abandoned the throne. We need a new king."

"His son," Sall said. "Will you obey him?"

The general grunted, and Umm-Sall spun a finger by the side of her head in reference to the rumors of the royal heir's madness.

"I have an idea." An molded a piece of dough into a ring, large enough to be a crown. "What about Sall?"

They looked at her, and Umm-Sall picked up her cup and sipped from it.

An looked at General Mazabi. "You agreed to lead the army he created. Why not follow his commands?"

Umm-Sall put down her cup. "What nonsense are you talking, girl?"

"Hold on," General Mazabi said. "Let her explain."

"I'm no king," Sall said.

"You're more than a king," An said. "You're the Elixirist."

"That doesn't give me the authority to issue orders."

"Yes, it does." An looked at him with an expression so explicitly loving that he wanted to kiss her again. "All the women of Edom are already following your orders. Didn't you see it last night? Your Male Elixir has given them the courage to cut their hair, make weapons and armor, and even collect snakes at night in the desert, just because you told them to do it. They think of you as their leader, we all do. And making decisions comes easy to you because you're smart and wise."

There was a long silence until Sall spoke.

"Me, the leader of Edom?"

"Yes," An said. "For a few days, until the Egyptians leave and the king is back on his throne, you should command Edom."

Umm-Sall, her lips curled in a slight smile, looked at General Mazabi. "Will you obey my son?"

The general turned to Sall. "Are you ready to lead?"

"How? I don't know anything about being a leader."

"Let me quote you," General Mazabi said. "Imitate until you mutate."

"How can I imitate a leader if I don't know any leaders."

"You know me. A king is more powerful than a general, that's all.

Use your imagination."

From the corner of his eye, Sall saw An nodding. He stood up, rested both hands on the table, and stared at the mockup of the valley. He tried to imagine what the king would think at this point, but couldn't come up with anything.

"General," he said. "What are my options?"

"That's exactly what the king would ask," General Mazabi said.

Umm-Sall, An, and Cook laughed.

Sall smiled. "And the answer?"

"You have three options," the general said. "Do nothing, prepare to defend, or prepare to attack."

"Do nothing isn't acceptable to me. It's down to defending or attacking. How do I choose?"

"It depends on the facts. Also, the two options aren't mutually exclusive. You could decide to prepare for defense, but also be ready to switch to attack if circumstances change."

Sall pointed to the road coming over the eastern hills from the trade route. "How do you know they'll be taking the road and not trying to sneak up on us over the hills from the south or west?"

"Moving an army through the rocky desert hills would be difficult and slow. Why would they go to such trouble? They've destroyed our army and obtained our king's surrender. In their mind, we're already defeated and defenseless." General Mazabi traced the road with his finger. "My guess is that they'll travel in a column on the road, chariots first, followed by the archers and foot soldiers, as well as the servants and supplies. When they arrive at Bozra, the Jabari will move into the king's palace, his officers will occupy the nicest houses, and the army will set up camp in the lower part of the city and outside the gates in the fairgrounds. They'll take a well-deserved rest while eating the fruit off our orchards, drinking the water out of our wells, and taking pleasure in our girls and young women."

"What if your guess is wrong?" Sall glanced at An, drawing confidence from her gleaming eyes. "What then?"

"A disaster," Umm-Sall said. "As what happened at the Sea of Reeds."

General Mazabi's face hardened, and he glanced at his right shoulder, where a new bandage wasn't yet stained with blood. "You're right. I could be wrong. They might be more cautious than expected, or suspicious of our king's intentions. In that case, they'll send spies to verify that there is no second Edomite army waiting for them."

"Spies?" Sall took a deep breath, suddenly nervous. "When?"

"They could be here already."

"Here?"

"On the hills." General Mazabi pointed at the lumps of dough. "Hiding and watching Bozra for any sign of military activity."

Sall knew what he had to do. "My first order is for you to summon whatever old men we have in the city, including the guards left in the king's palace, and divide them into two groups. One group will patrol the hills along the north part of the valley." He traced the hills with his finger. "The second along the south. They'll meet on the eastern hills by the road from the trade route, then retrace their steps, back and forth, searching for Egyptian spies. Keep the patrols going at all times."

"It shall be done." General Mazabi got up and left the kitchen.

An smiled at Sall, and his mother smiled, too, which pleased him. Cook made him a plate of bread, cheese, and sliced pomegranates. He ate while they watched.

The general returned. "The spy patrols will be leaving shortly."

Resisting the urge to thank him, Sall nodded and took a bite of the bread, as he imagined the king would do.

"What's next?" General Mazabi remained standing. "I need to know whether to train the army of women for attack or defense. Defending a walled city requires preparations that are very different from doing battle in the open."

Sall washed down the food with wine. "What do you recommend?"

"Defense. No question about it. We stay behind the walls and try to survive a siege. Any attempt to do battle with the Egyptians would end in annihilation." General Mazabi gestured at the mockup of the valley on the table. "If we march our army of women out of the gates and confront the enemy, we won't even get close enough to fight them. Their archers will release thousands of arrows in several waves, felling many of our troops. Then the chariots will storm our lines, the drivers running over us while the charioteers cut us down with long swords and impale us with lances. Finally, the foot soldiers will spring forward and slaughter anyone still alive."

"How long can we survive a siege?"

"Hard to tell. They'll hurl fireballs, ram our gates, and try to climb over our walls. I'll train the women to operate in formations, to fight with swords or whatever blades they have, and to shoot arrows from their bows. We'll hold up for a while, but we should humbly remember that many fortified cities have fallen before the mighty army of Pharaoh."

"How will the training be different for an attack?"

"The same basic elements, with the added drills of lining up to shoot arrows and fighting in the open, face-to-face combat, and tenacity under fears of likely defeat and certain death."

Sall drank the rest of his wine. "Train them both for defense and attack."

"Fine," General Mazabi said. "But you'll need to make a choice soon."

Staring at the table, Sall recalled the road north of Jericho, where the hostile soldiers of Manasseh had suspected him of being from the Judah tribe, and Li'uli and Li'iliti had burst out laughing, giving him the idea of launching into an imitation of their guttural throat-clearing, tongue-clucking language while gesticulating with his hands and contorting his face in a manner of someone making a passionate argument. The outrageous show had done the trick, and that night, Li'uli shared with him the principle that had saved them: "When facing a powerful enemy, always do the unexpected."

"You gave me three options," Sall said. "Do nothing, prepare to attack, or prepare to defend. Will the Egyptians expect us to choose one of these options?"

"Of course," General Mazabi said

"Then we need a fourth option, something they won't expect."

An picked up the pitcher and poured more mint water into their cup. "All those snakes," she said. "That's unexpected."

48

Sall and General Mazabi rode down the hill through the city, which was buzzing with activity, and out to the valley. The fields of wheat had been harvested, and those of barley had been plowed and seeded. The fig, pomegranate, and lemon orchards were heavy with fruit. The sun beat down with growing ferocity.

"Look." General Mazabi pointed. "There's one of the spy patrols."

Sall saw the small group on the hills bordering the south side of the valley.

"You'll have to choose soon, boy." The general gulped from his waterskin. "Do battle here and die, or crouch behind the walls and hope the Egyptians get tired and resume their campaign north to Canaan."

"How likely are they to give up?"

"Not likely. Pharaoh's army is immense in size, brilliant in structure, and meticulous in training. They'll break through our defenses in days and destroy us." General Mazabi drank some more. "It would take an army of equal might, organization, and skill to have a chance at defeating Egypt's army, but such an army doesn't exist. They are powerful without equal in the world."

At first, the words had a chilling effect on Sall, and a tremor rose from his feet to his chest. He sensed General Mazabi's eyes on him, seeking signs of weakness. Pressing his feet down on the stirrups, he shook the reins and swiveled his horse, urging it towards a fig tree. He leaned over and plucked a fig off a branch. It wasn't as sweet or as juicy as it would be in a few weeks, but it was edible, and he chewed deliberately to give himself more time to think. The general's words replayed in his mind. "It would take an army of equal might, organization, and skill to have a chance at defeating Egypt's army, but such an army doesn't exist." Ominous as they were, the words intrigued Sall with an underlying possibility, which he couldn't yet articulate. He repeated the words in his mind, searching for that possibility, for a thread to pull out until a different option unraveled.

General Mazabi joined him, tried a fig, and spat it out. "Let's go, boy."

Keeping his horse still, Sall pulled another fig off the tree and took a bite.

Stopping his horse a short distance away, the general spoke over his shoulder. "I said, let's go."

"I'm eating," Sall said. "You wait."

"Listen, boy—"

"Don't ever call me "boy" again." Sall turned slowly and locked eyes with General Mazabi. "You told me to imitate a leader, so you better imitate an obedient soldier."

They stared at each other for a long moment. In the end, the general grinned and made a shallow bow. He didn't fool Sall with this concession, which wouldn't last long unless he solved their quandary. However, forcing the mighty general of Edom to capitulate by quoting his own words against him made Sall feel closer to the elusive thread of a solution. Like a boy facing a general, the army of women would never equal Egypt's army, which even Edom's great army of men had failed to do. The choice facing him depended on answering a question that could not be answered: What army could defeat an army that had no equal in the world? And with that thought, Sall managed to grab the thread of an odd possibility: Could Egypt's army defeat itself?

General Mazabi shook his horse's reins. "If it pleases my leader, I'd like go back and drill our imitation army in the art of battle, for time is running short."

"One more thing."

The general looked at him, his eyes creased.

"Make sure that, from a distance, our army of women has solid military appearance."

"Appearance?"

"For an Egyptian general, standing in the middle of the valley and looking towards the city." Sall pointed at the fairgrounds outside the gates, where the women of Edom lined up in sixty rows of one hundred each. "He should see a solid army of men, ready to defend Bozra with proper weapons and orderly marching."

"I can do that." Starting towards the city, General Mazabi asked, "Are you coming."

"Not yet. You go ahead."

Sall watched him ride down the valley and inspect the women, row after row. A few women ran back into the city, presumably to correct deficiencies in their military attire.

Satisfied, Sall rode to the southern hills, urged his horse up the steep rocky slope, and intercepted the patrol. There were six men, all much older than him. He recognized one as a guard from the king's palace. They had stopped by a pile of charred wood.

"It's cold," the guard said. "Could be a day old, or a month."

Dismounting, Sall looked around and found a few pieces of pomegranate skins, which were dry but not crumbling as they would be after more than a couple of days. Nearby, he saw mice nibbling a half-eaten plum.

The guard pointed at a mound of feces. "More than one person."

Looking closely, Sall noticed that a few of the pieces were smaller than his pinky in both length and size. "At least one of them was a young child."

"Child spies," the guard said. "The Egyptians aren't afraid of us, for sure."

His friends laughed, but Sall didn't. He remembered Li'uli explaining how no one would suspect a man travelling with his wife and children. Had an Egyptian spy camped here with his wife and children to avoid suspicion in case they were spotted? What could he have seen from here? The previous afternoon, General Mazabi had marched the women in the fairgrounds. Was that enough to deduce the plan to form an army of women? He shaded his eyes and gazed towards the distant city, where a cloud of dust from the women's feet blurred everything.

"This spot is too far," the guard said. "Real spies would have snuck closer to the city. I think this camp was used by a family of nomads, coming to steal from the orchards, or snatch a goat from a farm."

Concluding that the guard was probably right, Sall told the group to keep going and remain vigilant. He rode back down to the valley and galloped across it to the other side and up the northern slopes. It took him some time to find the second patrol. They had found no sign of spies. Satisfied, he rode back to the city. It was early afternoon by now, and the heat was oppressive, but as he approached from the east, the women were chanting at the top of their voices, "Ee-Dom! Ee-Dom!

Ee-Dom!" while marching in straight rows at a fast pace set by the commanders, who shouted orders from the head of each row. He circled around to avoid the swirling dust, drummed up by thousands of feet, and stopped by the gates, where General Mazabi had taken position, watching the drills.

A lazy breeze came from the north, gradually carrying the cloud of dust towards the southern hills.

Sall was impressed with what he saw. The women had fabricated armor pieces for their chests, backs, and thighs, as well as leather helmets that brandished red rooster combs. At close examination, the armor pieces were imperfectly shaped, the leather helmets ill-fitting, and the rooster combs not altogether red or proportionally formed. From a distance, though, all those variations faded away, and the women looked like proper soldiers with long bows and arrow-quivers slung over their shoulders, and swords or axes strapped to their hips. Their short hair exposed their ears in the manner of men, and some had fashioned beards or stubble that could not be distinguished from the real thing.

Sheltering his eyes from the sun, Sall gazed at the women's faces, as fierce and determined as the faces of hardened men gearing up for battle. He marveled at the sight and wondered how much of it was the effect of his Male Elixir. The dwarf had said, "An elixir works by eliciting the recipient's confidence in its powers." Looking at the women of Edom, it was clear that they believed in his elixir.

While all the marching women stared forward, a single face halfway down one of the advancing rows glanced in his direction. It happened too quickly for Sall to see her features, but it left him unsettled, not because the face was less fierce or determined than any of the other countless faces under the helmets, but because the face was dark and somehow familiar. The row passed before him and General Mazabi, the women now facing away, looking identical with the red rooster combs on their helmets, the back-armor plates, and the weapons. Another row marched by, and another, but the face kept bothering him. Sall shut his eyes, concentrating on the fleeting glimpse of that dark face, which appeared behind his closed eyelids, gradually coming into focus, until he finally deciphered her features.

Li'iliti!

49

As soon as the recognition hit him, Sall rejected it as a trick of his imagination. How could Li'uli's wife, the mother of three young children, including a nursing baby, be here in Bozra, marching with the women of Edom?

General Mazabi was looking at him. "Are you feeling ill?"

"No."

"You look ill."

"There was a face." He gestured vaguely at the marching women. "It looked familiar."

"Why not? Many of these women have visited your father's workshop."

"This one reminded me of someone from my journey."

"Who?"

"The wife of a brown prince from Kush. We travelled together for a while."

"What was he doing in Canaan?"

"His ancestor was the last Egyptian governor of the region many generations ago. His father sent him to Canaan ahead of the Egyptian invasion to prepare—"

"To spy?"

Sall nodded.

General Mazabi kicked his horse's ribs, making it spring forward. He raced around the vast army, reached the front, and blocked the way. The front row halted, and the commanders yelled orders for each succeeding row to stop. The women continued to march in place, their feet raising copious dust that immersed them while they chanted, "Ee-Dom! Ee-Dom! Ee-Dom!"

Sall's first instinct was to ride over to the approximate area where he had seen the face, but there were many rows, an overwhelming ruckus, and thick dust that would smother him. Thinking quickly, he decided that an innocent woman would remain in place, whereas a guilty one would try to flee. Where would she go? Not towards the gates, where she had seen him mounted on his horse, or to the front, where General Mazabi was waiting, or towards the open valley, where she'd be spotted long before reaching the first orchard. There was only one direction open to her – the rear, where the breeze carried the dust towards the hills along the southern edge of the valley.

With a violent shake of the reins, Sall turned his horse to the right and galloped along the wall of the city, skirting the rear rows of women and the drifting cloud of dust. He didn't stop or change direction, but continued even after passing the last row, and only slowed down where the dust thinned out. Turning left, he came to a stop while covering his nose and mouth against the dust. He peered into the haze, which blocked his view yet allowed the sound of the chanting to come through. It occurred to him that he carried no sword or spear, but being mounted on a horse gave him enough of an advantage to stop a woman on foot, even if he had to trample her before she ran into the hills. Exposure of the true nature of Edom's second army would ensure Bozra's doom including, Sall realized with a pang of dread, his beloved An.

He waited for what seemed like a long time. The chanting subsided gradually and General Mazabi's booming voice sounded in the distance. Sall waited while his doubts grew with each moment. He began to rebuke his fanciful imagination, which had caused this unnecessary disruption in General Mazabi's training of all those brave women.

Sall turned his horse back towards the wall of the city when he noticed the outline of a single figure materialize out of the haze. She was running fast, but seeing him, turned around and ran back into the dust cloud. His doubts were gone. It was Li'iliti's face, dark-brown and beautiful, though not as tranquil and as graceful as he remembered it, but tight with mortal fear.

Recovering from the initial shock, Sall slapped the horse behind the saddle, causing it to leap forward and charge after her. The dust blinded him, but he kept slapping the horse, which neighed in protest. A moment later, he glimpsed her back just before the horse rammed her. She screamed while falling, and if not for Sall yanking the reins, would have been crushed under the hooves.

By the time he turned the horse around, she was back on her feet, sprinting away in her original direction. The horse took off after her, and they emerged from the dust, approaching the foothills. She pulled off her bow and quiver of arrows, hurling them back towards the horse, which almost tripped while dodging the weapons. With her helmet, however, she managed to hit the horse on the nose, and Sall had to jump off the saddle before being crushed by the falling horse.

He got up and ran. Without the traditional women's long robe, Li'iliti was swift, staying ahead of him. The hills were getting closer, and he wasn't catching up to her. Without stopping, he grabbed a stone and threw it, hitting the back of her leg. She cried, stumbled, but kept going as fast as before. He swept up another stone, a bit larger, and hurled it with all the force he could muster. It hit her between the shoulder blades, bringing her down. She began to get up, when he caught up and dropped on top of her, pinning her to the ground.

Both of them panting hard, a moment passed before she rolled sideways, toppling him over. They got up at the same time, but rather than running, Li'iliti drew a short sword and aimed it at his throat.

The sharp point of the blade prickled his skin. Death was only a quick stab away. He froze.

She smiled, panting. "It's really you, boy."

"This is my home," he said.

"Then stay here and let me go back to mine."

"You know our secrets."

"The army of women? It's a joke, not a secret."

"Li'uli gave me the idea," Sall said. "When facing a powerful enemy, always do the unexpected."

"By tomorrow night, these women will be like ants under Pharaoh's boot."

He was startled to hear that the Egyptians were so close, but kept his voice even. "Perhaps a few ants will survive. I can't let you go."

"Would you rather die? My husband will be upset a second time, having already thought his gift to the Cainite girl had failed to save you."

"If you kill me, your children will die, too."

Her eyes widened, which confirmed his guess about the origin of the tiny feces on the northern hills. If she only knew that he was lying to her because of another of Li'uli's lessons: "When lying is necessary, it's not a lie."

"My children?"

"They were captured on the hills near the trade route."

"And my husband?"

"He must have slipped away, leaving the children behind. I've resisted our priests' push to sacrifice them to Qoz." Sall glanced at the top of the city, where the temple was located. "It's a painful death, being dropped from high up onto the sharp spikes of Qoz's three-pronged thunderbolt."

Her arm shook, but she recovered, keeping the sword at his neck. "Are your people savage enough to murder a suckling baby?"

Sall almost answered in the affirmative, but something in her tone gave him pause. Had she left the baby with a wet nurse back at the main army camp before venturing with Li'uli and the older children on this spying mission?

"We only have your two little girls," he said.

Her eyes bore into him, clearly trying to figure out if he was telling the truth.

The drumming of horse hooves sounded through the haze.

She glanced at the nearby hills, hesitating.

"Think of your girls," he said. "The information you have is of little value. We're not going to fight Egypt again. This army of women is only for show, to help us negotiate better terms of surrender. Then, you'll be free, together with your children."

General Mazabi appeared, galloping towards them, his copper spear held high in his left hand, aimed at Li'iliti. Sall raised his hand to stop him, and she dropped her sword to the ground.

While the general watched, his spear ready, Sall made Li'iliti turn around. He tied her wrists behind her back with strings from her leg armor pieces, which he removed. Her belt fit around his waist, and he sheathed her sword against his own hip.

The army stood still in straight rows, the dust settling down, while General Mazabi and Sall rode back to the gates. The handbound prisoner walked in front of the horses, looking down at the ground. A few women hissed, then others joined, and soon all six-thousand women produced an earsplitting hiss. Sall was awed, not by their hissing, but by the fact that none of them moved out of formation, which demonstrated a level of discipline he didn't expect.

At the gates, Sall summoned the guards. "Lock her up in a room at the king's palace," he said. "Bind her legs, too, and let no one speak to her, not a single word."

Li'iliti looked up at him. "What about my daughters?"

General Mazabi looked to him, but said nothing.

"They'll remain unharmed," Sall said. "Unless you try to escape, or chat up one of your guards for information. They don't know anything, by the way."

"Don't forget that my husband saved your life."

Rage flooded him as he remembered the brown prince serving him hot milk, the stench of smoke waking him up later that night, the panicked donkey dragging him around the tree, tearing the skin off his back, and the fiery sun, searing his oiled face and chest until it sizzled.

Li'iliti must have seen the rage on his face. "We had to leave you behind and hurry for our next task."

"Sailing the Barada River?"

Her eyes widened.

He took a deep breath, struggling to imitate a man who wasn't boiling with fury. "What rendezvous did you arrange with Li'uli?"

She didn't answer.

"I'd like to give him the children before our eager priests prevail with the sacrifice."

General Mazabi grunted, nodding.

Still, she remained silent.

"Never mind." Sall gestured at the guards. "Take her."

"Wait." She wriggled out of the guards' grip. "How do I know that you won't arrest my husband, as well?"

Pressing his hand to his chest, Sall said, "I swear by Qoz not to arrest Li'uli or prevent him from leaving."

"Tomorrow at sunrise." Li'iliti tilted her head in the direction they'd come from. "Five thousand steps into the hills to the south."

50

"I'm impressed again," General Mazabi said. "Not only did you keep the spy from slitting your throat, but you manipulated her trust. Tomorrow, we'll catch her husband, question him, and burn them together."

Sall watched Li'iliti being led up the street. "I intend to keep my word."

"You promised not to arrest him. I didn't make such a promise."

"I'm your leader. My promise binds you, as well."

"Letting a spy go is dangerous."

"Not if we feed him false information."

General Mazabi laughed. "Do tell."

"It's an opportunity," Sall said. "Li'iliti revealed that the Egyptian army will arrive here by tomorrow evening. The Jabari would not lead his troops into a valley surrounded by hills unless he feels confident that we're defenseless and frightened. We can use the husband to bolster the impression that our city is on its knees."

"How?"

"I still need to figure that out." Sall dismounted. "Come with me."

He climbed the stairs to the guard tower. At the top, facing the railing where An had kissed him the previous night, Sall caught a whiff of lavender and had to shake his head to clear his mind. Behind him General Mazabi landed his copper spear on each step and was breathing heavily when he reached the top.

They stood together at the railing and looked out over the sea of helmets with red rooster combs in the open fairgrounds. Further up, where the fields and orchards began, the road bisected the valley all the way to the distant hills in the east. Sall tried to estimate the length of the valley. He decided on ten thousand steps beyond the first thousand steps of the fairgrounds.

"I want half the valley cleared up," he said.

General Mazabi turned to him. "Cleared up?"

"All the fields and orchards from the fairgrounds towards the eastern hills, about five thousand steps."

"Trimmed?"

"Cut off at ground level. Every wheat stalk and every tree must come down, leaving clear land between the fairgrounds and the middle of the valley."

"Why, in Qoz's name?"

"Tomorrow, when the Jabari looks down from the crest of the eastern hills, he should see half the valley ready for his great army to set up camp in comfort."

"Are you mad? These orchards are as old as Edom. They took generations of nurturing to mature."

"Would you rather Edom itself be cut down?" Sall didn't wait for a response. "Once the trees are cut, all the fruit should be picked off and set aside. The trees themselves should be dragged by donkeys or oxen and arranged as a barricade along the edge of the fairgrounds from one side of the valley to the other."

Shielding his eyes with his left hand, General Mazabi looked out at the valley. "You want to create a barrier preventing the Egyptian chariots from reaching the city, right?"

"That's one reason," Sall said.

"It won't stop their arrows or their foot soldiers."

"They won't shoot arrows or storm us with soldiers, because there will be no fighting."

General Mazabi nodded. "You chose defense, then?"

"Don't worry about my choices," Sall said.

"No? What else should I worry about?"

"Obeying my orders."

The general grunted, but didn't argue.

"About the fruit from the trees, I want it thrown around the cleared area where the Egyptians will camp."

"If you want to feed them, we should pack the fruit in sacks and keep it off the ground. Otherwise, it will attract rodents from all around the desert."

"That's my intention."

"You want to feed mice?"

"Mice, rats, gerbils, rabbits, bushy-tail jirds, and whatever else we can attract, as long as it's small. Any desert goats, jackals, or antelopes should be chased away."

General Mazabi looked at him. "What's this all about?"

"You'll find out," Sall said. "Make sure the women spread the fruit all over the cleared area, tossing it about on the ground throughout the whole width of the valley between the hills on the north and the hills on the south, and from the new barrier of fallen trees at the edge of the fairgrounds as far east as the end of the cleared area."

Pounding his copper spear on the wooden floor of the guard tower three times, the general summoned all the company commanders, who left their positions at the end of the rows and ran over, lining outside the wall below the guard tower.

Even at such close proximity, the sixty female commanders looked like men.

General Mazabi delivered Sall's orders without making any changes and divided the responsibilities between three groups for cutting the trees, dragging them to form the barrier along the edge of the fairgrounds, and spreading the fruit around the cleared area. The wheat and barley fields will be trampled in the process, pressing the stalks into the ground.

Sall took the stairs down and walked over to the king's horse stables, where the scar-faced snake-catcher's wife reported that the search teams had managed to find several viper dens, allowing them to gather over a thousand snakes, which were now packed into more than forty tall jars under the shade of a pavilion.

"Your efforts are admirable," he said. "Will the snakes survive in the jars until tomorrow night?"

"They can go without food and water for weeks if necessary, but this is their hunting season." She glanced at the jars. "They're not happy being trapped like this."

"What will they do when released?"

"Bite us."

He shuddered. "Assuming we get away quickly, what else will they do?"

"Slither away to find prey."

Satisfied, Sall got back on his horse and started up the hill along the main street, back and forth across the width of Bozra. At the same time, hundreds of women were rushing to their homes to pick up saws and axes for the massive tree-cutting work he had ordered, as well as animals to pull the trees over to form a barrier. The women bowed to him, some with a smile, others with awe, but none with any resentment or distrust.

Passing by the front yard where the previous night he'd seen a line of women waiting to have their hair cut short by the butchers' wives, he saw a pile of hair as tall as his horse and three times as wide.

He found his mother in the workshop, caring for a boy of about eight with a scraped elbow. Laundress was washing linen in a large bucket, and horseman was sweeping the front garden. Sall smelled food cooking in the kitchen.

The injured boy thanked Umm-Sall and ran off. She sat down with a sigh of relief. It was odd for Sall to see her sitting in his father's chair, but these were odd times in many ways. She looked at the sword on his hip. He wanted to show it to An, as well, and felt his heart beating faster as he imagined kissing her again.

"She's not here," his mother said.

He blushed. "Where did she go?"

"Where all the other girls have gone. To serve in your army."

"What?" He raised his voice. "Why did you let her go?"

"She asked nicely, and the needlework was finished."

"Not funny." He turned to the door. "She doesn't belong in the army. I'm going to bring her back."

"Don't you want her to become your wife – against her father's wishes and her brother's betrothal?"

"Yes."

"Then it's in your interest to nurture her independent spirit, not her obedience."

Sall hesitated, thinking of all the women of Edom, who now looked like men.

"Don't worry, son." Umm-Sall smiled. "I told her not to cut her hair."

51

Cook gave Sall a bowl of goat stew with bread and cheese. His belly full, he went to his room, which was kept cool by the curtains on the window, and lay down on the cot. He wanted to rest briefly before riding down to the valley to look for An, but fell into a deep sleep and dreamt that they were walking together along a riverbank, where her scent of lavender mixed with the aroma of blooming jasmines, and birds chirped in droopy willow trees.

He woke up when General Mazabi came into the room, propped his heavy copper spear in the corner, and sat on the bed, gulping water from a jug. Sall got up. Through the window curtain he could tell that the evening sun was low over the horizon, even though he felt as if he'd shut his eyes only a moment ago.

Umm-Sall appeared with two bowls, one with hot water and the other with a potion. She had several rags under her arm. General Mazabi groaned, loosened the strings holding his back and chest armor pieces, and turned slightly to allow her access to his right shoulder. She undid the belt holding the bandage, removed it, and washed the wound several times until the water in the bowl was red. After applying a layer of potion, she bandaged his shoulder and helped him lie down on his left side. He didn't complain of the pain, but his face was pale and sweaty. Umm-Sall pulled off his boots and covered his feet with a blanket.

Before leaving the house, Sall stopped at the kitchen for a piece of honey cake and a glass of goat milk. In the front yard, a line of women in armor waited to have their various injuries treated by Umm-Sall. He checked quickly to make sure none of them needed urgent help, relieved that all had suffered only minor cuts and scrapes.

Horseman had brushed the horse and replaced the old saddle with one made for the king's guards. It had sturdier stirrups for standing, a sheath for a spear, and red strings that dangled from the bottom edge of the saddle over the horse's ribs on both sides.

The day's heat had lingered, and as he rode down through the city, the afternoon sun cast long shadows across the road. He stopped at the butcher's house and stared at the massive pile of women's hair, remembering the humiliation he felt in Jericho when Timna shaved his head on his first day as a slave. He imagined how upsetting it must be for a woman to lose her hair, which was not only central to her beauty and essential for her feeling of attractiveness, but was the primary symbol of her femininity. He racked his brain for a valuable use for all this hair, a way to make their sacrifice useful beyond the necessary change in appearance.

The butcher's wife came out of the house. She noticed him and bowed. He bowed back excessively, making her giggle as she picked up a fistful of hair from the mound and headed back to the house.

"Wait," he said. "What will you do with the hair?"

"My commander told me to cook a meal for our company. My stove went cold, and it's much easier to start a fire with hair."

He clapped, excited. "That's it – start a fire! Thank you!"

The butcher's wife smiled and blushed at the same time, obviously confused.

"After you feed the women in your company tonight, have them help you move this mound of hair down to the horse stables and cover it with linen in case of wind. We'll need it tomorrow night."

Along the way downhill, he saw only children and young girls. At the gates, he dismounted and took the stairs up to the guard tower.

The valley had changed dramatically. Orchards that had stood for generations gave way to barren dirt. Swirls of dust accompanied groups of women and animals as they dragged fallen trees to the growing barrier along the far edge of the fairgrounds. The barrenness of the land shocked Sall. He had expected the work to proceed at the usual sluggish pace of farming, hampered by physical hardship and the beating sun. The women of Edom, however, had implemented his orders with dizzying swiftness, obliterating the verdant orchards and bringing total desolation to half the valley. He wondered how much of their destructive eagerness was fueled by his Male Elixir and felt a moment of paralyzing anxiety, remembering that his imitation of the ancient Elixirist was only that – imitation. If the plan his mind had conjured under this contrived identity ended up failing to save Edom from

Egyptian subjugation, the steps he had taken to implement it would add hunger and poverty to the suffering of his people.

Further up the valley, Sall noticed a woman on a horse, crisscrossing between various points of activity, gesturing at things that needed to be done. He recognized the horse as General Mazabi's giant steed, and as the rider swung around to head in a different direction, Sall's eyes caught the glistening gold of her long braid.

"Almighty Qoz!"

He was amazed, not only that she could ride a horse, which most women didn't know how, but that she had managed to charm the hardened general into handing her his prized mount, in effect delegating his command to her.

He skipped down the stairs, three at a time, and jumped into the saddle. Galloping out through the gates onto the road, he crossed the vacant fairgrounds, passed through the narrow gap in the new barrier of freshly downed trees, and raced up the cleared area of the valley. He had to slow down and veer off the road to avoid teams of women dragging more trees to the barrier with the help of donkeys or oxen.

An noticed him and waved. She was speaking with a group of women, who were busy cutting the branches off the trunk of a felled pomegranate tree. The fruit had been removed and tossed around the area, and the branches were broken into short sections.

He slowed down to a moderate pace to avoid stirring up dust and stopped near her. "Nice horse, General."

She burst out laughing.

The women around them stopped working and looked up. By their expressions he could tell that they had also fallen for her.

The two of them turned their horses towards the east so that the descending sun wasn't in their eyes. He noticed more branches arranged in neat piles, ready to serve as campfires for cooking food and keeping warm at night. There were many dozens of piles, spread out at about fifty steps from each other, dotting the cleared area that now encompassed the whole central bulk of the valley. He immediately grasped the way this addition advanced his goal of making the Egyptians feel welcomed to camp here.

"Setting up firewood is an excellent idea," he said. "The more they think we're bowing to them, the more relaxed they'll be."

"I also wanted to divert their attention from all the fruit we've discarded."

That was a benefit he hadn't thought of, and the ground was, indeed, littered with plums, pomegranates, figs, and other fruit.

An stopped her horse. "We're almost done. What should we do next?"

He turned his horse in a full circle, looking at the land being prepared for the enemy and the thousands of women who continued to set up firewood, drag fallen trees, and fortify the barrier in a straight line across the valley.

"Sunset is coming," he said. "They've earned a good-night's rest."

"And tomorrow morning?"

"Continue to improve their fighting skills before our enemy arrives."

"My father will arrive, too." Her hands gripped the saddle horn. "I can't go back to the way it was. I'd rather die than—"

"No." Sall reached over and rested his hand on top of hers. "You won't have to go back. We will be married with Qoz's blessing, raise a bunch of happy children, and stay together until we're too old to chew our food."

His words brought back An's smile.

52

With the first hint of dawn, Sall left the house on foot, walked downhill, and stepped out through the gates. He turned right and walked briskly along the whitewashed defense wall of Bozra towards the foothills. A long gray robe with a hood kept him warm. He avoided the crevices and climbed the first slope, heading straight up, counting his steps. Four-hundred and seventy-one steps later, he reached the top and glanced back. The city was dotted with early cooking fires, but the valley was shrouded in a bleak twilight. He resumed walking and counting, down one hill, and up another. One-thousand, three-hundred and ten steps later, a brightening dawn on his left told him he was still heading south. Another descent and ascent, more silent counting, and he knew by the radiance that sunrise was imminent. He hastened his steps.

At the peak of another hillcrest, barely three-hundred steps short of five thousand, the top edge of a new sun sparkled over the eastern hilltops. He walked down the slope and stopped by a boulder. Taking shallow breathes, he listened for an approaching horse.

Nothing.

Gradually, the day grew brighter, and the barren landscape around him came into view, but there was no sign of Li'uli.

A pair of strong arms locked around him from the back.

Sall froze in terror.

Someone kissed the back of his hooded head and uttered a staccato of guttural throat-clearing and tongue-clucking. In an instant, Sall's fright melted into laughter as he broke out of Li'uli's embrace and turned to face him.

Now, Li'uli was the one to be frozen in shock.

"Don't panic," Sall said. "I'm neither your wife, nor a ghost."

The two servants appeared, wearing only their loincloths despite the chill, followed by two horses. Sall greeted the two, but they didn't respond.

Finding his tongue, the brown prince uttered another sentence in the language of Kush. The two servants sprung forward, grabbed Sall, and pulled off his sword and his robe, leaving him, like them, in a loincloth.

Circling Sall, Li'uli touched his back, his chest, and his arms, mumbling, "Impossible. Impossible. Impossible."

"Possible or not, it's really me." Sall picked up his robe, put it on, and strapped on the sword. "A cold morning, isn't it?"

"I heard they dragged you behind a donkey until your back was flayed, then oiled you until the rest of you burned in the sun."

"I survived."

"But it was only—"

"Three moons ago."

"Where are the scars?"

"The hand of Qoz guided me to a place of magical healing."

"Where?"

"Do you really think I would trust you with such knowledge?" Sall adjusted the robe, which was a tad too big. "It's my hope the Gods of Egypt and Kush will one day punish you for what you did to me."

"Don't say that, my friend." Li'uli smiled, his teeth white against his dark skin. "My affection for you has always been deep and sincere. When I learned what the barbaric Hebrews had done to you, it hurt me more than it hurt you."

"A liar lies even when he tells the truth." Sall held up his hand to stop him from responding. "It's all in the past. Right now, I'm here to make a simple trade."

Li'uli looked around. "My wife?"

"I spotted her spying." Sall pointed at the sword he had taken from Li'iliti. "You recognize this?"

"Where is she?"

"Awaiting impalement on Qoz's three-pronged thunderbolt, but our general agreed to wait while I try to trade her for my father."

"Your father?"

"The healer of Bozra. He was with our army at the Sea of Reeds."

"The Jabari would never agree to release a healer."

"You're a resourceful man. Trickery, bribery, thievery, I don't have a preference, as long as you bring my father to this place when the sun is at its peak today, free and unharmed."

His sharp tone alarmed the two servants, who stepped forward, hands gripping the hilts of their short swords.

Li'uli signaled them to stay back. "What's the point of releasing your father? King Esau the Eighteenth has surrendered all of Edom to us."

"If things are all settled up, why did you send Li'iliti to spy on us?"

"Because I'm from a family that has learned the hard way not to leave anything to chance."

"You did take a chance on your wife's life, didn't you?"

"She's very capable, and I didn't expect anyone to recognize her. Why did you come home so quickly?"

Quoting the prince's own words, Sall said, "You only learn to appreciate home after traveling far away from it."

"It doesn't matter. By this evening, our army will arrive at Bozra for a well-deserved rest, the Jabari will move into your king's palace, and all your women and children will become slaves of Egypt, as will you and your father."

This was the moment Sall had prepared for, and he knew his words had to come out with the right balance of gravity and concern, neither agitated, nor indifferent.

"I wish it were that simple." Sall took a deep breath. "Our army's demise wasn't enough for the angry Gods, who brought sickness upon Bozra. Many of our women have taken ill. Perhaps the crushing grief for their fathers, brothers, husbands, and sons has weakened their will to live and ability to fight the sickness. They're dying by the hundreds in the city. We need my father, our healer. Only he can stop the red fever—"

"The red fever!" Li'uli grabbed the front of Sall's robe. "What about Li'iliti?"

It was hard not to smile with relief, seeing how easily the prince of Kush had accepted the false story as true. It was a clever ruse that explained the need for Sall's father to return to the city while also creating an urgency to get Li'iliti out, besides supplying a formidable reason for the Egyptians not to enter Bozra.

"I asked you—"

"Li'iliti isn't sick," Sall said. "Not yet, anyway."

"Get her out of the city. Right now."

"Our general will only release her after my father is back within Bozra's walls."

"No. We'll exchange them right here at midday. Bring her, or no trade."

"How can I trust you?" Sall thought of what Li'uli had said about necessary lies. "I trusted you once and suffered unspeakably for it – a worthwhile lesson for a naïve boy."

"What lesson?"

"That the same man could be simultaneously sincere and deceitful, kind and cruel, clever and a fool."

Li'uli's handsome face contorted with indignant fury. "You've changed, boy. Be careful how far you go, or the insults you hurl at me could soon apply to you, as well."

The warning was valid, Sall knew, because he was already acting with deceit and cruelty, though he wasn't the one being fooled here. Now, however, was not the time for self-reflection, not in front of this shrewd opponent who had easily manipulated two Hebrew judges and caused their fortified city to burn down. His secret – that he had dismantled Li'uli's planned flooding of Damascus – empowered Sall to keep his gaze firm and his lips pursed, making it clear that he would not negotiate.

"Fine." Li'uli's voice was bitter. "If your father is alive, I'll bring him to this place at midday. Tell your general to stand ready to release Li'iliti."

Sall looked down at the hand grabbing his robe until it let go. He nodded at the two servants and headed back up the slope. Behind him, there was silence, and with every step he expected to be stopped by a shout, a rock, or worse. Reaching the crest of the hill, Sall looked back. They were gone.

Before continuing on, he collected a few stones and piled them one on top of the other as a marker. From there on, he stopped at every hillcrest to erect another marker while making sure he could see the previous one so that he would be able to retrace his steps later.

53

The morning sun cleared the horizon as Sall returned to the city. He stopped at the king's horse stables. The scar-faced snake-catcher's wife reported having collected almost two thousand snakes. Rows of tall storage jugs, sealed with cloth, filled a whole pavilion. One of the girls had been bitten, but it turned out to be a dry strike.

"She was lucky," the woman said. "The snake had just used its venom on a prey."

"What kind of prey?"

She made a fist. "About this size, by the look of the bulge on the snake."

"Let's not push our luck. Tell everyone to stop looking for snakes. We have enough."

"What are we going to do with them?"

"All in good time." He pointed at the great mound of hair, which had been brought down as he had ordered. "Have the girls spread the hair along the bottom of the barrier on the side facing the fairgrounds and the city."

She had a perplexed look, but then her eyes lit up. "You plan to burn all those trees?"

"Yes, tonight."

"Don't we need the barrier to protect us from the Egyptian chariots?"

"That's a reasonable assumption." Sall smiled. "A wise man once told me that, when facing a powerful enemy, always do the unexpected."

Picking at her scar, the woman glanced back at the tidy rows of jars full of venomous snakes. It took a long moment before she guessed what his intentions could be and cried, "Qoz have mercy!"

Sall put a finger to his lips.

Sunrise brought a flood of women down the main street and out the gates. They wore armor and helmets with the red rooster combs, carried makeshift bows and quivers of crude arrows over their shoulders, and had bladed weapons of various types strapped against their hips. Unlike yesterday, when they had marched in succeeding rows facing forward, this morning each company lined up behind its commander in parallel columns. Sall kept glancing up the street, waiting for General Mazabi. Instead, it was An who appeared, mounted on the general's horse, with Sall's horse towed behind. She was clad in full leather armor, a short sword sheathed against her thigh. Her golden braid was rolled up and stuffed inside the helmet. Under the front rim of the helmet, her eyes were focused on him. It occurred to Sall that everything about her implied the royal bearing of a queen, and he took a deep bow.

An laughed, dismounted, and curtsied.

A sack was tied to his horse's saddle. He untied it and looked inside, finding a full set of leather armor pieces, boots, and a helmet. He noticed a few short hairs from Bozra's fur and could smell her on the sack, which gave him a good feeling. He went into the guards' room, took off the robe, and put on the armor and helmet. An helped him tie the straps that connected the chest and back armor pieces over his shoulders. He adjusted the belt with Li'iliti's sheathed sword.

An fixed the helmet strap under his chin. "You look strong and handsome – a brave young leader."

"An imitation of a leader. Where is the real one?"

Her face grew serious. "General Mazabi fell off the bed, and the wound opened. There was blood all over the floor. Your mother stopped the bleeding and dressed the wound again, but he's too weak to stand up."

Sall felt a pang of fear.

"Your mother asked me to remind you of something." An took a deep breath. "Fate is always a choice, except for cowards and slaves."

The words helped him recover. "It's up to us, then."

They mounted the horses and rode together through the gates to face the massive army of women, who broke into rhythmic chanting, "Ee-Dom! Ee-Dom! Ee-Dom!"

The horses stopped in front of the middle columns, standing close enough together that An's knee touched Sall's. He looked at her. She looked back at him and smiled.

Before them, six thousand women chanted in unison, "Ee-Dom! Ee-Dom! Ee-Dom!"

An reached over, took his hand, and held up their joined hands.

The gesture charged up the women, who shouted at the top of their voices, "Ee-Dom! Ee-Dom! Ee-Dom!"

He raised his other hand, fingers spread open, waited until they quieted down, and quoted General Mazabi. "Fingers are to a fist as soldiers are to an army – easy to break when separate, rock hard when clenched together."

As he clenched his fist, so did the women in all sixty columns of one hundred each, creating a vast field of clenched fists. They cheered, producing a deafening roar, as if a giant lion was asserting its territorial rights against a contender. It made the air reverberate, and Sall's heart swelled in his chest. Not that his fear was gone, or that the nagging voice in his head ceased warning him of the terrible risks he was taking with thousands of lives, but he steeled himself with the certainty that their lives under Egypt would be worse than death.

When the women quieted down, he pointed to the eastern hills at the far end of the valley. "This afternoon, the army of Egypt will descend from the hills behind its chief, the Jabari. It's a mighty army of many chariots, archers, and foot soldiers, all well trained and experienced, but still, they're only men of flesh and blood, as prone to bleeding and dying as your beloved men, who bled and died by the Sea of Reeds."

Sall paused to allow them a moment of grief.

"And so," he continued, "when you see our enemy's might, you must remember this rule." He quoted the old dwarf. "Courage is overcoming fear, not the lack of fear."

Murmurs of agreement raced up and down the columns.

"From now until midday, your commanders will continue to drill you in all the fighting skills that General Mazabi has taught you – marching, shooting arrows, and wielding blades if you have them – all the while obeying orders without question or hesitation. When the sun begins its descent, you will enter the city and stay low behind the walls, completely silent and out of sight. I will give my orders to your commanders, and then, go out to meet the Jabari and invite Egypt's army to set up their tents in the valley, cook their evening meals, and lie down to sleep."

He paused, his eyes moving across the sixty columns of soldiers, who stood in attention and looked back at him, their leader. He inhaled deeply and spoke as loud as he could.

"It will be a night like no other night in all the nights of our nation's life. By tomorrow's sunrise, fate will come into light, either in our favor, or theirs. Until then, no matter what happens, remember that you are soldiers who, like fingers, must stick together to form true strength. With Qoz on our side, we shall win freedom for Edom!"

The women raised their fists and roared, "Ee-Dom! Ee-Dom! Ee-Dom!"

54

An remained with the army, supervising their drills from her saddle. Sall lingered near the gates to watch. He noticed how the commanders glanced at her with reverence as they marched by with their soldiers. For them, she represented both the king's general and Qoz's high priest, a combination of the two powers that controlled their lives. For a moment, he was flushed with dread, realizing how presumptuous it was for a healer's son to think himself worthy of such a girl, but An smiled and waved, reminding him that he had captured her heart in the manner prescribed by the old dwarf: "To change a girl's heart, you must show her that your own heart has changed."

He waved back and rode into the city.

At home, Sall took off the armor, boots, helmet, and sword, and put his robe and sandals back on. He checked on General Mazabi, who was asleep, and ate a bowl of barley stew with bread and cheese, as well as a ripe pomegranate, which Cook sliced for him into bite-sized pieces the way she had done since his childhood.

Umm-Sall was in the workshop, taking care of injured and ill customers. He beckoned her outside and told her about his sunrise meeting with Li'uli and the trade they made. Her face went pale, and her eyes were drawn to the pantheon of effigies under the jujube tree.

"Don't worry," Sall said. "I know he cannot be trusted, but he won't hurt me, because I told him that my failure to return safely would cause his wife's death."

"A prince can easily find a new wife."

"He loves her. I've seen it while traveling with them."

His mother contemplated for a long moment. "If he won't take you as prisoner, what else can he do?"

"I tried to imitate the way he thinks. For a devious man, it's hard to trust others. If he doesn't trust me, he'll bring father to the meeting, but refuse to release him until I go back and bring his wife to make a simultaneous exchange."

"She knows too much. You can't hand her over."

"We'll negotiate. He'll see reason, I'm sure of it."

Umm-Sall took his hands in hers. "Don't go to meet him."

"I have to."

"Why? When the king returns to the city tonight, we'll ask him to plead with the Egyptians for your father's release."

"The king has made himself a slave. How can he plead for father's freedom?" Gently, Sall pulled his hands from her grip. "Don't worry, mother. I can match Li'uli, trick for trick."

"Didn't you tell me that he's the cleverest man alive?"

"Alive, yes, but there was a man even more clever than him who, before he died in Damascus, had taught me everything he knew."

As Sall mounted the horse, his mother knelt by the effigies and murmured prayers to the Gods of Edom. He hoped they would oblige her, because the confidence he projected was skin-deep.

He rode uphill and dismounted by the king's palace. A guard took him down a narrow hallway near the servants' entrance. At the end of the hallway, two guards stood by a closed door. It had a porthole, in which Li'iliti's face appeared.

"I want to see my children."

"You will," he said. "Very soon. In the meantime, have you been provided with enough food and water?"

"Don't pretend to care. When all this is over, I'll watch you burn at the stake the way the Hebrews would have done to you, if not for my husband's kindness."

"If not for your husband's deceit, I would have been fine in the first place."

"You're alive because he paid the girl. That's a fact."

Sall was determined not to let her throw him off his task. "Death comes to all, sooner or later."

"Sooner, for you."

"Perhaps," he said. "My father once treated a merchant from Persia, who said he wasn't afraid of dying, because our essence of life never actually dies, but leaps to another living creature when the last breath is taken."

"I hope you come back as a rat."

"Or a cat." Sall meowed. "I could be Pharaoh's next cat, or Li'uli's cat, if he decides to keep a cat like his fellow Egyptians."

He waited, hoping her response would answer the quandary for which he came to see her: was Li'uli unafraid of snakes, or was there another reason for the absence of cats from their tent?

Li'iliti disappeared from the porthole.

"That's interesting," he said.

From the darkness of the room, her voice came with an echo. "What's interesting?"

"The mention of cats unsettled you." He turned to one of the guards. "Go and find a couple of cats, bring them here, and put them in the room with her."

"No!" Li'iliti's face reappeared in the porthole. "Have you not been vindictive enough towards me already?"

"What do you mean?" Sall infused his voice with indignation. "How is a gift of cats' companionship vindictive?"

"Don't you know?"

He shook his head.

"Cats give me and my children a skin disease."

With a raised finger, Sall signaled the guard to stay. "I wasn't aware such illness existed among Egyptians."

"I'm not Egyptian." Her tone became bitter, but also proud. "My people lived in Kush long before the men of the Nile subjugated us. We have our own chiefs, whose blood runs through my heart."

"And now you help the Egyptians subjugate others?"

"I help my husband restore his birthright. It's my duty."

"Don't you care how many innocent people die in the process?"

Li'iliti didn't answer right away, and Sall didn't wait for her to contrive a response. It was enough for him to know that Li'uli feared snakes as badly as all Egyptians, whereas he didn't keep cats only due to their sickening effect on his wife and children.

He left the king's palace and rode downhill. At the horse stables, he dismounted and asked the scar-faced snake-catcher's wife to bring over one of the tall jars. She carried it with two hands, circling wide to come from the side of the horse, but when she put down the jar, the snakes inside hissed, and the horse neighed and skipped aside. Sall patted the horse until it calmed down. They secured the jar to the side of the saddle with straps. She tightened the cloth cover over the narrow neck and stepped back.

Rather than ride, Sall walked, pulling the horse along. Outside the gates, he turned right and proceeded south along the city walls. An waved at him from the fairgrounds, where about one third of the army was practicing face-to-face combat with swords, knives, and farming implements. Further north, another third of the army was lined up at the foothills, every woman down on one knee, shooting arrows towards the slopes. The rest of the army was marching across the valley in formation, changing directions at the call of a single commander who stood on a pile of wood.

At the south end of the valley, he started up the first hill at a slow pace to avoid the risk of the horse tripping, the tall jar breaking, and the irate snakes striking the horse and possibly him, too. At the top of the hill, he found the miniature tower of stones. Shading his eyes from the sun above, he gazed at the nearby hills until he spotted the next marker. Before starting the descent, he checked the straps that held the tall jar and the cloth over the open neck.

Four markers later, while descending a slope, one of the horse's front paws was caught between rocks. The horse managed not to fall, but the stumble shook the tall jar halfway out of the straps. As Sall was adjusting the straps and tightening them, the head of a gray-brown snake poked from under the cloth, which had loosened from the the clay lip of the jar. The snake's body was still inside, but its eyes and forked tongue took quick measures of the surroundings and focused on Sall's face, which was up close while he was tightening the straps.

Mesmerized by the snake's unblinking eyes, Sall froze while his mind recognized that the speed of a striking snake was much greater than his ability to dodge it. Almost immediately, a loud rebuttal came in Ishkadim's jovial voice: "Failure only happens when you give up." Without another thought, by instinct alone, Sall swung his hand and slapped the snake on top of its triangular head, which made hard contact with the Ring of the Fisherman on his index finger. The snake retreated into the jar. With trembling hands, Sall pulled the cloth over to seal the opening and retied the string around the neck of the jar to secure it. Touching the bulging middle of the tall jar, he could feel the tapping of tails and coils as the crowded snakes shifted irritably inside.

The sun was already at its peak when he resumed walking. The tremor in his hands, rather than subsiding, spread up his arms and down to his knees, while his chest tightened, and his breathing grew shallow and rapid. Heading up the slope towards the last hillcrest before the meeting point, he stopped and shut his eyes, trying to calm down. He realized that his anxiety, though ignited by the near-death encounter with the snake, was now being fueled by what was ahead. What if he had been wrong about Li'uli's intentions, and the brown prince was ready with an unexpected trickery? Was there a company of Egyptian soldiers, eager to grab Sall and use torture to extract the truth about Li'iliti and the defense preparations in Bozra? Would Li'uli take such a risk with his wife's life?

Inhaling deeply, Sall mounted the horse and urged it forward. He would not give up on his father, no matter what risks awaited, and if Li'uli had conceived an unexpected move, it would be an opportunity to think of a quick countermove.

At the crest of the hill, he stopped the horse by the stone marker and looked down at the boulder where they had met in the morning. Li'uli was already there with his two servants. One held the reins of two horses, and the other held a sword to the exposed neck of Sall's father, who was kneeling on the ground.

Forcing his eyes away from his father's sunburnt face, Sall surveyed the surrounding desert, making sure there were no Egyptian soldiers lurking nearby.

"Go back, boy," Li'uli yelled. "Fetch my beautiful wife and bring her here. Quickly, or your father's neck will be beyond healing."

As if by magic, Sall's anxiety disappeared, and he chuckled at Li'uli's clever wordplay. The situation was dangerous, but it was the danger he had prepared for, which left only the challenge of a successful execution.

He urged the horse to start down the slope while taking a long drink from a waterskin.

"You're wasting precious time," Li'uli said.

Sall plugged the waterskin while the horse continued downhill at a slow pace. "My father seems parched. Would you give him this water?"

Without waiting for a response, he tossed the waterskin to Li'uli, who caught it with both hands. Rather than give it to the kneeling man, the brown prince unplugged it and sniffed inside.

"What did you expect?" Sall stopped the horse about fifteen steps from them. "Warm milk with a sleeping potion?"

Li'uli handed the waterskin to his captive. "Turn around, boy, and ride fast. I'll count to five thousand, and if my wife isn't here, you'll have no father, and your sick people will have no healer for their red fever."

Sall's father, who started drinking from the waterskin, paused and looked up. "The red fever? In Bozra?"

The hoarseness and lethargy in his voice shocked Sall, who was accustomed to his father being happy and robust. "Don't worry, father. You'll be home soon."

"Not if you keep talking," Li'uli said.

"We had agreed on a simple trade this morning: you release my father and let me take him back to the city, and then, I set your wife free to join you. Why don't you honor our agreement?"

"Maybe this will convince you I'm serious." He turned to the servant with the sword. "Cut off his right hand."

The servant grabbed the kneeling man's forearm and held it up.

"Wait," Sall said. "I agree."

His father groaned as the servant put the blade to the wrist and looked at his master for a final go-ahead.

Li'uli signaled his servant to wait.

Sall reached down to the side of the saddle to loosen the straps holding the tall jar. "I brought a gift for you. Let me leave it here so I can ride fast for Li'iliti."

With some effort, he managed to pull the jar free from the straps. He held it up to his chest and turned halfway, raising his leg to dismount, but groaned, pretending his sandal was caught in the stirrup, and hurled the jar towards the group. It landed at their feet and shattered. A large ball of knotted snakes spilled from the clay shards and unspooled swiftly all over Li'uli's boots, his servants' bare feet, and the bent knees of Sall's father, who alone remained immobile, shutting his eyes tightly, while the three men jumped up and down, screaming while the enraged snakes struck rapidly at the servants' flesh and Li'uli's boots. A moment later, the three men ran off while the two horses reared up and bolted, disappearing into the hills.

Li'uli stopped on a slope about two-hundred steps away, but his two servants continued screaming as they ran around in circles, stumbling and getting up, pounding on their feet, calves, and shins, until they happened to collide and fell down. The one who had almost cut off the captive's hand was still gripping his sword. He plunged the blade into the other servant's abdomen. Pulling it out, he did it again and again, shouting and crying, then turned the sword around, the point of the blade against the center of his chest, and fell forward. As he hit the ground, the blade went through him, emerging out of his back.

The desert became silent again, but only for a moment.

Li'uli, who had avoided the snakes' venom with his leather boots, howled in sorrow and rage.

"Father," Sall said. "It's time to go."

Opening his eyes for the first time since the jar shattered, his father looked around to make sure all the snakes had slithered away. He stood with difficulty and reached up as Sall rode over and helped him up onto the saddle behind him.

Still shouting, Li'uli sprinted towards them, brandishing a sword.

Sall turned the horse and kicked hard, making it race up the hill. Near the top, he glanced over his shoulder. Down below, Li'uli had stopped, panting.

"It's your fault," Sall yelled. "You left me no choice."

The only response was a pantomimed slice across the neck with the sword.

"Your wife will be released tomorrow, unharmed, unless you engage in further trickery."

As they rode over the crest and down the next slope, Sall felt his father's arms embracing him from behind. They didn't speak while riding up and down the hills, from one stone marker to the next, until the last slope brought the city into view.

His father sighed. "How bad is the red fever?"

"There's no red fever."

"You lied?"

"A necessary lie to make Li'uli believe we needed you back urgently."

Down in the valley, Sall directed the horse along the wall of the city. Ahead was the army, standing in formation near the gates. An rode General Mazabi's steed up and down between the columns, as a general would inspect his soldiers before releasing them to rest after intense training.

"Mercenaries?" His father leaned forward, his chin over Sall's right shoulder. "Who hired them?"

"They're women, not mercenaries."

"What women?"

"The wives and daughters of our fallen soldiers. And the one riding General Mazabi's horse is An, the High Priest's daughter, who knocked me out with her eyes." He chuckled. "She's had a complete change of heart about me."

His father groaned and leaned back, his arms no longer embracing Sall.

Entering the city, Sall urged the horse up the street, crisscrossed the hillside while the view of the valley expanded. His father shaded his eyes and gazed at the barren land where the lush orchards had stood before.

"It was necessary," Sall said. "If the city survives, we'll plant new orchards."

Umm-Sall was in the front garden, kneeling before the effigies, looking the same as when he had left. With her were Cook, Laundress, and Horseman, praying together.

Cook was the first to see them and yelled, "Healer!"

While hugging her husband, Umm-Sall smiled at Sall. "I didn't want you to go, son, but now, I'm proud of you."

"The Gods clear the way for those who chase their dreams."

The servants took his father into the house.

Umm-Sall glanced at the effigies. "I think they love you as much as I do."

Her words made him think of General Mazabi, whom she loved in a different way. "How is the general?"

"He's a strong man, and he'll recover, but not by this evening."

"I'm not counting on him."

"But your army is made of women."

"They drank the Male Elixir and believe in its potency, which means they're as strong as men."

"Women don't need an elixir to be as strong as men."

"They need it to believe in their strength."

"But they don't know how to fight, and they'll face an army that has crushed our own."

"Defeat at the Sea of Reeds can turn into victory in the valley of Bozra."

They went into her room, where he changed back into his armor, boots, and helmet.

Umm-Sall handed him his sword. "How could a boy succeed where a general failed?"

"A boy couldn't, but the great Elixirist knows how to win."

"Against Pharaoh's invincible army?"

Sall buckled the belt and adjusted the sheathed sword against his hip. "The brown prince told me that history is littered with the ruins of invincible cities. I think the same is true for invincible armies."

She followed him outside and watched him mount his horse.

Turning towards the street, Sall said, "Tell father about my journey and show him the gold coins."

"I will, but don't expect him to bless your marriage to the high priest's daughter."

"Try to convince him. He'll listen to you."

"Why? Because he loves me?" Umm-Sall caressed the horse's neck. "A man's love for a woman will never be a match for his hate for another man."

55

The army of women was released to eat and rest until the evening. An waited for Sall outside the gates with the sixty company commanders, who sat on the ground, holding their bows, quivers, and bladed weapons. He stayed on his horse while speaking to them.

"The enemy will arrive soon. Normally, when a king surrenders his city to the Egyptian army, the Jabari moves into the king's palace and divides the loot and the women among his commanders and soldiers. This time, however, they'll stay out, because they believe there's a rampant epidemic of red fever inside the walls. As long as we can keep that illusion going, they'll be afraid to enter the city."

The women exchanged grim looks. There was no scourge worse than the red fever.

"Each of you command a company of one hundred," Sall continued. "We have sixty companies in all, which will now be divided into ten units. Each unit, therefore, will have six companies, which adds up to six-hundred soldiers. The six commanders in each unit will choose one of them to be Unit Commander. The ten Unit Commanders will report to me and receive my orders. If I'm not available, An will be in charge. Are you ready?"

They nodded.

"Unit One will start sixty small fires in safe places around the city, like yards or gardens, but far from the gates and the main street. You'll toss garbage into the fires and keep them going late into the night. The goal is to make it look and smell like we're burning the bodies of those who died of the red fever. It's important that you assign enough soldiers to each fire and you make sure everyone has enough wood to keep the flames burning and enough water to stop any fire spreading to nearby houses or trees."

An counted six of the commanders, and they moved aside to sit together.

"Unit Two, also one-tenth of the army, will be in charge of defending the gates."

They looked at each other nervously, but no one spoke up.

"If all goes according to plan," he said, "there will be no direct attack, but failing to prepare for it would be presumptuous. The great Elixirist taught me an important rule." Sall paused, recalling the exact words. "An error born of arrogance requires a correction devised in humility."

Many of them nodded.

"Unit Two's six hundred soldiers will stay in the army barracks near the locked gates, alert and ready to defend the gates with arrows and swords, if needed, while the commanders take turns watching the valley from the roof of the barracks."

An assigned the role to six commanders, who moved to sit separately.

"Unit three will be in charge of defending the walls from the gates to the north, going all the way around the city to the top of the hill behind the king's palace. You'll divide the wall into six sections and assign a company of soldiers to each section. Unit Four will do the same from the gates to the south, meeting up with Unit Three at the top of the city behind the king's palace."

Twelve company commanders, six for each new unit, moved over.

"This leaves us with soldiers for a total of six new units," Sall said. "Unit Five to Unit Ten will assemble in the main street after sundown. There will be no fires, torches, or even candles in the lower part of the city, so that the Egyptians will not be able to see our preparations. Each unit will line up its six companies in tidy columns. Unit Five will stand at the bottom of the street just up from the king's horse stables, followed by Unit Six, Unit Seven, and so on. I will issue my orders when the time comes for action."

Pointing, An counted aloud, dividing them into six additional groups of six company commanders each.

"My last orders are simple," Sall said. "Once you elect your Unit Commanders, they should wear a light-colored scarf to help me identify them in the dark. Second, you and your soldiers must blacken every piece of leather and skin. Use soot from stoves and ash from fires, mixed with water. The only exception is the back of the neck, which should remain exposed so that soldiers can follow each other in the dark. Now, go pass the orders to your soldiers and get some rest while I go with An to welcome our enemies to Edom."

The sixty company commanders went into the city, the gates closing behind them.

Sall and An rode across the fairgrounds, through the narrow gap in the barrier of chopped trees, and took the road east through the valley. The ground was flat, dotted with piles of firewood and strewn with discarded fruit, which the rodents were feasting on. An twisted her face in disgust, but Sall was delighted to see his plan coming to life.

At the eastern end of the valley, they took the meandering road up the hills, reaching the top just as the sun was halfway down in the west, hovering like a ball of fire above Bozra. The city was already overcast with plumes of smoke, rising towards the sun from the multiple small fires Sall had ordered Unit One to start.

"Look." An pointed east. "They're coming."

A double column of chariots was climbing the meandering road from the east. Behind the numerous chariots, soldiers marched in dense formations, darkening the road down the hills and back in the wide valley towards the distant turnoff from the main north-south trade route, which connected the Sea of Reeds with Moab and Canaan.

"So many of them," she said.

"The bigger the herd, the worse the stampede."

"I'm scared."

"Only a fool feels no fear."

An brought her horse close and leaned over to kiss Sall, which filled him with joy.

56

The Jabari travelled in a gold-plated chariot, drawn by four white horses and fitted with a cushioned armchair under a cloth sunshade. He wore a cotton skirt and leather sandals with interwoven straps up to his knees. Sall had expected the Egyptian military leader to be an imposing warrior, a mighty version of General Mazabi, but the Jabari was nothing of the sort. His extended belly and soft chest evidenced a sedentary life of good food and wine. His round head was bald except for a ring of gray hair, and his limp arms bore golden bracelets fit for a queen. His skin was lighter than Li'uli, resembling the color of desert soil, but glossy with oil. In his lap sat a white cat, which he caressed as his chariot came to a stop at the crest of the hill. A retinue of mounted guards flanked the gold-plated chariot.

An and Sall, dressed in their leather armor and helmets with red rooster combs, dismounted the horses and knelt down.

Sall said, "Welcome to Edom, Jabari of Egypt."

The cat jumped off and skipped over to them, sniffing at their knees.

The Jabari laughed.

Sall glanced up, unsure why the Jabari was laughing, and noticed that the charioteer and the guards remained blank-faced, as were the entourage of older men in gold armor and bejeweled saddles on beautiful horses. Right behind them, he recognized Li'uli, also on a good horse, as well as two men on donkeys – the king and high priest of Edom.

Clicking his fingers for the cat, which jumped back into his lap, the Jabari stopped laughing. "A girl dressed in a man's armor – is Edom that desperate?"

Sall pointed to Bozra. "The city is stricken with sickness. No one of importance was left alive to receive you."

At the other end of the valley, the plumes of smoke above Bozra had reached almost as high as the afternoon sun.

The Jabari gazed at the city for a long moment. "We heard about it. How many are dead?"

"More than we can count," Sall said. "The bodies are being burnt as quickly as possible. In the meantime, we cleared a large area in the valley and set up piles of firewood for your troops' comfort."

"The red fever is spread by the Demoness Ammit through unwed maidens." The Jabari clicked his finger at his charioteer. "Cut off the girl's head."

The charioteer looped the reins on a peg, stepped down from the chariot, and drew his sword.

Leaping to her feet, An unsheathed her sword and brandished it at the charioteer, who was twice her size. He smirked, angling his sword for a strike.

"Wait!" Sall put himself between them, raising his arms. "Another army is coming!"

The Jabari signaled the charioteer to wait. "What did you say?"

The charioteer's blade reflected the sun into Sall's eyes, distracting him. He had memorized the words, but now his tongue felt as heavy as a rock.

An cleared her throat.

"We received news," Sall said. "A traveling merchant told us that an army is coming from the north."

"What army?"

"The king of Moab heard of your campaign and gathered forces with all his neighbors – the king of Amon and the Hebrew tribes of Reuben and Gad. They're marching south to fight you here."

"When?"

"Two, maybe three days. That's why we put on armor and weapons – to help you in the battle against them."

The Jabari sneered and beckoned the charioteer. "Bring forward the donkeys."

King Esau the Eighteenth and the high priest rode their donkeys up from the rear. An's brother, Qoztobarus, walked along on foot. They looked tired and fidgety. The king and high priest dismounted the donkeys, and the three of them knelt by the gold-plated chariot.

Qoztobarus gave An a furious look.

"Go to your city," the Jabari said. "Kill all the sick, as well as anyone who cared for them and all their family members."

The king bowed his head. "It shall be done."

"Take all the bodies with their clothes, cots, linen, anything they used, and burn everything to ashes."

Sall saw his opportunity and spoke up. "We'll burn them with the trees that we've cut down to make room for your camp. You'll see them stacked up in a long line near our fairgrounds."

The Jabari waved his hand in dismissal, making the golden bracelets clink. "Go now, King Esau, and ride the donkey through the city for your people to see that you are Egypt's slave. In the morning, I shall move into your palace."

The king and the high priest mounted the donkeys while Sall and An went for their two horses. As she put her foot in the stirrup to mount her horse, Qoztobarus grabbed her arm and pulled her back. She fell to the ground, and he mounted her horse.

Sall, who had already mounted, jumped off and helped her up.

Qoztobarus jerked the reins, making the horse bump into Sall.

The Jabari clicked his fingers, and his guards surrounded them, spears in the ready.

"Back on your knees," he said. "All of you."

The five of them knelt by the gold-plated chariot.

"Forgive us," the high priest said. "It's a family matter. The girl is my daughter. Not only does she dress as a man, but she dares to ride while my son, who is both her brother and her future husband, walks. I will flog her when we're back home."

"You'll flog a brave girl who volunteered to fight for Egypt?" The Jabari chuckled. "Maybe she should flog you, a coward priest who sold his people for his own skin?"

The high priest blushed.

"Besides, I don't see a ring on her finger."

Qoztobarus answered. "A brother needs no ring to betroth his sister in Edom."

"Edom is no more, boy. Under Egypt, betrothal is always by ring, and it's valid only if the girl agrees." The Jabari looked at An. "Do you want your brother as husband?"

"She does," the high priest said.

"I don't want my brother." She pointed at Sall. "I want to marry him."

The Jabari clapped, and even his guards sniggered.

Sall pulled the ring from his finger and held it up. "I'm ready."

The Jabari held his hand out for the ring, which Sall gave him.

"He's a lowly healer's son," the high priest said. "Does a father have no say in his daughter 's marriage in Egypt?"

"A dead father has no say."

The implied threat hushed the high priest, who looked down at the ground.

The Jabari examined the ring. "What's an official seal doing on a healer's son's ring?"

"It's not official," Sall said.

"What do you call it, then?"

"The Ring of the Fisherman."

"I see now – a boat, a net, and a fisherman." The Jabari gestured around. "In this barren desert, where do you cast a net for fish?"

"It's not fish that I seek," Sall said.

"What, then?"

"I cast my net for loving hearts." He looked at An. "Her heart, in particular."

The Jabari gave him the ring back. "Put it on her finger."

As Sall was about to do it, Qoztobarus reached across and slapped An's hand away. One of the guards kicked him in the back, knocking him down.

Taking her hand in his, Sall slipped the Ring of the Fisherman onto An's index finger. He could barely breathe, having just fulfilled the dream that had consumed him since fainting at the high priest's house. With all his careful planning, he had not anticipated this strike of good fortune to be delivered by the leader of the enemy's army.

An and Sall looked at each other for a long moment while everything else faded away, and there was only joy.

"Splendid." The Jabari ran his hand over the back of the cat to its tail, which he held and pointed with the tip at the high priest. "You will marry them tomorrow at your God's temple."

The high priest bowed.

"It will be my first Edomite wedding. Make it worthwhile."

As they got up to go, the king swayed unsteadily. Sall helped him to the donkey. Meanwhile, the high priest mounted his donkey, ignoring his son, who remained on the ground, moaning. Two of the guards got off their horses, lifted Qoztobarus, and dropped him face down over the saddle of An's horse. She hesitated, unsure how to mount her horse, now that its saddle was taken. The Jabari clicked his fingers and patted the seat of the chariot beside him. The two guards grabbed her arms while the others positioned their horses to block Sall. He was about to fight his way through, but An looked at him.

"It's fine," she said. "I'll see you tomorrow."

He knew she was right — there was no point in fighting now — but he had to give An a hint about what to do when things started to happen during the night. A simple idea came to him. He walked off the road along the rocky hillcrest, picking up a few stones, and arranged them one on top of the other as a marker. To confuse the Egyptians, he knelt and bowed several times before the marker as if it was a potent deity.

Back on his horse, Sall glanced back at An, who was already seated by the Jabari in the chariot under the sunshade. She looked back at him, and he knew she understood he intended the marker as a meeting place. But then, he noticed Li'uli staring at him from further back and feared that the brown prince also figured out the true purpose of the marker. Sall drew the sword he had taken from Li'iliti and raised it, pointing at the marker to indicate he would bring her here, too, to reunite with her family.

Li'uli nodded once.

Kicking in with his heels, Sall sent the horse into a fast sprint down the road. The king and high priest, together with An's horse and her brother, followed through the swirling dust he left in his wake.

57

On the road through the valley, the horse grew tired and slowed down to a trot. The rodents were as active as before, nibbling on fruit and darting away at the sound of the horse's hooves. The sun was low over the city ahead, its rays reflecting from the copper roofs through the pillars of smoke.

When Sall passed through the barrier of chopped trees onto the fairgrounds, the gates ahead opened, and the ten Unit Commanders stood there, wearing light scarves. One of them pointed, and Sall looked back. The meandering road he had taken down from the crest of the eastern hills had turned dark with the forces of Egypt, descending into the valley.

Up close, he could see the anxiety on the women's faces. He took a deep breath, making sure his voice was calm when he spoke. "We met their leader, the Jabari, and convinced him that the city is filled with death from the red fever. No Egyptian soldier will cross the barrier. They'll set up tents in the valley, cook their evening meals, and go to sleep. Once they're completely relaxed, in the middle of the night, that's when they'll be most vulnerable."

One of them asked, "Where's the high priest's daughter?"

"The Jabari kept her with him."

Several of the women sucked their breaths, others covered their mouths, eyes opened wide. He expected this reaction, but the reality of their shock brought a lump to his throat and summoned back the tremor in his hands, which he pressed together, fingers interwoven.

"She'll be fine," he said, more to convince himself than the Unit Commanders. "An is strong and resourceful, but it won't hurt if you pray for her safe return."

They looked at each other, some of them murmuring prayers on the spot.

He needed a moment to compose himself. "Now," he said, "bring ten soldiers who are trustworthy without any doubt, as well as three empty sacks."

The commander of Unit Two ran to the barracks and returned with ten soldiers and empty sacks. Sall addressed them directly.

"The king and high priest will be here soon." He pointed at the road where the two donkeys and the horse were trotting towards the city. "As you know, they have surrendered to the enemy, which necessitates locking them up until we achieve victory. I want them covered up and mummed to prevent any attempts to give orders. Take them and the high priest's son to a house where there are no servants or children to be bothered. Put them under guard until I order their release."

The king, high priest, and Qoztobarus, who was sitting up in the saddle, were too stunned to resist the armed women, who pulled them down, slipped sacks over their heads, and rushed them through the gates and up the street.

Sall went up to the guard tower and watched the long column of chariots, archers, and foot soldiers descending the eastern hills. They reached the center of the valley, spread over the cleared area, and split into units, setting up tents and erecting corrals for the horses, which were released from the chariots. Eventually, the tail of the long column melted into the rest, and the whole Egyptian army was settled in dense squares of tidy tents, starting about two hundred steps east from the barrier of chopped trees. They filled up the whole width of the valley and almost half its length.

At the very center of the huge camp, a great white tent came up. Topping the center pole was a gold disc, which sparkled with the last rays of the sun. Sall imagined the interior of the tent, adorned with thick carpets, soft cushions, and hushed slaves serving food and wine to the Jabari and his beautiful prisoner. He imagined An, her leather armor replaced with a white cotton robe, her golden braid released from the confines of her helmet and freed to drop over her delicate shoulder and reach down the front her chest, ending with a red bow that rested between her thighs—

"Enough!" Sall pounded his fist on the railing. "Stop it!"

He turned and crossed the small platform of the guard tower to the opposite railing, which overlooked the open area inside the gates, between the king's horse stables and the army barracks. The air smelled of smoke and burnt garbage, but the foulness gave him comfort in the knowledge that the Egyptians also smelled it and believed the story about the red fever. Would the rest of his plan go as well? And if his plan succeeded, would An survive it?

Only now he grasped how clever the Jabari had been to let him betroth An and then keep her by his side to deter any attack that could result in her death. Was the king right to surrender?

As soon as the thought crossed Sall's mind, he imagined kneeling before the Jabari in formal capitulation while An glared at him with contempt a thousand times fiercer than before. He looked at the white tent in the middle of the Egyptian camp and knew that, as terrified as she probably was, An wanted him to stay the course and achieve victory tonight, even at the cost of her life and their future together.

The dimming twilight made the white tent fade into a ghostly pale patch while hundreds of campfires emerged, dotting the whole area between the darkening hills on the north and south sides of the valley. He looked up at the sky, where stars began to show, dotting it with points of light – an unexpected similarity between heavens and earth. For a moment, he concentrated on memorizing this view so he could describe it to An in the morning and, in years to come, to their children.

The lower part of the city was shrouded in near darkness in accordance with his orders to Unit One to keep all the fires higher up. He could make out the stream of armed women coming down to the gate area and splitting into three units to defend the gates and the walls around the city. Six more units congregated in formations up the main street, totaling three-thousand, six-hundred soldiers.

The six company commanders of Unit Two, led by their elected Unit Commander, climbed to the roof of the army barracks, where they had open view above the gates and the wall at the fairgrounds and beyond. Their soldiers sat on the ground below in rows, ready to be summoned to defend the gates from any attack.

Sall left the guard tower and went down to check on the progress of Unit Three and Unit Four, whose soldiers took positions to defend the city all around and repel any attackers from breaching the walls. It took him a long time to make his way along the inside of the walls up to the top of the city, behind the king's palace, and down the other side. The two units comprised of a total of twelve companies, which had taken positions in equal intervals, with lookouts stationed on rooftops, while roving commanders kept their subordinates alert and ready.

Satisfied, he walked up the main street to inspect the other six units. The women sat in long columns by company and unit, huddled together to keep warm. They were barely visible with their blackened skin, armor, and weapons. He stopped to chat with each Unit Commander, who were eager to assure him that their troops were ready to follow his orders.

Walking back downhill, Sall saw that the sliver moon had reached high up in the dark sky. Half the night had passed, the Egyptians didn't appear to have noticed the activity inside Bozra, and his army was eager for action. The grand plan of defeating the Egyptians had developed in the confines of his mind until now, never spelled out in words, like a lump of dough that could only rise to fullness under cover. Now, finally, it was ripe for execution.

58

At the horse stables, Sall collected soot from a cold firepit, spat on it, and smeared the black paste over every part of his body and armor. The snake-catchers' wives did the same. Having ran out of soot, they sent a few girls to bring more from elsewhere and used it to blacken all one-hundred and twelve tall jars and their cloth seals.

Sall summoned two companies of soldiers from Unit Five to carry the jars. He led them out the gates, up the road across the fairgrounds, to the gap in the barrier of chopped trees. He stopped there and peered at the Egyptian camp, its first line of tents about a hundred steps ahead. Their cooking fires had died down, and the crescent moon cast a meek glow on the quiet tents. He saw no guards, which made sense. The Egyptians had no reason to expect a threat from a city of sick women and children. They probably posted guards along the other three sides of the camp, especially after he had lied to the Jabari about an army marching down from Moab and Amon, but those guards were too far to notice what was happening along the barrier. To be safe, however, he instructed the women to make no sound and watch their steps to avoid stumbling or stepping on twigs.

Carrying the tall jars through the gap, they turned either left or right and put down the jars along the barrier in short intervals all the way to the north and south foothills. Sall and one of the snake-catchers' wives went to the far end in the north while the other two went to the south end. One jar at the time, they laid it down with the neck aimed at the enemy camp and pulled off the cloth seal, quickly stepping to the next jar. Numb from the night's chill, the snakes would be slow to crawl out, which suited his plan.

Sall and the three snake-catchers' wives finished opening the jars and crossed the barrier back to the side facing the city. Together with a few of the soldiers, he pulled some trees to block the gap where the road passed through. Now, the barrier completely separated the enemy camp from the fairgrounds across the whole width of the valley from north to south. He sent the snake-catchers' wives back into the city with instructions to have their thirty girls collect candles and oil lamps from houses, light them, and wait inside the gates for his orders.

Meanwhile, the rest of Unit Five emerged from the gates. He instructed the Unit Commander to arrange her six-hundred soldiers in a straight line facing the barrier, about twenty steps back from it, all the way from north to the south, and get ready with their bows and arrows.

"Tell your troops to stay completely quiet and do nothing until I order you to shoot."

When Unit Five was in position, Unit Six emerged from the gates in a single column. Sall took the lead, walking to the foot of the hills in the south, up the slopes and, just over the crest, to the left. He instructed the Unit Commander to continue east in total silence under the cover of darkness up to a point near the far corner of the Egyptian camp, about halfway up the valley. The goal was to form a line parallel to the south side of the enemy camp, just over the crest of the hills, and get ready to shoot arrows at it as soon as the women closest to the city saw Unit Five starting to shoot its arrows – but not a moment earlier.

The orders were passed down the line in whispers, and Sall watched the women, blackened with soot from head to toe – except for the back of the neck – follow each other into the darkness. The end of the column remained in sight from where he stood. He summoned Unit Seven and ordered them to form a second line behind Unit Six, get down on one knee, and be ready with their bows and arrows.

Back at the gates, he led Unit Eight, followed by Unit Nine, to form two similar lines on the hills parallel to the north side of the enemy camp. They were also instructed to watch Unit Five before starting to shoot their arrows at the Egyptians.

When Unit Ten emerged from the gates, Sall instructed the Unit Commander to form a second line behind Unit Five in the fairgrounds, facing the barrier and the enemy camp beyond, ready to shoot arrows or provide reinforcement to other units in case Egyptian soldiers attacked anywhere along the three fronts – south, north, or west through the barrier.

Next, Sall instructed the snake-catchers' wives and their thirty girls to go across the fairgrounds and light up the barrier. He stopped by the army barracks and instructed the commanders of Unit Two to alert their soldiers that action was about to begin. They were the last line of defense if his plan failed and the Egyptians made a full-blown attack, broke through the other units, and reached the gates.

Standing alone atop the guard-tower, Sall watched the girls crouch by the long barrier and put the candles and oil-lamps to the clumps of hair under the fallen tree. The tiny flames caught up rapidly and spread from the clumps of hair to the wood. The freshly cut trees, not yet dry, crackled and popped, breaking the silence of the night. It was noisier than he had expected, but he hoped any waking Egyptians would believe the fire was ordered by the king in accordance with the Jabari's vicious order to kill and burn all the sick, their caregivers and families, and their belongings.

Sall imagined the clay jars, lined up on the other side, becoming hot as the burning barrier radiated heat with growing intensity, the fearful snakes slithering away from the flames, their forked tongues tasting the night air, saturated with appetizing scents of various rodents. He watched in his mind's eye the slick serpents seeking prey to quell their hunger, crawling into tents, over cots, and under blankets, where sleeping Egyptian soldiers might shift a leg, bend an arm, or scratch a pulsating neck to unwittingly spook an irritable viper, causing it to part its jaws, aim its fangs, and sink them into warm flesh, injecting a full dose of deadly venom.

Banging sounds on the wooden stairs made him turn. A dark figure appeared at the top of the stairs. In the glow from the barrier fire, he saw only a left arm.

"This is madness." General Mazabi's voice was raspy, his back was hunched, and he breathed heavily. "You'll get them all killed, boy."

"There's no boy here," Sall said. "I am the Elixirist."

"You're imitating him."

"That's over. I have mutated. The Elixirist and I are one and the same."

"Perhaps, but just as I did at the Sea of Reeds, you underestimate Egypt."

"To the contrary," Sall said. "My humble plan depends on their superior training, excellent skills, and arrogant ruthlessness."

"You make no sense."

"You'll see." Sall gestured in the direction of the valley. "Soon."

General Mazabi stared at him, his sunburnt face illuminated by the flickering flames from the barrier. "Speaking of ruthlessness, I heard you locked up the king and high priest. Is that part of your delusional plan?"

Sall was offended, but not angry. "I'm neither ruthless, nor delusional. You can stay and watch, but insult me no more."

They stood at the railing in awkward silence and watched the burning barrier.

Moments passed.

The flames continued to consume the long heap of fallen trees.

The Egyptian camp remained quiet and peaceful.

Between the walls of the city and the burning barrier, the lines of kneeling women in the fairgrounds didn't move, but the Unit Commanders craned their helmeted heads towards the guard tower.

Still, the silence continued.

Sall began to worry that one of the commanders would lose her nerve and issue an order to shoot, which would cause other units to start shooting. The Egyptian army could sustain many injuries and still manage to mount a formidable counterattack, confirming the general's dire prediction. There was only one way to achieve victory over this monstrous army, Sall knew, and it didn't include direct confrontation.

General Mazabi leaned on the railing. "Call it off."

Sall put a finger to his lips.

"Call it off," the general repeated. "Now."

"They have my An," Sall said.

"I heard about it. That's why I came down here."

"To comfort me?"

"No, to stop you before you wake up a sleeping Egyptian lion and get us all eaten alive. Her life isn't worth six thousand lives."

"No, but it's worth yours." He drew Li'iliti's sword and put the point of the blade to the general's ribs, right under the bandage over his severed arm, in the space between the chest and back armor pieces. "Your next word will be your last."

Chuckling, General Mazabi said no more.

Moments passed.

The night remained silent, except the crackling of the barrier fire.

The Unit Commanders kept glancing up at the guard tower.

It was no use, Sall realized. His plan failed.

He lowered the sword.

"That's better," the general said. "Call it off, or I will."

A cry came from the Egyptian camp.

Then another.

And another.

It was too dark to see what was happening there, but the screams spread left and right and further up the valley. They also grew louder, which meant the bitten Egyptians were out of their tents, running around in pain and mortal fear the way Li'uli's servants had done after getting bitten by the snakes.

General Mazabi looked at him. "Why are they screaming?"

Sall made a slithering motion with his arm and a biting imitation with his hand.

"Poor devils." Shuddering, the general shook his head. "How many snakes did you release?"

"Over two thousand."

More and more agonized screams sounded.

Men wailed in terror.

Other men yelled in anger.

Below the guard tower, the Unit Commanders looked up at him, waiting for the order, but Sall held back, knowing he must give the snakes time to bite as many Egyptians as possible, drive them mad, and cause others to become convinced that the army of Moab and Amon was attacking them from the darkness.

The chaos in the Egyptian camp grew louder, and as Sall listened, he became convinced that some of the cries were of men stricken by weapons. He imagined Egyptian soldiers waking up, startled by the screams, blind in the dark, rushing out of the tents with swords in the ready, and starting to hack away at foreign attackers, who were actually their panic-stricken fellow Egyptians.

Horses started neighing at high pitch, followed by drumming of hooves as hundreds of terrified beasts broke free from the makeshift corrals and ran around blindly in the dark, trampling tents and crushing men.

General Mazabi knuckled on the railing. "Give the order to shoot. Don't wait."

Ignoring him, Sall shut his eyes and followed his father's advice: "A good listener opens not only his ears, but also his heart." He recognized the shrieks of men bitten by snakes, the howls of men stabbed by blades, the cries of men crushed by horses, and the shouts of commanders convinced they were under attack. He took in the reverberations of a thousand drumming hooves, the neighing of terrified horses, and the cracks of breaking bones, accompanied by the clinking of blades as men fought for their lives against invisible enemies. His heart swelled with a recognition that his mind could hardly believe – his plan was working! The Egyptian army was making war on itself!

It was time to turn their blind terror into unbridled hysteria.

Raising both arms, Sall paused, then gesticulated towards the enemy camp several times. It was the signal the Unit Commanders had been waiting for, and it took only a brief moment for a flock of arrows to take off from the kneeling women of Unit Five and fly in an arch over the burning barrier. The arrows, which had been blackened like everything else, disappeared in the darkness over the enemy camp. An instant later, a fresh wave of screams exploded in the night.

A second flock of arrows took off, and Sall knew that word was being passed down the lines of the other units to start shooting from the south and north sides of the camp. He shut his eyes again and imagined the deathly rain falling down from the dark sky on the faceless soldiers of Egypt, piercing their chests, backs, arms, and legs, fueling a desperate fight for survival against imagined invaders.

The deafening racket from the Egyptian camp confirmed what he imagined to be happening there. Sall thought of An, making her way through the madness towards the east, where the rest of the valley would provide her a safe passage to the hills and the marker he had set up while she watched from the Jabari's chariot. The white tent in the middle of the camp was a distant target for any of the arrows, reducing An's risk of injury from that menace, at least, but would she manage to dodge the blind terror of Egyptian soldiers, slashing at any moving figure in the night, or the crazed horses, stomping around in sightless terror?

Sall clutched his hands together, wishing her to run, run, run!

Below, he saw a company of Unit Ten get up and hurry northward. Someone must have alerted them to an attack. They knew what to do, and he watched with satisfaction as another company ran south to assist the troops there. Meanwhile, Unit Five and the rest of Unit Ten continued to shoot arrows into the night towards the mayhem, while no Egyptian soldiers could pass through the tall flames of the barrier.

"Ingenious," General Mazabi said. "Maybe you are the real Elixirist."

Sall sheathed his sword. "Don't tell my mother I threatened you."

"Don't worry." He chuckled. "I knew it was an empty threat."

"It wasn't," Sall said.

They stared at each other for a long moment before General Mazabi turned and, using his copper spear as a walking stick, made his way across the platform and down the stairs, one at a time.

Outside the walls, the soldiers of Unit Five had run out of arrows, and the Unit Commander ran over to the wall under the guard tower, looking up.

"You did well," Sall said. "Now, march your soldiers to the south hills." He pointed right. "Have them line up with the two units already there and hold the line, kill any wayward Egyptian soldiers who try to run to the hills, and stay put until sunrise. If the remains of Pharaoh's army approach the gates, all of you, the three units, will step forward and show yourselves to the enemy, nothing more."

While Unit Five marched to the hills in the south, he ordered the commanders of Unit Ten to do the same thing in the north.

All that time, in the dark Egyptian camp, the screaming and shouting continued, the swords kept clinking, and horse hooves drummed on with neighing and stomping.

Inside the city, Sall ordered Unit One, which had tended to hundreds of fires, now smothered, and Unit Two, which had waited in reserve near the gates, to climb onto the front wall and spread out from the gates north and south, all the way in both directions, forming two rows that faced east towards the fairgrounds, the burning barrier, and the valley beyond. He watched from the guard tower as twelve-hundred soldiers climbed onto the wall and lined up shoulder-to-shoulder as ordered, the front row kneeling, and the second standing.

59

It took a long time for the mayhem in the Egyptian camp to subside. While the burning barrier was gradually reduced to ashes, silence descended on the dark valley. The wait continued – Sall on top of the guard tower, the double line of armed, blackened women on the wall facing the fairgrounds and the smoky barrier, and thousands more lined up in the dark behind the hillcrests on both sides of the valley.

Dawn was breaking in the east when the Egyptians finally appeared. They advanced towards the city on foot, except for a single rider in the lead. It was the Jabari, mounted on a donkey, which had to be prodded to step over the smoldering remains of the barrier. In one hand, the Jabari held a pole topped with a golden disk, which didn't glisten anymore. With his other hand he caressed the white cat, which draped itself on the saddle between his master's knees. In all, the remaining Egyptian force numbered no more than a thousand men, who followed their leader in a haphazard formation.

Atop the guard tower, Sall stood at the railing with the twelve company commanders from Unit One and Unit Two in their full armor and helmets with red rooster combs. He spoke quietly without turning his head.

"Order the front row to get their bows ready with arrows, but not shoot."

The order passed down through the lines, and the women kneeling on top of the wall primed their bows with arrows and aimed at the approaching Egyptians.

"Good," Sall said. "Now, who is the best shot among you?"

The commanders pointed at one of them.

"Put an arrow in the ground before the Jabari."

She got her bow primed, aimed, and made the shot. The arrow whistled in the air and sank into the ground in front of the donkey, which stopped and brayed.

The Jabari made no attempt to advance further.

Sall was relieved. From that distance, the bleak light of dawn was enough for the enemy to see the full force of armed soldiers on top of Bozra's walls, but not enough to see that they were women.

The Jabari looked up, his head moving from side to side, taking in the sight of over a thousand well-armed soldiers, whose existence he hadn't known.

Peering hard, Sall surveyed the Egyptian force in search of An, but could not find her.

Raising the banner with the gold disk, the Jabari yelled, "In the name of Ra, surrender to the army of Pharaoh, or die!"

Sall yelled back, "In the name of Qoz, leave the land of Edom, or die!"

A long silence ensued.

Putting his hands forward, Sall clapped once. When he clapped a second time, the commanders joined him. On the third clap, the woman standing in the second row along the top of the wall joined him, clapping together as if their hands were controlled by a single brain. Then, an echo came from both sides of the valley, where nearly five thousand women stepped forward on the hillcrests, emerging from the bleak twilight like apparitions, clapping at the same deliberate, unnerving pace, which reverberated across the valley and shook the air.

From the donkey's saddle, the Jabari looked over his left shoulder at the hills on the south, then to the right at the hills on the north, and again to the left, and to the right. He must have been stunned by the immense size of this new army because, when he finally looked back to the guard tower, the banner of Ra slipped from his hand and fell to the ground. The white cat sat up, craned its head up to glance at the Jabari, and jumped down from the saddle, sprinting between the legs of the soldiers, away from the city.

The army of Edom continued to clap in unison, one roaring thunder after another. Behind the Jabari, the Egyptian force began to crumble as individual soldiers broke away, then large groups, and eventually, the whole lot, running east towards the distant hills under the first rays of a new sun.

60

The women knew not to cheer, lest their voices expose their femininity and give the Egyptians an excuse to return for a future attack. They kept clapping rhythmically while the Jabari, now alone, turned his donkey and rode away.

For Sall, victory brought no relief as his mind turned to An. He ordered the Unit Commanders to keep clapping until all the Egyptians were out of sight. Hurrying down from the guard tower, he jumped on his horse and raced up the street to the king's palace, where he ran inside and got Li'iliti.

She refused to mount his horse. "Not without my daughters."

"I lied," he said. "We never had them."

She was quiet for a moment. "You're a good liar."

"I learned from the best, and I know where he's waiting for us now. Pray that I'm right."

With her in the saddle behind him, he sprinted back downhill, out the gates, across the fairgrounds, and over the strip of embers that remained from the barrier. The clapping hit them in waves, echoing from all directions, the raucous only diminishing as they galloped further up the valley towards the early sun.

The road passed between collapsed tents, broken corrals, dead horses, and countless fallen Egyptians. Everything was pierced by arrows, including the ground, which in some places looked as if it grew arrows instead of wheat. Most of the bodies were naked except for loincloths. They were olive-skinned and lanky, with black hair but no beards. In addition to the arrows, many of them were stabbed by swords, hacked by axes, or crushed by horses that left indentations in their heads, or caused broken ribs to poke out of their chests. He noticed a young solider, not older than himself, still kneeling, face up to the sky, an arrow in his eye.

Sall looked away, shaken. He had imagined them as faceless, coldblooded invaders, their weapons still stained with the fresh blood of Edom's fathers, brothers, husbands, and sons, arriving to kill and enslave the widows and orphans of Bozra. These pitiful corpses were also fathers, brothers, husbands, and sons, whose loving families would soon weep bitterly for them on the banks of the River Nile.

"Nice work," Li'iliti said from behind him. "How does it feel to kill thousands of men?"

"I meant to scare them, make them run away, not kill so many—"

"Don't lie to yourself. A little shower of arrows is scary. A massive downpour is meant to kill."

Bending to the side, Sall vomited.

At the east end of the camp, they passed by several hundred chariots, which had been detached from the horses the previous evening, standing unguarded in tidy queues. Here and there, he saw a snake lying limply, bulging with a rodent it had swallowed.

Li'iliti did not say another word, not even when they passed the lonesome Jabari on his donkey. None of his soldiers accompanied him, but the white cat had somehow returned to its perch on the donkey's saddle. Sall could see the soldiers far to the right, crossing the valley in an east-south direction, likely in hopes of melting into the desert to avoid capture by the victorious Edomite army and a life of slavery, as was customary after battles.

At the eastern hills, the tired horse struggled to walk up the meandering road with two riders in the saddle. A wind began to pick up, stirring up copious dust. They covered their faces against the stinging grains, and the horse lowered its head and snorted unhappily.

As the road leveled at the top, the swirling dust blinded them.

Sall yelled, "An? Can you hear me?"

There was no response.

He remembered the approximate distance and direction to the marker. Dismounting, he gave Li'iliti the reins and walked along the crest, bent over, sheltering his eyes while he searched for the marker through the haze of dust.

"An? Where are you? An?"

There was no answer, only the shriek of the wind and the hiss of dust whipping his leather armor.

The marker appeared to his left, but as he approached it, a pang of fear stopped him. Coiled around the marker was a thick snake with a dark head.

He stepped back. "An? If you can hear me, don't come near!"

No reply.

Picking up a stone, he threw it at the snake. The stone hit the marker and toppled it on top of the snake. It didn't move. He threw another stone, and another, but the snake remained still. Sall drew his sword and approached slowly. Grain of sand stung his face, the wind whipping him. He reached forward to poke the snake with the tip of the sword. The blade went through it, and that's when he recognized what he was staring at: An's golden braid, snipped off at her nape, the end still tied with the red bow, which he had mistaken for the head of a snake.

Sall shook the braid to clear the sand and pressed it to his face. The scent of lavender was as clear as if she were there with him. Tears welled up in his eyes. He kissed her braid and noticed that the hair felt warm as if it had been resting inside her robe, pressed to her back, only moments ago.

Sheathing his sword, Sall ran back, only to hear the horse's hooves drumming on the road.

"Li'iliti, stop!"

He kept running until the road appeared under his feet. The sound of the hooves was growing distant on the right, but he couldn't see through the haze of churning dust.

"Stop!"

His shouting caused no interruption in the steady staccato of the hooves. He could only see a few steps ahead, but he remembered how the road descended in a switchback pattern over the east side of the hills. Stuffing An's braid under his chest armor, Sall ran straight downhill. There were rocks, some of them too large to hop over, forcing him to go around, and thorny shrubs that he plowed through, scraping his exposed shins. The horse's hooves, which had grown distant, were coming back now, and he knew there was little time for him to reach the road and intercept Li'iliti. Without her and the horse, he would have no way to catch up and nothing to trade for An, who might be lost forever.

The sound of the hooves was coming fast from his right when the road appeared below. Sall jumped down just as the horse passed. He managed to grab the left leather strap of the reins, but lost his footing and was dragged along for some distance while the horse neighed, twisted its head sideways and down, and came to a stop.

As Sall got up, Li'iliti pulled her leg from the stirrup and kicked him in the head, knocking him down. He lost his grip on the leather strap, and she rattled the reins and kicked the horse, which moved on.

"Stop!" Panting, Sall couldn't get up. "Stop!"

After a few steps, the horse stopped.

Li'iliti kicked in, shook the reins, and shouted in the language of Kush, but to no avail. She leaned forward and slapped the horse on the side of the neck. The horse whinnied, reared up, and tossed her out of the saddle. She landed with a yelp on the road near Sall. They stayed down, breathing heavily. The wind lashed at them, and they lay on the road, covering their heads until the tempest passed and the dust settled down.

The sun shone brightly, the air cleared up, and the vast desert below them came into view.

Sall got up and drew his sword.

Li'iliti stood and walked backwards, away from him.

He turned the sword around and held it with the handle towards her. "We're not enemies, not anymore."

She reached to grab the sword, but changed her mind. "Is this a trick?"

"You served your husband, and I served my people. We did our duty. It's over."

Passing her hand through her thick curls, she asked, "What do you propose?"

"You return to your children, and my girl returns to me."

"And if Li'uli refuses to release her?"

"Then we'll have another war, but this time, Edom will crush Kush."

That made her grin. "With your army of women?"

"Have they not beaten the army of Egypt?"

Her grin faded. "Kush is very far."

"I'll go to the end of the earth, if necessary."

"You, maybe, but why would the women of Edom go?"

"For love." He pulled An's golden braid from under his chest armor and shook it in Li'iliti's face. "For love!"

To his dismay, she buried her face in her hands and burst out crying. She sobbed bitterly, her shoulders shaking. Sall went to the horse, got a waterskin from the saddle, and gave it to her. She drank some water and wiped her face. When she spoke, her voice trembled.

"Li'uli and I agreed on an alternative meeting spot." She gestured downhill. "That's where he and the children are waiting for me – if they survived."

The horse rocked its head and whinnied, but relented and allowed them to mount. They rode in silence while the sun rose higher. Sall had looped An's braid around his neck, and the scent of lavender made him hopeful. At the end of the long, meandering descent, Li'iliti directed him off the road to a goat path along the foothills.

Li'uli appeared from behind a boulder, aiming a long charioteer's spear. He came closer, the tip of the spear pointing at Sall's chest. His robe was torn and soiled, his legs were stained with dry blood, and his bloodshot eyes darted about as if he feared attacks from multiple directions.

Li'iliti dismounted. "Put the spear away. The boy comes in peace."

"He's not a boy." Li'uli spoke hoarsely. "He's a demon. A demon!"

She paused, remaining by the horse. "What are you talking about?"

"Only a demon could have made Pharaoh's army turn on itself."

"Calm down, husband. It was cleverness, not magic." She looked around. "Where are the children?"

The two little girls stepped out from behind the boulder, followed by An, who was holding the baby. Sall was relieved to see no blood on her robe and, even better, a smile on her face. Her loose hair, cut straight above her shoulders, sparkled in the morning sun.

Sall adjusted the thick braid around his neck. "Does it look good on me?"

An laughed, handing the baby to Li'iliti, who showered it with kisses while crouching to hug her girls. They buried their faces in her bosom.

Li'uli glanced back at his reunited family, but immediately returned his eyes to Sall while aiming the spear.

Keeping his hands visible, Sall dismounted. "Do you really think a wooden spear can bring down a demon?"

Li'uli looked at his spear, grunted, and dropped it. "How did you do it?"

"By following your advice," Sall said. "When facing a powerful enemy, always do the unexpected."

An came over to his side. "You're being modest."

"My single achievement was understanding that an army capable of defeating all other armies could only be defeated by itself. The rest required a few simple steps." Sall counted on his fingers. "First, the women of Edom had to believe that they were as strong as men. Second, they fabricated the armor pieces, bows, and arrows in order to learn basic military skills – march, fight, and shoot arrows. Third, a group of girls collected two-thousand snakes in clay jars. Fourth, I invented a deadly red fever epidemic to keep the Egyptians out of Bozra and tipped the Jabari about a great army marching down from the north. The rest was easy – the snakes drove the Egyptians mad, showers of arrows terrified them, and the darkness of the night caused them to see enemies where their brothers stood and utilize their fighting skills to kill each other."

Li'uli sat on the ground, hugging his knees. "You killed my dream."

The utter sadness in his voice would have upset Sall, but he recalled another thing the brown prince had once said and repeated it out loud: "One person's dream is often another person's nightmare."

The little girls came over and sat by their father, leaning against him while he rocked back and forth. Li'iliti joined them and put the baby to her breast.

Sall and An climbed into the saddle.

Li'uli mumbled something.

"What did you say?" Sall leaned forward to hear better.

"Come with us to Kush."

"Why?"

"My father will give you good land and many slaves. You'll be happy and safe in Kush, and your cleverness will help us turn the harsh land into another Canaan."

"Bozra is our home. We have to go back."

"You'll both be killed – she by her father for her disobedience, and you by the king for your popularity."

"The king and high priest are my prisoners. They'll be grateful when I grant them freedom."

"Kings and priests are never grateful to anyone."

"That's true," An said. "But why do you care?"

Looking up at them, the brown prince's eyes glistened. "It's all my fault. The Jabari didn't plan to fight Edom at the Sea of Reeds. He accepted your king's offer of safe passage to Canaan, but I convinced him to breach the agreement, destroy your army in a surprise attack, and come here to take Bozra and subjugate Edom."

Sall felt An's breath on his neck as she asked in a stunned voice, "What made you do that?"

"The question is, who made me do that?" Li'uli chuckled sadly. "The boy from Edom, who told me about his beautiful city of Bozra, the fertile valley outside its gates, and the rich copper mines of Edom – that boy made me realize that control of Edom would bring abundant trade to Canaan, which I was due to govern for Egypt at the end of our victorious campaign."

At first, the words shook Sall to the core with crushing guilt and debilitating confusion, but a moment later, he remembered who he was dealing with.

"Trickery and manipulations," he said. "You want to lure us to Kush and make us your slaves, because you seek revenge. Otherwise, why would you chop off her braid?"

"You were cruel to my woman, so I was cruel to yours."

From the back, An pressed his shoulder. "It doesn't matter. Let's go home."

"Truth matters." Sall pointed at Li'uli. "How dare you complain of cruelty when you were going to flood Damascus and drown all its people?"

Li'uli's eyes widened with dismay. "How do you know about that?"

"I'm a demon, remember?"

61

On the ride back through the valley, Sall asked An to pull the headdress down over her eyes to avoid seeing the dead Egyptians. He kept his eyes on the road ahead, never once looking left or right at the remains of the enemy camp.

The sun was high in the sky when they approached the city. No one was in sight, and the gates were shut. Sall brought the horse up to the gates and turned sideways so that he could use his hand to bang. There was no response.

He cupped his mouth and yelled, "Open up!"

Nothing.

Again, he banged several times. "Anyone in there?"

The locking bar inside rumbled as it was lifted, and the left gate cracked open. The limping snake-catcher's wife let them in, shut the gate, and reset the bar.

She pointed uphill. "The high priest summoned everyone to the temple."

Sall was surprised. "Why was he released without my orders?"

"I don't know. Maybe the king ordered it."

"He's free, too?"

"Why not? The Egyptians are gone. He's still the king, isn't he?"

An's grip on his shoulder tightened, and Sall felt dread forming a lump in his chest. Had Li'uli been right about the danger they faced? Should they turn around and ride away from Bozra?

"It'll be fine," An said. "I'll talk to my father. He can be harsh, but I know he loves me."

Her words reminded him of what his mother had said: "A man's love for a woman will never be a match for his hate for another man." Was the same true for a man's love for his daughter?

An tapped his shoulder. "Let's go."

Shaking off his worries, Sall urged the horse up the street. He had saved Edom from Egypt. The army of six thousand women was his army. They loved him and admired An. Their gratitude, no doubt, made him and An invincible.

He pushed the horse hard, following the street from one side of the city to the opposite, higher and higher, until they reached his family home. Entering the front garden, he saw Cook kneeling by the effigies, praying with closed eyes. She heard him and got up. He pointed at the workshop, but she shook her head and gestured uphill in the direction of the temple, implying that his parents had gone there. Bozra ran out of the house, barking. He dismounted, played with her for a moment, and got back on the horse. Directing it back to the street, he turned it uphill and sped up.

At the top, next to the king's palace, a tall white wall separated the temple from the street. They tied the horse to a tree, went through an arched entry, and climbed a long flight of stairs. An adjusted her headdress to cover her face as befitting a modest maiden in the temple. Near the top of the stairs, Sall stopped her, and they listened to the booming voice of the high priest.

"Qoz, almighty God of Edom, accept this sacrifice as a token of our eternal gratitude for saving our nation from slavery to the Pharaoh. May you forgive our wretched women for their evil presumptuousness in wearing men's armor and carrying men's weapons and marching as an army of men, all in sinful violation of men's divine supremacy over them."

The words made An groan, whereas for Sall, they fanned the embers of dread from Li'uli's warning.

They took a few more steps and paused at the top, still out of sight. The stairwell connected to the end of a long, high balcony overlooking a sandy arena and a circular amphitheater with tiered benches. In the center of the arena, a giant copper statue of Qoz sat on a massive stone throne with armrests carved to form a bull and a cow. Its head was topped by three stubby horns, its bulging eyes were blank, and it held a three-pronged thunderbolt, on which a dead goat was impaled, blood dripping from it down to the sandy arena below.

The moment Sall and An stepped onto the balcony, the packed amphitheater exploded, thousands of women cheering from the tiered benches.

Sall took An's hand and raised their joined hands high.

The women erupted in rhythmic chanting, "Ee-Dom! Ee-Dom! Ee-

Dom!"

It was a roaring welcome that filled him with joy and melted away the lump of dread in his throat.

The high priest and the king stood at the railing, dressed in their ceremonial attires – the high priest in a black robe and headgear, and the king in a red coat and a gold crown. Qoztobarus stood behind his father, wearing a similar black robe, but no headgear. At the far end of the balcony was General Mazabi, leaning on his copper spear, as well as Sall's parents, who wore grim expressions.

The crowd continued to chant, "Ee-Dom! Ee-Dom! Ee-Dom!"

The high priest raised his hand to silence the chanting, but the women persisted.

"Ee-Dom! Ee-Dom! Ee-Dom!"

Sall and An stepped up to the railing and waved at the crowd, which responded with even louder chants. The women were no longer wearing armor or bearing weapons. They were back in their usual robes and headdresses. He looked at An, who smiled back at him. They continued to wave, and the chanting persisted, though it gradually changed into a different chant.

"Kiss-Her! Kiss-Her! Kiss-Her!"

An laughed and pulled off the headdress, revealing her cropped hair.

The chanting interrupted by widespread yelps and cries, but immediately, the chanting resumed even louder, "Kiss-Her! Kiss-Her! Kiss-Her!"

Holding both her hands in his, Sall gazed into her eyes while they leaned towards one another and locked their lips in a kiss that made his body tremble with pleasure. Here he was, kissing the girl who had, more than four full moons ago, knocked him down with a contemptuous gaze, igniting a dream about a tower and an old dwarf, who said, "If you wish to change how another person feels about you, start by changing yourself." That advice had sent him on a quest that was finally reaching its destination – winning An's heart. And with her warm lips pressed to his, Sall finally knew what real happiness was.

With a violent jerk, An tore away from him and rose up in the air. It was Qoztobarus, who gripped the back of his sister's robe and lifted her above his head. Before Sall had time to do anything, Qoztobarus turned towards the arena and hurled An over the railing. She flew in an arch and landed with a thud on the sand in the arena below.

The crowd roared in shock.

Sall bent over the railing and shouted, "An!"

She didn't move.

He turned to run to the opposite end of the balcony, where a circular staircase led down to the arena, but Qoztobarus grabbed his back armor and lifted him as he had done with An. Facing up, all Sall saw was a blue sky. He kicked his legs and flailed his arms in the air, but in vain.

"Put him down." It was Umm-Sall's voice.

Qoztobarus laughed. "Down is where he's going."

"Don't hurt him." Her voice was closer now. "They'll rip you to pieces."

"These women?" He laughed harder. "They wouldn't dare."

The crowd quieted down.

"Don't!"

Qoztobarus stepped to the railing.

Exploding with fury, Sall lurched to the right, to the left, and to the right again, loosening the straps that tied the back-armor piece to front one, and managed to turn his upper body, twisting far enough to reach down and poke Qoztobarus in the eye.

Qoztobarus cried and let go, and Sall landed on the railing. He grabbed the top plank, climbed back into the balcony, and ran to the circular stairs and down to the arena.

A few women from the nearest benches had already rushed to An's side. One of them had a waterskin, which she used to wet the girl's face. Sall dropped down and put his ear to her mouth. For a moment, he felt nothing, but then, a soft puff on his ear told him she was breathing. He searched for bleeding from her mouth, nose, or ears, finding none. Her arms and legs seemed not to have been broken due to the softness of the sand.

His father joined him and lifted An's legs off the ground, as Sall had seen him do with fainted people.

The amphitheater grew quiet until it was completely silent.

Gazing up at the giant statue of Qoz, Sall held An's limp hand and prayed. The women sprinkled water on her face and caressed her hair.

An sighed. Her eyelids fluttered, then opened, and she looked at him.

"You're back," he said. "Praise Qoz. Do you feel any pain?"

Her lips moved soundlessly, and her gaze shifted, looking up. Craning his head, Sall saw the king and high priest above, looking down over the railing.

She coughed. "What happened?"

"Your brother threw you over."

Pulling on his hand, she tried to sit up.

"Stay down," he said. "You need to recover."

An shook her head. "Help me up."

"But—"

She turned her hand to show him the Fisherman's Ring. "It's now, or never."

He understood what she meant. This moment, when they were surrounded by a huge crowd that ached with sympathy for them after the violent attack of Qoztobarus, was their best chance to get her father to marry them.

Leaning on him, An stood up. Water dripped from her chin, and her hair was matted with sand. One of the women used her fingers to comb An's hair and brush away the sand. They stepped slowly to the center of the arena, near the giant statue of Qoz, and turned to face the balcony.

Sall spoke loudly enough to be heard around the amphitheater. "This girl is betrothed to me. I wish to marry her now."

"No!" The high priest gripped the balcony and yelled, "She's betrothed to her brother!"

Sall's father crossed the arena to stand by them and looked up at the balcony. "That betrothal was declared invalid by the Jabari."

The arena was completely silent, thousands of women holding their breath, listening.

The high priest sneered. "Qoz smote the Jabari and his army."

"Qoz chose my son to smite Egypt, while you ran off to kneel before the Jabari and accept Pharaoh's laws, which require a girl's consent to betrothal. Your daughter never agreed to marry her brother. Therefore, at the time my son betrothed her, she was available."

Hearing his father make the argument filled Sall with gratitude, because it implied support for the marriage.

"I'm her father." The high priest pounded the black robe over his chest. "I'll never allow her to marry a healer's son."

To that, Sall knew what to say. "I am proud to be a healer's son."

The crowd cheered, but the high priest gestured in dismissal.

"Peace," Sall's father said. "On this glorious day in particular, I extend my hand to you in peace and forgo our enmity. There should be no conflict between the healing powers of the Gods and the healing properties of the plants and animals that the Gods have created. Your father and mine hated one another, and their fathers before them, for too many generations. This marriage between our children can put an end to our needless hatred."

"Bow before Qoz," the high priest shouted, pointing at the statue. "He is the one you insult every time the sick and infirm receive fake potions and empty promises from you and your wretched wife."

General Mazabi pounded his copper spear, shaking the balcony. "Wretched are your empty promises, priest, which failed to help us at the Sea of Reeds."

Silence returned the amphitheater.

The general pounded his spear again, glaring at the high priest. "What father wouldn't marry his daughter to the young man who pulled victory from the teeth of certain doom?"

The crowd broke into chanting again. "Ee-Dom! Ee-Dom! Ee-Dom!"

Umm-Sall made her way down the spiral stairs and joined her husband, Sall, and An in the arena. She put her arm around the girl's shoulders.

Sall raised his hand, and the crowd quieted down. "Marry us now. Marry us before Qoz."

Turning to the king, the high priest said, "Our wise sovereign will decide whether a commoner may strive to betroth a noble girl, for this is a dangerous precedent. What's next? A commoner demanding the hand of a king's daughter, or granddaughter?"

It was a clever argument, appealing directly to the king's self-interest, but it didn't weaken Sall's resolve. He kept his eyes on the high balcony, but intended his words to be heard by the thousands of women around them.

"Our nation has lost its men," Sall said. "We need new families to replenish our ranks. We need a new generation to create a future in this land. Let the two of us, An and myself, be the first new hope for Edom."

The king adjusted the crown on his head, straightened the red coat over his chest, and rubbed his hands at length. It was obvious he was stalling, unable to choose between two unappealing options.

The women clapped once, twice, and a third time at the same deliberate rhythm as they had done in the final confrontation with the army of Egypt. This time, however, their clapping wasn't meant to scare away foreign invaders, but to force a wavering king to make the right choice.

General Mazabi began to pound his copper spear on the wooden floor of the balcony in tandem with the crowd's clapping. The king gave him a stern look, but the general persisted until the king held forth both hands to signal that he was ready to rule.

As soon as General Mazabi rested his spear, the whole amphitheater stopped clapping. The king gripped the railing. All eyes were on him.

"The Gods gave this land to my forefather, Esau the First, eighteen generations ago. Our monarchy has lasted because we respect tradition above all. In our tradition, a girl marries a man chosen by her father. Therefore, we would never compel the high priest to give his daughter to a healer's son."

The high priest grinned, beaming with satisfaction.

"However," the king continued, "this boy is no longer the mere son of a healer. He is the savior of kings. He is the liberator of nations. He is the great Elixirist. If we had a daughter to give him, we would do so gladly. Surely the high priest doesn't think his daughter is better than a king's daughter, does he?"

The high priest's face reddened as he shook his head.

"Very well," the king said. "We shall observe the marriage ceremony right now."

The crowd went wild with cheers while King Esau the Eighteenth and the high priest took the stairs down to the arena and joined Sall's parents and the young couple at the foot of the giant statue of Qoz.

Sall's eyes were drawn to the old boots on the high priest's feet, and their foul odor assailed his nose from memory. Another memory surfaced, that one from the night aboard the Sailor of Barada, of the old dwarf's didactic voice, which Sall proceeded to quote out loud: "Smelly feet should be soaked daily in hot water mixed with equal parts of lemon, mint, rosemary, and salt."

The ensuing silence was broken by the king's laughter. An covered her mouth and also laughed, and Sall's parents joined, as well. Sall's words were repeated by women around the arena, and soon the whole crowd was hollering while the red-faced high priest glared at Sall, who kept a straight face.

"It's true," he said. "You should try it."

The high priest extended his hand with an open palm and yelled, "Pay my daughter's dowry – two thousand silver coins!"

The crowd quieted down, the women leaning forward in their seats to hear better.

He repeated. "My daughter's dowry shall be two thousand silver coins!"

The enormous sum drew a collective groan.

Turning to the king, the high priest said, "The law of Edom gives a father the right to demand a price for his daughter's hand, doesn't it?"

"Correct," the king said. "Bride-price payment is due from the groom's family to the bride's father before the wedding in coins or in labor, as the bride's father may determine at his sole discretion. That is our law."

"Father, please," An cried. "Let me marry him!"

"Silence, girl," he said. "You belong to Qoztobarus, my heir, the next high priest of Edom."

"But he just tried to kill me!"

"That was your fault. You made him angry." The high priest grabbed her arm. "Let's go!"

Sall's father raised his hand to stop him. "We agree to your dowry demand."

The crowd groaned again, because accepting such an outrageous demand was as astonishing as making it in the first place.

"Do you?" The high priest laughed, extending his open hand. "Two thousand silver coins?"

"Yes, we will pay it."

"You must pay now, or my daughter will be married to her brother in a moment."

An looked at Sall, her eyes wide with fear. He smiled and gestured at his father, who pulled a purse from under his robe, untied the string over the top, and reached inside.

"These coins," Sall's father announced, "which had been kept out of circulation since new by the great Elixirist in Damascus, bear the image of Pharaoh Nebhepetre Mentuhotep the Second, who ruled Egypt many generations ago. Each coin was honed from pure gold and is worth at least a hundred silver coins."

Mesmerized, the whole arena watched as he counted twenty of the sizable honey-colored coins, handing each one to the high priest, who needed both hands to hold them. One of his servants rushed over with a piece of cloth to wrap the gold coins.

"What about tax?" The king held out his hand. "One in ten from each side should do it."

Sall's father and the high priest gave the king two coins each.

"Splendid." The king peered closely at the coins and slipped them into his coat pocket. "Let's get on with it, priest. Marry them."

The servants brought a red cloth canopy, a bowl of ripe figs, and a goblet of wine. They gave the goblet to Sall and the bowl to An. The canopy was held above them as a symbolic roof of a new home.

The high priest sprinkled copper dust on the couple to imply future wealth and murmured a marriage blessing. When he finished, An held a fig by Sall's mouth, and he took a bite of the soft fruit, whose abundance of crunchy seeds foretold the couple's plentiful fertility. Sall, in turn, held the goblet to An's lips, and she took a sip of wine that sweetened her palate and spread warmth in her chest to herald a lifetime of happiness.

A red drop of wine trickled down her chin. Sall dabbed it with his finger and, while still touching her chin, leaned forward and kissed his new wife.

The End

NOTE TO THE READER

When readers ask what happened to Sall and his beloved An after their marriage, I suggest they go on to read *Deborah Rising* (HarperCollins, 2016) and its sequels. That series of novels, which tells the dramatic story of the first woman to lead a nation in known human history, features Sall (at an older age) in a leading role as a friend and mentor to young Deborah.

To ensure accuracy in describing how people lived in the ancient Mideast, I consulted countless books and articles. They are too many to list here, but I am particularly indebted to the scholarly works of William F. Albright, Yigael Yadin, Avraham Biran, Israel Finkelstein, Benjamin Mazar, Amihai Mazar, William G. Dever, Joyce Salisbury, Carol Meyers, Thomas E. Levi, George Hart, Bruce Routledge, Richard Elliot Friedman, Geraldine Harris, Richard Wilkinson, Boyd Seevers, Gale A. Yee, Brian Schmidt, Alan Dickin, Monroe Rosenthal, Isaac Mozenson, Diana Vikander Edelman, Hershel Shanks and Claudia Valentino.

We are blessed with wonderful friends and family members, who read my manuscripts at various stages, provide insightful observations and, most graciously, offer enthusiastic support. They include (in alphabetical order) Margie and Arie Adler, Sarai Azrieli, Talya, Ben, and Elan Azrieli, Hagit and Michael David, Rabbi Dr. Israel Dreisin, Don Eddins, Monica and Prof. Michael Finkelthal, Risa and Dr. Opher Ganel, Rachel and Joel Glazer, Prof. Sharon Glazer and Tamas Karpati, Julie and Hanan Gur, Dr. Jennifer and Nir Margalit, Linda and Dr. Bernard Rosenbaum, Glenna Salisbury, Wendy and Avner Skolnik, Stephen J. Wall, Stephanie and Ernie Wechsler, and Carol Wilner.

As always, this novel would not have come to life without the tireless support of my wife, Fiona, a dedicated physician who finds time to read the first draft of every new novel and provides astute critique, perceptive comments, and inspiring encouragement. Fiona and our children fill my life with love and laughter, which sustain me daily.

Last but not least, I owe a debt of gratitude to you, my readers, for choosing to spend your precious time with my books, for sending me intriguing comments through my website, and for posting thoughtful insights on social media. There is no greater reward for a writer (beside the writing itself) than to find positive readers' reviews and ratings on Amazon.com and similar websites. Thank you!

ABOUT THE AUTHOR

Avraham Azrieli is the author of books and screenplays. His first novel was *The Masada Complex* (a political thriller), followed by Israeli spy novels *The Jerusalem Inception* and *The Jerusalem Assassin*, as well as *Christmas for Joshua* (an interfaith family drama), *The Mormon Candidate* (a political thriller), *Thump* (a courtroom drama featuring sexual harassment and racism), and *The Bootstrap Ultimatum* (a mystery involving the commercialization of Memorial Day). Most recently, he has written a series of novels inspired by the true story of the first woman to lead a nation in human history, starting with *Deborah Rising* and *Deborah Calling* (HarperCollins, 2016 and 2017), and continuing with *Deborah Slaying* and *Deborah Leading*.

Beside fiction, he has also authored *Your Lawyer on a Short Leash - a guide to dealing with lawyers* and *One Step Ahead – A Mother of Seven Escaping Hitler's Claws* (an acclaimed WWII true story, which inspired the musical By Wheel and by Wing).

While growing up in Israel, Avraham received extensive Talmudic education, before attending law school and serving as a law clerk at the Israeli Supreme Court in Jerusalem. He later earned an advanced law degree from Columbia University in New York City, served as a law clerk for the Federal District Court, and started his legal career with Davis Polk & Wardwell. He has represented clients in numerous complex court cases before trial and appellate courts, including the United States Supreme Court. He currently lives near Washington DC with his wife and children. Like Ben Teller, the protagonist in *The Mormon Candidate* and *The Bootstrap Ultimatum*, Avraham often rides his motorcycle in the mountainous forests of western Maryland. To learn more, please visit www.AzrieliBooks.com

BOOKS BY AVRAHAM AZRIELI

Fiction:

The Masada Complex
The Jerusalem Inception
The Jerusalem Assassin
Christmas for Joshua
The Mormon Candidate
The Bootstrap Ultimatum
Thump
Deborah Rising
Deborah Calling
Deborah Slaying
Deborah Leading
The Elixirist

Nonfiction:

Your Lawyer on a Short Leash – A Guide to Dealing with Lawyers
One Step Ahead – A Mother of Seven Escaping Hitler's Claws

Author Website:

www.AzrieliBooks.com

Map of Sall's Journey:

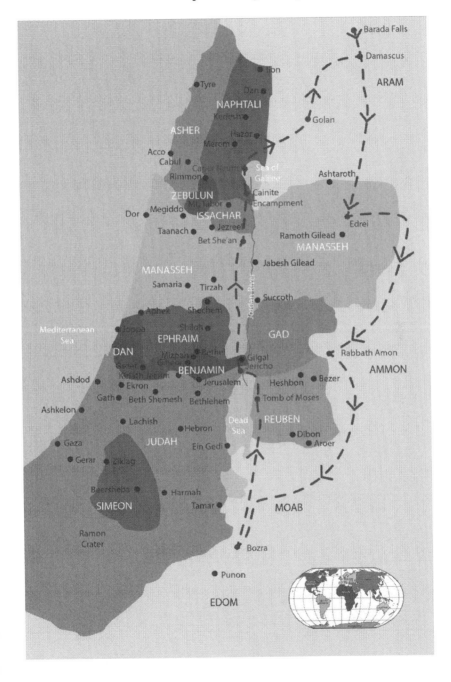